BESTSELLING ROMANCE AUTHORS LAVISHLY ACCLAIM SHIRL HENKE:

"*Terms of Love* is a sexy, sensual romp that will keep you enthralled from first page to last. Without a doubt, Shirl Henke at her best."

—Katherine Sutcliffe

"Rigo is my kind of hero. *Return to Paradise* swept me away!"

—Virginia Henley

"Shirl Henke goes big time with a grand and glorious novel of Columbus' Spain, and the swashbuckling New World. I couldn't stop reading."

—Bertrice Small

"A riveting story about a fascinating period. I highly recommend *Paradise & More.*"

—Karen Robards

"Warm, savvy and perceptive, Shirl Henke's wonderful plots and characters never let you down!"
—Maggie Davis, aka Maggie Deauxville, Maggie Daniels

"*Return to Paradise* is a story you'll remember forever...definately a book you'll keep to read again and again!"

—*Affaire de Coeur*

STUD FEE

"You damn Yankee!" Cass said with loathing.

Steve shrugged dismissively. "I'm getting no lady wife in this bargain, am I?"

"No gentleman paws a woman the way you did, so we're even!" After retreating a pace, she stood her ground defiantly.

"One thousand," he said quietly. "That's my stud fee. And if you want to fulfill your father's will, you'll not only have to pay me, you'll have to suffer my *pawing* you a lot more after we're married. I assume a woman with your colorful vocabulary understands barnyard facts of life?"

She hated him, standing in front of her so calm, so overbearing, daring her! Cass was caught in her own trap and she knew it, but she would never let him know how badly frightened she was.

"One thousand it is, but I'll tell you when you may 'be of service,' Mr. Loring. Try touching me any other time and I'll show you how well I wield a blacksnake!"

Other *Leisure Books* by Shirl Henke:

RETURN TO PARADISE
PARADISE & MORE
NIGHT WIND'S WOMAN

TERMS OF LOVE

SHIRL HENKE

LEISURE BOOKS   **NEW YORK CITY**

A LEISURE BOOK®

October 1992

Published by

Dorchester Publishing Co., Inc.
276 Fifth Avenue
New York, NY 10001

Cover Art by Pino

Printed in the United States of America.

For Hildegard Schnuttgen, director of reference, The Maag Library, who would dig through the Rockies to locate any book I request.

Prologue

Pueblo, Colorado,
1870

Cass appraised him with seeming detachment, trying to convince herself that he was just another mule or horse to be bought and broken. She noted that his hands, resting on the pommel of his saddle, were bound. As he dismounted, she could see he was tall and lean. When he awkwardly doffed his dusty headgear, a longish thatch of sun-streaked brown hair fell across his forehead. His lower face was covered with a thick brown beard, giving him a hard, grizzled look. Still, he seemed well-formed and young enough.

Steve watched the woman on the porch of the large building as she stepped confidently down the stairs. She was dressed oddly in a crisp white shirt and tan pants, scandalously tailored to fit her long, slim legs. Impatiently she tossed a fat plait of pale copper hair over her shoulder and approached them. High arched brows rose over wide-set, clear amber eyes. Eyes just a hue lighter than his own. Her skin bore the golden kiss of the sun and her lips were well molded. He amended that: all of her was well molded and clearly revealed in the mannish clothes that only made her femininity more apparent. Her stride was bold, but not the swishing invitation of a whore or the teasing mince of a society belle. Here stood an enigma.

"Cass, this here's Steve Loring. Steve, meet Miz Cassandra Clayton, owner of Clayton Freighting," Kyle said measuringly.

"Hello," she greeted him coolly, tilting her head slightly to look in his eyes. Two golden gazes locked for a moment.

"Hello, Miss Clayton. I assume you'll be the one to explain why I've been snatched from the jaws of death and brought here?" His smile went unanswered.

Ignoring him, Cass turned to Hunnicut. "Where did you find him?"

"Tumbleweed wagon down in th' Nations. Seems he got hisself set up fer killin' a feller who wuz fixin' ta rob him. Out west on a fool's errand. After some Copperheads." Over the past few days on the trail, Kyle had grown to like the quiet Yankee. But still, Cass must know what she was getting into.

Her eyes narrowed to golden slits as she inspected Steve from head to foot. "So, a dude on the run from a hanging. He'll do, Kyle." She sniffed. "If only he didn't smell so bad—and weren't a damn Yankee. Have him cleaned up and find some decent clothes for him. Bring him to the house for dinner."

With that curt command, she turned and walked back to the house. Once inside, she collapsed against the door and breathed deeply. She could still feel those cold brownish gold eyes raking down her body—as if he knew! But she was sure Kyle had followed her orders and not told him. Damn, even with his wrists tied the Yankee had been insolent, but she would break him!

While Cass and Kyle discussed him as if he were an imbecile or a piece of livestock, Steve seethed inwardly in spite of his outward show of casual bravado. Hunnicut he understood—a man who hired out his gun, a professional. But the Texan was only doing an errand for this enigmatic woman. What the hell did she intend to do with him?

Chapter One

"Palmer's Owls" rode into the winter, seventy-five ragged and frozen Federals, wanting nothing so much as a warm bed and a cooked meal. The icy rain had not relented since they left Kingsport at the end of September. Slippery mud and freezing rain were lethal foes, as dogged and deadly as the Confederate cavalry that pursued them. The Union column left Tennessee behind and ascended the tortuous pathway through the mountains of Virginia, moving north toward Kentucky.

William Jackson Palmer leaned on the pommel of his saddle, painfully shifting his weight as the wet leather creaked and groaned in protest. There was no shelter and no dry wood for a fire—not that they would dare light one anyway in this

14

stronghold of the Confederacy. "Damnable weather, but nothing in this accursed fratricidal strife is less than damnable," he mused as a young private's horse stumbled, then regained its footing on the mud-slick ground.

The trail they followed took them higher and higher toward the passes that led to the Cumberland Plateau. To reach General Burbridge with their urgent dispatches they must find one of those passes free of Rebel sentries. At the moment the prospect seemed as bleak as the weather.

Palmer's Owls had earned their name as fearful night skirmishers who raided the length and breadth of the Tennessee-Kentucky border. They struck, then vanished into the darkness, relying on Federal sympathizers for shelter and intelligence. East Tennessee and Kentucky were sprinkled with pro-Union farmers and tradesmen. Today the Owls rode to a rendezvous with just such a man, Abner Henderson.

Palmer looked through the slackening rain at Henderson's cousin, Steve Loring. Born and bred in Philadelphia, Loring ran in the same social circles as Palmer himself, but his mother was a Graham from Louisville. The colonel often wondered what his quiet young lieutenant felt about a war in which his family fought on both sides.

Steven Terrell Loring reined in his mount beside the colonel. Doffing his hat, he shook water from the soaked brim, then gazed up at the gradually clearing skies. A few faint streaks of pink and gold in the slate gray sky hinted at a break in the weather. He observed his commander's bone-weary visage, old beyond its twenty-eight years, knowing that the harsh lines of exhaustion were mirrored in his own face.

Rubbing the stubbly beard on his cheek, Loring said quietly, "Abner should be at the shanty on the west fork by full moon."

Palmer grunted. "If we *have* a moon." His keen blue eyes held the darker ones of his lieutenant. "He's taking an awful chance leading a whole column of bluecoats through the Crow's Nest."

Loring's face was taut for a moment as he thought about his boyhood companion. Then he smiled. "No more of a chance than you took when you spied for McClellan at Hagerstown."

Palmer's voice was edged with grimness as he replied, "Yes, and when I tried to repeat the fool-hardy feat in Virginia, I was captured and spent three months in Castle Thunder. You know it's dangerous for Henderson, Steve. The Confederates hang spies."

Steve shrugged. "They shoot us in uniform, hang us without. Dead's dead, Will. Abner can't join the Federals. His father serves with Johnston."

Palmer muttered an oath under his breath, then sighed. "I guess he needs to do his duty as he sees it without shooting Confederates."

"Especially considering one of them is real close kin," Steve said quietly.

Palmer looked at Loring as they resumed their slow ride. "You have any other family with the South besides your cousin Abner's father?"

Steve shrugged uncomfortably. "No, only my uncle by marriage and his kin—except for his son, Ab. I may have spent my childhood on the border, but there was never any doubt of my loyalties when I came back from England."

"Ever regret joining the Army?" Palmer asked.

Steve let his chiseled lips relax in a grin. "Every day."

Just then Sargeant Simms came galloping up, followed by a man in civilian clothes. Abner Henderson's homely face was wreathed in smiles as he sighted Steve. "Hell, cuz, thought you fellers had clean been washed away in the rain. Been waitin' at the shack for over an hour."

Abner's huge, callused hand clasped Steve's slimmer one in a firm shake. Although first cousins, they looked nothing alike. Steve resembled his father, the Philadelphia aristocrat, slim and elegant with the refined features and graceful carriage of a man born to privilege. Abner, by contrast, had grown up in the mountains on the Tennessee-Kentucky border. Like his father he was a strapping hulk of a man with the blunt face and raw bones of a farmer.

"How's Aunt Fay making out, Ab?" Steve asked.

"All things considerin', she's right pert, Steve, but you know Mama. Nothin'll ever keep her down in the mouth."

As they rode, Abner explained to Steve and Colonel Palmer about the circuitous route they must follow to avoid local Confederate patrols and still get through the formidable barricade of the mountains.

"You think we can make our way up this perpendicular path by the light of the moon?" Palmer asked after Abner had finished.

Steve grinned. "Ab's half mountain goat. If anyone can get us through, he will." His face darkened and he rubbed his chin thoughtfully. "Of course, there is Prentice dogging our heels, but we've lost him, at least for a while. That heavy rain was good for one thing."

"Prentice, yes, but there is the other . . ." the colonel said softly.

Abner looked from Palmer to his cousin. The evening air had grown silent and only the sucking squish of horses' hooves broke the calm at twilight as they wended their way through the autumn-brown woods. "You got more troubles 'n the rebs trailing you? Seems ta me that ought ta be enough."

Palmer exchanged a look with Loring. "We'd be willing to consider Colonel Prentice sufficient chastisement," he replied drily, "but we've been plagued by too many accidents in recent months."

"Ever since the Ohio Tenth was transferred to this command," Steve added darkly.

"Copperheads?" Abner whispered, shifting uneasily in his saddle.

"We've had rather unexpected encounters with Confederate patrols on two occasions," Palmer replied.

"In places they weren't supposed to be." Steve's face was harsh in the dying light.

"You know who?" Abner asked. "I rightly mislike havin' my face marked down by a feller who'll describe it ta the garrison commander back home."

"That's why we've not used your name or let any of the men but Sargent Simms see you up close," Palmer replied.

The colonel's aide, Simms, had met Abner at the cabin and escorted him to Palmer and Loring. The column of men rode behind them, with the Ohioans placed at the rear.

"We're sure it's an Ohio man. Nothing like this happened with our Pennsylvania regulars," Steve added. "But out of nearly twenty men, one Copperhead is hard to pin down. I think it's Vince

Tanner. He's been away from his bedroll one night too many."

"You can't court-martial a man on suspicions like that, Lieutenant. The way we skirmish and live off the land, if I tried a roll call every morning and night, I'd have to shoot half my command in a week," Palmer remonstrated.

"Still, there's something about Tanner," Steve insisted. "My guts tell me it's him."

Palmer's face was pensive. "In the last two years of fighting you've developed good instincts, I know."

"If you mean I've become edgy, you're right." Steve rubbed his neck, stiffened in the night chill. The trio lapsed into silence.

At full dark Palmer called a halt. They rested their horses, ate cold, moldy biscuits, and washed them down with brackish water. Everyone waited expectantly for the moon to rise. Traveling over the treacherous mountain passes of the Cumberland was dangerous enough in daylight. In pitch blackness it was insanity.

The wind came up with a low, eerie howl as they mounted up, but the sky was clear. A full moon cast a faint silver haze over the steep, winding trail. Tortuously they plodded up the switchbacks toward the Crow's Nest, the only pass not held by the Confederates. It would allow them access to the broad plateau of eastern Kentucky, access to General Burbridge's army.

When they crested the last ridge, Abner stopped and pointed west, down a steep twisting trail clearly delineated in the brightening silver light. "Follow this down till ya hit the creek, then veer to the right. Creek'll take ya ta Pine Knoll."

Palmer nodded. "We can find Burbridge from

there. You've rendered a great service to your country, Mr. Henderson. My men and I are most grateful."

"Only doin' what I got to, Colonel, just like you 'n Steve."

Loring reached across to clasp the brawny arm of his cousin. "When this damn war's over, I'm coming down to Clinch Creek for some of Aunt Fay's gooseberry pie. Then you and I are going squirrel hunting."

"You got you a deal, cuz," Abner replied warmly.

With a final wave he turned his horse off the trail and headed south down another twisting ravine, staying clear of the column of men. He'd be back in Clinch Creek by sunup with no one the wiser. Abner considered his cousin's parting words about squirrel hunting. Although Steve was a natural marksman, he'd never had Abner's woodsmanship and cunning, but after two years as a skirmisher, Steve's skill just might have improved.

The wind was still blowing, and then the rain renewed its assault, a stinging mist that added to Abner's misery. He thought of the warm bed at journey's end and nudged his horse to a faster pace. Exhaustion combined with the unfriendly elements to dull his hunter's instincts. Abner Henderson never heard the men behind him as one raised a .44 caliber Henry rifle and fired.

Denver, October 1864

The sound of soft weeping seeped beneath the heavy walnut door of the bedroom. Rising over the woman's softly sobbing remonstrance, Rufus Clayton's angry voice cut like a lash.

"Another girl child and dead at that! Bad enough you stillbirthed two sons for me, madam, now you can't even produce another puling live female!"

Cass leaned her ear against the door to hear her mother's soft voice, weak and exhausted. "Rufus, I've given you a fine healthy child. Cassandra is—"

"A female! My only heir, a seventeen-year-old girl, spoiled rotten and headstrong as one of my unbroken mules. I need sons, Eileen, sons to run my business. I've built the largest freighting firm in the biggest gold rush territory in the nation. The future's full of opportunities—opportunities for a man to grab with both hands. I survived a fire last year and a flood this spring. I'll be damned if I won't own half the territory in another decade.

"But what do I work for? A wife who wears silks and jewels but can't give me an heir. A daughter who spurns dresses for muddy boots and plays at doing a man's job. Dammit, it takes a *man* to do a man's job!"

Cass's knuckles whitened on the doorknob, then she abruptly released it. She'd spent half her life defending her mother against her father's vicious tirades. All it had ever earned her was Rufus's condemnation, followed by Eileen's pleading to "act like a lady."

"Damn them both!" she whispered to herself, fighting against the tears that clogged her throat.

She'd just returned from a two-week trip into the mountains, delivering general mercantile goods to the mining camps. Of course, her father's wagon master, Chris Alders, had been furious when he discovered her disguised as one of the stockboys tending the extra mules, but by then it was too late to send her back. Cass was there to work. And work she had—driving a team and wielding a whip with the skill of a man. Her vocabulary rivaled the most blistering compound adjectives of the muleskinners.

When her brothers were alive, they'd taught her well. Even Rufus himself had indulged his baby daughter, laughing at her attempts to emulate her older half brothers, even encouraging her interest in the freighting business. Bitterly she remembered how swiftly everything had changed when her brothers both died in a cholera epidemic four years earlier. Her beautiful mother became the target of Rufus's abuse and single-minded obsession to replace the sons he'd lost.

Cass walked down the hall to her room at the far end of the huge brick mausoleum Rufus Clayton called his city house. First she would soak two weeks' worth of mud and grime off her body and exchange her baggy trousers for a suitable dress. Nothing set Rufus off more than seeing her in boy's clothing.

On the subject of her behavior, her parents were in agreement. Eileen Quinlen came from a fine old Missouri family and was bred to Southern gentility. Ladies did not wear pants, swear, or even sweat. They certainly did not aspire to run a freighting business, which required all three!

As she luxuriated in scented hot water, every aching bone in her body cried out from the cold nights spent sleeping on hard ground. Her flesh was soothed but not her spirit. Her father had been notified of her return before she had even been able to undress. Immediately he had summoned her to his study.

"Let him wait," she muttered as she lathered her hair with lilac shampoo. Once, his vicious abuse of her ill mother would have sent Cass flying at him with claws out, but no more. She had her own battles to fight with Rufus Clayton. If her mother was spiritless and endured his tirades, so be it. Unable to please either parent, Cassandra Clayton had long ago decided to please herself.

When she knocked on his study door an hour later, she was dressed in a plain linen day gown of deep yellow and her light coppery curls were piled high on her head in a style she hoped added an aura of maturity to her nearly eighteen years.

Without waiting for permission to enter, Cass strode in. Rufus sat behind the big oak desk that dominated the room, thumbing through a sheaf of legal papers. Without looking up at her, he snapped, "You took your own sweet time obeying my summons."

"I needed a bath, Father."

He slammed down the papers and stood up, bristling at the self-possessed chit of a girl who stood defiantly before him. He was a big man, nearly six feet tall with heavy bones and a thick, muscular body. His dark brown eyes glared at her.

At five feet six inches, Cass was tall for a girl and thoroughly unintimidated as she glared back. "Well, get it over with. You're going to yell about my going with the train."

"If you'd stayed at home and not worried your mother half to death, perhaps the delivery would have gone better. The child might have lived," he accused cruelly.

Fighting down the rage his hateful words engendered, she bit out her reply. "What would it matter to you if the child had lived? It was only another worthless girl! I heard you cursing her for having another stillborn female. Your concern is really touching!"

As he stared at her, his ruddy complexion flushed, then paled. "I take it you've added eavesdropping to your already outstanding list of undesirable traits?"

She walked across the large, masculine room and stopped in front of the window overlooking the street. "Let's discuss my desirable traits for a change, Father. I rode the nigh wheeler on a ten-span and pulled a Murphy wagon with a trailer. Even Chris said I'm learning to work a jerk line as well as any of his new men. I can run this business, from loading the wagons to buying the goods. I can hire the drivers and keep the books. You don't need a son to run your empire. I can do it!"

She stood with her feet planted firmly apart, her fists clenched at her sides, and her chin thrust out—a most unladylike stance. "Ask your wagon master." Her golden eyes blazed the challenge at him as she waited for his reply.

Rufus Clayton strode across the room toward her. His iron-hard expression and menacing walk had cowed many a man, but not this reckless girl. He had not slept since his wife had gone into labor two days before, and he was exhausted and bitterly disappointed. Eileen was delicate and weak, but Cass was *his* daughter, tall and strong, a tough survivor. What splendid grandsons she would give him! But only if she learned her place as a female.

"I've been remiss raising you as I did, letting you run after your brothers, thinking yourself capable of besting a man." He shook his shaggy head, and the thick mutton chop whiskers on his jowls gave his face the look of a tenacious bulldog. "It's time you learned your place—and it is *not* on one of my freight wagons!"

"I suppose my place is simpering at gentlemen callers in the parlor or sipping tea with Abigail Simpson and her mother. I hate parties and dances and making vapid conversation with addle-brained women."

"You *are* a woman—at least you should be! Soon you'll be eighteen. Old enough to marry," he said levelly.

She replied with withering scorn, "How very convenient. Marry me off and then turn your attentions to my poor mother again. How many times will you endanger her life? She's had three stillbirths since my brothers died—you'll kill her in your quest for a son!" Cass squeezed her eyes shut for a second in an effort to regain control. She didn't see the blow coming.

Rufus slapped her across the cheek, knocking her back against the bookshelves that lined the study wall. As she struggled to stay on her feet and shook her head to clear it, he felt an immediate stab of guilt. He'd always had an abominable temper, but so did Cass. She goaded him beyond reason.

Her cold, curt words broke the silence that had lengthened between them as she daubed at the blood on her cut lip. "I will never marry. No man will do to me what you've done to my mother."

Rufus bristled defensively. "I took that woman from what is politely called genteel poverty and lavished everything on her—stylish clothes and grand houses, everything her lazy, worthless father lost for his family. She was glad enough to be Mrs. Rufus Clayton, and no matter to her or her fine Southern family if I was a crass Yankee."

Cass sneered. "You bought her from Grand-father Quinlen. Just you try and sell me like that, Father!"

"I'll do whatever I damn well please with you—including marry you off! *If* I can find a man stupid enough to want an unnatural woman like you for a wife," he said, fighting the red rage that danced behind his eyes like licking flames.

"I'll get a job as a bullwhacker before I let any man own me!"

Suddenly the room seemed to go dark and Rufus sank to his knees, then fell face forward at Cass's feet. He could hear her scream for help, but when she knelt and rolled him over, cradling his head in her lap, he could not utter a sound.

"A stroke is an uncertain thing, Miss Clayton. He's regaining some use of his right arm and can talk a bit now, but . . ." The elderly doctor let the sentence fade. His expression revealed the hope-lessness of Rufus Clayton's situation. "A real trag-edy, first your poor mother losing the babe, then your father stricken so suddenly. Do you have any kin we can notify? Rufus will need someone to manage business affairs for you and your mother."

Cass stood in the hallway outside her father's bedroom. It had been over a week since their ter-rible argument and his collapse. She shook her head and began to usher him toward the stairs. "No, Dr. Simpson. I'm the only Clayton left. Fa-ther had no family, and my mother's people are all dead now. My last cousin on the Quinlen side was killed at Gettysburg."

The doctor made clucking sounds of sympathy.

"I suppose Attorney Smith will have to appoint someone," he said vaguely. "Your father asked to speak with him."

Cass let it pass, nodding in agreement as she bade the doctor farewell at the front door. "Let him do his worst, calling that puling old lawyer," she whispered beneath her breath. "As God is my witness, I swear I'll run Clayton Freighting and I'll make it into the biggest shipping empire in the Rocky Mountains. Just let them try and stop me!"

Virginia, April 1865

"It's a hell of a note, Will, you ordering men to tear up railroad tracks," Steve Loring said with a quirky grin at General Palmer.

The two officers stood watching their men at work, destroying a vital link in the Confederate rail system just outside Lynchburg. They had just received word of Lee's surrender at Appomattox the day before, but Johnston still ravaged through North Carolina and Jefferson Davis had fled further into Georgia. The war neared its end, but still the destruction continued.

"As a railroad builder I must confess a certain reluctance at doing this duty, but when this war's over, I'll make up for these few miles of track," Palmer replied gravely. Then his eyes lit up as he spoke of his great dream. "The railroad is going west. Just think of it, Steve, linking California with Philadelphia, Chicago with Mexico. Rails will stretch the length and breadth of America. The future's in the West."

Steve ran his fingers through his sweat-dampened hair and replaced his hat. His face was hard and weary for a scant twenty-four years of living. Still, he smiled at his commander's faith in the future. "You go west and build your railroad, Will. I'll be happy to raise good horseflesh and wake up each morning in a real bed."

Palmer's eyes were kind as he looked at the younger man. "You're not so lacking in ambition as to settle for life as a Kentucky farmer? If I know Robert Loring—and I do know him well—he's already making more grandiose plans for his only son."

Steve shook his head. "After the past two years, I just want breathing space, Will."

Before Palmer could frame a response, one of the sentries called out a warning. Several men in tattered gray uniforms rode slowly into the midst of the Union soldiers, who now stopped their work to observe the confrontation.

"Colonel Prentice, I believe?" Palmer said, indicating with a nod that the officer could lower his hands.

The sentry stood behind Prentice with his rifle ready, his eyes never leaving the enemy officer as he dismounted.

Prentice smiled thinly. "And you are now risen in rank to general, I believe, sir. I have the rather dubious distinction of being a messenger for General Johnston. He's arranged a truce with your General Sherman."

Palmer turned to Sargent Simms. "Bring some water from the spring and have the cook fry up some of that side meat we had for breakfast. Please, Colonel, you've had a long ride. Let me see your documents while you and your men refresh yourselves."

"I thank you, sir. We've eaten nothing but moldy

corn dodgers for weeks on end," Prentice said as he followed Palmer to the shade of a large oak where the men could sit on the clean grass and rest.

Palmer read the papers and nodded. "This seems to be in order, Colonel. I'll send a messenger to General Sherman and request further instructions. I hope we do not have to become your general's jailers."

Evening fell soft as a kiss, and the hum of the katydids blended with the wistful sound of a harmonica played by one of the enlisted men. Steve sat in the shadows of a willow copse near the stream, slowly chewing his food but not tasting it. Finally, he set the tin plate down and took a swallow of hot coffee. In the last days of the war's mop-up operations, their rations were better than they'd been since he joined Palmer's fast-moving raiders in 1863. "And that reb complained of moldy bread. What the hell did he think we've lived on all these years?"

Just then one of Prentice's aides, a young boy, approached him. Ragged and pale, he looked no more than fifteen. Loring's forbidding countenance lightened. "What can I do for you, son?"

"You be Cap'n Loring—Steve Loring?" the boy asked nervously.

Puzzled, Steve nodded.

"I heerd them men say yore name. I know a lady back in Clinch Creek who's kin."

"Fay Henderson is my mother's sister," Loring replied.

"You might want ta look ta her once't the war's over, Cap'n, her bein' a widow woman with no other kin."

"I knew my uncle was killed, but she has a son, Abner," Steve replied uneasily.

The boy shuffled in obvious consternation. The man was a Federal, but he did have kin in his home county. "Abner's been kilt, Cap'n. Last fall. Miz Fay, she's alone."

Steve grabbed the boy's frayed jacket in reflex before he could stop himself. "Abner's dead? When? How did it happen?"

The boy's story poured out in a rush of frightened words. "It was last October. We was followin' you fellas, but we lost you in the rain. We come on his body in a ravine. He'd been shot in the back. Colonel Prentice said he was a Federal spy, but I saw ta gettin' him home, him bein' from Clinch Creek 'n all."

Steve released him and then asked softly, "Your colonel knew he was a Federal sympathizer?"

The youth began to back away. "I only know what he said, Cap'n. Don't know if'n it be true or not."

Steve looked at the boy for a moment, then said, "I thank you for seeing to his burial." Then he turned and walked across the grassy hillside to where Palmer and Prentice were sitting.

"Prentice, I understand you found a dead civilian last October when you were chasing us into Kentucky," he said without preamble.

Palmer's large hands tightened around his tin cup. "Lord God! Not Henderson?"

Prentice looked from Palmer back to Loring. "Yes. Several of my men knew him. He was a Kentucky boy but a Federal spy. I'd heard rumors about his guiding you and other Union troops through the passes. We never caught him. Apparently someone else did."

Steve's face was granite hard as he knelt before the Confederate colonel. "He was shot in the back?"

"Yes. We found the shell casings nearby. They were from a Henry rifle, .44 caliber rimfire. None of my men had the means to obtain such a fancy gun, Loring. You know that," Prentice stated in a tense voice.

General Palmer stood up and ran his hand through his hair. "O'Brien, Tanner, and Wortman all carried those fancy Henry rifles."

"And they deserted before we reached General Burbridge," Steve added. "They *were* our Copperheads. I knew it!"

Palmer sighed wearily. "I always suspected your instincts were right, Steve. Damn, I only hope they've been meted out justice for their treachery!"

Steve's face was devoid of all expression now, its chiseled planes and angles ice cold. "Oh, justice will be meted out, Will, never fear. I swear it!"

Chapter Two

Denver, 1868

"And to my daughter, Cassandra Eileen Clayton, as my only living heir, I bequeath Clayton Freighting Lines, my ranch and all its livestock in Pueblo, my city house in Denver, and all my other worldly goods, with the exception of the following cash sums." Attorney Thurston Smith was a thin, officious man with a moustache that seemed to outweigh his cadaverous head, which always hung forward, causing him to pause as he was doing at the moment and push his spectacles up over the bridge of his nose.

Cass fidgeted in her chair, a lumpy monstrosity of horsehair with gargoyles carved on its arms and legs. *Get it over with*, she fumed to herself, loathing Smith's sense of drama as he slowly turned the page and read off the small bequests to various household servants and men who worked for Clayton Freighting. Twisting the small lace hankie in her hands until it shredded, she forced herself to be calm. After nearly four nightmare years it was over. She had proven herself worthy, if not of his love, at least of his business.

If only Mama could've lived! Now she'd be free. But, paralyzed and bitter, Rufus Clayton had outlasted his frail wife, who nursed him devotedly while Cass attended to the daily operation of the freighting company. Less than a year after his stroke, Eileen had died of influenza. Cass had scoffed at the diagnosis. Her father's vitriolic rages had sapped her of the will to live.

While Eileen had grown listless and pale, Cass had bloomed. House-bound and under heavy medication, Rufus Clayton had tried to control his vast holdings, but such work required a boss who could meet with salesmen, ride the wagons up to the mining camps, and check on the livestock at the road stations. Never a man to trust subordinates, Rufus had summoned one of his longtime wagon masters, Chris Alders, and charged him with the duties. It quickly became apparent to Cass and to Alders himself that he could not handle the job. Increasingly as the years wore on, he deferred to her judgment.

She traveled east to Kansas City and Council Bluffs, even Chicago, and arranged wholesale shipments of everything from yard goods to laudanum. She went to St. Louis and ordered twenty new wagons from the foremost manufacturer in the nation, Joseph Murphy. She hired several clerks to oversee the bookkeeping, bought mules and oxen, harnesses and yokes. At first she needed Chris's help in hiring muleskinners and bullwhackers, but her ability with a blacksnake and the accompanying inventiveness at swearing gradually allowed her entry into their rough society. She was "ole man Rufus's daughter and no doubt about it!"

Sitting in the cluttered dark office of her father's attorney, Cass didn't at all resemble the hoyden who scandalized Denver society by parading down Larimer Street in men's mud-spattered pants and boots. Her wildly curly mass of copper hair was swept up into a sleek chignon with a tiny black lace hat covering it. She wore a severely tailored black silk dress that bespoke mourning even as it accented her unmistakably feminine curves. She looked subdued and ladylike, but those who knew her could understand the determined set of her chin and the golden luster in her dry eyes. It was too late to cry for her father, just as it had been for her mother. Fear, tension, and sheer grit had carried her through the huge, ostentatious funeral. Now she only wanted it done. Everything she had toiled for in the last four years would finally come to her.

As Thurston Smith paused again and swept the room with a pregnant glance, a sudden prickle of unease rippled through her. There was more. She looked over at Chris Alders, who smiled in reassurance. With no other family left to inherit, only Chris and half a dozen of the household servants sat in the stifling room with her.

"The conditions of my daughter's inheritance are as follows," Smith continued smugly. Did Cass detect a smirk in his voice as her heart began to thud in her chest? She gripped the carved arms of the hideous chair until her fingers whitened and ached.

"First, she has a three-year grace period from the date of my death in which to find a suitable man to wed. Being cognizant of my daughter's willful temperament and manipulative nature, I further stipulate that her husband will henceforward control all operations of Clayton Freighting and have at his complete disposal all the resources I herein bequeath my daughter. To assure that this be no marriage of convenience in which she will command a weak-willed man unfit to carry on my work, I further stipulate this union produce a male child within the three years following my death."

Although several audible whispers and gasps echoed in the high-ceilinged room, Cass sat stock still and silent. Small cuts on her fingers from the splintered edges of the chair arms oozed blood. But the coarse wood soaked it up. She did not feel the pain as Smith continued reading.

"Let her choose the man she weds well, for he will get children on her who must one day inherit all I have striven for. In the event Cassandra Eileen Clayton fails to fulfill the conditions of this will within the time given, she will forfeit all claims to Clayton Freighting and all other of my worldly goods. Everything bequeathed to her will then go to Clark Matthews, nephew of my beloved first wife, Mathilda Matthews Clayton."

Chris Alders swore beneath his breath as Smith droned on with the conclusion and verifications of the will. When the old man looked at Cass, she nodded woodenly to him, indicating that she was not about to have an attack of the vapors. Yet Chris knew what Rufus's cruel provisions had done to her. *He's reaching back from beyond the grave to punish her for not bein' born a boy. Damn him to the hell I already know he's in!*

Thurston Smith looked up at Cass and rubbed one elongated, thin finger across his bristly moustache in a nervous gesture. Damn, he always had disliked the brazen Clayton woman! "Are the terms of your father's will quite clear, Miss Clayton?"

"Quite clear, Mr. Smith. Also quite monstrous, as well you know." Her eyes had ignited with golden flames, and she stood up and glared furiously at him. Still her composure did not break. "Of course, I will fight the terms of this will. No reasonable court in the territory would uphold it."

Smith too stood up now, but with far less assurance. He was several inches shorter than Cass Clayton and had always hated looking up into her haughty, beautiful face. "The will is quite legal and not at all unreasonable, my dear. Your father's body had grown frail, but his mind was quite sound. No court will ever question a father's concern for providing a protector for his only daughter."

"We'll see, Mr. Smith, won't we?" Her tone of voice indicated the slow-simmering rage that she held agonizingly in check for the moment. Chris, who had seen her in tempers to make a muleskinner quake—not to mention the mule—feared she would erupt with little more provocation.

"We can get the best lawyers from back east, Cass. We got us years to beat this," he said stoutly.

Nodding to the gnarled old wagonmaster, Cass turned one last scathing word to Smith. Looking his immaculate gray wool suit up and down, she asked irrelevantly, "Do you know what would perfectly accessorize your ensemble, Attorney Smith?"

Dumbly he shook his head. Had the chit lost her wits?

"A large, rabid timber wolf at your throat!" With that she turned sharply on her heel and walked rapidly through the office door.

When they had emerged into the bright morning sunlight on the crowded street, Robert N. Byers of the *Rocky Mountain News* headed toward her, note pad and pencil ready. Byers's precisely trimmed beard and piercing gray eyes reflected the crusading zeal with which he approached his job. News about the last will and testament of one of Denver's leading citizens was obviously the story of the week.

"Miss Clayton, a moment, please," he asked politely, tipping his hat in deference. "Would it distress you too greatly to tell us the disposition of your dear father's estate?"

The crowd pressed in on her. Many of them were her employees, stock handlers, clerks, muleskinners, and bullwhackers, abetted by an overflow of riffraff from the saloons in the neighborhood, and sprinkled liberally with curious merchants and shopkeepers, even well-dressed matrons with small children in tow. The whole city avidly awaited word of the final duel between Rufus Clayton and his outrageous daughter.

Vultures, she thought, then amended the condemnation. They were merely curious, and some even feared for their livelihood, depending on what happened to one of the city's largest businesses. "I plan to fight my father's will, Mr. Byers," Cass said clearly for all the crowd to hear.

"Surely he didn't disinherit you, Miss Clayton!" the publisher asked, startled.

Cass's eyes blazed, but her face was coldly set

as she replied. "No, he did not. But as to the terms of the will, you may discuss them with Attorney Smith. Soon they'll be a matter of public record. Now, if you'll excuse me, gentlemen."

As Byers politely nodded and again offered his condolences, Cass turned toward her waiting carriage. Just as Chris cleared a path for her and she reached for the step up, Bennett Ames's big beefy hand reached for her elbow to assist her inside. She flinched away and glared at him with undisguised hostility.

"Keep your paws to yourself, Mr. Ames."

His round, florid face broadened even more as he laughed. "You never could abide men touching you. From what I hear about your daddy's will, you'll be changing your tune real soon."

Cass paled, but recovered quickly. "What did you do, get Thurston Smith drunk so he'd tell you?"

His blunt fingers spread in a placating gesture, causing his garish ruby and sapphire ring to wink obscenely in the sunlight. "You know I keep abreast of everything going on in the territory. A man has to, to run a business as big as Ames Freighting. This ain't no business for a woman alone, Cass. Now you and me could make a deal. Marry me and I'd do my duty by you to keep the terms of the will. Then I'd let you free with a large cash settlement. You could travel, go to Europe—"

Her scornful laughter cut him off, but her skin crawled in revulsion. "I'd as soon bed with a spider—a big *fat, hairy* spider!"

His face darkened. "Keep this up and you'll be out begging in the streets. That cousin of yours'll have the line, Cass. I can run either one of you out of business in a year or two."

"By sabotaging my wagons so the brakes fail, or cutting through the ropes on drag logs down Court Hell Pass?" she shot back. "You're a bully and a thief, Bennett Ames, and I'll see *you* begging in the streets before I'm done! Now get the hell out of my way or I'll put a bullet in your fat gut." She pulled a .22 caliber Remington Zig Zag from her reticule and pointed it levelly at the straining middle button of his satin vest. "It's smaller than what I usually carry, but they aren't usual accessories for mourning wear." When he hesitated with a livid grimace, she added, "At close range, even a pop gun like this would seriously interfere with your digestion, Bennett."

A long, low chuckle emanated from behind her and then a slight man with frizzy reddish hair stepped up on the walk beside her. "I reckon I'd mind th' lady, Mr. Ames. I seen whut one o' them pea shooters kin do ta a feller. Rightly messes up his clothes. Rearranges his innards some, too."

"Who the hell are you?" Ames rounded on the much smaller man, then backed up a step when he saw the hard gleam in the man's blue eyes. His hand rested ever so lightly on the Colt strapped to his hip. Freckle-faced and bandy-legged though he was, the stranger commanded respect.

"Name's Hunnicut, Kyle Hunnicut." He shoved a greasy Stetson back on his head and smiled at Cass, ignoring Ames.

Her gold eyes widened into a shocked smile. "I must say you look nothing like the ogre my father portrayed."

"Ole Rufus 'n me go back a ways. I wuz jist a tad in Texas when I worked for him. Can't say yew favor him, Miz Cass, but that's all the better!"

Cass laughed heartily, ignoring Ames now as she tucked the Remington back in her handbag and reached out to shake his hand. "Welcome to Denver, Mr. Hunnicut."

Ames's eyes narrowed as he watched the exchange. "This man's a hired gun. I've heard about him! What the hell are you doing with him, Cass?"

Chris Alders, who had been silently observing the confrontation, let out a chuckle of his own. "Why, Bennett, doncha know Mis Cass hired his gun!"

Ames looked at Cass for confirmation and was aghast at her nod. "I've been trying to catch up with Mr. Hunnicut ever since my father began to decline last month. I figured once he was dead, I'd need his, er, unique talents."

Ames nodded to the man who stood slightly shorter than Cass Clayton, then turned to her. "So, it's to be a war, then. Winner take all. Good enough for me. Don't say you weren't warned."

"You already 'warned' us at Court Hell Pass. That's why Mr. Hunnicut is here," Cass said levelly.

When Ames had stomped off, she turned to the slightly built man. The way the ruthless freighter had backed down from Hunnicut had not escaped her. "You do seem to have a fearsome reputation, Mr. Hunnicut," she said as she climbed into the carriage and motioned him to join her. Chris followed them into the coach and the driver took off.

"I'd admire it if'n yew'd call me Kyle, ma'm. Folks like Ames kin call me mister," he said with a crooked grin that made his ageless face seem almost boyish.

Cass let a breath of relief escape. "All right, Kyle.

I have a feeling you and I are going to deal famously together."

Cincinnati, 1868

As he reached for the heavy brass door knocker, Steve Loring took a deep, calming breath. After three years of searching, he must not fail.

When a big blonde woman wearing a brassy smile and a sheer silk robe opened the door, he grinned rakishly and doffed his hat. "Hello. I'm looking for someone." He paused and scrutinized her ample curves consideringly.

With a throaty laugh she ushered him in, saying, "I'm her. Name's Kitty."

It was raining outside and the inclement weather provided him with an excellent excuse for wearing a coat that concealed the army revolver in his belt. Men seldom came to the poshest bordello in Cincinnati to shoot anyone.

Kitty Boyle looked at the handsome stranger who seemed busy brushing raindrops from his clothes. Expensive coat and boots, well barbered, with elegant, aristocratic features. He reeked of money. "Well, sugar, you decide you've found who you're looking for? I sure have!" Her eyes devoured him as she reached for his coat.

Refusing his hostess's offer to take the coat, Steve scanned the opulent parlor through the big arched doorway. A piano was being played surprisingly well by a pretty brunette. The long, elegant silk sofas scattered about the large room were filled with women in various stages of artful dishabille, their bodies draped over men in expensive suits.

"O'Brien around?" he asked casually of the blonde, but the dangerous glint in his eyes warned her something was badly amiss.

Kitty stroked his wet coat sleeve, trailing her fingers down onto the back of his hand in an intimate gesture. "Mick O'Brien's a mean sucker. What do you want with him? We could go upstairs..." She stroked his wrist again.

"O'Brien upstairs?" he asked without emotion.

She dropped her hand from his abruptly, knowing after long years of experience when to give up. "He's out back in the kitchen stuffin' his ugly face with supper," she answered with a curt nod toward the long gaslit hallway that led to a heavy oak door.

He favored her with a devastatingly white smile. "Thank you, I'm obliged."

"Wait," she called out as he turned down the hall. "O'Brien didn't get to be the doorman here by fighting fair. He carries a sleeve gun and a knife sheathed on his back."

Steve's eyes narrowed in consideration and he nodded at Kitty again. "I appreciate the information. I won't fight fair either."

She watched his retreating back with a sense of dread tightening her chest.

Steve put his hand on the doorknob. The polished brass felt cool to his touch. Holding the knob with his right hand, he reached inside his coat with his left, reassuring himself as he cocked the revolver and pulled it free from his sash.

O'Brien looked up, his watery gray eyes squinting at the dark figure looming in the doorframe. The lights behind the stranger were dim, obscuring his face. The big kitchen was brightly illuminated as the German cooks fussed with the elaborate foods for the buffet tables in the dining room. The thin Irishman remained seated behind the large oak table. If necessary, it would be good cover when overturned. A prickle of unease washed over him as he studied the stranger. He wiped his mouth free of grease from the fat capon he had been devouring and started to lower his hand to the gun at his waist.

"Don't," came the low rejoinder. Both men knew what was meant, and O'Brien paused with his hand on the edge of the table.

Steve raised his right hand slightly and Mick relaxed a tiny bit. "You remember me, Corporal?" he asked softly.

The harshly chiseled face with its fierce golden tiger's eyes suddenly came into focus, jarred into familiarity by the use of the old military rank. "Loring, Lieutenant Loring, ain't it? You ain't out to catch deserters, are you? War's been over for three years." O'Brien watched the tall man take a step into the room. Now the noise level in the kitchen subsided as the German cook and his helpers sensed the eminent confrontation.

"War's been over three years, yes. And Abner Henderson's been dead for four years. You still carry that .44 caliber Henry rifle, corporal?"

O'Brien stiffened for a split second, then lunged up, flinging the heavy table forward with surprising strength for so slight a man. With blinding speed Steve grabbed the edge of the overturned table and toppled it away from O'Brien. Robbed of his cover, the startled man raised his hands as Loring's gun flashed into sight, leveled in his left hand.

O'Brien began to back away as Loring advanced on him, his eyes now as cold as polished amber. "Look, Lieutenant—"

"Captain," Steve interrupted. "After you and your pals killed my cousin and deserted, I was promoted. Now, about Wortman and Tanner..." He let the gun barrel loom ominously near Mick's face.

"If I tell you where they are—Vance, he done the shootin', not me. He was our leader. Said Henderson was a traitor. It was war, Loring!" O'Brien's voice took on a pleading note as he backed near a wall of open cabinet shelves.

"It took my agents three years to find you. Now you're going to take me to Wortman and Tanner. Then we'll decide who was the leader."

Just as Steve prodded the gun barrel sharply into Mick's throat, the wiry man smashed it aside with one hand while his other hand groped behind him for a heavy cut glass pitcher. Grabbing it, he swung at Loring's face. Steve dodged as O'Brien dropped the pitcher and threw himself to the floor. As he rolled, Mick freed his Colt from its holster, but Loring was on him, kicking the weapon away. Steve pinned his foe's wrist painfully to the hard wooden planks and ground his booted foot down on it.

With his gun once more prodding Mick's throat, Steve appeared barely winded. "As I was saying, where are your friends?"

"Let me up, let me—ooh!" O'Brien let loose a volley of profanity as Steve applied more pressure to the wrist. "I can't talk if you break my arm!"

"You can't talk if I shoot you either, but that won't stop me once I run out of patience. Where are Tanner and Wortman?" Steve asked hoarsely.

"All right, Wortman's in St. Louis! Works for a brewery near the levee. Just let me up, goddammit!"

"What about Vince Tanner?" Steve asked, lessening the pressure on O'Brien's wrist slightly.

"West—he went back out west! Franz knows his people—where he's from, all that." O'Brien sat up when Steve released his arm, waiting for the agonizing throbbing to stop. As he massaged his wrist, he moaned and slumped forward, hoping to distract his tormentor while he went for his sleeve gun.

Steve let him free the gun and raise it before he fired. His bullet knocked O'Brien backward like a mule kick. As he landed on the floor, the sleeve gun, still clutched tightly in his hand, discharged harmlessly into a wooden cabinet.

Dispassionately Steve rolled the dead man over with his foot and noted the beautifully carved stiletto in its sheath on his back. "Thank you, Kitty," he murmured as he replaced his Colt in his belt and left the kitchen by the rear door.

Louisville

"It's disgraceful, I tell you! And dangerous! You could've been killed, Steven—shooting a common criminal in a...a..." Amelia Graham Loring stumbled over the distasteful word.

"Bordello," Steve helpfully supplied for his mother as he stared out the big window. He could sense her shudder of revulsion even though his back was turned.

"Yes, well, the fact remains, you were fortunate those criminals didn't all attack you! Oh, Steven, give up this insane blood feud. Fay's passed on to her reward now, and you can't bring Abner back."

"But I can bring the men who caused their deaths to justice," Steve said levelly.

They'd had this argument often in the past three years as he relentlessly pursued every lead his paid operatives brought him. His Aunt Fay had grieved herself to death, losing her husband to the Confederacy and her son to the Union. At first, when he returned from the war, a hardened veteran with the cool golden light of the damned glowing in his eyes, his parents had left him alone, hoping he'd find himself. But he had never settled down. He couldn't, knowing that those traitors, the three men responsible for the destruction of his most beloved kin, were walking free.

Amelia twisted a fine lace handkerchief in her delicate fingers and began to pace, her dark gray skirts rustling softly. She was still in the final stages of mourning for her husband. Robert Loring had died nearly a year ago, and everything rested on his son's shoulders. Steve had begun by turning over his interest in the vast Loring banking empire to his father's brother, Lucas. That had pleased Amelia, for it meant her son had come home to Louisville after so many years in that cold, dreadful Philadelphia. How she had hated the East and longed for soft, warm Kentucky nights. Since Robert's death, she and Steve had returned once more to her ancestral home, Graham Hall.

Steve turned and looked at his mother's delicate magnolia complexion. The soft blonde hair and patrician features hid a will of iron. *The steel butterfly*. That's what his father had called her, and it was an apt description. Outwardly a flighty and charming Southern belle, Amelia was different from her sister. Fay had been strong in an honest, generous way. Amelia was manipulative and frigid beneath the facade of beauty and grace. He'd known since he was twelve years old that his father had kept women and visited bordellos. By the time Steve was fifteen, he'd understood and forgiven the proper Philadelphia banker for his one real vice.

Now mother and son confronted each other across Robert Loring's study. It was the one room in the Graham family mansion that he'd left his stamp on, the room Steve always retreated to, as if trying to capture the essence of the distant man who had been his father. The study was dark with deep burgundy drapes and a Turkish carpet of midnight blue. The furniture was all of walnut and leather, the walls lined with bookshelves, filled with volumes covering every subject from ancient history to modern banking law. It was an orderly, erudite room, masculine and quiet.

Amelia had always disliked it. Last year when she wanted to redecorate, they had argued. Steve won and it became his office. The headquarters from which he dispatched detectives, and in which he sifted through reports, searching, searching.

Not deterred by her son's casual indifference and seeming preoccupation, Amelia again launched her suit. "Since your father died and Barbara married, I'm all alone, Steven. You have responsibilities to remain at home, see to the running of your family estate."

He quirked one brow sardonically. "Oh? You were more than eager for me to relinquish the running of father's estate in Philadelphia. And as to my sister, she lives scarcely an hour's ride away.

Soon you'll have grandchildren to occupy your
time."

"You are the one to carry on the family name,
not Barbara," she replied plaintively. "Since the
war, you've become a stranger, full of brooding
silences, obsessed with this . . . this mission of
yours."

"War changes people, Mother." He shrugged
and poured a small glass of sherry, then a larger
dollop of bourbon. He handed her the sherry and
took a long sip of the whiskey. "Anyway, I have
been attending to 'my family estate' here. The stud
farm is flourishing and I've repaired virtually all
the damage done to the outbuildings during the
war."

Amelia took a drink and grimaced at the acid
sweet burn of the wine. "Those filthy animals, destroying property just because we remained loyal
to our country."

"This is rebel country, mostly, Mother. The Confederates only did here what the Federals did all
over the South," he replied tiredly. At least he had
diverted her from the tirade about the shooting.
He'd been lucky his attorneys were able to get him
free in Cincinnati by claiming self defense. It had
been a near thing to jail. If his mother knew how
close, she'd have even more apoplexy.

Amelia switched tactics. "Why don't I have Marcia and her parents to dinner this Saturday? I'm
sure they've heard rumors about your . . . altercation. We need to put the scandal to rest, Steven."

Steve chuckled mirthlessly. "By all means, let's
not have my fiancée's genteel parents upset at the
prospect of a jailbird son-in-law!"

* * *

Dinner was sumptuous and elegant as always when Amelia Loring was in charge of the affair. Paul Coleman and his wife chatted of inconsequential matters with his mother while Marcia exchanged confidences with Steve. The crystal chandelier over the dining-room table reflected on Marcia's glistening chestnut curls. She was exquisitely lovely in a pale lavender dress that displayed her more than ample bosom. Her delicate lily white skin and enormous china blue eyes only added to the allure.

Her parents owned the estate adjoining Graham Hall, and since Steve's return to run the stud farm, he had bought several brood mares from Paul. The two men were both war-hardened and practical. Despite his initial reserve at dealing with a Federal, Paul Coleman had needed the sale and found he liked Steve and enjoyed doing business with him.

Then his only daughter had ridden into Steve's life, waiting regal as a princess to be helped down from her sidesaddle. Clad in an elegant riding habit of royal blue velvet, Marcia had a waist he could span with his hands, and smelled of expensive French perfume. It had been love at first sight.

At least Steve had thought so six months ago. Now he was not so sure. Unlike his frigid, iron-willed mother, Marcia was warm and vivacious, a natural born flirt. The first time he kissed her she had melted in his arms. She was innocent, yet possessed a fiery temperament that had more than once tested his dwindling reserve of honor. He had vowed not to touch her until their wedding night.

Now he had to postpone setting the date. He shifted uneasily in his chair, wondering how to bring up the delicate matter. The Colemans knew nothing of his oath of vengeance, indeed they knew little of the dark side of his nature. He was a man raised with split allegiance who'd had to choose a flag in the senseless bloody carnage they'd all lived through. Paul Coleman, a colonel in the Confederate Army, had forgiven him his choice, but could he understand and forgive this quest to bring three Copperheads to justice? Could Marcia?

"What a bore I must be, Steve." Marcia interrupted his reverie with a saucy flip of her curls. "You're a million miles away while I've been rambling on about our engagement ball. You *are* an interested party, aren't you, darling?"

Steve could feel the heat stealing into his face. The very subject he had to broach was laid conveniently open before him. He looked from his fiancée to her parents and his mother. *No, not here.* "I'm sorry, Marcia. I've had a lot on my mind lately."

"Could it have to do with what happened in Cincinnati last week?" Marcia asked, holding her breath and casting a furtive glance toward her father.

"Now, Marcia, you know we agreed that Steve and I would discuss that over brandy and cigars later. It's nothing ladies should concern themselves with," Paul Coleman remonstrated.

Steve sighed. He'd avoid a scene with his mother and take on Paul and Marcia one at a time. "Yes, Paul, perhaps you're right. We do need to discuss what happened in Cincinnati. Please excuse us, Marcia? Mrs. Coleman? Mother?"

He kissed Marcia's soft hand and gave it an affectionate squeeze, then nodded at Amelia, who smiled her most gracious smile. "Yes, child, let's do let the men discuss their business while we plan that ball."

On cue, the women rose, Marcia and Mrs. Coleman obediently trailing after his mother toward her sitting room while he and Paul adjourned to the study. His future wife was nothing if not biddable. Of course, whose orders she would choose to follow, his or his mother's, remained to be seen. The thought gave him a twinge of unease as he poured two brandies and handed one to Paul.

"Now, Steve, tell me about your run-in with the police. What in hell possessed you to shoot a man in a whorehouse?"

Chapter Three

Dark purplish clouds massed in a threatening slate gray sky. "No wonder the horses were so skittish this morning," Steve muttered aloud as he led his favorite stud, Wind Racer, to the paddock where Southern Beauty awaited his service. A natural horseman since childhood, Steve had always preferred working outdoors with livestock to being confined in his father's office back in Philadelphia. But he also knew that without the Loring banking fortune, he'd not have been able to rebuild Graham Hall after the ravages of the war.

Or hire all those men to comb the country searching for three killers. He shook off the reverie. What was done was done. He'd left his business in Philadelphia in the capable hands of his uncle, and now the farm could practically run itself. He'd hired experienced men and seen to the selection of a fine new line of thoroughbred horses. Amelia was ensconced in her completely refurbished mansion, and he was free. Or was he?

He heard hoofbeats and looked up to see Marcia riding much too fast down the lane between the long rows of whitewashed board fences. When she reined in her lathered filly, he grabbed the bridle. He calmed the skittish animal by crooning low endearments and stroking her muzzle. In spite of growing up in Kentucky horse country, Marcia had never been a good rider.

He scowled up at his fiancée. "What the devil's gotten into you? You could have broken your neck, or killed a fine animal." He helped her dismount from the awkward sidesaddle and handed the reins to Hank.

One look at her tear-streaked, hysterical face made him contrite. She sobbed and leaned on him for support until the groom was out of earshot.

"Oh, Steve, I'm sorry, but I had to talk to you!"

He knew the reason for her tears. The scene last evening with Paul Coleman had been less than pleasant. Gently he led Marcia toward the small tack room near the paddock so they could talk in private. "Calm down, Marcia, and tell me what's wrong," he said, motioning her to sit on a long wooden bench against the rough plank wall.

He sat down next to her and she snuggled close. Dabbing at her eyes with a lacy kerchief, she hiccupped, "Daddy said you were going off to St. Louis chasing some man, and after that, off again. That you were risking your life and reputation and he wouldn't allow me to wait for such an irresponsible man. He wants me to break our engagement! Oh, Steve, tell me what he said isn't true," she implored, her small hand clutching his arm with surprising strength.

He took a deep breath. "I'm sorry your parents made the decision they did. Paul said he and your mother would discuss my plans and—"

"Your plans—then it is true!" she accused in a shrewish voice. "You are going to traipse all across the West looking for some horrible men to settle some silly old feud from the war!" Her eyes, teary and pleading before, now shot sparks and her cheeks reddened with anger as she stared impatiently at him, rather like a child denied a toy at bedtime.

"Yes, Marcia, I'm going to St. Louis and from there perhaps someplace else. It may not be more than a week—or it may mean another dead end. I may come back here and send out agents to search again," he explained carefully.

"In the meanwhile, what am I to do? Sit home knitting and hope you don't end up murdered in some—some bordello or gutter!" Her voice had a hysterical edge now.

"I'm not going to be murdered, Marcia. During the war I learned how to survive. I can take care of myself," he assured her.

"But who's going to take care of me?" she wailed pitifully. Then her voice changed from teary to wheedling. "Oh, please, darling, I know I can bring Papa and Mama around if you only say you'll stay home. We can have the grandest ball to announce our engagement. After all, the sooner we're betrothed, the sooner we'll be married..." she let her voice trail away suggestively as she embraced him, showering his neck and cheek with warm, wet kisses.

Steve firmly disengaged himself, rising from the bench to pace across the floor. *The manipulating little . . .* She was using him, using his physical attraction to her, encouraging it, just to bring him to heel.

"At least I'll give my mother credit for refraining from sexual bribery with my father," he said in a deadly quiet voice. Ignoring her hiss of shocked anger, he continued, "I must see two men brought to justice. If you can't wait a matter of weeks while I go to St. Louis and check out O'Brien's story, I see little hope for our future together, Marcia. I need your trust, not cajolery."

"Trust!" she spat furiously, standing up and gathering the long train of her riding habit with a swish. "What you don't need, Steve Loring, is me! I'll be the laughing stock of Louisville when our engagement is called off. I've already told all my friends! They tried to warn me not to marry a Yankee. I should have listened to them!" She stamped her foot in a childish gesture.

"Yes, my dear, you certainly should have listened to them," Steve replied coldly, turning his back and striding angrily from the tack room.

Denver, 1870

"Shit, he ain't drunk 's long 's he kin still make a noise," one of the men in the Bucket of Blood Saloon said of the figure slumped across the bar.

The big man lurched upright, wobbling from one leg to the other until he regained his balance by gripping the heavy oak lip of the bar top. "Let him whosh wifout sin cash th' firs' stone," he said in a nasal, slurred voice.

The Reverend Charles Filbert, dubbed "Sour Mash Charlie" by his friends in saloons the length and breadth of the territory, was a tall, corpulent man with a bulbous red nose, thinning white hair, and thick white eyebrows. Now he rose to his full majesty, brows arched and nose glistening, as he struggled to focus his unsteady gaze beyond the press of the crowd.

"Mish Clayton, your humble servant, ma'm," Sour Mash said with a flourish, bowing to greet her, hat in hand. Unfortunately, his protuberant stomach and its load of tangle-leg whiskey caused him to continue his face-forward descent toward the sawdust-strewn floor. Only the agility of his companions, one grabbing his arm and another his suspenders, saved him.

"Reverend Filbert, I had your word that you'd be ready to roll at dawn tomorrow. It looks to me like you won't be able to find your wagon, much less drive it." Cass eyed the weaving countenance before her with resignation. Damnblast! He was her only cook and she needed him for the long haul down to Fort Union in Arizona Territory.

"Aw, Miss Clayton, he'll be fine come mornin'," Dog Eating Jack volunteered as he held valiantly to the elastic suspenders threatening to give way with every lurch of the fat preacher's body.

All the other teamsters and miners in the Bucket of Blood hooted their agreement. If anyone in Colorado Territory had ever questioned the propriety of Cass Clayton storming into a saloon, that day was long past. Dressed in a crisp white shirt and tan trousers that were tucked smartly into her high, mud-covered boots, Cass looked businesslike and efficient. Her career in the two years since Rufus died had cemented acceptance of his daughter as proprietress of Clayton Freighting.

Cass nodded and slapped the looped blacksnake she always carried against her thigh. "Jack, you and Hog Leg see that he doesn't get another drop of forty rod tonight. Is that clear?"

Both men nodded, chorusing assurances that by morning Filbert would be preaching up a storm at his mules. She turned to leave, then paused for a moment and said, "That means no bouts of rheumatism as well as no hangover! Just remember that mule I whipped into shape last year," she added with a wicked grin.

Dog Eating Jack finished the now-familiar tale for her. "Yup, he got so skeered of you he jumped clean outta his skin. You backed him back inta it, but he's never been the same critter since!"

She shook her whip at the room full of roughened miners and teamsters with the mock severity of a schoolmarm threatening a class full of children. "And don't forget there isn't a man here I can't handle as well as I handle a mule!" Grinning, she left the saloon.

The big wagon yard behind Clayton Freighting was chaos. Mules brayed and horses skittered. To each set of Murphy wagons, swearing men harnessed ten pairs of wiry mules, called a ten-span. The first wagon of the set was called the leader. The second, attached to the rear of the leader by a short tongue, was the trailer. The average payload for each wagon was five tons. They carried all manner of staples for the isolated military posts, from flour to ammunition, salted meat to stove pipes. For the long trek, everything was carefully packed with the weight evenly distributed.

"If'n I wuz offered a chance ta work in a nitroglycerine factory or harness up a ten-span o' mules, I'd jump at th' chance fer th' factory job," one muleskinner said as he wound his blacksnake into a wide coil and draped it over one shoulder.

"Shit, here comes ole Sour Mash. Reckon we'll be prayin' for our grub this trip," another man said, spitting a big lob of tobacco juice into the churned-up mud of the yard.

"At least he don't give out them little bitty Bibles like old man Majors did," the first man said grudgingly.

"Just the right size for rollin' cigarettes," his companion rejoined with a chuckle.

Sour Mash Charlie Filbert lumbered toward the large mess wagon, where he began to check his supplies: repair tools for the wagons and harnesses, food and cooking utensils for the men. Then he opened the medicine chest and examined its contents: calomel, laudanum, and epsom salts, along with a few crude surgical tools. Having satisfied himself that all had been loaded in good order, he sat down on the wide plank porch backing the offices and rubbed his swollen knees.

"Whoohee! Thet stinks worse'n a possum eatin' shit, Sour Mash," Kyle said, wrinkling his nose at the red flannel rags, soaked in some odoriferous liquid, wrapped around the fat man's legs.

"My rheumatism has been paining me, sir. This remedy is from my sainted mother. Red flannel and kerosene. It will never fail to bring relief."

Kyle backed away, holding the cigarette he had been preparing to light. "Yew'll go up like Fourth o' July fireworks if'n anyone tetches a match near yew, yew dumb fool!"

"The Lord protects his own," Sour Mash averred resolutely.

"Yep, fools, preachers, 'n jackasses," Kyle muttered, walking across the yard to where Cass was preparing to mount the nigh wheeler on the lead wagon in the train. He eyed the wicked blacksnake casually slung across her slim shoulder and said, "Now, remember, go easy. We don't need ta break our fool necks keepin' up with yore crazy drivin'."

Cass grinned. "Yep, I know. A wagon as much as possible oughta stand upright when travelin'." She mimicked his east Texas twang perfectly. "Just so we make twenty miles today!"

It was a typical early spring day on the high plains. The sun was blindingly brilliant in an azure sky where fleecy clouds skittered across the wide horizon. On the ground the wind-driven dust peeled the skin from man and beast. The men complained, but it was the even-tempered grousing of everyday life. No one expected conditions to be easy.

The winter snows were melting in the high mountains. Rivers once a mile wide and an inch deep were becoming swift and treacherous to ford with cumbersome wagons. Cass pulled her lead wagon up and looked across the Purgatoire. "Hellsfire, I think we're going to have to uncouple, Kyle."

Hunnicut edged his buckskin gelding into the rapidly moving shallows to test the bottom. "It's a pretty considerable o' a river if'n it wuz tipped on its side. Right muddy, though. I reckon I'll give it a try." As he urged his horse out further, he caught sight of a lone wagon across the river, down around its curving bank.

"Wait here," he said and goaded the big horse deeper into the current. Taking no chances, Kyle slipped his Colt from its holster. Even with what looked to be one broken-down old wagon, a body could never be sure of a friendly welcome. Bennett Ames had any number of tricks up his sleeve.

When he crossed the river, he rode around the
bank to where a man, obviously a miner down on
his luck, was struggling in vain to free his wagon
from axle-deep mud.

"You look ta be in trouble, friend."

The man spat a wad of tobacco and scratched
his gray beard. "I been in worse, but they's two
other wagons under this un and they's in one hell
o' a fix!" He let loose with a hoot of laughter at
his own hyperbole and Kyle joined him.

"Rest them mules, an' after we cross, we'll pull
yew out."

They had been on the road for over a week and
had been lucky with the earlier crossings. Now the
time had come for a tedious "slow cross." When
Kyle returned to the train, Cass had already begun
the preparations. All the sets of wagons had to be
uncoupled and each individual wagon pulled
across one at a time with a ten-span of mules.

Kyle watched, half in admiration, half in vex-
ation as Cass issued crisp orders. Muleskinners
and stock wranglers methodically stripped down
to their longjohns, some even further. They were
as complacent about doing it in front of Cass as
she was impervious to their actions. Men had to
pull the mules by their harnesses and goad them
through the deep water. The teamsters had
learned early on that a man saved wear and tear
on his clothes, not to mention reducing the risk of
drowning, if he was lightly clad. There sat Cass,
perched on top of one particularly heavy wagon,
issuing orders to dozens of half-naked, swearing
men, calm as a church deacon directing a Christmas pageant.

Kyle remembered the first time he'd made a
deep river crossing with her. A couple of new men

had balked at her orders to undress. She'd backed them into the water with her whip, where they were carried under because of their heavy denim pants, wool shirts, and leather jackets. When her regulars hauled them coughing and choking back to the bank, they stripped and went to work with no further complaints—at least none voiced aloud near the woman with the whip and the fearsome temper.

By nightfall they had all the freight wagons across the Purgatoire and even pulled old Max Hancock's traveling home up on dry land. Campfires winked and the smell of baking biscuits wafted on the breeze, mixing with the moldy sweat of river-dampened men and the excrement of mules and horses.

Cass leaned back against the wheel of her big wagon and stretched like a contented cat. Her hair was still wet and tangled, her clothes muddy. She pulled her boots off and wiggled her toes near the fire with a sigh.

Kyle sat across from her, watching the way she adapted to a life most women would hate, even toughened pioneer women. After two years, she was still in many ways a mystery to him. He poked the fire. "Whut yew gonna do if'n them fancypants lawyers cain't git ole Rufus's will broke? Only got yew one more year, Cass. It's been draggin' on too long."

Her placid relaxation of a moment earlier evaporated and she sat up. "We'll win, Kyle. We have to!"

He considered as he sipped his coffee. Bitter. Sour Mash was a dreadful cook when his rheumatism acted up. Kyle's shrewd gaze noted the coiled tension in her body. "Don't mean to borry trouble, Cass." He paused, at a loss for words. "But, even if'n yew git ta keep runnin' th' freight lines, don't yew ever want ta get hitched—have a family? Yew treat men like they's jist so many span o' livestock. Niver seed one yew fancied?" He'd never been so bold as to put his worry and curiosity into words before, but they'd spent nearly two years in fruitless court battles and he feared what the outcome would be.

Cass took a steadying swallow of the inky coffee. "No, Kyle. I never want to marry. I've told you what hell Rufus made my mother's life. I'll never be at any man's mercy. As to how I treat men, I try to be fair, a good boss to my employees, a good friend to you." She paused and looked worriedly over at the little gunman. Then comprehension lit her eyes. "You're just bothered about the men undressing in front of me. Honestly, Kyle, whether a pack of scraggy muleskinners are clothed or buck-ass naked hardly signifies!"

Kyle knew she'd avoided the question. "I ain't talkin' 'bout our bein' friends or 'bout how them scraggeldy muleskinners look. Yew met lots o' fine fellers in Denver City 'n lots o' other places, too. Real gents. Yew oughta think again, Cass. Might git right lonely when yew git old."

"When I get old, I'll own half of Colorado, Kyle. You just see if I'm lonely!"

The clang of the dinner chime cut the discussion short. Kyle and Cass filed in line with the rest of the men, taking their turns democratically with the muleskinners. The Reverend Filbert always said a brief grace before he'd allow anyone to touch a spoon to his food. Silently Kyle said his own prayer that it would be tastier than the coffee.

Sour Mash, now sober and chastened, looked

balefully around the assembled multitude. "Oh, Lord, this gathering is a miserable excuse for humanity. Men of foul habits and low morals. Have mercy on them. Come down and save their souls from perdition—and please do not send your son, Jesus. This is no job for a boy! Amen."

The men surged forward for their dinner. Starved after a day of pulling recalcitrant mules through muddy water, few questioned the quality of the fare. When Kyle saw the grayish mass of lumpy matter ladled on his plate, he quirked one red eyebrow at Filbert. "Whut is it?"

"The best sonofabitch stew you ever sank a tooth into, you young rapscallion."

"Whut's in it? I cain't recognize nothin'," Kyle said peevishly, nudging one gray lump off another green one.

"Fool! That's what sonofabitch stew should be— if it's good, you can't recognize the hog chittlins from the cow's heart. Are you complaining or will you eat it?"

Kyle shrugged and took a bite. "I kin eat biled crow, but I don't hanker after it."

Men with their mouths stuffed full of stew and biscuits slapped their thighs and guffawed, spewing half-chewed food in their mirth.

Cass only winked at Sour Mash.

The rest of the trip proved uneventful, and by month's end they were back in Denver, having stopped at their Pueblo road ranch to check the new mules and oxen Cass had purchased that spring. The stock had been delivered in good condition, but she had Kyle post extra guards and leave strict instructions to watch out for rustling. One of Bennett Ames's favorite tactics was to sabotage competitors by depriving them of livestock.

"Some day we'll ketch thet greasy Ames, Cass," Kyle said as they walked toward the freight office. "Near did last fall if'n it warn't fer thet gulley-whomper thet washed out th' trail."

Cass shrugged in frustration. "Well, at least you've slowed him down with the men you hired to guard our outposts. Sooner or later, Mr. Ames will make a mistake and we'll have him by the bal—" Cass stopped short as a tall, gangly young man emerged from behind the counter, clearing his throat with an embarrassed cough.

His reddened face indicated that he had over-heard her crudity. "Miss Clayton, I presume?" He nodded stiffly in a disjointed yet oddly prissy man-ner, rather like an effete Ichabod Crane.

"Yes, I'm Cass Clayton," she replied coolly. "Who are you and what are you doing behind the counter in my freight office?"

"I'm Clark Matthews. Your daddy was my un-cle. His, er, first wife, Mathilda, was my daddy's dear sister."

Kyle could sense Cass stiffening and searched his brain for the significance of the vaguely fa-miliar name.

"So, aren't you a bit premature, *Cousin* Clark? The terms of my father's will give me another year before you inherit," Cass replied with icy irony.

Clark Matthews retreated a step at the obvious hostility in the bedraggled female's voice. Her long plait of hair was snarled and filthy, her scan-dalous pants and mannish shirt muddy and wrin-kled. He reconsidered the purpose of his journey, then looked again, through the thick lenses of his glasses, at her face with its clear golden eyes, del-icately arched brows, and firm ripe mouth. Of course, the chin was far too pugnaciously set and the eyes narrowed in anger, but the unorthodox clothes did reveal a startlingly well-proportioned woman's body.

"I realize the specifications of the will, Cousin Cassandra—I may address you as cousin although we're not truly blood kin, I trust?" Without waiting for her assent, he plunged on, "I've journeyed here all the way from Kansas City to meet you, not to see you disinherited. As a matter of fact, my intention is quite the opposite." He paused and looked at the menacing little banty-legged gunman standing beside Cass. He coughed nervously again. "Er, could we perhaps meet somewhere more private to discuss this matter?"

Noting the way Kyle made Matthews nervous brought a twitch to Cass's lips. "Oh, forgive my bad manners, Cousin Clark. This is my general manager and friend, Kyle Hunnicut."

Kyle shoved his dusty wide-brimmed hat back on his head and said, "Howdy," without breaking a smile. He instinctively disliked the skinny weasel.

Cass ignored the men's curt exchange and said, "I have some pressing paperwork to do this afternoon. We just returned from a long trip to Fort Union in Arizona Territory delivering army supplies." She turned to Kyle. "Why don't you go to the bank and get the men's payroll while I see to 'Cousin Clark'?"

"I'll be back soon's I pay off them ornery muleskinners. Blackie Drago'll have his Taos lightnin' all poured 'n waitin' fer them galoots." He nodded to Matthews and sauntered out.

The tall man made a grimace of distaste at Kyle's back. "Quite a crude fellow," he said in a patronizing tone of voice. "Whatever do you need him for in a freight business? He looks to be a common gunman."

Cass laughed. "He's a gunman, but believe me, he's anything but common. He's my most invaluable employee." Her face turned grave. "He takes care of people who bother me."

Matthews blanched and sputtered, "Now, Cassandra, er, Cousin Cassandra, I didn't mean to offend. It's just that, well, I hoped we might have a pleasant visit and discuss some matters of mutual concern. Perhaps over dinner tonight?"

He looked suddenly like a half-grown pup begging for table scraps. In the space of a breath he moved from imperious snob to bumbling suitor—suitor!

Warning bells clanged in Cass's mind. She sauntered past him and leaned on the counter with studied ease. "Just exactly what mutual concerns do you want to discuss over dinner?"

"Well..." he began to approach the counter, then reconsidered and moved back to stand near the window. "As you know, if you fail to fulfill the terms of Uncle Rufus's will within a year, you'll lose everything to me. I realize you've engaged in costly litigation, thus far unsuccessful, attempting to break the will. I propose a far more felicitous solution for your dilemma. No more legal expenses, no more worries about running this far-flung, dangerous business. This life is certainly unsuitable for a woman of your obvious education and beauty." At her look of amused skepticism as she ran her fingers through her matted, filthy hair, he realized how false his prepared speech sounded.

"Pray, do continue," she said coolly.

With dogged persistence, he slogged on. "You cannot win in court and you must marry. But you have obviously found no one here in Denver who meets your high standards. Nor should you be forced to wed some stranger who will only want your money. I'll inherit anyway, so I do not have that motive. If you and I marry, the whole matter would be resolved, whether or not you were able to provide the male child stipulated in the will."

When he came up for air, Cass was rounding the corner of the counter, contempt stamped on every feature.

"You're damn lucky I left my blacksnake out back or I'd peel a layer or two off your hide! I've run this business for six years and I've built it into a bigger, more prosperous enterprise than Rufus Clayton ever imagined. You puling, spineless, money-grubbing son-of-a-bitch! You think I'll just lie down like a sick mule and let you take over? I don't know how they grow ladies back in Kansas City, but I'll tell you how we grow women in Colorado Territory. We take care of ourselves! I'll win this fight—in court or outside of it! I'll keep Clayton Freighting, and you'll never see one . . . thin . . . dime." She punctuated each word with a sharp jab of her index finger against his bony chest. By the time she had finished her speech, he was halfway out the door, gulping like a banked trout.

Cass slammed the door on the miserable weakling and let her seething fury abate. Walking slowly back to the big desk in her office, she slumped into the worn leather chair and laced her fingers through her hair. "I've got to think . . . figure it out. There has to be a way!"

Finally she began once again to sift through the pile of papers on the desk, cursing at Henry Suttler, doubtless off on another of his fool errands. When he returned, she'd skin him for letting that weasel Matthews in *her* office.

Just then the object of her wrath walked through the door. Henry was an aging man with a shiny bald head and a perpetual stoop. He never ran when he could walk nor walked when he could amble at a snail's pace. "Hello, Miz Cass. Glad to have you back," he said as he strolled leisurely toward the counter where she waited. "Your cousin leave?" he asked, looking around the big, cluttered office.

"Yes, Henry. And he's not really my cousin, only distantly related to my father by marriage. I would appreciate it in the future if you'd lock up and not let strangers loose in my office when you have to leave during the afternoon."

He bobbed his head perfunctorily and offered her a handful of mail. "I won't let anyone stay while I'm out again, Miz Cass."

"See that you don't, Henry," she replied crossly and began to scan the mail. Her hands froze on a thick official-looking envelope with the seal of the largest law firm in the territory in its upper-left-hand corner. Clutching it tightly, Cass looked up at Henry. "I have a lot to think over this afternoon, Henry. Why don't you take the rest of the day off?"

It took little encouragement for him to turn and plod slowly toward the door. She gritted her teeth until it slammed, then tore into the envelope. A wave of apprehension washed over her as she began to read.

It was nearly dark when Kyle returned. Cass sat alone in the twilight, rocking back and forth in an old chair in the corner. Squinting to see, he walked over and turned up the gaslight on the wall. "Cass, I been ta th' house 'n Vera said hew niver come home. Whut in th' hell's wrong?" He walked quickly over to where she sat rubbing her temples and avoiding the bright glow of the light. "Hey, somethin's bad wrong, ain't it? Did thet scrawny feller—"

"No, no, Clark Matthews is easy enough to handle, Kyle. At least for another year," she added darkly. Then she handed him the letter from the attorney.

Never a great scholar, the little redhead began to read the first line or two and then gave up, knowing what it must mean. "Reckon th' bottom line is thet yew lose 'n ole Rufus's will stands?"

She nodded bleakly. "I've been thinking, Kyle . . ." she began.

"Yew cain't do thet in th' dark, on a empty stomach, with a month's worth o' trail dirt weighin' down yore brain." He squatted on his heels beside her chair. "I got me an idee. I'll walk yew home 'n while'st yew take a nice long soak in a tub 'o' hot water with them fancy smellin' bath salts, I'll have th' cook fix us some vittles—real food, so's we kin know whut we're chewin' on. Then you kin tell me 'bout yore plans. Deal?"

His blue eyes twinkled as he pulled her up from the chair, but once she nodded and preceded him to the door, his countenance became troubled. It wasn't like Cass to sit alone and brood in the dark. He didn't like it, and he didn't think he was going to like her plan either.

"Yew are a goin' ta do *whut*!" Kyle dropped his knife onto his plate with a clatter that brought Vera Lee, Cass's Chinese housekeeper, swishing through the swinging door from the kitchen.

With a nod of dismissal to Vera, Cass turned to her friend and said calmly, "I said I am going to send you to the Nations to find me a man who's about to be hanged, get him released—bribery, a jailbreak, whatever it takes—and then bring him to Colorado to marry me.''

Hunnicut shook his head. "Marry a murderer?— Some ornery galoot who'll like's not rob yew 'n take off like a scalded dog right after th' weddin'? Cass, thet's plumb crazy!"

"No, Kyle, it's the only logical choice I have left. By the terms of Rufus's will, any man I marry automatically takes over the freight lines and everything I own. But," she persisted, "if he's wanted by the law and we make it clear to him that you'll track him down and see that he hangs, he'll have to abide by the terms I dictate. He'll be a figurehead supposedly in charge of my business, but I'll still run it."

Kyle took a gulp of Vera's rich coffee to wash down a lump of mashed potatoes and cream gravy that had lodged in his throat. Carefully he cleared it and forced himself to look eye to eye with Cass. " 'Pear's ta me they's one little thing yore fergit- tin'. This here ain't a weddin' jist fer show, Cass." He paused, his face redder than his hair. "Yew gotta get a baby from him." His voice croaked on the last words, but he persisted doggedly, "Whut kinda father wud some yahoo from a tumbleweed wagon make?"

"What kind of father was Rufus Clayton?" she shot back. "Any man, no matter how rich or re- spectable, could do the same horrible things to me that my father did to my mother. Kyle, I swore I'd keep what I've earned and by God, I will!"

Kyle sighed. One night not long after he'd come to work for her, after a narrow brush with death on a steep mountain trail, the two of them had shared a bottle of whiskey over a campfire. Unused to spirits, and having no women friends to confide in, Cass had spilled out the brutal story of Rufus and Eileen, and of her own sad and lonely childhood. It explained much about the grit and coldness of the woman he worked for. After that he'd seen her through far more tolerant eyes. Kyle Hunnicut, born in an east Texas whorehouse, denied a mother's love and a father's name, had been cast adrift by the age of eleven. He understood what it meant to stand alone and live by his wits.

Cass sat watching him consider her carefully reasoned plan. "I can control a fugitive, Kyle. I— I'll have to be his wife—but only until I become pregnant. At least there's a fifty-fifty chance it'll be the male child my father so devoutly wished. If it is, I can be through with him—pay him and send him away, never have to fear he'll come back to lord it over me or claim my birthright."

She held her breath. Kyle had spent much of his youth in the Nations, the wild and lawless territory to the southeast. It was just distant enough to render her prospective groom anonymous in Colorado, yet under the jurisdiction of Fort Smith and its hanging judge, a palpable threat indeed! Surely in all that wide-open country he could come up with one fugitive to suit her purposes.

Kyle leaned back in his chair and scratched his head. "Yew got yew any idees 'bout looks 'n sech? Should I check his teeth? I niver bought a man afore, only horses 'n mules."

"Just so he's clean and reasonably intelligent. I don't want to birth a moron," she replied tartly.

Chapter Four

The Nations, 1870

"Damnation, I plumb fergot it's hotter'n Texicali chilies here'bouts," Kyle swore as he loped his gelding across the sun-baked red earth, pulling the lead rope of a sway-backed nag that followed him. The wind whipped gritty dirt against his cheeks and stung his eyes. He'd grown up on the hot plains of the Southwest, but since he'd become accustomed to the dry, cooler air of the Rockies, he found the Oklahoma landscape as bleak as his mission. Some mission: fish a jailbird out of a cell and drag him back to marry Cass! Kyle swore again as he scanned the flat, barely rolling horizon for any sign of life.

A speck appeared in the distance. Always cautious, Kyle checked the Winchester on his saddle scabbard and the Colt strapped to his hip. Grunt-

ing in satisfaction, he reined his mount to a stop
and waited. Soon he recognized the iron bars of a
large tumbleweed wagon, one of the mobile pris-
ons commonly used to transport criminals across
the vast, lawless Nations to face justice in Fort
Smith on the Arkansas line.

Smiling grimly, he considered his chances of
success with this lot. So far the jail cells of the
territory had yielded no one he'd even consider—
filthy brutes and ice-hearted killers, pathetic boys
and drunken old men. Cass had sent him on a fool's
errand. This was perhaps his last chance.

The man driving the wagon looked tired. His
countenance was gray and wind-blasted. He wore
a tarnished federal badge and wrinkled, dusty
clothes, but in spite of his weary appearance, his
cold eyes were alert as he appraised Hunnicut's
weapons and manner. He knew the little Texan by
type, if not by name. "Howdy," the marshal said,
pulling the team to a halt, jolting awake the prisoners who had been napping in the stultifying
noon heat. As muttered curses and groans filtered
from behind him, he kept one hand on the butt of
his gun while he waited for Kyle to make the next
move.

Hunnicut leaned forward, careful to keep his
hands in clear sight. The deputy studied him intently. "How do, yerself, marshal. Name's Hunnicut, 'n I'm lookin' fer a feller."

"This feller have a name?" the deputy marshal
asked levelly.

"Reckon so, onliest problem is, I don't know
whut it is." Having the lawman's attention now,
Kyle smiled broadly and nodded toward the men
stirring in the wagon. "Cud I have me a looksee?"

"You know him by sight?" the deputy inquired.

Kyle shrugged. "Wal, yew cud say thet." He dismounted carefully and strolled slowly over to the wagon as the lawman watched warily.

Steve struggled to focus his eyes as the monstrous throbbing in the back of his skull tortured him. The jolting of the wagon had driven him nearly blind with pain. When the deputy had reined to a stop, he had banged his injured head on the bars. God, what now?

In answer to his question, a small, banty-legged man with frizzy red hair stood peering through the bars, apparently checking each of the prisoners. Loring put his head down and held it gingerly between his hands.

Kyle looked at the four filthy, disheveled men in the wagon. He dismissed a toothless old drummer and a pimply-faced boy at once. The third fellow was the right age, but fat and wheezing. Hunnicut turned his attention to the figure in the far corner. "Hey, yew, got a name?" When the man failed to respond, Kyle asked the lawman, "He sick er somethin'?"

Rikert laughed. "Er somethin'. Got himself one hell of a hangover. Seems him and another fellow had a fight over a whore back in Sweetwater. Claims it was self-defense, but the town sheriff found him passed out drunk next to the dead man. Woman's gone. He'll hang for sure." He shrugged carelessly.

Kyle raised a brow. "No witnesses yew say? I heerd thet new judge, Isaac Parker's, a mean un."

Rikert grinned. "Yep. We don't have us no overpopulated jails since he come on the bench. What you want with Loring?"

"Thet be yore name?" Kyle asked, turning back to the prisoner.

Steve raised his head and ran his fingers through his sun-streaked brown hair, careful not to touch the lump on the back of his skull. "I'm Steve Loring. What's it to you?"

Kyle looked at the narrowed golden brown eyes and chiseled features. Behind the stubbly growth of whiskers was an arresting face. He was long-legged and lean; that was apparent even in the cramped wagon. "I jist might cud save yew a neck stretchin'. Yew married?"

A slash of even white teeth showed as Loring grinned insolently. "No. Are you proposing?"

"Let's leave thet be fer now. If'n yew ain't hitched, I cud save yore life."

"And what would prompt that act of Christian charity? You haven't even heard my story yet. Maybe I'm a cold-blooded murderer."

His voice was deep and resonant with the obvious accent of an educated man. "Yer teeth er good 'n yew got book learnin. I reckon yew'll clean up all right." Kyle turned back to the deputy marshal. "Cud we palaver fer a minute?"

The blazing sun offered no respite and it was a long ride to the night's camp at a wayside cabin on Turkey Creek. Impatiently Rikert replied, "You got something to say, spit it out."

"If'n I wuz ta take thet one off yore hands, it'd be one less mouth ta feed 'n body ta tend on a long haul. Easier ta jist say he escaped when yew get ta Fort Smith. I'll give yew two hunnert fifty dollars fer him."

Rikert's thin gray brows rose contemptuously. "Shit. That ain't even the price of a good mule."

Kyle shrugged. "With one good mule I cud buy me Denver City."

"Why don't you just go do that?" the lawman asked.

"I ain't got th' mule." Kyle grinned. "But I purely want thet hombre. Go as high as three hunnert American 'n a pint o' real fine tangle laig whiskey."

The deputy looked dubious, but was obviously weakening. It was a long trip to Fort Smith, and the tall stranger with the odd Eastern accent had been nothing but trouble since he'd taken him into custody. He scratched his head uncertainly.

"I'll even throw in a couple o' tins o' peaches 'n sweet syrup I got in my saddlebags. Slide down real cool on a hot evenin'."

"Done." Rickert unlocked the wagon while Hunnicut counted out the money.

As the tumbleweed wagon vanished over the eastern horizon, Loring eyed the bony old mare with obvious distaste. Fly-bitten and footsore, she probably looked no worse than he did. Hunnicut had tied his hands securely in front of him and he mounted with difficulty. Looking questioningly at his savior, he said, "Where to?"

"Northwest a piece," was the taciturn reply.

They rode in silence for a while as Steve fought the hammering in his head. Kyle observed his sad physical state and assumed his new companion had the prince of hangovers. In spite of that and his Eastern accent, he rode well. To a Texan that was a big mark in his favor.

"Why'd you buy me off?" Steve finally asked. "I've never even seen you before."

The little man chuckled. "Wondered when yew'd git yore tongue ta flappin' straight agin.

Sorry I give th' lawman thet hair o' th' dog. Looks like yew cud use a swaller er two."

Loring grimaced. "I'm not suffering from the excess of drink, contrary to what that idiot sheriff told Rikert. I'd never drink the bilge they call whiskey in this hellhole."

"So, yer not a drinkin man 'n yer fer shore not from 'round here'bouts. Whut yew doin' in th' Nations? Ain't a likely place fer a lone dude ta pick fer a pleasure trip."

"I was looking for a man," Steve replied grimly.

"An' yew kilt him."

"No, not that man—at least he wasn't the one I was hunting. The man in that Sweetwater saloon was trying to rob me after his whore lured me up to her room. We struggled and the gun went off. Then the light went out. Hell, I guess his girlfriend brained me. I woke up minus my money belt, with a split skull, laying in a pile of broken glass. Next thing I knew, the sheriff was there saying I'd shot whatever his name was. The blonde had vanished, of course."

"Course. If'n thet feller warn't th' one yew wuz after, who wuz?" Before Kyle took this stranger to Cass, he was going to have to make a careful judgment about his character.

"It's a long story," Steve replied with a shuttered look on his face.

"Try me."

Something in the tone of the little Texan's voice caused Steve to reconsider. Hell, what did he have to lose? From what he'd heard about Judge Parker, he'd been bound to hang before Hunnicut had intervened.

Steve began with the war and Abner, telling

Kyle about killing O'Brien in Cincinnati. "When I found Wortman in St. Louis, I beat the truth out of him before turning him in as a deserter. He and O'Brien and Tanner ambushed Ab. Tanner was the leader, the one who actually pulled the trigger. I want him." His voice was low and ragged, filled with hate.

" 'N this here Tanner—yew think he's in th' Nations? No place fer a dude all alone."

Steve shrugged. "I learned to survive in the war. So did Tanner," he added grimly.

" 'Pears ta me O'Brien 'n Wortman didn't learn so good," Kyle said consideringly. "Yew ain't done so great yerself." Men on vendettas made him nervous.

"I only have to find Tanner. Then it's over," Steve replied doggedly. "I told you my story. Now what's yours? Why did you buy my freedom?"

"Wal, it shore warn't cause o' bein' on th' same side in th' war. Yew bein' a bluebelly 'n me bein' a reb."

"Why do I get the impression you're avoiding the issue, Mr. Hunnicut?" Steve asked with a chilly smile. Then, changing tactics, he added, "I can wire back east for money and repay you—"

"Fergit yer fight with thet Tanner feller," Kyle interrupted. "Leastways fer now. Said yerself th' trail went cold in Sweetwater. I got plans fer yew, and they purely don't include yew gittin shot, 'less I do th' shootin'! After yew finish a job o' work fer my boss, then yew kin go after this here Tanner feller. Chase him clean ta Californy fer all I keer."

Steve looked at the gunman. "And exactly what is this job of work?"

Kyle grinned cryptically. "Jist cool down. Yew'll find out soon 'nough."

Pueblo

Cass crumpled the telegram in a ball and threw it in a corner. She let out a volley of oaths damning Bennett Ames by several rather ingenious methods. Two more shipments of expensive mining supplies lost over the side of a mountain. Sabotage! It was costing her money to sit here in Pueblo waiting for Kyle. He'd been gone nearly a month. Every chance of breaking the will had been exhausted, and she was running out of time. "Please let him bring me a man," she murmured to herself.

Hearing hoofbeats outside, Cass thought it was Chris Alders, back from his latest stock purchasing trip in Arizona. The Pueblo place, located at a convenient midway point in the territory, was their main road ranch, or livestock supply center. Clayton Freighting owned over one hundred thousand oxen and mules to pull its wagons from the heights of the western mountains all the way south to the Arizona army posts. From the San Luis Valley's agricultural centers to the Wyoming border where the Union Pacific Railroad needed supplies, Cass ran her wagons. Denver housed her main business office, but Pueblo was where the livestock was wintered over and new mules and oxen were broken and trained.

Pueblo was also isolated and small, a good place for meeting her doubtlessly reluctant bridegroom. When she opened the front door and stepped onto the porch, she recognized Kyle riding in with a stranger. Her heart began to pound, and she gritted her teeth in self-loathing at the fear knotting her belly. She must let him get a child on her, but only if he passed muster, she resolutely assured herself.

Setting her mind to put on a show of bravado, she stepped down from the porch to meet her fate. "You've handled barrooms full of drunken mule-skinners. You can handle one man," she gritted out beneath her breath.

Steve was baffled by his introduction to Miss Cassandra Clayton. She had inspected him like he was one of the Loring racing stable's most expensive studs, then dismissed him as if he were a down-on-his-luck drifter riding the grub line. Even as Hunnicut untied his hands, Steve suspected his deliverance into this nest of unreconstructed rebels might not be such a blessing after all. He decided to get the lay of the land as quickly as possible.

As they walked toward the long log building at the far side of the maze of corrals, Steve looked over the road ranch. Clayton Freighting was one hell of a big operation. That much was clear, even to his untrained Easterner's eyes. Cassandra Clayton must be one rich young woman, he mused.

Anxious to defuse the tense confrontation between Cass and Loring, Kyle began to explain the operations of her Rocky Mountains freight empire and how she had made it prosper since her father's untimely stroke and subsequent death.

Steve shook his head as he considered the foul-mouthed, hard-drinking teamsters he'd met in his travels west. Hard, dirty, and dangerous were the kindest terms that could be used to describe them, and she worked side by side with such men on the road. They respected her as their boss!

He considered his own appearance, then grinned. He no doubt looked as bad as the worst of them. It might be interesting to take Cass Clayton's measure. He decided to play the role of desperado to the hilt. Treat him like some damn gelding, would she!

While Steve soaked away his prison grime in a tub of hot water and shaved three weeks' worth of beard off his face, Kyle posted guards from among his own hand-picked men to watch the prospective bridegroom. Lober, one of his men, was roughly Steve's size and agreed to lend a pair of dress pants and boots to the mysterious stranger, as well as a clean shirt. Besides Kyle, only two of his men had seen Loring brought in tied up for the first meeting with Cass. The inspection in Pueblo was planned so there would be no gossip when they arrived at Denver City for a very public wedding.

As Kyle walked up to the big house for a talk with Cass, he wondered if she was happy with his choice. "What a son-of-a-bitchin' pickle," he muttered.

He found Cass in the parlor, a plain, functional room with rough-hewn masculine furniture and bright Mexican rugs spread across the plank floor. She had changed into a dress and had her hair swept up in some sort of fancy concoction. He could smell the fragrance of Rosario's home cooking wafting from the kitchen.

He smiled to himself as he realized she planned to soften Loring up with feminine wiles. "Shore smells better 'n Sour Mash's sonofabitch stew," he said, sniffing deeply.

Cass's fingers whitened as she gripped the back

of a big oak chair. "After days on the trail, the least I can do is feed him before I present my deal to him."

" 'N ta make it more appealin', yew decided ta dress th' part." His face was guileless. "Good idee, Cass." Maybe this would work out after all. If Loring cleaned up half as well as he suspected the Yankee would, he and Cass would make a striking couple.

Cass dismissed the Texan's remarks and began briskly ticking off a list of details. "We should reach an agreement this evening. If so, I'll ride to Denver tomorrow early and notify that wretched Attorney Smith. He'll need to witness the ceremony. I'll contact Father Evans at the Episcopal church. The marriage will be private and small. This has to be legal, but I don't want any more publicity or questions than absolutely necessary. Oh, yes, another thing. He'll need a complete wardrobe. I'll send the tailor from Denver with a selection of clothes to be altered. We received a shipment of men's suits and accessories recently. Loring's 'trousseau' will be ready before he arrives." She smiled with sardonic humor.

Damned if she hadn't given this a lot of thought! "Whut yew gonna tell folks 'bout how yew met yore bridegroom?"

Cass shrugged. "I'll just tell Attorney Smith and Father Evans that we met back East when I was making that wagon deal last year. I'll concoct a few more details with Loring tonight." She hated the nervous edge to her voice.

Sensing her tension in spite of her veneer of control, Kyle hesitated, then said, "Yew shore yew don't wanna wait a few days? Sorta git ta know one another a mite first?"

"No. I've wasted too much time as it is."

"Whut if he says no?" Sensing the stubborn toughness in the Yankee, Kyle feared the possible consequences.

Cass's face looked pale and strained, but her expression was hard. "Then he'll hang."

Still under guard, Steve was escorted to the big house. *Damn, this is an armed camp!* He looked around the corrals full of mules and horses. Plenty of stock to steal, but too many armed men guarding them—and him. He was as much a prisoner in Colorado as he'd been in the Nations. "At least I'm clean," he muttered under his breath as he was ushered into the house by Lober. The two gunmen then withdrew, leaving him standing like a dunce in the big open room that served as a parlor of sorts. The smell of food wafting from the kitchen made his mouth water. He wondered how many people were here in the house with Cass Clayton.

His thought was interrupted by a soft swish as she entered the room from a side door. Cass was dressed in a simple yellow muslin gown, plainly cut, yet revealing an ample amount of creamy skin and outlining the softly swelling curves of her willowy body. Bright masses of coppery curls were piled high on her head, adding to her already considerable height. Dressed in the outlandish shirt and pants she had been attractive. Dressed as a woman, she was breathtaking.

Cass steeled herself for his perusal. Men had always found her physically attractive, but all the simpering dandies and leering miners in the territory had never upset her as this man did. She countered his inspection by giving one of her own.

Bathed and shaven, he was much more than passable looking. The crisp white shirt stretched tautly across broad shoulders. Plain dark wool pants outlined his long, rangy legs. If she didn't know him to be a dude, she'd envision him as a horseman. His every move was lithe and graceful. That chiseled face, with the grizzled beard removed, was arrestingly handsome.

Not liking the train of her own thoughts, she addressed him brusquely, "We might as well have dinner before we discuss business. I assume you're hungry?"

Puzzled, he let her mention of "business" pass by and admitted, "I'm starved. Neither Hunnicut nor I have had anything but charred jackrabbit and beans for a week."

"Rosario is a good cook," she said as she preceded him into the dining room. A long table was set with only two places at one end. It looked embarrassingly intimate to Cass as she sat down. As if by habit, Steve pulled out her chair and assisted her, then seated himself across from her. His unconscious manners were not lost on Cass. He was obviously a man of some refinement.

The short, plump Mexican woman named Rosario served them roasted pork with candied yams and crisp green beans. The meal was delicious, and Steve found himself voraciously hungry. Not knowing what lay ahead, but glad of a reprieve from prison and its meager fare, he decided to enjoy the meal before they discussed whatever her business was. He noted as he took a second helping that she ate sparingly, methodically cutting the tender meat, then chewing and swallowing it slowly, as if forcing herself to do so. *What the hell's going on here?*

Cass watched him eat. In spite of his obvious hunger, his manners were impeccable. She asked him about his trip through Colorado with Kyle and again noted the educated quality of his voice. Back East he would have been a master of small talk, a real charmer with the ladies. She prayed her nervousness didn't show as she prodded him with a barrage of simple questions. Some he answered, some he evaded.

"I've given you an Easterner's impression of the barren waste of the Great American Desert. Now you tell me about your life in the West," he said with a frankly disarming smile.

"I run a freight line—the biggest in the territory. We ship everything from calico to dynamite—up in the farthest reaches of the Rockies, all the way down to the Arizona desert." The pride in her voice and glow in her eyes as she described the freighting business made her even more beautiful. She became so animated in describing her freight lines that the cold, calculating facade of earlier vanished. Steve began to feel he could genuinely like a woman who possessed such a passion for her work, unorthodox as it was for a female.

Lord knew, Cass Clayton was nothing like Amelia or Marcia. Still, she was holding something back, and a warning prickled his spine when she nodded for Rosario to clear the table and asked him to follow her back to the parlor.

"Now, I think it's time to discuss some important matters," she said as she turned to face him in the middle of the big, comfortable room. "Have a seat, Mr. Loring. I promise not to eat you," she added tartly, indicating the sofa and seating herself briskly in a chair across from it.

He grinned lazily and took the proffered seat,

noting how she had chosen to distance herself from him. "But I haven't said a word about not eating you."

Her head jerked up from fussing with her skirts and her eyes flashed. "After the dinner you just polished off, I should think you'd have had your fill. Besides, if I snap my fingers, three rifle barrels will be leveled on you before you can blink," she replied sweetly.

Steve's grin faded, but his voice betrayed no emotion. "You obviously take pleasure in brutalizing people you have at a disadvantage, Miss Clayton." Cass's cheeks appeared scorched, as if they had been touched by a torch.

He leaned forward, placed his arms on his knees, and stared witheringly at her. "Why don't we end this little charade right now? Your hired gun paid three hundred dollars and change to get me out of a tumbleweed wagon. He escorted me at gunpoint across the most godforsaken wilderness west of the Sahara, just to deliver me to you. Why, Miss Clayton?"

His eyes bore into her like posthole spades into soft mud. She swallowed and forced herself to return the hard stare. Facing down mean drunks, even armed bandits, had never been this difficult!

She willed herself to answer his question with one of her own. "Are you married, Mr. Loring?" Her voice was cool and steady. Good.

He quirked an elegant brow until it almost met the straight, thick lock of hair falling across his forehead. "Odd. Hunnicut asked me the same question. I wasn't desperate enough to marry him. In your case, Miss Clayton, I don't think I'm desperate enough either. Care to elaborate a bit further?"

She stood up, fury flashing across her face. "Just answer my question, damn you!"

He smiled coldly. "No."

"As to being desperate enough, Mr. Loring, I think you'd better reevaluate your options." She paced swiftly across the floor to the fireplace. Gripping the mantel with one slim hand she stated, "You'll marry me or you'll hang. Kyle rescued you. Kyle can return you, right to Judge Parker's waiting gallows."

Again that chilly smile slashed across his hard, handsome face. "Don't you think, under the circumstances, we might at least be on a first name basis, Cass? Call me Steve. It isn't every day I get proposed to. Why me?"

She didn't move, but did avert her eyes from his harsh, questioning glare. Ignoring his attempt at familiarity, she said, "That should be pretty obvious, Mr. Loring. You're completely in my power."

A look of honest bewilderment crossed his face as he watched the beautiful woman's profile. He could see her swallow painfully. There was a great deal more going on here than she was telling him. "I still don't understand, Cass. Why would a wealthy, beautiful young woman force a wanted man to marry her?"

Now it was her turn to smile coldly. "Precisely because you *are* a wanted man. I could marry any one of hundreds of men in the territory—and they'd get everything—everything I've slaved to build! Clayton Freighting is my birthright, and I won't give it over to any man." She bit off each word as if it was wrenched from deep inside her.

Dawning comprehension spread across his face.

"To keep your 'empire' you have to marry. Your parents' decision?"

"My father's decision. His will was quite explicit. My brothers would have inherited, but they died in childhood. A mere female was all he had left. Of course, I was deemed unworthy."

"So he wanted a son-in-law to take over—and you want to keep control yourself. Neat. I'm under your thumb but the will's fulfilled. A docile husband. Very neat!" He stood up and walked over to a side table where he saw a decanter and glasses. He needed a drink. Maybe the ice princess with the incongruously volcanic temper could use one, too.

"There's more," she said softly, still unable to look at him. Suddenly he was standing much too close to her, handing her a glass of sherry. She took it and sipped, then coughed.

He swallowed the amber liquid in one clean gulp. Leaning against the mantel, he let the empty glass dangle casually in his hand. "How long must this marriage of convenience go on? Is it a life sentence?"

She stiffened and took another fortifying swallow. "No. Only a year, maybe less..." She hesitated and then steeled herself, "It won't be a 'marriage of convenience,' Mr. Loring. My father's will was not only unbreakable, but very thorough. I have to produce a male child to inherit. I...we have only a year left in which to accomplish it." She forced herself to look at him.

At first his dark gold cougar's eyes widened in amazement. Then, to her utter mortification, he threw back his head and roared with laughter. If she'd been carrying her blacksnake, she'd have peeled off his lips!

"I used to work on a stud farm in Kentucky before the war. How ironic!"

"Now you'll learn how the stallion must feel," she shot back coldly.

He stopped laughing and reached out to touch her cheek in a soft caress. As she flinched back instinctively, he said, "And you, my dear Cass, will learn how a mare feels."

She sensed the color stealing into her face and swore aloud. She hadn't blushed since she was twelve! "Don't think you can threaten me, Mr. Loring, or think you can escape. Kyle Hunnicut can track fly sign over cracked pepper. If you do anything to hurt me, I'll have you hunted down and killed—and believe me, out West you'll find hanging is one of the pleasanter ways to die!"

He strode over to the decanter and poured another glass of sherry. Tossing it down with a mock salute, he said, "To our wedding day, Cass . . . and night." His lips smiled, but his eyes were glacial.

She returned the cold stare. "We have an understanding, I assume. Good. As soon as you've . . . fulfilled your marital responsibilities, you'll be allowed to leave. I'll even see to it you receive ample compensation and safe passage back East—wherever you want to go to escape hanging," she added with a hint of spite to cover her humiliation. Discussing the subject of producing offspring with this hateful stranger was unhinging her usually unshakable nerve.

"How much?" His question was a flat, bold insult and he knew it, but if he was reduced to being a stud, he would damn well receive a decent fee for services rendered.

Cass flinched, but recovered quickly. "I hadn't considered the amount. You say you worked on a breeding farm. The irony doesn't escape me, either, I can assure you. What did your employer receive for the services of one of his thoroughbred stallions?"

He saluted her with his empty glass. "I'll give you your due, lady. You've got plenty of nerve. At least as long as I don't get too close."

With that he set the glass down, strode over to the mantel, and swept an arm around her waist pulling her against him. She didn't back down or struggle as he studied her strong, beautiful face. Her cold, level stare indicated she was damn sure of her power to control him.

As he bent down and savaged her mouth, he could feel the soft pressure of her breasts against his chest. Her long, slim legs pressed to his thighs as he pulled her tighter into his embrace. God, she fit so well, felt so good, smelled so sweet! It had been months since he'd had a woman, and the beautiful, infuriating one in his arms inflamed his senses with a sudden rush of passion. His tongue teased her tightly clamped lips. He pulled her hair loose from it pins and buried one hand against her scalp. She gasped in outrage and he took advantage, plunging his tongue inside to taste her mouth. His ardor was rewarded with a sharp bite. Simultaneously, she dug a wickedly pointed heel into his instep, forcing him to release her.

Cass backed off, panting and shivering with loathing as he touched his bloody tongue with one hand and cursed fluently.

"I might have known your stupid Yankee army couldn't even teach a man how to swear," she said contemptuously. "Now, if you have the brains of a piss ant and the discipline of a half-broke jackass, you'll keep your filthy hands to yourself, you misbegotten son-of-a-bitch dog in the heat of hell's lowest level!''

The whole diatribe of epithets was delivered so fast and effortlessly that Steve realized it had to be a reflex action born of much practice. He smiled nastily. "I never heard a woman cuss that well . . . too bad your voice isn't deep enough!"

Cass's triumphant sneer turned to fury. "You damn Yankee," she said with loathing.

He shrugged dismissively. "I'm getting no lady wife in this bargain, am I?"

"No gentleman paws a woman the way you did, so we're even!" After retreating a pace, she stood her ground defiantly.

"One thousand," he said quietly. "That's my stud fee. And if you want to fulfill your father's will, you'll not only have to pay me, you'll have to suffer my *pawing* you a lot more after we're married. I assume a woman with your colorful vocabulary understands barnyard facts of life?"

She hated him, standing in front of her so calm, so overbearing, daring her! Cass was caught in her own trap and she knew it, but she would never let him know how badly frightened she was.

Her mother's face, wan and listless, flashed before her eyes, then her father's scowling, harsh countenance. She forced the images to recede, then clenched her fists and said, "One thousand it is, but I'll tell you when you may 'be of service,' Mr. Loring. Try touching me at any other time and I'll show you how well I wield a blacksnake!"

Chapter Five

Steve awakened the next morning to the swearing of men and the popping of whips. Disoriented, he looked at the crude log furniture in the spacious room. The sheets were clean, the bed comfortable, and he remembered the magnificent meal he had eaten last evening. After weeks of filth and near-starvation on the journey to Forth Smith, this was a decided improvement. But he remained a prisoner.

The incredible conversation with Cass Clayton replayed in his mind as he sat up and rubbed his eyes. Would he actually have to go through with a marriage to that whip-wielding, foul-mouthed termagant? The alternative was even less appealing unless he could wire his uncle in Philadelphia for an attorney. That option had been summarily denied him by the sheriff in Sweetwater and the deputy marshal on the tumbleweed wagon. From

what he'd heard of Judge Parker's court, he
doubted he would be treated any differently in
Fort Smith.

The insanity of the whole situation almost made
him think he was still asleep, dreaming some
ghoulish nightmare, like the ones he'd suffered
since the war. He swung his long legs over the side
of the bed and rose, then walked over to the wash-
basin on the table. As he splashed icy water on his
face, he turned over plans in his mind. If he
couldn't escape, he'd have to marry that manipulating bitch and perform in her bed. God, the
thought of fathering a child with a woman like
Cass Clayton! He shuddered.

Steve had told neither Hunnicut nor Cass about
his family's money and influence back East. Since
they thought he was just a common soldier bent
on a vendetta, he might throw them off guard.
Today he'd get the lay of the land around this
ranch and look for ways to steal a horse and escape. He chuckled mirthlessly, realizing that horse
stealing, too, was a hanging offense. "Oh well, in
for a dime, in for a dollar."

Perhaps if the luck that had so long deserted
him returned, Will Palmer would be in Denver
with the railroad by now. But first Steve would
have to find a way to get to Denver. Surely the
Clayton woman couldn't complete her wedding
arrangements for a week or two. Then again, considering Cass Clayton, maybe she could!

He smiled grimly into the mirror as he shaved.
"Well, my man, you'll just have to cool your temper and try charming your blushing bride until
you can shake the dust of Colorado off your
clothes." And he'd thought his mother was ma-

nipulating and frigid! He laughed. Even Marcia's simpering wiles were an improvement over Cass's iron-willed, icy disposition. At least his former fiancée didn't flinch at his touch. His tongue still ached from that bite!

Steve realized he must be careful—if he was too forward, she might decide he was dangerous and ship him off for a fast hanging. He must seem to capitulate until he could devise an escape, or he'd end up saddled with a most unwelcome wife. "I'll act the gentleman if it kills me."

Cass was down at the corral watching her trainers work a batch of wild mules just brought up from Mexico. To weaken them and make them slightly more docile, the animals had been given neither food nor water for over twenty-four hours. Now the men were hitching the span to a special, heavily laden wagon. After they pulled it around the corral for a few hours, the mules would get used to the harness, then to pulling with other mules, leaders in front, wheelers behind.

Kyle walked up to where she sat perched on the corral fence. "Mornin'." He paused, trying to gauge her mood. "How'd it go?"

She kept staring at the mules but murmured, "It's all settled. I'm leaving for Denver to make the arrangements today. I'll send Chris back with word for you in a few days."

"Thet soon?" He grinned slightly. "Loring cleaned up real good, if'n I do say so. Eddicated, too. Cass, I believe him 'bout shootin' thet feller in Sweetwater," he said earnestly.

She turned to face him. "It hardly signifies whether he's innocent—the important thing is he'll hang if he doesn't follow orders."

Kyle scratched his head. "Cass, yew gotta ease up on th' jerk line jist a mite. Loring's a dude, but he wuz a soldier, even if'n he wuz a bluebelly. He's not some fool boy like Clark Matthews. He ain't gonna take it good if'n yew try 'n make him crawl."

Cass hissed, "The only way Steve Loring would ever crawl is if I sawed off his legs at the knees— then he'd come after me on the bloody stumps! You know how much I hate this, but I'll do what I have to, Kyle."

"Mebee yew oughta accept one o' them fellers from Denver," he began uncertainly.

"Who would you suggest I marry? Bennett Ames?" She sighed. "No, Kyle, you brought me an intelligent, healthy male. He'll do."

The little gunman could tell by the stubborn set of her chin that the issue was settled. He caught sight of Steve Loring strolling casually across the dusty ground toward the corral. Lober and Ernie were with him, discreetly guarding him.

Loring nodded to Hunnicut. "Sorry I overslept, but it's been a while since I had a good meal and a clean bed." He looked up at Cass who seemed engrossed in what was taking place in the corral. She gave him a perfunctory glance, but said nothing.

Just then one of the mules being harnessed broke free and the man working the animal used his whip with brutal impact. Steve took in the sight of the terrified animal's frantic struggle.

"What a stupid way to treat good livestock. I always use carrots or sugar lumps, not whips. Those animals are dehydrated and terrified."

Cass looked at him scornfully. One of the mule-skinners, overhearing his remarks, snickered.

"Wild mules is broke by starvin' em, mister, not feedin' em."

Steve looked up at Cass for confirmation. She nodded. "Standard way to break mules to harness. We have no time to bottle-feed them. We buy mules and oxen by the thousands every year. A day without food or water makes a mule more tractable."

Steve gave a low, silky laugh. "Seems to me a soft touch and a little kindness would work better—sort of like gentling a woman." His golden eyes held a dare.

Cass stiffened, then turned and gave him a blinding smile. "All right, fancy Eastern stockman. Why don't you try it your way?" She swept her hand toward the corral where the two handlers were holding the harness and struggling to get the last mule strapped in. Everyone around the corral was watching.

Climbing between the rough log poles, Steve walked over to one of the bystanders munching on an apple. "Mind?" He put out his hand for the apple. After a cursory glance at Cass, the teamster gave over the half-eaten apple with a wink at the man standing next to him.

Steve approached the mule, held tightly by a handler's none-too-gentle grip on the bridle. The animal put his ears back, but didn't move. Talking in a low, soothing voice, Steve reached for the bridle and then, seeing that the mule remained stationary, eased his grip and offered the animal the apple, which was received in one fast snap, nearly taking at least three fingers along with it. Several men snickered and one called out, "He likes meat with his fruit, dude."

Steve remained calm and continued talking to

the animal as he pulled gently on the bit, easing the mule toward the harness. Lord, the contraption looked complicated! He'd never seen harness gear like this before; in fact, he'd never worked with anything more cumbersome than an Army-issue saddle. Cursing himself for the stupid blunder, he quickly scanned the harness on another mule already secured in the rig. The trick seemed to be to get the mule's neck into the harness—or the harness over the mule's neck, depending on how one chose to approach the intricate problem. He debated another bribe and dismissed the idea. Even if someone could spare an apple, he couldn't spare any fingers. Firmly he pulled the mule toward the harness, deciding he'd worry about the fastenings once he had it over the animal's head.

"Raise that contraption up while I pull him forward into it," he directed the man standing beside the mule that was already hitched. The man nodded with a knowing grin and obligingly raised the heavy harness. Steve almost had the mule walked into the headgear when the eruption came without warning.

The mule seemed to go in every direction at once. The beast twisted like an unleashed cyclone, breaking free of Steve's grip on the bridle just inches shy of the harness rig. He snapped at Steve's arm with big yellow teeth. As Steve dodged the attempted amputation, the mule seemed to curl around until his backside was where his head had just been. Razor-sharp hooves came flying at Steve's face. He threw himself to the ground, rolling in the thick dust, then came up coughing and gasping for air. Two of the handlers succeeded in beating the mule away from his prey with their cracking blacksnakes. One man got a hold on the

bridle and hauled on the bit until the animal subsided. The laughter around the corral took a while
longer to die down.

Kyle was there, reaching down his hand to help
Loring rise. With a grim nod of thanks Steve stood
up, quickly checking his body for damage. Only
his pride was seriously injured. The hoots and guffaws of the men bothered him a great deal less
than the quiet smirk on Cass Clayton's face as she
jumped from the corral fence and strode over to
where the handlers were restraining the thoroughly unrepentant mule.

With an even more amazing string of oaths than
she'd thrown at him the preceding evening, she
cussed the mule and cracked her whip until the
beast was backed over to where two handlers held
the harness rig. With amazing deftness, one man
reached for the bit and yanked the mule's head
through the harness while Cass continued with her
loud harangue and cracking whip. Before Steve's
amazed eyes the whole elaborate rig was fastened
with blurring speed and efficiency.

"Now, Whitey, make those sons-of-bitches pull
until their legs drop off." Coiling up her whip, she
walked across the large corral to where Steve was
dusting himself off.

Steve grinned manfully. "It seems I have a lot
to learn about mules and freight wagons."

"And women," she said with one slim coppery
eyebrow arched wickedly.

He replied insinuatingly, "I'll remember you
prefer a whip to a carrot, Cassie." When she tightened her grip on the blacksnake, he knew the comment had hit home. What was it about her—crude
and full of bravado one instant, hurt and flustered
the next?

She looked at his rumpled, dust-coated body disdainfully and said, "I hope Lober has a lot more pants and shirts. You're going to be real hard on his wardrobe. I'm sending a tailor from Denver in a couple of days. He'll outfit you with suitable clothes. Try to stay out of trouble until then." With that, she walked over to another cluster of men and left him standing with Hunnicut.

Kyle chuckled and said, "Cass is goin' ahead to arrange thangs, but I'm stayin' here. Don't go gettin' no idee 'bout headin' out. Tenderfoot like yew'd be buzzard bait inside two days."

"I may be a tenderfoot in Colorado, Kyle, but I think you'll find I'm a fast learner," Steve replied grimly.

The banty-legged gunman studied his hard face as Steve's eyes followed Cass. "Yep, reckon yew jist might be at thet.... Don't hurt her, Loring," Kyle warned softly.

Steve guffawed. "I think you'd be better off giving that admonition to her, not me. I wonder if she's planning to bring that blacksnake on our honeymoon!"

During the next few days Steve learned a good deal about running a vast freight business in the Rockies. He watched the handlers break mules and realized the seemingly brutal treatment was short-lived and that a five-hundred-dollar animal was too valuable to abuse. Once broken to harness and trained to command, the mules were well cared for and worked an average of twenty years. He talked with the bullwhackers, too, learning how they worked the much slower moving but stronger oxen, used primarily on the long hauls over flat country where speed was not deemed essential. From everyone he gleaned information useful for his escape plans.

Clayton Freighting supplied the miners high in the Rockies, and the Army outposts dotting the isolated frontier. Cass's wagon master at Pueblo, Chris Alders, gave him one surprising bit of information. Cass was in a cutthroat, desperate race with Bennett Ames to obtain the lucrative new contracts supplying the grading crews for Colorado railroads—railroads that a young entrepreneur with British backing planned to build. His name was General William Jackson Palmer!

Steve had hidden his surge of pure delight behind a series of casual questions about the general's whereabouts. Palmer was busy shuttling back and forth between Denver and the fast-approaching Kansas-Pacific tracks being laid in eastern Colorado. At once Loring began to consider various ways to get word to his old commander. Being constantly guarded, well over one hundred miles from Denver, presented significant obstacles. The loyalty of Cass's employees surprised and frustrated him. He couldn't believe these rough, unlettered men were so fond of a woman who swore like a muleskinner and lorded it over them like a princess.

He knew Cass was going to send for him in a few days. Taking three precious days to learn the routines of the ranch was chancy, but he had to know when he would have the best opportunity to steal a horse. Mules were more plentiful, but after his first encounter with them, he had given up the idea of ever getting near one again.

The tailor arrived the second day after Cass departed. He spent the best part of the next morning outfitting Steve with a complete wardrobe, everything from the casual denims and shirts so practical for outdoor wear in the West to the most elegant three-piece suits and dress shirts. He could feel the marital noose tightening when the small, fussy tailor fastened the top shirt stud at his neck and stood back to inspect the suit Steve would wear to the wedding. If the little man thought it odd to be outfitting a groom at the bride's expense, he said nothing.

On the fourth night, Steve had his plans laid. The routine had been established, he and Kyle eating their supper in the big ranch-house kitchen with Kyle's men, Lober and Ernie. Except for Chris Alders and the old cook Rosario, these were the only people who knew he was being held against his will. When he returned to his bedroom each night, either Ernie or Lober guarded the door. The other man watched outside his window. Neither seemed to require sleep, and both, he was certain, were more than proficient with guns. At least Hunnicut seemed to require his sleep. Steve was grateful for the small favor.

Two nights ago he'd been able to convince Ernie he needed to walk out back to relieve himself. Lober insisted he use the chamber pot, but Ernie was easier-going and had strolled along with him past the back fence.

Praying he could find a way to overpower the gunman without awakening the household, Steve slid from his bed and slipped on his denims. He acted sleepy as he shuffled to the door and leaned against the frame, rubbing his eyes. "Mind if I walk out and water the grass? You know how I hate those damn pots."

Ernie shrugged. "Why not? Gits borin' sittin' round here ever' night." He eyed Steve's bare feet and chest and decided the dude wouldn't do anything rash.

Once they had passed the back fence, Steve turned, as if to unbutton his fly, then doubled over with a sudden grunt of pain. Ernie reacted as he'd hoped. Instead of yelling for help, he reached out to grab for him. Steve whirled from his half inert position and brought his knee up with wicked impact, connecting solidly between Ernie's legs. He followed that blow with a second and third to the gunman's jaw. Ernie went down, out cold. "Sorry, pardner. At least you'll sleep through the worst of the pain down below," he whispered apologetically.

Being considered a helpless tenderfoot who had been bested by a mule had its advantages, he decided grimly as he stripped off Ernie's boots and shirt. Because they were roughly the same size, even the man's boots fit him well enough. He strapped on the gunbelt and then pulled several handkerchiefs from his pockets and proceeded to tie and gag his captive.

With any luck, he could steal a horse and be halfway to Denver by the time they found the gunman or he worked his way loose. Knowing where the guards were posted, he stealthily circled the corral and slipped inside the big barn where the riding stock was kept. The inside of the barn was dark, with only a few thin slits of moonlight to help him get his bearings. He'd already marked out a strong, quiet-mannered gelding kept near the rear door. He'd have to walk the horse a good ways before he could dare mount up and ride.

Having only a few matches, he conserved them. Groping his way to the tack wall where the bridles and saddles were stored, he pulled down the necessary equipment after using one precious match to aid in his selection. Lugging the heavy saddle across the dark floor, he stumbled twice and several horses whickered softly. He quieted them with a few soothing words and was grateful for the superior intelligence and amenability of horses. Thank God these weren't mules!

It seemed to take forever to saddle the bay in the dark. When he was finally finished, he led it slowly out the back side of the barn. Waiting until the moon went behind a bank of clouds, he crossed the open corral area and headed for the stand of cottonwoods near the small stream behind the barn. With that cover between him and the guards, he could quickly move far enough out of sight to mount up and ride like hell for Denver.

"Easy, boy, easy, Reddie, we're almost there," he crooned, glad he'd learned the bay's name. It was all coming together. He walked into the sheltering embrace of the trees and pulled the canteen from his saddle, heading to the stream to fill it. Just as he knelt by the burbling water, he heard the unmistakable click of a hammer being cocked.

"Not bad fer a tenderfoot. Wondered if'n yew'd recomember ta take water along. Now, drop th' gun, real easy."

Kyle Hunnicut's voice held a trace of admiration, but Steve knew he was bested. Still, he had one more ace to play. "If you kill me, I'm no good to her, Kyle. And I won't give up without a fight." He stood up slowly and turned to face Kyle, but made no move to drop the gun.

The Texan chuckled. "Bluebelly, yew purely are a caution, yep, thet yew are. I don't figger on killin yew. I cud just put a bullet in yore laig. How far'd yew think yew'd git then?"

"I won't be a fit bridegroom if I'm shot full of holes, Kyle."

This time Kyle laughed broadly. "Cass said yew'd crawl on bloody stumps if'n both laigs wuz cut clean off. Reckon she wuz right." His eyes took on a devilish gleam. "But jist think on it, yew bein' an eddicated feller 'n all. Cass only needs one part o' yew in workin' order, 'n I reckon I'm a good 'nough shot ta miss thet general area."

Loring swore and tossed his gun away in utter disgust. "Just how long have you been waiting for me to try this?"

Kyle shrugged. "Figgered yew'd make a break fer it after yew got th' lay o' th' land. Been watchin yew 'n Ernie last couple o' nights. Not a bad job o' work fer a greenhorn, takin' down a man like him. An' yew didn't try to kill 'im. Reckon I needed ta know thet," he said consideringly.

Steve replied sourly, "Thanks for the vote of confidence. When I come up before Judge Parker, I hope you'll be there to testify in my behalf."

"Might at thet, bluebelly. Jist might at thet, but fer now, we got us a weddin' ta git ta."

Denver

Once in a city the size of Denver, it should be easier to escape. Steve's eyes focused on the trail as he turned over various plans in his mind. Surely hotel clerks and restaurant waiters would be more amenable to persuasion than Cass's hand-picked hired help. If all else failed, he vowed to make a break for it down some back alley on the way to the church. Mayhap he would be fortunate enough to run into Will Palmer when they reached Denver.

As soon as they arrived in the sprawling gold town on the banks of Cherry Creek, they wended their way through the crowded streets toward the freight offices. Steve was fascinated by the motley assortment of humanity that filled the town. Having never been in a city further west than St. Louis, he was unprepared for the bizarre mix of burly miners in plaid shirts and denim pants, slightly built Chinese clad in loose, baggy trousers, corpulent German merchants in expensive wool suits, and quiet Jewish shopkeepers wearing yarmulkes and severe black clothing. It might have a population of only five thousand, but Denver was amazingly diverse.

The city's architecture matched the population. After the floods and fires of the 1860s, Denver had been rebuilt with brick and stone—solid Victorian structures of impressive dimensions. But even here, the unique Western flavor of the gold camps prevailed—the skyline was mutilated with steeples and cupolas, Italianate towers and Gothic spires. Every structure seemed to have elaborate cast-iron trim weighing it down.

Before he knew it, they reined up in front of Clayton Freighting and Kyle dismounted. "I need ta handle some thangs here. Chris, yew, Lober, 'n Ernie take Steve ta th' house."

Now warned of Loring's skill and stealth, Ernie was every bit as wary as the other men. The trio crowded in on three sides as they rode across town to an impressive Victorian house on a quiet, tree-lined street.

Once inside, Steve realized his hopes for escape were ended. The place was decorated with flowers and all the trimmings for a wedding, probably within a few hours.

* * *

Vera fussed with Cass's wedding gown as her mistress toweled herself dry. Cass had rushed from that damnable lawyer's office back home to prepare for the ceremony. Thurston Smith had all the necessary papers ready. Rufus's accursed will would be fulfilled to the letter, she thought with a vengeful oath.

Hearing the downstairs door open and close, then the sound of footsteps on the front stairs, she knew Steve Loring had arrived. "Vera, I can manage until I have to put this dress on. Please go and see that the men have everything they need."

"Bath water is hot. Lots of it. The tailor left the suit in Mr. Loring's room, pressed and ready. Same for Mr. Kyle. But I'll see if there is anything else they need." She bobbed her head and left Cass alone.

"Just being in the same house with him, I can feel his presence," she whispered as she took a seat at her dressing table. The face staring at her from the mirror was pale and haunted. "I have to go through with this, so I might as well do it with pride." She pinched her cheeks and stuck out her chin pugnaciously. Vera had taught her how to use the tiniest hint of kohl on her eyelids to enhance her big amber eyes. She had a few other cosmetics—powder, and even a pale pink stain to rub on her lips.

Thinking of the Denver society matriarchs' disapproval of such a whorish practice, she began to apply the makeup with relish. If only she had another kind of firsthand knowledge, that possessed by the "ladies of the line!" Prostitutes outnumbered society belles in Denver and probably always would. After all, it was a city in which the fanciest bordello and the largest Methodist church had been designed by the same architect. But Cass had only a few respectable society friends and knew no prostitutes. As if either category of female could or would be able to help her deal with an arrogant man like Steve Loring!

Grabbing the hairbrush, she began to run it through her waist-length hair. She had almost gone to visit Dr. Elsner yesterday. The kindly Jewish physician had become a friend since she had donated generously to his hospital for the indigent, but her situation was just too humiliating to confess to a man. Fleetingly she thought of her mother, then quickly dismissed the image of Eileen Clayton, who would no doubt have told her in euphemistic terms to do her duty. It was a woman's lot in life, wasn't it? "Maybe for you, Mama, and for others, but not for me!" Her hair crackled as she drew the brush through it, electrifying her whole body with resolution.

Kyle introduced Steve to Father Evans as they waited for Cass in the large front parlor. The tall, white-haired clergyman was smiling and gracious, acting as if this Monday-afternoon marriage ceremony between one of the wealthiest women in Denver and a complete stranger were an everyday occurrence.

Hunnicut looked wretchedly uncomfortable in a three-piece suit with a tight starched collar. Surprisingly, he wore no gun—at least none in plain sight. The hovering presence of Lober and Ernie, stationed discreetly at the front and rear doors, was sufficient warning to Steve.

Earlier, as he had bathed and dressed for the ceremony, he'd considered his options. Appalling as the forced marriage was, it sure beat hanging or dying with a bullet in his back. Cass Clayton was an icy, domineering bitch, but she was still a woman, and a damn fine looking one at that. He would have to wed her, bed her, and fulfill her insane bargain. Uneasily he patted his pocket where the simple gold wedding band rested. She had arranged everything, even selecting the functional ring. Once she had control of her precious freight empire, he could leave, clear his name, and get a divorce.

Of course, that left two unsettled issues—the nameless child he might leave and Vince Tanner. He would be able to hire new men to trace Tanner's cold trail. The most disturbing thought was deserting a son or, worse yet, a daughter who Cass might truly hate. He felt oddly vulnerable and bereft, but forced the disquieting thoughts aside.

Kyle's face split in a broad grin and he walked toward the hall door. "Wal, lookee at yew!" He took Cass's hand and admired her. Dressed in pale ivory satin, and clutching a small white leather prayer book, she was exquisite. The gown was plain, not designed as a wedding dress, yet its very simplicity set off her loveliness, emphasizing her slender curves and flushed complexion. Her hair was pulled into a sleek roll at the back of her head, with a small, frilly hat perched atop it. The rich ivory color of her ensemble set off the tawny beauty of her copper hair and amber eyes.

Cass scanned the room nervously, her eyes sweeping past the hateful Attorney Smith to Clark Matthews. The attorney had assured her that her "cousin" was an essential witness to her marriage. Chris Alders beamed and Father Evans nodded with a smile. She looked over Kyle's shoulder to where *he* stood, tall and handsome in the rich charcoal wool suit she'd selected. A stray sunbeam from the big stained-glass window behind him highlighted his freshly barbered hair and made the thick brown waves gleam. He was elegant and nonchalant in the way only a man born to privilege could be, a man with power and breeding behind him.

A frisson of fear shot through her. How little she really knew of this man. Had she chosen wrong? She looked at scraggly Clark Matthews and then thought of fat Bennett Ames. Steve Loring was her only choice.

She whispered to Kyle, "Let's get this over with and send Thurston Smith back to shuffle his papers."

Kyle gave a low chuckle, "He'll hotfoot it over ta Byers's office first, yew kin bet. Hope yew got a story fer th' *Rocky Mountain News*, 'cause yore gonna need it by tomorra."

She nodded as they walked across the long room to where the others waited, her fingers clutching the prayer book in a death grip.

Steve took her hand from Kyle's arm, noting the way she held on to the book. He murmured low, "Good thing that isn't a bouquet or you'd have crushed it to paste by now."

His eyes danced with a mocking light, and she hated him for his seeming calm. *Of course he's calm. He knows what's going to happen tonight. I don't.* Even more, she hated her own fear.

The ceremony took only a few moments. When Father Evans made the final benediction, Cass turned quickly from Steve to avoid the customary ceremonial kiss and looked at the lawyer. "I believe you have some documents for us to sign, Mr. Smith?"

The legalities did not take long, but Thurston Smith, officious as ever, said to Cass as she signed, "You do understand that this is only the first step in fulfilling the terms of your father's will."

"We understand perfectly," Steve interposed before Cass could reply. He took the pen and affixed his name, then shoved the documents back at the little weasel. "Now, if you'll excuse Mrs. Loring and me..."

Thurston Smith scooped up the papers and vanished with Matthews in tow. Father Evans congratulated them, as did Chris and Kyle. Then the three men departed, leaving Cass and Steve in the large room, all alone.

He raised one eyebrow and cocked his head. "Well, what now, Mrs. Loring? Do we go upstairs and—"

"No!" she interrupted with a furious hiss. "It's scarcely the dinner hour yet." The minute the words escaped her lips, she wanted to call them back, remembering her comment to him, *I promise not to eat you*. The laughter in his eyes indicated he recalled the incident too, and his rejoinder that he had made no such promise.

"Vera Lee, my housekeeper, has arranged an evening meal for us. There are still a few matters we must iron out," she said quickly, ignoring his suggestive chuckle.

Steve shrugged. "Whatever milady commands ...for now. You can't hide forever, Cassie." He made no move toward her, but the soft insinuation in his voice seemed a palpable threat.

*   *   *

If the simple dining room at the Pueblo road ranch had seemed intimate, the high-ceilinged walnut-paneled one in the city house was impressive. The chandelier was a mass of prismed crystal, winking with dozens of soft golden lights. A fragrant bouquet of fresh yellow and white roses filled the center of the table. Two places were set, one at the head, the other intimately beside it.

Steve escorted Cass to the table and pulled out the side chair for her. Then he took the master chair at the head of the table as if born to it, knowing how it must grate on her pride to see him where old Rufus used to sit—where she wanted to sit and now could not.

Two Chinese maids served the elaborate meal of roast prairie chicken with spicy sage dressing and fresh vegetables. Neither of them was particularly hungry, but he noticed how Cass sipped the iced champagne rather freely. Bridal nerves. Good. He smiled as he nodded dismissal to the servants.

"Now, what matters must we discuss until it's properly dark enough to retire for our wedding night?" he asked innocently.

If he hoped she'd choke on the bubbles, he was disappointed. "We have to meet Denver society, such as it is, especially the estimable William N. Byers, an old family friend and editor of the *Rocky Mountain News*," she replied coolly.

"Ah, yes. Tongues must be clacking because you've held such a hurried, private ceremony, dragging a groom in from nowhere," he said tauntingly.

She smiled coldly. "After all I've done in past years, I doubt bringing my bridegroom from back East straight to a wedding will matter much. We should agree on a story, however—for your protection as well as mine," she added with schoolmarm primness.

He snorted. "We can hardly tell them I'm one jump away from a hangman's noose and you're blackmailing me, can we? So, how did we meet, Cass? Am I a long-lost love from your finishing school days?"

His golden eyes were dancing, but she felt the undercurrent of derision and hated him for mocking her. "As a matter of fact, I never attended any insipid Eastern girl's school."

He raised his glass. "Yes, I know, you're a self-made woman, not a vaporing lady."

Ignoring the barb, she said, "Last year I went to Chicago to close a wagon deal. Have you ever been there?"

"I know the city," he said noncommittally.

"Good. That's when we met. We've corresponded since, and you asked me to marry you. When I accepted, you came to meet me in Pueblo. But because of the . . ." she hesitated and stumbled with words ". . . the nature of my problem with the will, the wedding had to be witnessed by Attorney Smith and several others. Therefore we had to come to Denver. I do trust it's not taxing your memory too much to tell that simple story when asked?" She smiled caustically.

"Touché, Cassie," he said, again lifting his glass and draining the last swallow of bubbling white wine from it. "Yes, I'll remember we met in Chicago last year. Is a specific date essential, or am I to improvise summer walks under the stars?"

"Try crackling fires in the cold of November," she replied tartly, also draining her glass.

He reached over to the ice bucket and pulled out

the bottle to pour refills. "I neglected to thank you for the elegant trousseau, Cass. The tailor did an excellent job," he added, brushing a speck of lint from the sleeve of his immaculate dark gray coat.

She colored at the idea of buying a husband, which the mention of the clothes evoked. "You could scarcely arrive in Denver in those filthy rags Kyle found you wearing." She dabbed daintily at her lips with the napkin and began to rise from the table.

Instantly he was beside her, assisting her with the chair, always the perfect gentleman. His hands brushed her arm, and she forced herself not to jerk away. Cass found his presence more disturbing, his touch more frightening with every tick of the ormolu clock on the fireplace mantel. He had not tried to kiss her or manhandle her in any way since they'd been left alone for their wedding supper, but his barbed wit and facade of courtly concern disturbed her in ways she did not care to analyze.

Steve looked down at the soft swell of breasts that rose gently beneath the rounded neckline of her gown. If she had chosen the simple wedding dress in an attempt to get him to desire her, damn her, it was working! He still remembered her tall, slim body pressed intimately against his that day at the Pueblo ranch. He could taste the mellow honey of her mouth, smell the wildflower fragrance in her tangled coppery curls.

He could also sense how much she disliked his hands on her, even in the most casual gestures of courtesy. For all her fiery nature, this strange, driven woman had proven impervious to his charm. He certainly hadn't wanted to marry her, but his male ego was stung at her cold dislike of him.

"Cassie, Cassie," he chided, knowing how she

hated the endearment, "what are you going to do tonight?" He was rewarded with a soft gasp and the reddening of her cheeks.

"I am going to do as little as possible. I believe it's up to the man to perform his husbandly duty, is it not?" Her eyes met his in a duel of wills.

"Is that why you chose such an alluring wedding gown and fixed your hair this way?" She had removed the saucy hat before dinner. Now he reached over and tucked an escaping tendril of copper behind her ear. "Are you afraid I'll be so repelled by our shotgun wedding that I'll be unable to perform 'my husbandly duty'?"

Cass stood her ground by sheer force of will, feeling her temper boil. "Kyle picked well. You'll manage to perform, Mr. Loring. I'm confident I need not seduce you." She turned to swish from the room, but his words stopped her.

"You're too much an emotional cripple to ever seduce a man, *Mrs*. Loring," he said scornfully. "But you're right. I'll manage. I have to, don't I? See you upstairs, say in about thirty minutes?"

Chapter Six

Cass sat before her mirror twisting and untwisting a coil of hair nervously. She pressed her fingers to her temples, dreading the night to come—so many, many nights to come. Perhaps it wouldn't take long. Her mother had been fertile enough to conceive often, just too frail to carry a healthy baby to term. But Cass knew she was stronger than Eileen—no miscarriages or stillbirths for her! There was no time.

Oh, why had she waited so long, investing two years in feckless court fights? She knew the answer, of course, could feel it welling up inside her now. At first she had convinced herself that she was simply too strong, too independent to submerge her identity beneath the will of some foolish man. Rufus Clayton had never cowed her. No man would. But now, faced by her wedding night with

Steven Terrell Loring, Cass's courage was rapidly evaporating.

She knew so little about him—only when they signed the marriage documents had she learned his middle name! What she did know was not reassuring. He was a man who had killed without qualms, a man obsessed with some sort of blood feud, used to command, educated and arrogant—everything she had despised in her father and more.

But above all, he was a very physical presence, sensuous and handsome, teasing her with the soft liquid baritone of his voice, the steel-clothed velvet of his hands when he touched her. There was a power there . . . and something more, something she feared to name.

"I've just got a case of nerves over the first time. I'll let him do what's necessary and then send him away." She compared human mating to what she'd observed with livestock and tried to put it in perspective. Unappealing certainly, but manageable.

Softly, without knocking, Steve opened the door and stepped inside. Her head shot up and she stood, facing him furiously. "How dare you come in here without asking permission?"

He watched the rise and fall of her breasts through the clingy satin of her dressing gown. She hugged her arms protectively across her chest, as if trying to conceal what the luscious peach silk revealed. "Lovely," he breathed, feeling a sudden surge of tenderness in spite of his angry resolve. She was virginal and frightened, and it moved him. "I told you thirty minutes, even gave you an extra ten, Cassie." He grinned crookedly. "For all I knew, you might have barred the door on me."

She let her arms drop and walked stiffly to the big bed in the center of the room. The covers had been turned back and pillows plumped up high.

"I'd scarcely marry you to get a child and then be so stupid as to lock you out," she said in asperity. "Just get it over with!"

She reached to the wall to lower the gaslight, but his words stopped her. "Don't. I want to see you." Before she could touch the stem, his hand was covering hers, gently pulling it to his warm lips. He dropped soft, nibbling kisses on her fingertips while his other arm embraced her, pulling her against his chest.

Cass felt dizzy, drowning, knowing this seductive pleasure had nothing to do with the essential sex act. She wanted only that, nothing more. She dared allow him nothing more.

Twisting out of his embrace, she again reached for the lamp. "I want to have this done. You should, too. We're scarcely lovebirds!"

He again stayed her hand, more roughly this time. "No, we're not lovebirds, Cass. But in all your unladylike haste to consummate this union, you're overlooking a few basic facts." He paused until her eyelashes fluttered open and she forced herself to meet his gaze. "You are a virgin, aren't you, Cass?"

Her sharp intake of breath would have convinced him if her nervous reactions hadn't already. "Yes," she hissed tersely.

"Well, then," he continued silkily, as if explaining to a half-bright child, "I must take some time, go slowly and caress you, build up to the act gradually—ready you so nature can take its course."

At her look of anger and alarm, he sighed and drew her stiff body to him once again. Finding it too humiliating to face him, she allowed her head to fall against his chest. His hand stroked her hair, then followed the curves of her spine down to her buttocks. Although her body quivered, she made no attempt to move away.

"I fail to see what this has to do with nature," she whispered crossly.

His chest vibrated with a suppressed chuckle. "I imagine you're thinking of horses and cattle, aren't you?"

Her face flamed again. She was relieved to have it hidden against his chest. "It only takes a few moments and they don't..." she grasped for words "... they don't touch this way."

"That's because the female comes in heat and the male takes her. Animals have a much simpler cycle of reproduction than humans. A woman has to be made ready for lovemaking. If a man just takes her—especially the first time—it can be quite painful, and physically damaging." He felt her stiffen and knew she must have overheard a few horror tales from her mother or some matronly friends. "It doesn't have to hurt, Cass, not if I go slow and you let yourself relax and enjoy it."

"I can't," she gritted out. "Don't you understand? You married me to escape a rope; I married you to gain my inheritance—this is not for pleasure. It's business! A thousand dollars' worth for you."

Stung as if she had slapped him, he replied coldly, "All right, take off that robe and lie down." *So, you think you're immune to pleasure?* The frigid, castrating bitch! He vowed to make her whimper and plead, and not to give her satisfaction, even if she begged for it!

To his surprise, when he looked at her long, slim body lying on the bed, his fury began to abate. The sheer peach silk gown outlined each curve and hollow of breast and thigh. She was breathtaking and he wanted her. More than that, he wanted her to want him.

Now he reached for the gaslight's stem and turned it down ever so slightly. Then he shed his heavy robe, carelessly letting it fall to the floor in a heap. Cass's eyes remained fixed on the ceiling. "Look at me, Cassie," he whispered as he placed one knee on the edge of the bed and reached for her chin, tilting it so she had to do as he commanded or squeeze her eyes closed.

She complied, letting her amber eyes travel from the harshly chiseled planes of his face down the tan fur on his chest. When it narrowed below his belly, she quickly raised her eyes to study his broad shoulders and the flexing muscles of his arms. A shiver of tingling pleasure washed over her. He was beautiful—hard and lean, male to her female, compelling. She was shocked by her sudden urge to reach out and touch the springy hair on his chest, to feel the muscles bunch and flex as he moved, but she held back.

Steve slid onto the bed beside her and began to stroke her arm. He lay on his side, his head propped up by his other hand, watching her breathing become more erratic. Her skin tinged pink with heat as his hand traveled ever so lightly across her collarbone, then down to quickly brush over her breasts. He was rewarded with an involuntary gasp and the hardening of her nipples, clearly visible through the sheer silk.

He lowered his head to one breast and teased with his tongue, then shifted to the other until the

silk turned translucent from the wetness of his
mouth. "Pink, pale, pale pink like spring rose-
buds," he whispered as his lips roamed up her
throat. Cass felt on fire with stabbing frissons of
pleasure, helpless as he worked blistering magic
on her body. When his lips centered over hers and
began brushing them, she moaned without realizing it. His hand cupped an aching breast and she
gasped, giving him entry to her mouth. His mouth
was warm and firm over hers, but not savage as
it had been before. His tongue did not plunder,
but gently teased. With a will of its own, her arm
came up to rest lightly on his shoulder just as her
tongue darted against his, touching his mouth.

Steve groaned and deepened the kiss, twining
their tongues together as he pressed his hard chest
over her soft breasts. She could feel his labored
breathing, sense a desperation in him, in herself
too. She wanted, she wanted . . . what?

When his mouth left hers, she felt bereft, but he
blazed a path down her throat with hot, wet kisses,
peeling the silk gown down her arms as he kissed
his way back to her now naked, aching breasts.
He caressed them alternately with his mouth, then
his hands, all the while easing the gown yet lower,
until he had it worked below her slightly bucking,
writhing hips.

"Ah, Cassie, yes, that's the way. You are so beautiful. It'll be good, so good, I promise you," he
murmured against the silky texture of her concave
belly.

His passion-roughened voice, her gradual
awareness that she had been stripped naked, the
teasing brush of his fingers in that alarmingly wet
and sensitive core of her body—all of it suddenly
awakened her to a terrifying sense of powerless-

ness, a complete capitulation to mindless passion. This was what he meant by "preparing her for lovemaking." He had robbed her of her mind, her will, her self!

Steve felt Cass stiffen when he touched the soft curls between her legs, but he murmured reassurances and probed gently again. "Mmm, you're almost ready now, Cassie."

Cass began to push him away, humiliated, furious, and frightened. "Stop it, stop all of this! Just do it. I don't want to be ready! I won't be your ... creature!"

Her hissing, breathy voice cut through the warm haze of his passion like a cavalry saber through flesh. He raised himself up with an arm on each side of her. His fingers caught in the tangled silk of her fanned-out hair, immobilizing her thrashing head. Now blazing with fury, his face loomed over her. "Oh, that's right, good women aren't supposed to enjoy this, are they, Cass?" His voice was rough as cedar shingles, a low feral growl as he added, "But we both know you aren't a good woman, don't we?"

With that he bent down again, crushing her breasts beneath his chest, savaging her mouth as his knee slid up between her legs.

"Open for me, dammit! I'll do it your way," he rasped as her thighs instinctively parted. He thrust inside her in one fast, hard plunge that left them both breathless.

She was wet and slick and the barrier was slight. They both felt the brief tearing as he buried himself deep inside her. Her eyes were closed tightly now, her body rigid, lifeless, giving no indication of how badly he had hurt her.

For Cass the pain had been only a brief twinge,

the greater discomfort being the stretching fullness and pressure when he thrust so deeply. She willed herself to remain still and unresponsive. Let him perform his duty and leave, she prayed in shame.

Very slowly he began to move, as if testing her—or himself, she could not tell which. What had been terror and pain only moments earlier slowly metamorphosed into heat and pleasure, spiraling outward from the center of her body. She lay very still, willing the agonizingly sweet sensations to abate, but they only grew stronger.

Steve watched her face, sensing her internal struggle to remain immobile. Her damn pride, her dislike of him kept her from letting go. Grimly he renewed his vow to teach her a lesson in wanting. He stroked slowly, evenly, rhythmically, all the while waiting for a signal that her body was winning control over her mind.

Finally he was rewarded with the slight lifting of her hips. Her eyelashes squeezed more tightly closed, like thick, dark brushes on her cheeks. "Losing the war, my little rebel, aren't you? History repeats itself," he whispered as sweat beaded his brow. It took every ounce of concentration not to plunge over the brink himself—not yet, not until he had her just where he wanted her—wanting *him!*

Suddenly something snapped inside her mind and she gave in, arching up in an agony of need, uncaring, unable to stop herself as her hips raised to meet his thrusts. She heard a low moan like an animal in pain, but did not recognize her own voice. Abruptly she felt a surge of pressure inside her as his whole body seemed to shudder and tense. He collapsed on top of her, then quickly rolled away, leaving her empty and aching.

With shame she realized her body was still writhing as he stood up and carelessly tossed a sheet over her nakedness. The caress of the cover only inflamed her already screaming nerve endings and she gasped, her eyes flying open.

Steve stood over her, fastening his robe nonchalantly, a sardonic sneer on his face. "I trust my husbandly duties were performed adequately? As you said, Cass, you didn't have to do a thing." With that he turned and strode through the adjoining door to his bedroom.

Never in her life had she felt so tense, coiled tightly like a spring about to snap. Finally, unable to endure the bed with all its hateful, humiliating memories, she arose before dawn the next morning.

Cass decided to visit Dr. John Elsner at his small hospital. The kindly older man had always had an air of Old World courtliness and tolerance about him. As county physician he had become the champion of the indigent and ill, and she, as one of the wealthiest subscribers underwriting his charitable endeavors, had become his friend. Of course, what she needed to discuss with him now strained the outer limits of even the most unconventional friendship.

Cass shrugged as she slipped into a plain green linen day dress. "He is a doctor and I need some medical information. It's as simple as that!" Observing the dark circles under her eyes and the haggard, exhausted look on her face, she realized it was not as straightforward an issue as she wished it to be. There was no help for it; she simply had to talk with John.

Once she was seated in the small, cluttered office, Cass's nerve began to desert her. As she waited for the doctor to finish his morning rounds with patients, she rehearsed her speech again.

The door opened and a small thin man with graying hair stepped in, a broad smile wreathing his face. John Elsner was an Austrian Jew who immigrated to America and spent over a decade serving the medical needs of Denver with selfless devotion. His slight German accent only added to his aura of subdued charm and gentleness. "What a surprise this is, Cassandra. So early in the morning you wait for me—you are not ill?" His face lost its smile as he walked over to take her hand and look at her wan face.

Cass smiled at his concern. John Elsner was the only man in Colorado who could call her Cassandra and not anger her. "No, I'm not ill, John. That is . . . not exactly. I don't imagine you've heard, but I was married yesterday . . ." Floundering for words, she looked up at his startled face.

"Are congratulations in order, or not so?" he asked gently.

Cass sighed. "You know about the conditions of my father's will?" It was a foolish question. Two years ago the newspapers had carried all the details given out by Thurston Smith.

"This is why I ask. This man you married, it is not for love, but for business, ya?"

She nodded, relieved at John's tact and understanding. "I lost the court fight to break the will, John. Marrying Steve Loring and having a child are the only ways I can keep Clayton Freighting."

"So, where did you meet this Steve Loring? He does not live in Denver?" There was obviously more to her problem than he could surmise and it related to her marriage.

"No, no . . . that is, he's from back East. Oh, John, it is a business arrangement as you said, but you know the conditions of the will—I have to get pregnant—within the next few months!" Her face flaming, Cass stood up and began to pace.

John Elsner was feeling a twinge of discomfort himself. Assuming his most professional mien, he looked at the distraught young woman. She had always been a rebellious, shockingly unconventional female, but her goodness of heart and generosity to those less fortunate had won him over. When Rufus Clayton called him a "worthless kike nursemaiding lazy trash," Clayton's daughter had brought injured teamsters to his office and offered to pay for their care out of her own pocket. When Rufus had his stroke and she took over the business, she had become a patron of Elsner's hospital. Now she needed help.

He began very carefully, "This new husband— you fear he may not be able to give you children, is that it?"

Cass gave a bitter, choking sob, "Hardly that! He . . . he can 'perform' most adequately! Too adequately." She swallowed and forced herself to finish before she lost her nerve. "As I said, this is a business arrangement. We don't love each other. In fact, we heartily detest each other. I want to know some medical facts—about human reproduction." She couldn't face him so she turned and ran her hand along the shelves of leather-bound volumes that ringed the office. "I want as little to do with him as possible—but I want to conceive as soon as possible so we can end this sham marriage. Can you help me?"

He cleared his throat. "Well, there are times

when a woman is more fertile than others during
her monthly cycle. Cassandra, has he . . . hurt you,
this husband? Did you know there is some discomfort—it varies depending on the woman—but
after the first night, it will not be so."

Cass remembered Steve's seductive voice as he
explained how she needed to be made ready so he
wouldn't hurt her. Her face flamed and her guts
knotted in outrage. She could never, never confess
the humiliating craving she had felt at her husband's touch! "I'm not concerned about the discomfort, John. It wasn't that bad. It's just that . . .
well, I want to get it over with." She paused, then
forced herself to look at him in mute entreaty.

"You are a very well read young woman, Cassandra. This I know. But I will give you some
things you never have read before—medical books
and some others. Maybe you will find them . . . enlightening, ya?" As he scanned the shelves searching for several slim volumes, he considered her
tense, drawn features and the way she had answered—and not answered—his questions. He
knew her for a warm and compassionate woman
who hid beneath a rough businesslike exterior.
Could it be that she shared with so many women
the foolish fear of experiencing pleasure in the sexual act, or of showing her husband that she did
so? The more he considered the proud, lonely
woman, the likelier the idea seemed. Now, if only
he could find that new text and a few very rare
old books . . .

Cass slammed the book closed with a resounding thump and fairly threw it on the table, then
at once checked to see she had not damaged the
binding. It was no doubt a treasured and very ex-

pensive possession of John's. But after spending
the entire day alone in the study reading what he
had given her, she was so furious she wanted to
smash something—no, someone! Steven Terrell
Loring!

He had deliberately done that to her, humiliating her, working her body to a fever pitch of
desire and then denying her the same completion
he had obtained. Of course, the books with their
cold, clinical language were rather inadequate in
explaining exactly how this orgasmic thing felt,
but she understood enough to know that her restless misery last night had been intentionally inflicted. And he could do it every time he bedded
her—telling her she had to be "made ready" so he
wouldn't hurt her! Damn him!

"All he wants to do is get revenge for being
forced to marry me," she gritted out to the empty
study. The words echoed off the walls. She shoved
aside the shadowy memory of her cold words and
attempts to stop his tenderness at the height of
passion, choosing to recall only the frustration and
humiliation she felt when he left her.

"Damn you to hell, Rufus Clayton, if you aren't
already roasting! This is all your fault! You saddled me with a husband who hates me!" She sat
down with another book—on male physiology.
John's reading list was thorough. There must be
a way to fulfill the terms of the will and still exact
retribution from her husband. She had a tray
brought to her and read through dinner, telling
Vera to serve Mr. Loring alone in the dining room.
By late that evening, a plan had begun to form in
her mind.

* * *

Steve sat staring morosely at the thick rare steak on his plate. Shoving it perfunctorily about, he ate a small piece, never tasting the juicy rich beef. God, she was so sickened by the sight of him she couldn't even bear to sit at the table with him, and he couldn't blame her. Taking another generous swallow of red wine, he let his self-loathing overflow. *What a bastard I've become.* Being faced with a hanging and railroaded into marriage, then finding himself attracted to his shotgun bride had not exactly brought out the best in him.

As he sat reviewing the past seven years, he realized that the senseless violence of the war had changed him, hardened him into a man whose only peacetime ambition had been to pursue a deadly vendetta. Had he become so fond of killing that he deliberately turned the Hendersons' tragedy into an excuse for continuing his own private war? Now his quest had embroiled him in a war against a woman—his own wife.

The vision of Cass flashed before him, writhing on the bed in shame and misery as he cruelly tossed a sheet over her nakedness. In spite of his parents' loveless match, even after his near-disastrous brush with marrying Marcia, he had never thought himself capable of degrading a woman as he had Cass Clayton.

Part of him defended his actions. She was a tyrannical, unnatural woman who had blackmailed him into marrying her and then had scorned his attempts at tenderness. She was also a frightened virgin who had plenty of reason to fear what he could do to her, his conscience whispered.

He shoved the plate away in disgust and rose unsteadily to his feet. Several brandies and a bottle of wine had soused his brain quite thoroughly.

Feeling sure she would not want a repeat performance of his husbandly duties tonight, he decided to go straight to his bed and pass out. Tomorrow he'd try to talk with her. Lord knew they couldn't go on living the way they'd begun.

Cass heard his uneven footsteps come down the hall, then enter his room. She had slipped the bolt on her side of their adjoining door. From the sound of his gait, she knew that he was sufficiently drunk not to disturb her that night. She sighed in relief.

Earlier that evening she'd had a visit from Chris Alders with disturbing news. General Palmer was in Cheyenne, conferring with the Union Pacific Railroad about the last stages of the Kansas-Pacific track expected into Denver in a few weeks. Bennett Ames was on his way to Cheyenne to meet with the general and make him an offer to supply the grading crews for his new railroad.

Cass knew how much that kind of a supply contract could mean to the freight line that received it—thousands of tons of food, equipment, and explosives, not to mention the lucrative business of supplying whiskey for the tent saloons that followed railroad camps across the West. If the rumors about the extent of Palmer's English backing were correct, he was going to build his narrow-gauge rails through the farthest reaches of the Rockies and all the way south to Mexico. She vowed to get that contract and put Bennett Ames out of business once and for all.

Of course, it meant her plans for dealing with Steve Loring would have to wait until she returned. She wrote a note to Kyle and had one of the houseboys deliver it to his hotel before she retired.

* * *

"So I'm supposed to stay here in Denver and behave myself while my bride goes chasing off to Cheyenne," Steve said to Kyle.

The Texan grinned. "'Pears ta me it's a mite safer 'n workin' mules at th' ranch."

Steve grunted, ignoring the barb. "Now that I'm legally married to your boss lady, how much slack will you give me, Hunnicut?"

"Yew know we got wanted posters with your pitcher on 'em. I'd rightly hate to give 'em ta th' territorial marshal. Whut yew fixin' ta do?"

Sighing in resignation, Steve replied, "I won't run off, Kyle. Knowing how easy it would be for you to track me or for any gun-happy bounty hunter to kill me, I'll be good. But I need to have some kind of work—something to pass the time. You said Cass has a big office here in town. Who handles the paperwork for her while she's off with her muleskinners or chasing after railroad contracts?"

"Got a clerk name o' Suttler." He scratched his head. "Yew bein' an eddicated feller 'n all, mebee yew cud help out at th' office, I dunno."

When Steve walked in the door of Clayton Freighting, a stooped, bald man sat with his feet propped on the large desk in the corner. A glass of warm beer was balanced precariously on the chair arm and his head was lolling to the side at an odd angle. If not for the loud, even snores, Steve might have considered him dead with a broken neck.

Reaching quickly for the beer, he knocked the man's feet from the cluttered desk. "You Suttler?"

"Who wants to know?" the man asked angrily, sitting forward in his chair and rubbing his bleary eyes.

Steve's smile unfolded slowly. "I'm your new employer."

"I work for Clayton Freighting," the man said, looking the fancy dude up and down with contempt.

"Yesterday Clayton Freighting became Loring Freighting. Allow me to introduce myself. I'm Steve Loring, Cass's husband."

The bald man stood up quickly and glanced over at Kyle Hunnicut, who lounged negligently against the front door. "He's tellin' yew straight, Henry."

"Er, what can I do for you, Mr. Loring?" Suttler asked nervously, reaching down to begin shuffling papers in pointless stacks.

"Begin by getting a broom and cleaning out this office while I go through the mail. Oh, Henry, I may have a few errands for you to run later," he added casually.

The afternoon was most enlightening for Steve. He sorted through the mail and was amazed at the volume and variety of merchandise the firm handled. One letter began, "Der Sirr, I am senning yoo a orgun. It be for my wife Clorinda whut alwas likes moosic. She will come to Denver at Crismas and pik it up then. Thank yoo. Geo. Watts." The letter was addressed from a remote mining camp in the mountains.

"Guess we'll just have to see if the organ arrives and then wait for the happy couple," he muttered, sticking it in a folder marked "Transfers."

The business was basically sound. Cass kept the books balanced and up to date, seeing that payrolls and outstanding bills were met, but the handling of correspondence and the organization of the daily office operation had grown woefully inadequate over the last two years. It seemed that as the business grew, Cass spent more time on the road and less time attending to paperwork.

Henry Suttler was obviously worthless as a clerk. Steve planned to fire him and asked Kyle to keep his eyes open for a likely young man to take his place. In the meantime, while Henry made a feeble attempt at sweeping the place clean, Steve and Kyle strolled to the telegraph office. Steve explained that he needed to send a wire about one of the freight orders. While the Texan waited outside, Steve wired Will Palmer in Cheyenne explaining his whereabouts and other bits of pertinent information. Smiling grimly, he walked out the door and said to Kyle, "Got time for a stop at Klein's General Store?"

Nodding, the short man said sourly, "Keepin' up with yew's like ta kill me with all this here walkin'. Fer ever' step yew take, I gotta hop three times."

"You could trust me not to run off. As you and my bride both clearly explained to me, those wanted posters would get me shot inside a week if I deserted my husbandly duties."

The Texan considered a moment, then looked Loring in the eye. "Yore momma didn't raise no dumb chil'ern, I reckon. Yew jist stay put in Denver 'n keep outta harm's way till Cass gits back."

As Kyle headed across the street, Steve called after him, "Don't worry. I'll stay clear of mules!" then added beneath his breath, "at least until my wife returns."

Early the next morning a crowd gathered in front of the freight office to watch two men hoisting up a new sign. Painted in bold letters were the words, "Loring Freight, Ltd." The weathered Clayton Freighting sign was unceremoniously carried to the back of the building and broken up for firewood.

Steve nodded to the onlookers and then headed inside to begin his day. As usual, Suttler was late. He really must find a new clerk. Shortly thereafter, as he pored over the mountain of correspondence, a trim, bearded man with a high forehead and piercing blue eyes entered and nodded briskly.

When Steve stood and approached the counter, the man reached out his hand and said, "Good morning, Mr. Loring. I am William N. Byers, editor of the *Rocky Mountain News*. I understand you are the new owner of Rufus Clayton's empire."

Steve's brows arched. "I understood that it was Cass Clayton's empire—that is, until I married her."

"Well, yes, of course. But obviously Rufus Clayton felt a woman could never be expected to continue running a business of this magnitude. That's the reason he made the provisions he did in his will."

Clayton was a pompous ass, Steve thought with annoyance, feeling a surprising twinge of empathy for Cass. "More like her father made his will to spite her for being born female, Mr. Byers."

Now it was the editor's turn to look surprised. "I certainly meant no offense to your bride, Mr. Loring. She's done a commendable job holding together the business. Of course, being of secessionist sympathies, she's been influenced by some of the wrong elements in our fair city."

"Such as?" Steve asked, ushering Byers behind the counter and offering him a seat. The man might well prove a repository of valuable information.

"Well, Blackie Drago, for one. He owns the Bucket of Blood Saloon," he said with a grimace of distaste.

"Oh, yes, I found an invoice for an immense shipment of whiskey for his place yesterday. I'm afraid he's a good customer, Mr. Byers."

"Are you by any chance a Democrat, sir?" Byers asked as if inquiring whether Steve had a venereal infection.

He smiled broadly. "No, I'm a Republican, Mr. Byers, Federal Army, and Temperance, sir."

Byers face split in a beaming smile. "I am so pleased to hear that! Your wife's father shared your views, but her mother was a Southerner. In girlishly romantic rebellion, Cassandra chose to follow her misguided principles."

Steve suppressed a chuckle, finding it impossible to imagine Cass being "girlishly romantic" about anything. "Well, I do hope you understand that even though I'm taking over the freight business, I must deal in the whiskey trade. If I don't sell to Mr. Drago, Bennett Ames and a number of other competitors will have no compunction about doing so."

"Yes, well, at least it will be out of the hands of a young woman. Do you know she has actually gone inside that odious place to drag her drunken teamsters to work? Dealing with those men is most unacceptable for a lady. They are seldom sober."

"Never touch the stuff myself, Mr. Byers," Steve said piously. "Of course, now that I must save Cassandra from the sordid freight business, I will have to occasionally frequent a saloon or two—

just to see we're not being robbed by those cut-throats."

"Perfectly understandable, Mr. Loring, perfectly understandable. Now, might I ask you a few questions about your background for our society page? This marriage was most sudden, and everyone in the city is interested in the details."

Steve gave a brief version of the false story he and Cass had agreed upon and then turned the conversation back to Cass and her family's involvement in Denver politics.

"Politics is like the whiskey of our fair city, Mr. Loring. Plentiful and most villainously adulterated. Take that unscrupulous Blackie Drago, for example . . ."

By the end of the hour, Steve had a great deal of information that might prove useful to him, but he felt assured that William N. Byers had very little accurate information about Cass's new husband.

That evening he strolled down to the Bucket of Blood Saloon after another solitary dinner. The house seemed empty without Cass. Odd, how quickly he'd gotten used to her spitting at him. She was a mystery and a challenge as no other woman had ever been. But then he ruefully added, he'd never married any other woman! He had a great deal to accomplish before she returned from Cheyenne.

The Bucket of Blood was enormous, gaudy, and noisy, with a three-foot-high beveled glass mirror running the length of the bar, two pianos plunking out a verisimilitude of harmony, and a genuine polished oak floor. As Mr. Byers had said, "After all the shootings in the place, imagine what a gorgeous shade of red that floor must be!"

Steve saw no evidence of fresh gore, but the men lining the bar looked rough and surly, many of them sporting long bullwhips or blacksnakes wound around their shoulders. An arsenal of knives, handguns, and longarms bristled on virtually every patron. Even several of the satin-clad "ladies of the line" carried small but lethal "pepperboxes" or stilettoes.

He sauntered to the long, intricately carved oak bar and ordered a beer.

"Wall, lookee here. It's th' dude whut married up with thet man-eatin' female muleskinner o' ole Rufus Clayton's. She carry her blacksnake ta bed with 'er? Mebee ya like yer wimmen ta treat ya rough, huh?"

The speaker was a mountain of a man with a curly black beard and close-set dark eyes that gleamed with a feral light. He wore the plaid wool shirt and denim pants of a teamster, and the four-foot-long hickory stock of his whip marked him as a bullwhacker.

"For a man twice as stupid as the oxen he drives, you sure can talk a lot. You're ugly, too," Steve said with surprising geniality. "You work for my estimable competitor Bennett Ames, don't you? I can smell his stink on you. Or is that ox shit?"

"You done cut a hog in th' ass now!" one small man called out nervously as the big bullwhacker lunged at Loring with a furious oath.

Steve sidestepped the first roundhouse punch and hit the offender in the back of the head with his heavy beer mug. It only stunned the bearlike man, who climbed back to his feet shaking his head, apparently sobering up with distressing rapidity.

"I'm gonna make ya a new face, greenhorn!" With that he came at Steve again. Each time Steve dodged his larger, slower foe, he landed a number of savage punches, but none seemed to deter the enraged giant.

Scanning the bar, Steve grabbed a full whiskey bottle out of a patron's hand. When the teamster lunged, Steve feinted high, then struck in a zigzag arc to the man's knee. The bullwhacker went down on the injured knee with a grunt of agony. Just as quickly, Steve struck again, smashing the bottle against the man's very large, bulbous nose. Blood flew everywhere as the bone gave a sickening thunk. The teamster collapsed backward, spread-eagled on the floor.

"Now, I'd like another beer, please," Loring said to the bartender. "Charge *him* for the bottle of whiskey," he added, motioning to the unconscious man on the floor.

"They're both on the house," a gravelly voice said from behind him.

Steve turned and looked at the man. This had to be Blackie Drago. Small and dapper with a thatch of curly ebony hair and a waxed moustache, he wore a maroon brocade vest that softened the severity of his plain black suit. Diamonds winked on his fingers and from the stick pin in his cravat.

Steve raised his glass in a salute of thanks. "Obliged, Mr. Drago. Steve Loring's the name."

"So you're the man who married Cass. Come with me," he said with a peremptory toss of his head as he walked to the rear of the long, crowded room. "I'll be servin' you better than beer."

"It'll have to be private then. I just this morning convinced Bill Byers I'm Temperance."

At that Drago let out a lusty roar of laughter. "Let's talk in my apartment." He led Steve up a long staircase to the second floor and then through a heavy walnut door. After Drago closed it, the noise from below was startlingly muted. A henna-haired woman, her ample bosom spilling over the top of her tightly laced corset, slid one black-silk-clad leg off the other and stood up, allowing Steve to peruse her bounty as she inspected him.

Before the mutual appraisal went very far, Drago interrupted. "Junie, bring us my best Irish whiskey from the liquor cabinet and then leave us alone."

He raised an eyebrow at Loring appraisingly. "You fancy her?"

"No. I already have enough trouble with one redhead."

Again Drago laughed. "It's glad to hear it I am! Not the trouble part, for I know Cass can be a trial—but that you are right and properly married. I was always wonderin' what kind of man would end up gettin' her."

Steve took the crystal glass from the redhead and sniffed the whiskey. "I don't exactly have her," he said as he took a sip and let it burn a warm, mellow trail down his throat.

"It'll take some doin', that it will—tamin' her," Drago replied as he studied Loring over the rim of his glass. He, too, sipped and then said, "I think you're the man for the job. No one around here she couldn't be leavin' her boot prints all over— exceptin' a few who'd beat the spirit out of her as old Rufus did Eileen." There was a wistful sadness in the way he said *Eileen*.

Steve looked sharply at the infamous Irish machine politician who ran the Denver underground.

"You loved Cass's mother?"

Drago nodded. "From a distance, I assure you. She was married to Clayton when I met her. A real lady she was, Eileen."

"Then the only thing she and Cass had in common was their politics, I assure you!"

Drago's face lost its momentary haunted look. "Yes, Cass is full of piss 'n vinegar. She's niver had it easy, Loring. Rufus Clayton was a real bastard, all the way down to bedrock."

"So I've heard, but he did business with you, didn't he?"

"Better him than Ames," Drago replied in disgust. "At least he didn't water the whiskey or short me on barrels. About six years ago it was, he up and took a stroke. Pure meanness I called it. Cass was only a lass of seventeen, but she took over the whole of it—drivin' the teams and handlin' the men. And a right fine job she's done, too. Better than himself ever did."

Steve looked at Blackie Drago and then asked levelly, "You know about the terms of the will?"

"Doesn't everyone in Denver? Yes, I know. Why, I'm wonderin', besides the pretty cast of your face, did she choose you to husband?" He waited.

Steve shrugged. "Let's just say I was convenient. I won't let her run roughshod over me, but I won't beat her into submission either. Now, having that settled, I'd like some information. As one of her best customers and the man who, rumor has it, hears everything that happens in Denver, what do you know about Bennett Ames?"

"Already run afoul of him, eh?"

"I've been going over records in the office the past couple of days, and it seems he's been running neck and neck with Cass for a lot of business.

There's also been some talk about sabotage on the trail—broken wagons and stolen livestock."

"And as the new owner of Loring Freight, Ltd., it's protection for your backside you'd be wantin' now, is it?"

Steve laughed. "For me and for Cass, Blackie. Ames seems to know every time she bids on a new contract or ships a valuable payload. I've fired Suttler."

Drago nodded shrewdly. "I told Cass he was worthless, maybe even in Ames' pay. But it's a soft heart she has beneath that fierce temper."

"You'll find I'm not similarly afflicted," Steve said drily. "Cass also has a decided aversion to delegating authority. You should see the paperwork she lets pile up while she's on the trail. Even if Suttler wasn't in Ames' pay, his laziness was wrecking the business. I need a clerk. Someone I can trust—bright, quick, good with figures, and able to write a clear, legible hand."

"It's your own man in her camp you'd be wantin'. Someone to offset Kyle Hunnicut?" Blackie asked.

"Kyle's a good man. I figure on winning him over to my side soon enough. But a clerk he's not."

Chuckling, Blackie said, "And well you might win him over, bucko. As to the clerk, I think the Widow Wilkes might have just the boy you need. Name's Ossie, and he always votes a straight Democratic ticket." He raised his glass and drained it.

Steve followed suit and Blackie poured them both refills. "Now as to Bennett Ames and his shenanigans..."

Chapter Seven

Cass climbed off the Denver Pacific train from Cheyenne, soot-covered and bone-weary. For all the vaunted progress the trains brought, they were still rough, dirty, noisy means of transportation. But they were fast and big; one car could carry three times the payload of a freight wagon. They were also relatively safe. Stagecoach passengers risked life and limb on the careening coaches, while train passengers risked only dirt and discomfort. Still, Cass preferred honest dust churned up by horses and mules to the sooty filth belched from locomotive smokestacks.

"Tired, Cass?" Chris asked solicitously as they walked across the platform. He knew how she felt, not so much from the rigors of the journey, but because of their lack of success in Cheyenne.

Smoothing the wrinkles in her dark blue traveling suit, Cass smiled wanly. "Nothing a good hot bath won't fix, Chris. First I want to stop by the office and check on the mail, see how things are going." She scanned the crowded street looking for her driver and carriage.

If Chris suspected her cowardice in not going to their city house to face her new husband, he did not mention it. "I sent a wire to Vera saying we'd be on the twelve-fifteen train, Cass."

She caught sight of the Clayton carriage as it rounded the corner. Turning to Chris she said, "Wait for my luggage and take it to the house. I'm going to walk to the office. I need time to think."

As she strolled down the bustling streets, wending her way through the raucous crowds, Cass waved absently to acquaintances, mostly teamsters and other men she did business with in town. Then the peacock plumage of Selina Ames caught her eye, swishing directly her way. Bennett Ames's sister was decked out in a royal blue silk gown that made Cass's darker blue suit look like a hermit's sackcloth. A feathered concoction of froth that passed for a hat perched jauntily on her glossy black hair. Her voluptuous curves were shown off to perfection as she preened, inspecting a bedraggled Cass.

"I heard you'd been out of town on business. So has Bennett. Perhaps you saw him in Cheyenne?" Selina's dark eyes glowed with a strange, dancing light, as if she knew a delicious secret Cass did not.

Nodding coolly, Cass replied, "Yes, Bennett and I both met with General Palmer, and no, neither of us received the contract, Selina. Your brother wasn't on the twelve-fifteen train, so I haven't seen him since we left Cheyenne."

"Ah, well, no matter. I'll catch up with him this

evening. What I really wanted to do was congratulate you on your marriage. Steven Loring is quite a find." Her tone of voice and her inspection of Cass's rumpled clothes indicated just how unworthy she thought Cass was to have landed a man like Loring.

"Yes, we met in Chicago last year. You really ought to travel east, Selina. Who knows? You might find a husband, too...if you went far enough," Cass added sweetly.

Selina drew back, then forced a smile as she played her trump card. "Well, I don't have to travel at all. I have dozens of suitors in Denver, but then I'm not in the unfortunate position of having to marry." She stressed the word maliciously. "Bennett does take such good care of me, I can quite pick and choose among gentlemen until I decide I want a husband."

Cass's palm itched to smack the beautiful woman. "I chose Steve, and as you said, he is quite a find. No man in Denver can even compare. I looked them all over first and rejected them. Now, if you'll excuse me, I have to get to my office. Business, you know?"

Selina smiled a bit too broadly as she nodded farewell. "You may find one or two surprises at your office, Mrs. Loring."

Not wanting to give the harpy any further cause to gloat, Cass quickly departed in the direction of Clayton Freighting. When she rounded the corner of Cherry Street, she stopped dead in her tracks, staring up at her big brick office building.

Steve looked across the counter when the front door slammed open with a deafening crash. Ossie, who was helping several customers, smiled nervously at the boss's wife, whom he had seen chastise drunken muleskinners with blistering skill. Even without her whip she looked formidable—and very, very angry. The men in the room parted like the waters of the Red Sea as she advanced.

"Welcome home, Cass," Steve said coolly, one eyebrow arched, waiting to see what she'd do. He was leaning back in a chair, a cigar clenched between white teeth and papers in both hands, surrounded by neat stacks of invoices and carefully organized accounting ledgers.

"Who the hell gave you permission to put up that sign?" she grated out in a low, furious hiss.

Several men looked nervously from Cass to Steve, a few with poorly hidden grins, more than one in avid anticipation of the impending showdown.

Steve calmly laid his cigar in a clean ashtray and deposited the papers on the desk. "No one had to give me permission. I own this business, or had you forgotten, *Mrs. Loring*." He stressed her name contemptuously.

"That is not part of our deal and you damn well know it!" she shrieked, fists planted on her hips.

He stood up slowly, forcing her to raise her face to look him in the eye from the disadvantage of her inferior height. "Do you really want to discuss our, er, deal in front of all these witnesses, Cass? Why don't we go into the stockroom and continue our discussion?" Without waiting for her assent, he locked his fingers with iron tightness on her elbow, guiding her toward the back hall. He turned briefly and called over his shoulder, "Ossie, see to those orders and then finish with this correspondence. There's a good lad."

Cass yanked her arm from his painful grasp but strode quickly toward the back room before her temper led her to blurt out enough to ruin her plans—not that she would regret seeing Steven Terrell Loring dancing at the end of a rope at that very instant!

The minute the heavy oak door was closed and they were alone in the enormous crate-filled stockroom, she whirled like a cornered bobcat. "How dare you try to take over my freight business! Who's that boy working the counter? Where's Henry?"

Steve smiled lazily and threw up his hands in mock surrender. "Which question do you want answered first? Calm down, Cassie." He stepped toward her and she backed up a step, spitting mad but still afraid of his touch.

"Calm down! Calm down! I'll see you hang if you keep this up—the whole idea of our agreement was that I retain control of my business—"

"And so you shall," he interrupted. "But remember, Rufus's will says you're to give over control to your husband. Now, how would it look to Thurston Smith or Bennett Ames if I didn't put my name on the freight line? And as to Henry, I replaced him with Ossie Wilkers. He's a good clerk—quick with figures, writes a legible hand, and works circles around that lazy, conniving noaccount you hired. I'm only filling in as a manager for you, Cass. You'll still be the real boss," he said soothingly.

"If I'm still in charge, why didn't you talk to me about all these changes first?"

"Because you'd have refused," he answered matter-of-factly. "You won't delegate one ounce of authority, Cass, and it's draining you. How do you think the business will function after you're well into pregnancy? Expectant women can't go bouncing around on Murphy wagons, you know. What about recovery after the baby's born?" He could see her whiten and flinch at his words and pressed his advantage ruthlessly, reaching out to take her by the shoulders firmly. "You forced me into this, Cass. I didn't choose it, but by God, I'm learning the rules. Forget your father and your fears about men—if you don't have a son, you'll lose everything. You have to ease up on the reins, lady."

"Don't you threaten me, Steve Loring!" She couldn't stand the way he held her, more by force of will than with his hands lightly cupping her shoulders. She raised her arms and broke free, willing herself to return his stare. "You don't know about my father anyway. Leave him out of it."

"I do know that his twisted travesty of a marriage has led you to repeat his mistake with your own." At her look of sudden suspicion, he said, "I had a long talk with Blackie Drago the other night. Like I said, Cass, I'm learning the rules. I have to if I plan to survive this 'arrangement' we have."

"I can't believe Blackie'd talk to you!" she said incredulously.

"Better than that, we tied one on together. Quite a hangover, but it was worth it. He recommended Ossie for the job. The boy's an eager worker, Cass. Give him a chance."

She seemed to wilt for a moment, then took a deep breath and faced him with her chin defiantly high once more. "You win this round, Steve. Organize the paperwork in the office. I'll keep the boy on Blackie's say-so, but from now on, ask me before you make any more changes."

Cass walked regally through the now hushed front office. In spite of her dirty, rumpled clothes and the tired circles beneath her eyes, she looked proud and fully in control of the situation. Managing a cool smile at the assembled men, she opened the front door and headed toward her city house. A bath and some clean clothes would give her a whole new perspective on how to handle the infuriating and frightening man she'd married.

Vera Lee greeted her at the front door. "Mr. Chris brought your bags. I have a bath waiting."

"That sounds wonderful, Vera," Cass replied, heading for the wide curving staircase at the center of the large marble foyer. Just as her hand fastened on the newel post, the card tray on the table caught her eye. It was piled high with calling cards and invitations, highly unusual for Cass, whose social life seldom extended beyond sharing campfire tales with her teamsters. Even when her parents were alive, Cass had detested parties and dances.

Quickly she began to flip through the pile of invitations. Selina Ames's invitation for tea on Friday she consigned disdainfully to the trash. As she read the names of several prominent matriarchs, it quickly dawned on Cass that her now respectable status as a married woman had once more placed her within the pale of society. She began to smile. Perhaps a few occasions to dress in her best clothes and have Steve squire her about might not be such a bad idea after all. After reading Dr. Elsner's books, she had planned to make him suffer by setting up a careful schedule of nights when he would have to come to her room during her most fertile time, then denying him his rights all the rest of the month.

Perhaps she could now add an extra bit of punishment by making him jealous. Her every instinct told her that Steve desired her. If only it didn't also work the other way around!

She quashed that treacherous thought and said to Vera, "What would you say to my giving a ball—a rather gala affair to celebrate my marriage and introduce Steve to Denver society?"

Vera Lee smiled and nodded. "I will begin by planning the menu. Mr. Loring will be most pleased, I am sure. He has enjoyed meeting so many of your friends already."

Cass's eyes narrowed, recalling his plying Blackie Drago with liquor to learn about her childhood. "What friends, Vera?"

Vera shrugged with exaggerated innocence. "You saw some of the cards—the Ameses, Attorney Smith, the Dortons, Mrs. Jared, the Byers—"

"The Byers!" Cass echoed incredulously. "But William Byers's wife is the leading temperance crusader in town and his paper has always railed against the freighters who pander to saloons like Drago's!"

Smothering a smile, Vera replied gravely, "Well, he and Mr. Loring had luncheon here yesterday, Miss Cass. Of course, Mr. Loring told me to hide the liquor in the pantry and serve lemonade instead of wine."

Cass seethed through the elaborate courses of Vera's welcome-home dinner that evening while Steve ate with his usual relish.

Finally, shoving away the remains of flaky crust from a peach pie, he looked over at Cass, waiting. Until now they'd had a desultory conversation about the details of some new orders for heavy machinery and the general store supplies to be delivered to Gold Hill and Fairplay.

It was evident by his repeated casual references to the city's leading commercial figures, both respectable and not-so-respectable, that he'd spent the week of her absence far more profitably than she had. Everyone seemed to like him!

"Something bothering you, Cassie?"

"Don't call me Cassie. You know I hate it," she said, throwing her napkin down. "I read Mr. Byers's laudatory article about Denver's newest freighting tycoon! You'd best watch out what he learns or you'll end up dangling from the end of a rope," she added coldly.

"And where would that leave you? In search of another husband? Time's running out, Cass," he said softly, his dark golden eyes running appreciatively over the swell of her breasts above her emerald green gown. Her cheeks flushed with embarrassment at his bold perusal.

"As to our marriage agreement, that's a separate issue we can discuss later," she replied with feigned coolness. "Right now I want you to understand something: You are to stay in the background as much as possible and let me run my business. That goes double for granting newspaper interviews and mingling with men like Blackie! If Byers doesn't have R. G. Dun investigate you, Drago'll get you drunk and find out about your past!"

He smiled grimly. "So you don't like a taste of your own medicine, do you? It seems I've won a few friends. You were right about one thing, Cass. It's easier for a man in a man's world—and Denver is a man's town. Tell me, just what did you think you were going to do with me? Stuff me in Kyle Hunnicut's hip pocket like a sweaty bandana and just pull me out when you wanted my 'services'?"

His smile had turned into a scowl.

Steve's loss of control helped Cass bring her own fury in check. She could tell by the way he had watched her through dinner that he desired her. Didn't his own words betray him? "As to my 'wanting your services,'" she began acidly, "we both know that is not a matter of choice, but we do need to discuss a schedule for completing the atrocious terms of this farcical marriage."

Now she had struck a nerve! "Just what do you mean, 'schedule'?" he asked in a voice that snapped like a blacksnake.

"Precisely what I said. I've been doing some reading about physiology. One of my best friends is John Elsner—Dr. Elsner. I trust you haven't met *him* yet?" she inquired sweetly and was rewarded with a low negative growl. "It seems human females have only a certain number of days through the middle of their monthly cycle when they're fertile." So far, so good. Her nerve was not failing her. Watching the tic in his cheek helped bolster her courage. "It's quite useless to attempt impregnation with 'your service,'" she paused to lace the words with contempt, "for the next two weeks." She stood up, noting with relish that this time he had forgotten to assist her with the chair.

Steve simply stared at her as if seeing her for the first time. "You said *human females* were only fertile during the middle of their cycle. Well, darling wife, that doesn't really apply to you, does it?"

Without warning his hand shot out. He grasped her slim wrist in a bone-crushing grip and yanked her onto his lap.

Too stunned to fight, Cass parted her lips to yell and his mouth covered hers in a harsh, punishing kiss. His hand tangled in her hair, pulling it loose and kneading her scalp as his tongue explored and tantalized the soft, hot interior of her mouth. Something about the savage suddenness of his assault triggered her own response, making her accept, even return, the passionate embrace. Her breasts arched against his chest and her tongue dueled with his as the kiss deepened.

Steve could feel her heart pounding in rhythm with his, feel the hard points of her nipples through the thin silk and lace of her clothing. She wanted him all right, her body did, even if her calculating bitch's mind rejected him! Before he lost control and took her right there on the dining-room carpet, he had to end it. But when her arms, now freed from his grip, stole up to encircle his neck, he plundered her mouth again. He was rewarded by an incoherent sob as her soft body molded to his.

Abruptly he stood up. He would have dumped her onto the floor, except for her arms clinging about his neck. With cold deliberation he reached up and disentangled them, pushing her away and turning quickly to put the heavy walnut captain's chair between them lest she see visible proof of his need for her.

Cass stood, dizzy and stunned, as he said, "Do summon me when you feel my 'services' are required, wife." He walked several paces toward the door before her strained voice halted his retreat.

"Next week . . ." She hesitated, gripping the table while air rushed into her lungs, fortifying her. "Next week I'll require services of another sort from you. I'm giving a ball to announce our marriage. Since you've already met most of the people

I've invited, you should enjoy it far more than your other marital duties.''

The week before the ball passed in misery for Cass and Steve, neither one willing to lower the defenses so pridefully erected after that last hurtful confrontation. After a day going over paperwork in the office, Cass was happy to retreat from the efficient domain that Steve had created. The system that he and Ossie had set up worked like an oiled machine. She had only to make major decisions and leave the details to her young clerk.

Cass and Kyle attended several stock auctions, and Steve insisted on joining them. Although he stayed quietly in the background while she inspected mules and oxen, she knew he was absorbing and storing knowledge about every facet of the freight business. Everywhere they went, people smiled in greeting, offering the newlyweds congratulations. Smiling in return, Cass counted the days until the ball. Every evening she shared dinner in icy silence with Steve, discussing only what she had to about business operations. They retired to their separate bedrooms each night to toss fitfully.

The day of the ball, Steve left for the office early as was his routine. Cass remained at home to oversee the final preparations. Nervously she issued orders to the two pretty Irish girls Vera had trained as upstairs and kitchen maids. For that evening, a dozen other men and women had been hired as butlers, maids, cook's assistants, and doormen.

"Yer dress be pressed out an layin' across the bed, missus. I'll be drawin' hot water up for yer bath now, if that's all right?" Kate asked, tiredly running her hands through her frizzy blonde hair.

"Yes, that'll be fine, Kate. Please see that Peggy goes to the kitchen to assist Vera first." Cass liked the quiet, hard-working Kate, but pretty, giggly Peggy had altogether too saucy a manner when it came to Steve, whom she watched with lascivious cow's eyes whenever he entered the room.

Huge vases of fresh mountain wildflowers filled the hallways of the Loring city house. In the dining room, the buffet tables groaned beneath a lavish feast being set out. Saddle racks of venison, rare beef, glazed capons, and even fresh trout in almond sauce were accompanied by all the bounty of summer, fresh garden vegetables and elegant fruit compotes. A champagne fountain burbled on a nearby table, set with rows of sparkling crystal goblets. There was fresh citrus punch for the teetotalers, and expensive bonded whiskey for those who preferred stronger refreshment. In the front parlor, now cleared of furniture to serve as a ballroom, Eileen's elegant piano was being played by a young musician from one of Blackie's saloons. The youth was accompanied by two violinists whose music was airy and sweet.

Standing at the top of the stairs, Cass surveyed the crowd below with nervous anticipation. Never, even at her first party, which Eileen had given on her fifteenth birthday, had Cass been so tense. "I'd rather face a saloon full of drunk mule-skinners than these people," she croaked to herself as she fussed with the amber satin ball gown.

Suddenly a warm, strong hand gripped her bare shoulder. "Talking to yourself, Cassie?" Steve asked in mock reproval.

"I was thinking of ornery tempered mules," she

replied. "Small coincidence that you should arrive at the moment. You're late."

He inspected her gown and hairdo critically as he replied, "And of course, we must present the facade of joyous newlyweds to the assembly, mustn't we, Cass? Allow me?" Bowing formally from the waist, he offered her his arm with a flourish.

She placed one dainty hand around it and felt the electric tension flare again as it always did when they touched. Her knees felt weak and she knew she was trembling, but Cass buried the fear deep inside, coiled in a hard, cold knot. She smiled brilliantly at her husband.

He was dressed in darkest midnight blue, the suit impeccably tailored with a snowy ruffled shirt emphasizing his tawny good looks. Everything about him, from his elegantly booted feet to the gold watch fob that glinted discreetly at his waist, whispered style and breeding. Again she was struck by the mystery of why such a man would end up in a tumbleweed wagon.

"You've done 'a real job o' work,' as Kyle would say, Cass." Steve's eyes quickly scanned the lavishly decked out rooms unfolding below them and returned to peruse her with a brooding stare.

"Do you refer to the ball arrangements or my appearance?" she inquired, uncomfortable under his hypnotic eyes, so deep a gold they matched her gown.

"Both," he replied. His hand reached up and lifted the heavy russet lace that fell provocatively from her décolletage. Her hair, a glowing shade between the deep amber and rich russet of her gown, was coiled in intricate curls, laced with delicate gold filigree combs. A few long soft curls fell over one shoulder, inviting a man's hands to touch, to caress. Steve fought the impulse as they descended to the bottom of the long fan of carpeted stairs. The crowd of wellwishers closed in on them. Remembering his own additions to the guest list, Steve smiled in anticipation.

Finally breaking away from the press, they entered the large front parlor where dancers were waltzing in graceful cadence. "Shall we?" he asked, but gave her no opportunity to reply before sweeping her smoothly into the rhythm of the lilting strains.

Pressed so closely to him, Cass could smell the crisp aroma of shaving soap and a faint hint of tobacco. She had rehearsed her plans ever since her visit to John Elsner. Why was it so difficult to put them into action now? Why did his nearness have this unnerving effect on her, leaving her addle-witted and out of breath? When she raised her head and gazed at his face, she was jolted by the hot golden liquid of his eyes.

"I was wondering how long it would take for you to work up the courage to look at me," he said in soft derision. "You're beautiful, Cassie, but then you know that. Did you perhaps dress to entice me?" Ignoring her indignant gasp, he continued smoothly, "If so, you have. Satin and lace are much more becoming than mud and blacksnakes."

"You are insufferable and vain! I did nothing of the kind. We have an agreement, and if I were ugly as Medusa and rolled in the mud nightly, you'd still have to fulfill your part of the bargain—or hang!" she finished spitefully.

He threw back his head and chuckled as if at some secret lover's jest. In an ironic way, he realized that the circumstances of their marriage were a secret jest of sorts. "How brutally you state matters, Cass."

"I learned at an early age it does no good to sugar a jackass's medicine," she whispered tartly, then stiffened as she caught sight of Selina Ames's glossy black head across the room. "Who invited *her*?" she accused Steve, knowing full well. "I suppose her slimy brother is also partaking of my hospitality."

"*Our* hospitality, sweet, and yes, I did invite them. Bennett Ames is our biggest competitor and utterly ruthless. It pays to keep an eye on him," he murmured as he scanned the crowd.

"More words of wisdom from Blackie Drago?" she said, knowing that the asperity in her voice betrayed how much she hated Steve's encroachment into her world.

"Blackie and I did discuss Ames and how to handle him," he replied.

"I've been handling Bennett for years. I'd think you'd be far more interested in 'handling' his sister. Selina does seem your type—all fluff and glitter. She keeps her claws concealed in lace gloves until she's ready to strike."

He touched her jaw, ostensibly a tender gesture, as he said, "Unlike my wife who keeps her whip in plain sight—most of the time. What game are you playing tonight, Cassie, I wonder?"

She shrugged and turned casually from him as the dance ended. Just then Norman Jared and Able Wise, two prominent bankers, approached her. Before Cass could make introductions, it became apparent that Steve had already met both men. When the music resumed and Norman asked her to dance, she accepted, flashing him a blinding smile.

She was playing a dangerous game with a volatile man and Cass knew it as she watched Steve's narrowed eyes follow her across the dance floor. He stood near the bar, holding a whiskey, a long thin cigar clenched in his teeth. Forcing her gaze from his lean face, she turned her attention to her current partner and laughed at his inane conversation as if he were the wittiest man alive.

"Well, hello again. I wasn't expecting to find half of the joyous bridal pair alone," Selina purred, placing one slightly plump hand on Steve's arm.

Wryly he remembered what Cass had said about Selina's claws as he returned her smile. "Hello yourself, Miss Ames. My wife seems to be enjoying her party. Mightn't we do the same?" He motioned to the dance floor, and Selina immediately took his cue.

The raven-haired beauty was dressed to emphasize her abundant endowments, nearly spilling out of a rose silk gown. She pressed her creamy flesh against his ruffled shirt front and whispered conspiratorially, "Your shirt studs are sharp, but I don't mind, Steve, not at all." With a low, rippling chuckle, she held him far closer than propriety allowed.

Bennett Ames's spoiled sister had a shady reputation at best, but Steve recognized the game his teasing wife played, and knew exactly how to play back. He also knew who would win at evening's end.

Never sit in a high-stakes game unless you can afford to lose, Cassie, he thought mirthlessly. Steve had despised the hot surges of jealousy he'd experienced earlier, watching all those adoring men fawning over his wife. She could have chosen any man in this room and had him with a snap of her fingers, yet she chose to wed a wanted criminal, a complete stranger whom her hired gunman brought to her in chains. Just so she could have total control. What kind of a twisted woman had he married? And worse yet, why did he still burn with desire for her?

Cass watched Selina's lushly rounded curves puddle at Steve's chest. Spitefully she thought the tramp spilled out of her dress like melted vanilla ice cream at a Fourth of July picnic. When Steve's sun-streaked hair fell forward, Selina reached a beringed hand up and brushed it back proprietarily, like a wife would do. He laughed and led her from the dance floor toward the open French doors to the garden.

Something inside Cass snapped. With a quickly murmured apology to Norman Jared, she followed them, her mind racing furiously for an excuse to drag Steve from Selina's clutches without utterly humiliating herself. Just then the perfect answer appeared in the person of General William Jackson Palmer.

The fine-boned, intense man with the shrewd blue eyes smiled courteously at Cass, who returned the smile with a warm greeting. "General Palmer, I'm so happy your busy schedule permitted you to attend our little celebration. I must introduce you to Steve. Perhaps between us we can convince you to give us the supply contracts for your railroad."

Palmer's eyes twinkled for an instant as he greeted Steve's wife. The cryptic telegram he'd received from his old friend the day before her arrival in Cheyenne had told him little.

Once he'd met the very cool, businesslike Cassandra Loring, even more questions had filled his mind. Steve had been engaged to a Louisville belle only a few months ago. Marcia was quite the opposite of the whip-wielding frontier woman who employed a gunman Palmer would have appreciated riding beside during the war. In peacetime, however, men like Kyle Hunnicut made Palmer decidedly uneasy. So did the unlikely Mrs. Loring.

But now, she was dressed in satin and looked like a goddess. The general was struck anew with curiosity. Perhaps Steve had not chosen so precipitously after all. They left the crowded ballroom and walked into the cool garden.

"Oh, Steve, I have someone I want you to meet." Cass hailed him in a dulcet but ringing voice that carried on the quiet night air. Steve and Selina stood, far too close together, beneath the whispering branches of a willow tree near the garden wall.

Just then Bennett Ames came striding down on them with a predatory grin etched across his features. "Well, well, General Palmer, what a pleasure to see you here, sir. I was just looking for my sister, as Mrs. Loring was looking for her bridegroom, it would appear."

"So fortunate you found us together, Bennett," Steve said as he walked with Selina toward the approaching trio.

"Yes, isn't it," Cass echoed innocently. "General Palmer, may I present—"

Steve reached out and slapped Palmer expansively on the back. "How the hell are you, Will?"

As Bennett, Selina, and Cass stood mute in amazement, Loring and Palmer laughed boisterously and shook hands. Then the general turned to Cass and said, "Please excuse my captain's bad manners, Mrs. Loring, but you see we've been friends since childhood and served in the army together."

"And I asked Will not to tell you. I wanted to—"

"Surprise me yourself," Cass cut in with venomous sweetness. "How thoughtful you are, darling," she fairly cooed, moving over to take his arm and lead him away from Selina. "I suppose you also mentioned the small matter of my . . . our freight contract for his railroad." Her voice was gritty now as she battled to control her temper.

"Ah, yes, dull men's talk, Cassie," Steve said with a wink at Selina. "If you and your brother will excuse us, I do believe I must explain some things to my wife and my old comrade at arms."

Before either Bennett or Selina could say anything, Steve had one arm slung around the general's shoulders and the other around Cass's waist. They walked toward the rear of the formal gardens where a small musical fountain splashed.

Cass had always hated Rufus's taste in ornate marble statuary, but seating herself on the cool stone bench, she was grateful for the soothing sound of the water. All else failing, she could always drown her perverse husband in the pool!

The two men briefly mentioned their years as Federal skirmishers, but Steve concluded with mock reproof, "Cass doesn't approve of that chapter in our careers, Will. I'm afraid you're looking at an unreconstructed little rebel here. She doesn't hold with Yankees."

"But, darling, how you misunderstand. I married you, didn't I? Please don't listen to him, General. The war's been over for five years, and it never really touched us here in Colorado anyway."

"What she means is it's good business to let sleeping dogs lie, especially if they were the victors."

Sensing the antagonistic undercurrents between Steve and his new wife, Will decided to move to safer ground. "As you say, all that's past. Like you, I look forward to a long and prosperous life in Colorado. This fall I'm getting married, Steve. Her name is Queen Mellon and she rivals your own lady here in beauty and grace. We're both very fortunate men."

"Congratulations, Will. I'm very happy for you," Steve said sincerely. Did the surge of his own loss, of his frustration, register in his voice? he wondered.

"You deliberately set me up, you chamber pot with ears, you sneaky, whoreson cur!" Cass's voice hissed as she whirled on Steve after closing the study door.

He stood in the corner, a glass of brandy in his hand, leaning against the massive walnut desk. "It's late, Cass. The party's over, the guests have gone home . . . to bed. So should we. That's what this whole little charade was about, wasn't it? To dress up, flirt with a pack of men, and entice me into a jealous rage? Ah, Cass, you've worked at being a man too long to be good at feminine games," he said with a laugh.

She seethed with fury at the accuracy of his assessment. "Don't change the subject! You and Palmer cooked this whole scheme up—toying with me. You let me traipse all the way to Cheyenne on a fool's errand while you sat back waiting to spring your past association with him on me! 'Ah, yes, dull men's talk, Cassie'!" she spat, mimicking his hateful voice. "Let's get one thing straight, Steve! I make the decisions about the freight line, not you."

"But without me, sweeting, Will won't give you the contract, will he?"

She sputtered, "He couldn't be so stupid as to give it to Bennett Ames!"

"He will if I ask him to," he replied with maddening calm.

"Are you and that slut Selina in this to fleece your old war comrade? Would you stoop so low as to deal with a thief like Ames?"

"Why not? You stooped so low as to marry me—a man on his way to hang, as you frequently point out, love."

"You are disgusting!" She turned toward the door, but before she reached it he caught up with her and pulled her to him roughly.

"I think not *so* disgusting—else you'd not set out to make me jealous and be jealous yourself when you found me with Selina. You don't like to taste your own unsugared medicine, do you, Cass?"

She pushed furiously against his chest, wrenching free. "Get your hands off me! I'll tell you when you may touch me!"

He gave a harsh, ugly laugh. "So that's your game—entice and then turn a cold shoulder when I respond. God—" he ran his fingers through his hair. "When I listened to Will talk about Queen Mellon...a woman who loves him..." He looked up at her with raw anguish on his face. "A woman he *chose* for a wife. I never realized until tonight what I've been cheated of, Cass. The pity is, you never will!"

"What do you know of love?" she lashed back in pain. "All you know is how to paw and rut like an animal!" With that she opened the door and fled.

Steve stood listening to her footsteps echo on the marble floor of the foyer.

"Paw and rut, is it, Cassie? Well, you'll get your share tonight, and your fertility schedule be damned!" He reached for the snifter, finished the brandy in one gulp, and smashed the crystal against the fireplace. It exploded in a flash of diamond-bright shards, broken like his dreams.

Cass sat at her dressing table massaging her temples to ease the pounding pain in her skull. "Too much champagne and all those hairpins and combs biting into my scalp," she whispered, running her fingers over her aching head. Her hair hung down in coppery splendor, picking up the light from the glowing coals in the fireplace.

Like Steve, she had been touched by the way Will Palmer had spoken of his fiancée. She knew that Rufus had never felt that way about Eileen. Steve would never feel that way about her, either. Shocked at the unexpected turn of her thoughts, Cass stood up, discarding her long velvet robe in preparation for bed. Carelessly she tossed it across a chair and reached for the coverlet, already turned down by a maid.

Steve entered so quietly she did not hear him. He watched her slim, lithe body, outlined by the fire's glow through the sheer white silk nightrail she wore. As her glorious hair fell in shimmering waves to caress the pillow, he felt a tightening ache in his loins.

"You play with fire, you get burned, Cass." At her startled gasp, he laughed and walked silently across the heavy carpet toward her bed. "God, you are beautiful," he ground out against his will.

Cass's eyes flew to the adjoining door. The bolt was not slipped! How could she have neglected it? *Maybe you wanted him to come*, a voice taunted inside her head. "Get out, Steve. I told you Dr. Elsner—"

"To hell with Dr. Elsner and his damn fertility schedules! You're my wife and I have the right—the duty—to bed you." He reached for her and she slapped his hand.

"You danced and teased all night, Cassie. Now it's my turn to 'paw you like an animal.'"

"Don't you touch me. I'll have you shot for this! Get out—get—"

He cupped her shoulders with his hands and his fingers dug into the soft flesh as he shook her rigid body. "Too bad Rufus's will specified my stud services—you'd love to have a husband you could castrate and then lead around like one of your more docile oxen, wouldn't you? Wouldn't you?"

Her eyes were enormous golden pools, glowing with fear, but she held her chin high and refused to flinch from the rough shaking, even if he loosened her teeth.

Suddenly, in a wave of self-loathing, he stopped. Cass took the instant to say coldly, "Go on, then. Get it over with."

He looked at her blankly for a second, then began to laugh. "Isn't this where we began the first time, ice princess?" His face became serious. "No ...I don't think so. You wanted attention...attention you'll get, but on my terms, Cassie ..."

Steve pulled her to him and began to nibble softly at her throat, tangling her hair in his hands. Her arms were caught to her sides, trapped and immobilized by his strong embrace.

She felt herself growing dizzy and warm, trembling. It's the champagne, she told herself. *It's him*, a small, truthful voice niggled. When he began to unfasten the silk frogs on her gown, caressing her bared flesh with his slim but strong, fingers, she allowed it. When he took one aching breast in his mouth and suckled it, she arched to meet the wet heat, unaware that her silk nightrail had whispered to a puddle on the floor.

Now she knew what to expect, what he would do, what she wanted him to do. That first night he had set her body aflame and he was doing it again, only this time it would be different. Cass gave herself over to the longing that had kept her restless and ill-tempered the past weeks. What a fool she'd been to think she wanted to deny him!

Steve reached down and swept her into his arms, laying her across the open invitation of the bed, then shrugged his own robe from his body and knelt over her, stroking her breasts, belly, and thighs until she writhed in response to his touch. When he lay beside her and pulled her to him for a slow, searing kiss, he felt her open eagerly for his questing tongue, even return the caress as her arms wound about his shoulders.

They rolled across the bed, both breathless and seeking, feverish in their need. His hands followed the delicate curve of her spine to her silky buttocks. He cupped one, squeezed it gently, and was rewarded with an insinuating undulation of her pelvis.

Cass could feel the hard length of his shaft against her belly. A hot surge of pleasure frissoned through her as she felt the proof of his desire, his need that matched her own. She arched against him instinctively as he rolled her onto her back and kissed her.

When his knee slid up between her thighs, she parted them and raised up to welcome him, hot and hard into the weeping core of her body. This time there was no pain, unless she counted the desperate aching need he had created deep inside her. The wanting did hurt, just as the waiting had.

Feeling her ardent, almost desperate response, Steve thrust deeply inside her wet sheath. How tight and smooth its grip, how exquisite the sensations, blinding, delirious.

No other woman had ever affected him this way. He felt himself slipping over the abyss, afraid of her hold on him—not just the blackmailing marriage that could one day be dissolved, nor even the child they might create. He would take the child with him, for Cass wanted only her empire. He gazed with passion-glazed eyes at her beautiful face, lashes squeezed tightly closed, lips caught between small white teeth, her whole being concentrated in absorbing him and the pleasure he was giving her. She took but did not give, desired but did not love. He had awakened her body, but could he touch her soul?

Cass could sense the urgency in his movements as they suddenly accelerated. Through a haze of desire and pleasure, her conscious mind remembered the textbooks. He would finish too soon—without her again! With a moan of anguish, her eyes flew open and she clenched her fingers into his hard, narrow hips, digging her nails in until he slowed, then stopped, still hard, buried deep inside her.

Steve stared down at her in amazement as she pulled him from the edge of maddening ecstasy.

Cass looked like a wounded fawn, with big amber eyes round and pleading. She wet her lips with the tip of her tongue, but no words came out. Instinctively he knew what she wanted, and some viciously perverse part of him felt compelled to deny her.

"What, Cassie?" he whispered, again resuming his slow inexorable rhythm that her hips followed. When she didn't answer him, he again began to thrust rapidly.

"No!" The cry was torn from her. "No, please." Her nails again dug into his hips.

"No, what, Cass? What do you want? Say it," he rasped out raggedly, wanting her admission even more than he wanted release.

"I . . . I want you to go slow . . . for me . . . for me to have time . . ." the words were agony for her, made worse by the ripples of ecstasy he sent through her with every slow, sleek movement.

"Oh, so you want pleasure, too . . . sexual satisfaction . . . release? As Kyle would say, Cassie—" he leaned down to nip at her ear with warm, persuasive lips, "—'that's another job o' work.' You've paid me to make a baby, not give you pleasure. What price for pleasure, Cass?" He straightened up over her and appeared to debate. "How much?"

If he'd dunked her in Cherry Creek at Christmas he couldn't have dashed colder water on her passion. Rage, sheer, blinding red rage replaced the sweet, intolerable ache. Cass levered herself up on her elbows and twisted her hips sideways, dislodging him from his seat.

Steve reached out for a handhold, but the flailing, swearing woman succeeded in pitching him headlong off the bed before he could grab the headboard. His hand grazed the bedside table as he fell, causing the pitcher to wobble.

Without thinking, Cass responded to his visual lead, only her hand connected solidly with the pitcher handle and she raised it above her head and threw it at her husband as he rolled backward onto the carpet. It struck him squarely on the head, then broke into several large, jagged pieces. Steve lay very still, flat on his back.

Chapter Eight

Cass knelt up, teetering on the edge of the bed, staring in horror at Steve's unconscious body—at least she prayed he was only unconscious. Lord, what if she'd killed him! With legs shaking, she cautiously stepped onto the floor and then knelt beside him, feeling for a pulse. He was breathing.

Silently she offered up a prayer of thanks, then returned her consideration to more practical matters. She looked at the shattered pieces of the ceramic pitcher and wondered how badly she'd brained him. Long accustomed to treating trailside injuries, Cass knew that the only way to find out was to examine him.

Hesitantly her fingertips brushed across his forehead, then gingerly worked their way up into his hairline. She was rewarded with a ragged moan as she touched the rapidly swelling lump just over his right temple. Luckily it was hidden by his thick hair, for it was the size of a goose egg. Again he moaned, but showed no signs of regaining consciousness.

Just as well, she considered, fearing the rage he'd be in, but what was she to do with him? She couldn't just let him lie there. He could roll over and seriously cut himself on the broken glass, or at the least catch pneumonia after spending the night naked on a cold floor. Anyway, she certainly couldn't have Peggy or Kate walk in tomorrow morning and see him this way.

Quickly she began to gather up the larger pieces of the pitcher, which she deposited in a small trash basket near her dressing table. Then she dug an old brush from her bureau drawer and swept the smaller fragments up. He had fallen on his heavy dressing robe, and getting it from beneath him proved difficult, but finally she managed it.

Cass stood up to drape the robe over his naked body, then stopped, almost against her will—almost, but not quite. With his hot golden eyes mocking her, she had never before dared to look at him. Really look at him. Certainly not when he was splendidly naked. Her eyes traveled from his tousled brown hair with its long, heavy sideburns to those beautifully sculpted lips. The burning eyes were closed, and the elegant brows had no sardonic arch to them now. Lord, it was an arrestingly handsome face!

She suppressed the urge to stroke the bold jaw line and let her eyes move lower to examine his broad chest with its curly pelt of tan hair that narrowed into a thin line that descended to his navel, leading her gaze lower yet to the bush of slightly darker brown hair at his loins. Lying as limp in unconsciousness as the rest of his body, his phallus did not appear menacing to her now. Still, she could recall the rock-hard, pulsing life in it when it had swelled and filled her. Cass quickly let her eyes travel lower still to trace the contours of his long, sinewy legs.

All of him was splendid, she thought with a sudden rush of despair—splendid, intelligent, educated. And he despised her with every fiber of his being. His tauntingly cruel words about pleasuring her being "another job of work" came echoing back, and she felt defiled and painfully hurt.

Cass let the robe drop over his naked length, then stifled a sob and rushed to don her robe. She would have to drag him back to his own bed. Let him wake up with the mother of all headaches in the morning, but it would not be in *her* room, in *her* bed! Quickly opening the door between their rooms, she walked back to him and reached down to grab his body beneath the shoulders, preparing to drag him.

Cass was a strong woman, tall and used to hard physical labor, but even counting her hair, she weighed at most one hundred and twenty pounds. For all his lean, rangy build, her six-foot husband had to outweigh her by fifty pounds. One fierce tug moved him about three inches and nearly gave her a hernia. She took a deep breath and tried again. Barely two inches further. At this rate she'd have him to the door by sunrise.

Admitting defeat, Cass decided to ring for help, then quickly stopped. The very last person she wanted to see this debacle was that simpering Peggy. No, she'd have to go upstairs to the servants' quarters and ask Vera to assist her.

Cass felt like a criminal tiptoeing through her own house in the dark of night. Fortunately, Vera

Lee was a faithful employee who asked no questions. She quickly pulled on her robe and followed Cass back to her bedroom. Unfortunately, she was Cantonese, barely five feet tall with the bone structure of a wren. After several unsuccessful attempts to drag Steve with one woman pulling on each arm, they gave up. Each time they stopped, his already injured head bounced on the carpet when they released his arms.

"We're going to kill him at this rate," Cass sighed in exasperation.

"Or dislocate both his shoulders," Vera said sagely. "We must call Kate and Peg. They're big, strong girls. That way we can each take an arm or leg and lift him. That is, if you are certain you do not wish me to summon Dr. Elsner?"

"No," Cass snapped quickly. Then she amended contritely, "That is, he isn't that badly injured. I want him in his own bed first. Oh, damnblast! Call Kate—but not Peg!" she added quickly.

With as near an amused look as her carefully schooled Oriental face would allow, Vera went to summon the older maid.

Cass knelt and dabbed Steve's head with a cool cloth as she waited, again straightening the robe, which had pulled halfway down his chest in their exertions.

"You're doing this on purpose, you perverse man," she gritted out.

Vera returned with both of the sleepy-eyed maids in tow. She shrugged helplessly at Cass's angry stare. "They sleep in the same room. Anyway, we will need them both."

Cass issued crisp orders, as if dragging an unconscious man naked from her bed was as usual as hauling a wagon of freight from Denver. "Kate, you take his right arm, Peg, his left. Vera and I will take the legs."

"But, mum, what if we drop him?" Kate whispered in a horrified voice.

"Don't," was Cass's succinct reply.

That was easier said than done, for several times before they reached the door Vera's hands slipped. So did the robe covering Steve. Once when it caught on the edge of a chair and was nearly whisked completely off his body, Cass dropped his other leg to retrieve the cover.

Both Irishwomen's eyes were round with amazement, and Peg's filled with more than a little honest, lustful curiosity.

Cass quickly secured the robe across his lower body and then snapped at Peg, "Keep your eyes off him. He's my property." The minute she saw the smug laughter in the maid's eyes, she could have bitten her tongue. *I sound like a jealous shrew!*

Kate suppressed a nervous giggle, and Peg cast her eyes downward to hide the flash of resentment, but mumbled beneath her breath, "A fine way to be treatin' yer property, brainin' him."

Kate's strangled giggles kept Cass from catching Peg's censuring words, but Cass and Peg understood each other's hostility perfectly.

"Now, be careful getting him through the door," Cass directed, fearing the flighty maids would cause him further injury. Just as they eased him through the close confines of the doorway, Cass could feel Steve's leg stiffen. He emitted another moan and opened his eyes.

"What the hell—"

Steve's words were cut short when Kate's giggling turned to a shriek of dismay and she dropped his arm. "Jasus, Mary, and Joseph! He's awak-enin'!"

Tiny Vera Lee, carrying his right leg, felt the sudden jerk and her hands lost purchase. Steve tumbled sideways to the floor with Cass tripping over his left leg and falling headfirst on top of him. When they hit the floor, Peg's firm grip on his left arm yanked her forward into the welter of thrashing limbs.

Kate stood back, wringing her hands in horror. Vera stood in serene detachment as Cass swore and elbowed Peg off her, then clambered to her knees to inspect her hapless "property," who had the distinct misfortune to be on the bottom of the heap. He was out cold again.

With a string of oaths that would have done her best bullwhacker proud, Cass had her trio of unwilling teamsters hefting their cargo once again. This time when the robe slipped, she ignored it, daring Peg to look as they struggled toward the bed with their burden. "Why didn't I ever notice how enormous these damnable rooms were before?" she gritted to herself.

"Because it ain't yerself who's cleanin' them," Peg muttered in reply.

Ignoring the impertinent maid, Cass gave orders to heave Steve's body onto the big, high bed on the count of three.

"Now mind you, don't toss him clean over the other side, poor man," Kate remonstrated in a hoarse whisper as they began to swing their heavy burden in cadence.

"One . . . two . . . three . . ." With a combination of grunts and squeals they tossed him onto the center of his bed. He landed none too gently right on target, but his robe willfully continued wafting across the bed, fluttering to the floor on the opposite side. Ignoring her aching back, Cass bent from the waist and yanked the bottom edge of the coverlet up to drape it across a strategic portion of his anatomy.

"Are you certain he'll be all right?" Cass asked, worriedly chewing her lower lip as Dr. Elsner briskly replaced his instruments in his medical bag.

"Just a slight concussion, Cassandra. You say he tripped on the carpet and fell, knocking the bedside pitcher onto his head?" He parroted her unlikely story gravely, not believing a word of it. Lucky for Steve Loring his scalp was still intact!

"Yes, the pitcher shattered so hard, I was afraid ...and then the stupid maids dropped him carrying him—never mind. As long as he'll be all right." She turned and began to walk nervously toward the door. "How long until he regains consciousness?"

"By morning, if not sooner," the doctor replied in his precise English. "If still he sleeps at noon, send for me again." He paused and took her trembling hand in his as they stood in the hall. "Not to worry. I do not think I will be needed."

After seeing Dr. Elsner out and giving instructions to Vera, Cass trudged upstairs once more and wearily slipped into his bedroom. Pulling up a chair near the bedside, she sank exhaustedly into it and began to doze, only to be rudely awakened by a low masculine whisper.

"So I tripped on the carpet and bashed my own brains in with *your* wash pitcher."

Cass sat up with a start, greeted by Steve's narrowed eyes, now sunken and dark-rimmed from his harrowing experience. "You have no brains to bash in, beloved. I said you hit your head—it's lucky you have such a thick one."

Steve rubbed his eyes to clear his blurring vision as vague memories of the past traumatic night flashed across his mind. "You bloody, hypocritical bitch—you had those damn giggling maids dragging me, buck-ass naked out of your room. Wouldn't it have been a lot easier to put me in your bed?"

"After last night I don't ever want you in my bed again," she hissed furiously.

As she started to rise, Steve reached out to grab her wrist, but the whole world seemed to explode behind his eyelids when he sat up so abruptly. He fell backward with a strangled gasp and passed out. The next thing he could feel was a wet compress being none too gently slapped across his throbbing head.

"Ever since I came west I've been afflicted with headaches, it seems," he mumbled. "Must be the dry air."

"Especially all of it between your ears," she replied tartly, hiding her relief that his lapse into oblivion had been brief.

"Could you send one of the maids to do that? I'm certain Pegeen has a gentler touch," he groused as she reapplied the compress.

"Could you tell that by the way she fell on top of you in the doorway?" Cass asked sourly.

He managed a cheeky grin through his stubbly beard and said, "And here I was so sure it was these delectable breasts pressed onto my chest." He reached up inside her robe for a deft examination.

Cass yanked her robe closed and slapped the

offending hand away as he added, "But then, maybe not. I think they *were* larger..."

"Dr. Elsner was right! You'll recover in plenty of time." She yanked the cloth away and turned to slop it into the basin on the bedside table.

"In time for what?" This time he made no attempt to sit up.

"Why, in a week we're delivering a load of freight in the mountains. You wanted to learn the business. Since you've already mastered office procedures here in Denver, I thought it was time you learned how we really earn our money—on the trail."

"You don't like me winning over your friends here in town," he said with a low chuckle.

"Let's just say I think you'll have a harder time impressing my teamsters, tenderfoot."

"But there is one city fellow you need me to impress, Cass. Will Palmer."

She looked at him with narrowed eyes and a set jaw. "Would you honestly be so stupid as to let Bennett Ames have that contract?"

He put his hands up and gingerly slid them behind his head, cradling it carefully. "If I use my influence, I expect to be paid, Cass."

She rent the air with a volley of fast, low profanity and then stood towering over his reclining figure with her arms akimbo. "What's the price for your influence, Loring?"

"I'm thinking, Cassie...I'm thinking. I have all week to consider my options before you whisk me off to the Rockies' high peaks."

She glowered at him. "Maybe I'll shove you off one of them!"

* * *

"So that's the story, Will, wildly improbable as it is," Steve finished with a sigh.

As he leaned back in the overstuffed chair in General Palmer's hotel suite and closed his eyes, his old friend studied Steve with shrewdly measuring eyes. He looked haggard and haunted. Palmer considered his words carefully before replying to the incredible tale of Steve's forced wedding. Although he had flatly told Will he detested Cass and she him, something did not ring true. There was more that he was not confessing. Of course, Steve had always been a taciturn man, ever since their boyhood days in a Philadelphia prep school.

"When I met your wife in Cheyenne, I must confess I was surprised—not by the fact that you had gotten married, but by *whom* you married. Miss Clayton's reputation is known across the territory and as far east as Kansas City."

Steve exhaled smoke from his cigar and said wryly, "I can imagine what you expected Cass Clayton to be—a foul-mouthed, mannish-looking hellion wielding a blacksnake."

Palmer's eyes danced in amusement. "Something like that. I couldn't for the life of me imagine why you'd marry her—until I met her. Yes, she was all business. Very professional in handling her bid for the contract, as a matter of fact. If you hadn't asked me to withhold a decision, I'd have given it to her over Bennett Ames, believe me."

Steve's face became shuttered as he replied, "Yes, she's all business . . . when she wants to be."

"She's also a real lady. Nothing at all like I'd heard her described," Will remonstrated.

Steve snorted in disgust. "That's only because you've never seen her with her muleskinners.

Now, *that's* the real Cass Clayton!"

Will gave an impatient wave of his hand. "To take over her father's business I imagine she's had to do some pretty unconventional things."

"You should hear her cuss," Steve interrupted.

Will ignored that remark and continued probing. "She's beautiful, Steve. Strikingly so. If I weren't so smitten with Queen, I might consider courting the lady myself. I always liked a woman with a mind and will of her own. That's why I chose the one I did."

Steve stood up and began to pace across the floor to the window overlooking the bustling Denver street scene below. "It's not that I want a simpering, vapid woman. God knows I'm well rid of Marcia, but, dammit, Will, you *chose* your wife! I didn't have any say in the matter."

Palmer chuckled broadly now. "So your male ego's been wounded! This is the West, Steve. It's wild and unconventional and even dangerous, but it's the future—the future of the United States, the future for me—for you and Cass, too. You can build a whole new life together. Why, the possibilities are as limitless as the plains and mountains themselves."

Steve threw up his hands and turned to face Palmer. "I know, I know all about your plans. And I've been considering the business possibilities in Colorado, too."

"Only the business possibilities?" Will asked dubiously. "Not your relationship with your wife?"

A sardonic smile etched Steve's chiseled features. "Let's just say I'm working on that, too. God knows how it'll end, though. She is the most maddening, impossible female I've ever met! For now, let's leave Cass out of this. I wanted you to understand how I came to be involved with this freight business. You said you favored Cass over Ames for the grading crew supply contract. Will you give it to me?''

Palmer's eyes twinkled. "So you want to take the reins from your wife's capable hands and wield the whip yourself. I imagine, considering all she's put you through, that isn't completely unreasonable. Of course you have the contract, Steve!''

As they shook hands, Steve said with a wintery smile, "I'll tell Cass the good news tonight.''

"What about the other matter? You are still a wanted man in the Nations," Will said with gravity.

Steve shrugged. "That's a long way from Colorado. Anyway, I've wired Uncle Lucas and he has some good agents investigating. Let's just hope they can clear me.''

"What about Vince Tanner?''

All the facade of casual indifference erased itself from Steve's face. His expression was granite hard as he replied, "I also have men tracing him. It may take years, but I have a gut feeling that we'll meet again, Will. Like you said during the war, my instincts have always been damn good.''

"Now remember, keep your coat in your bedroll and your mouth closed," Cass said to Chris as they walked out back toward the loading yard.

"I don't like it, Cass. Steve's likely ta—''

"Exactly," she interrupted with grim glee.

In the week since his encounter with Cass's ceramic pitcher, Steve had spent a good portion of each day in the freight yard, watching the teamsters and stock handlers who worked with the mules. The second day, she'd come out of the office to the sounds of a snaking contest. It was a common diversion for the men to set a small object such as a silver dollar on a post staked in soft ground and compete with their whips to see who could knock the coin off without toppling the shallowly mounted post. Steve had been taking lessons from Sam Marsh and Dog Eating Jack. Although she smirkingly watched him knock the post over every time that first day, by the third day he had been able to cleanly snick off the coin one time in three.

Yesterday he had Jack helping him harness a pair of mules—trained ones, not the unbroken variety that had led to his downfall in Pueblo. Already possessing an uncommon skill and empathy with horses, he was now set on learning how to handle the infuriatingly perverse but vital mules used so extensively in the freight business.

Nevertheless, Cass convinced herself, he had a long way to go before he could come close to a good muleskinner's skill. Certainly he could never rival her own. *Could he?* She squelched the thought and smiled inwardly as she and Chris walked across the chaotic freight yard early that morning. Today the supply train of twenty wagons was leaving for a series of deliveries in the remotest mining camps of the Rockies.

"It sure looks to be a scorcher, doesn't it, Chris?" Cass said, looking up at the fiery orange ball rising in the east.

"Well, it was a mite hot yesterday here in town, but—ugh!"

Cass's nudge to the ribs with the stock of her blacksnake quickly silenced him as they stopped beside Steve, who was harnessing a ten-span with Bully Quint.

"Careful. Try not to let a jackass brain you, Steve," Cass said sweetly as he struggled with the elaborate straps and buckles on the restive animals.

He turned to her with a sardonic grin and said, "A bit late for that advice, isn't it, my little Rocky Mountain canary?"

Bully guffawed at the new boss calling his missus by the nickname that the teamsters had given to mules, not having an inkling of the full implications of the insult. Her killing look squelched his mirth.

"We about ready ta roll?" Chris asked quickly, sensing that there was more to the exchange between Cass and her husband than he wanted to know.

"I have to leave a few instructions with Kyle about Ames. Then we can leave," she replied.

"Why aren't you taking your watchdog along, Cass?" Steve taunted in a low voice only she could hear as he stood close beside her.

She looked into his golden eyes and matched their steely glint with her own. "I think you'll have your hands full just driving a team of mules and surviving camp life, Loring. What's your alternative, jumping off a cliff?"

"Considering my alternative, jumping off a cliff might be the act of a rational man," he said with a grimace as he swung up onto the nigh wheeler's saddle.

They climbed steadily for the first day, heading southwest from Denver. The ascent was very gradual, and the looming high peaks seemed no closer by nightfall even though they had made a record-breaking twenty-one miles. Loaded down as they were, that was excellent time, but Cass always pushed relentlessly, Steve learned from the other men who had driven for her the past six years.

Every bone in his body ached as he climbed from the saddle that night. His shoulder was virtually dislocated, and his hands were raw from pulling on the jerk line to slow and direct the lead mules. Their noon break had been short, only enough time to rest the animals and eat a cold meal. Watching Cass as she jumped from the nigh wheeler she'd been riding, Steve vowed to hide his misery. Although dusty and windblown, she looked as energetic as she had at dawn.

It was dusk and the blistering heat of the day on the windswept high plains was fast fading. Nights in Colorado's high altitude were always blessedly cool. Steve had never been so appreciative of the fact as he was that evening. His clothes stank of sweat and were plastered to his body.

"Lord, a bath would be welcome," he said conversationally as he squatted before a campfire.

Cass took a swallow of bitter coffee from a battered tin cup and looked at him disdainfully. "No frills and fancy stuff on the trail, greenhorn."

"Then I'll just have to stink like you," he said with a smile. "At least we'll not offend one another when we sleep together tonight."

She tossed the dregs of her coffee into the fire and stood up. "Pitch your bedroll wherever you like, but we sleep separately on the trail, Loring."

"Not private enough for you, Cassie?" he taunted. "Or are you afraid of what I might do to you after our last little bedroom tussle?"

Her eyes flashed furiously as she recalled his humiliating words and her even more humiliating needs.

"I've never been afraid of you, Steve Loring. As

it happens, you're a failure as a stud. My courses came three days ago, so I can't use your 'services' even if we did have privacy!"

He counted, very obviously, on his fingers and then replied with a lazy grin, "Then I guess tomorrow night's the night for making up, isn't it, Mrs. Loring? Surely you weren't so naïve as to think you'd conceive miraculously the first time? It might take dozens..."

She wished she'd not wasted those hot coffee dregs on the fire as she turned silently and stomped off. *Just wait, Mr. Loring. You'll have other things on your mind besides that by tomorrow night,* she thought smugly in consolation.

The sun hung low in the eastern sky, tingeing the clouds with violet and pink. Already sounds of the awakening camp turned the morning air blue with curses as men waged their endless battle against mules. Steve sat up and stretched. God, the rocky ground was hard and the thin bedroll little enough protection from the chilly night air. If he had not been stiff and sore from riding the nigh wheeler yesterday, the night beneath the stars would have accomplished the same end.

He quickly slipped on his boots and rolled up his sleeping gear, wishing he'd thought to bring an extra blanket. Of course, tonight he could use Cass for body heat, he considered wryly. It was past time he bedded her again after that last disastrous encounter. He had to show her who wore the pants, at least figuratively, in their family. But never again would he let his guard down around the woman, lest she cave in his skull permanently!

As they climbed higher, the terrain began to change. The gradually rolling hills dotted with stands of evergreens began to give way to jagged outcroppings of rock that resembled the broken-off fingers of some netherworld giant thrusting mightily from beneath the earth's crust in a feckless bid for freedom. The striations were frozen in time countless eons ago, he knew from his studies of the geologist Lyell, but nothing could prepare a man for the raw majesty of the Rocky Mountains. Compared to them, the Smokies he had fought through during the war seemed like pretty stage scenery. Even the Alps he'd visited in Europe were humbled by these peerless mountains. Will was right, he mused, this was the future, rugged and untamed, waiting for the hand of man to cultivate the wilderness, to tame the land. He thought of Cass and smiled.

When they began their ascent through the first narrow pass, their path was little more than a hacked ledge with a nerve-jangling sheer drop to an icy stream hundreds of feet below. Steve noticed that the dry, hot air that had so bedeviled him the first day was now growing decidedly cooler. Dressed in a thin cotton work shirt with the sleeves rolled up, he began to feel a chill. By the time they stopped for midday rest, he had rolled his sleeves down. The buckskin driving gloves, so hot and uncomfortable yesterday that he'd risked blisters rather than wear them, were now blessedly warming.

Cass was standing by her big wagon talking to Chris. Both of them had donned sheepskin jackets. As Steve looked around at the other men, most of whom sported heavy lined vests or coats of some sort, he realized with sudden anger that he had once more been set up as a greenhorn.

"Tell me, how much colder does it get before we

reach Fairplay?" he asked, refusing to let his teeth chatter.

Chris started to reply, but Cass stopped him. "You'll see for yourself by tonight. Didn't anyone think to tell you to bring heavy gear for the mountains?" she asked innocently.

"I can just bet why no one told me, Cass," he said grimly.

"Well, everyone in Colorado knows how cold it gets up in the mountains."

"Considering it was hot enough to fry eggs on the rocks yesterday, I can't imagine why it eluded me," he snapped. "I may be a greenhorn, Cass, but just remember, I am very adaptable and I learn quick!"

By late afternoon Steve's lips were turning blue when they rode into the tunnel. It was a peculiar formation, too smoothly rounded to fit the jagged outcroppings of the surrounding mountains. The opening was hacked in the narrow trail's pathway, almost as if a landslide had blocked the shelf of a road and the teamsters had simply dug through it.

"Damn, it's cold in here," he groaned.

Dog Eating Jack, on the wagon in front of him, heard his words echo in the tunnel and laughed, calling back to him, "What'd you expect. We're ridin' through solid ice."

"Ice!" At once Steve lowered his voice and cursed in monosyllables until they cleared the tunnel. On the far side, the roadway widened onto an open meadow dotted with patches of snow and scrubby evergreens. He pulled over and stopped, motioning the muleskinner behind him to go on. Extracting a small knife from his pants pocket, he scraped on the tunnel wall near its opening. Beneath the thick coating of tan dust lay the grayish white gleam of ice.

"This place is a bloody oxymoron," he said savagely to Chris Alders when they stopped for the night.

Chris gave him a puzzled look, but Cass, overhearing, explained, "Oxymoron is a literary term, Chris. It means a contradiction in terms . . . like a tunnel of solid ice still standing in July." She looked smugly at Steve, who was feeling ridiculous with his saddle blanket wrapped around his shoulders.

Chris's face creased in a grin. "Oh, yeah. I reckon you never seen a ice tunnel back East. In winter storms we get us lots of snow slides up here. Got ta keep the roads open ta th' mines, so the miners use their pickaxes ta dig 'em clear. Summer comes 'n the bigger ones this high don't never thaw, just get covered with dust 'n last till th' next winter."

"Actually they partially thaw and refreeze, harder than ever, into solid ice. We'll drive through several more over the next few days," Cass said with relish.

"And you, madam, are an expert on solid ice, as we both know," Steve replied savagely. "Where's the goddam manifest?" he asked, turning to Chris, whose face was now devoid of humor.

"In Cass's wagon. I'll get it for you," he replied, beating a hasty retreat.

"We're not bringing coats to the miners this trip, Steve, don't waste your time," she said levelly.

Ignoring her, he grabbed the large inventory list from the wagon boss's hand and began to scan it, then nodded and stalked off.

After over an hour of searching the carefully loaded, tightly packed wagon, he found a cache of blankets. Thick winter woolens, not the thin summer sort of which his bedroll was made.

"I may look like a goddam Indian squaw, but I'll be damned if I'll freeze," he gritted when he walked up to the campfire just before dinner. "And if anyone laughs at me, I'll use him for target practice," he added in a feral growl to the assembled group of muleskinners as he pulled a Colt Thuer Conversion revolver from its hiding place beneath the heavy plaid blanket.

"Where did you get that gun . . . ?" Cass stopped short, remembering the cases of handguns and rifles in the last wagon. Damn and double damn! "Are you going to shoot me, Steve?" she asked with wide golden eyes daring him.

He grinned like an Apache about to scalp a trooper, then uncocked the gun, returning it to his belt. "No, Cassie, I have other plans for you," he replied softly.

A few quiet guffaws echoed around the campfire, but were quickly muffled as Cass glared at the assembly while caressing her whip stock.

When it came time for sleep, Cass laid out her bedroll near the main campfire, close to a number of the men, including Chris Alders. Steve calmly walked over to where she knelt spreading it and reached for one slim wrist. "This is awfully public, Cassie," he whispered low, "but if you want us to . . . sleep here . . ." He shrugged and tossed down his bedroll alongside hers, releasing her wrist.

She froze in mortification. "I told you," she whispered in a breathless voice, "I've just had my courses. It'll do no good yet. Wait until we get to Fairplay. There are some tents or even cabins we can use."

"Fine with me, but since you didn't prepare me

with the right gear to keep warm, you'll just have to curl up with me for body heat. Couldn't have your property freeze to death before you're done with him, could you?'' He began arranging both bedrolls, laying them out so she would have to share hers with him.

Mortified to create a scene when she instinctively knew she couldn't win, Cass capitulated, thinking her thick layers of clothing would protect her. Surely he wouldn't be so vindictive or crude as to attempt to strip her naked in front of several dozen muleskinners! *Would he?*

Chapter Nine

Cass awakened to the first faint noises at dawn, aware she was wrapped in a warm cocoon—perhaps trapped was a more appropriate word, for Steve's long, hard body was entangled with hers. In a welter of blankets, they lay like two spoons with his arm draped possessively over her breasts and his leg stretched over her thigh. For all his blue-lipped shivering yesterday, he was a veritable furnace now.

When she stirred, trying in vain to wriggle out from beneath his grasp, his low voice whispered into her tangled hair, "You sure do keep a man hot, Cassie."

She stiffened and spit out, "Get off me, you oaf!" Pushing his arm off her, she sat up awkwardly, looking around to see how many of her men had witnessed the intimate tableau. Dog Eating Jack and Bully Quint were hunched beside the campfire with tin mugs of Sour Mash's bitter coffee in their hands. Chris Alders stood apart from them watching the faint streaks of orange reach out jagged fingers, pulling down the night sky. Sour Mash clanked pots and pans as he readied breakfast. All the men who came shuffling toward the cook wagon near the fire studiously avoided looking directly at Cass. She threw off the covers and stood up, smoothing out her wrinkled shirt and pants as best she could, shivering in the high altitude now that she was deprived of Steve's body heat.

With an angry glance at her unperturbed husband, who sat up and stretched like a satiated lion, she reached for her coat and slipped it on, then grabbed her boots and hobbled in sock feet toward a wheel of the nearest wagon. She balanced herself and yanked them on, stomping her feet into the ice-cold leather vengefully.

Steve sat up and pulled on his boots, then rolled up their gear, keeping out the heavy blanket he'd appropriated in lieu of a coat. He slid the gun into his belt before wrapping the blanket about his shoulders. Whistling casually, he sauntered over to where Cass was pouring herself a generous slug of coffee from a large granite pot. He reached for a cup on the back end of the cook wagon and held it out to her. "I'd appreciate some of that coffee, Cass." Then seeing the mutinous gleam in her eyes, he added in a low voice, "And if you have any ideas about scalding me, forget them unless you want me to pull down your pants in front of this whole crew and paddle that delectable little backside."

"Just wait till I get my blacksnake. I'll shred you up so good Sour Mash can make sonofabitch stew out of you," she hissed back. Then, sensing the eyes of the muleskinners on them, she poured coffee quickly into his cup, slamming the pot back onto the fire grate with a resounding clunk.

As soon as he had the quick breakfast of biscuits and bacon ready, Sour Mash banged on a tin plate to summon everyone, but not before Cass had watched him walk over to confer with Steve. As the day passed, she noted several other of her men talking to her husband in friendly deference. The relationship between her and Steve was subtly changing the relationship between her and her men.

She bitterly resented that fact, but without turning him over to the law—which would defeat her plan—she saw no way to stop him from acting the role of her husband. As a man among men, even if he was a dude, he had an advantage over her, especially since he'd been proving himself the past weeks by working with the mules, even driving with credible skill on the rough mountain trail the last two days.

Worst of all, her men had seen them actually sleeping in the same bedroll. Her cheeks flamed and she fumed, plying her whip with unnecessary vigor over the heads of her mules while they hauled the cumbersome wagons up steep switchbacks. Only another five miles and they'd arrive in Fairplay, a small mining town that was their first stop on the delivery route.

Cass's thoughts of a warm shelter in Fairplay, away from the prying, curious eyes of the men, were cut short as a shot rang out in front of her. As her lead mules rounded the curve of the trail, two men stood blocking the way. They were mounted and heavily armed. Beyond them, at the narrowest part of the road, was a makeshift gate made of a big log with a crude rope pulley attached to it.

"Just pull up and pay the toll, little lady," the larger of the two men said genially. He was a great, unshaven brute with hard, flinty eyes. An ominous ten-gauge shotgun pointed in her general direction as he spoke.

"This isn't a toll road. The miners from Fairplay and Gold Hill cut it so our wagons could reach them. Who the hell are you?"

"Now, now, temper, missy," the smaller fellow said sibilantly, showing a wide expanse of yellow teeth. "It be only a dollar a wagon, plus twenty-five cents for each extra horse or mule."

Cass swore inventively, then scoffed. "You can't count that high! Get out of my way or I'll peel your hide."

"Now, little hellcat, you listen good," the burly man on the buckskin said, moving alongside her team, nearing where she sat. Her whip cracked with blurring speed and his shotgun went flying out of his hands, over the side of the mountain with a clatter of loose rocks.

His partner took aim at Cass and prepared to squeeze off a shot, but a yell from behind her caused him to switch his sights. A bullet knocked him cleanly off his horse. Two more men opened fire from higher ground behind the toll gate where they were hidden as Cass jumped from the nigh wheeler, whip still in hand. The spokesman for the road agents turned his horse around as best he could on the narrow ledge and retreated.

Suddenly Cass was flattened to the ground as Steve knocked her beneath the wagon, lying partially over her body as he aimed his Colt at the men firing on them. "You idiot! What in hell were

you doing attacking him before we could see how
many of them there were?" he shouted over the
whine of bullets.

"I never back down to highbinders like that,"
she hissed back, coiling up her whip as she
crouched beside her would-be protector.

Ignoring her, Steve took a bead on one man who
stuck his head from behind a jagged outcropping
of slate at precisely the wrong instant. The man
dropped backward without a sound, obviously dispatched. Bully and Chris came up behind Cass,
crawling on all fours to keep out of the line of fire
still raining down on them. "What should we do,
Mr. Loring?" Chris asked.

Bristling, Cass replied, "Slip under the wagon
and keep them busy with your rifle while Bully
goes between the mules for a clean shot. They can't
hold up a whole train with only a handful of men."

"Six I'd judge by the gunfire, but two of them
are out now," Steve said levelly. Ignoring Cass, he
turned to Chris. "Get her back to safety. I'm going
to use that ledge down there to get around them.
Cover me, Bully."

Cass pulled a .36 caliber Colt revolver from her
hip and cocked it at Steve. "I'm still giving the
orders here in case anyone forgot that fact! He's
never climbed on thin, crumbly mountain terrain
before," she said to Chris. "He'll be tumbling to
the bottom of the canyon in two minutes."

"We haven't got time to argue," Steve interrupted as another bullet whirred too close for comfort, causing the mules to skitter in their heavy
harness. "I've had plenty of experience under fire,
and I don't want a woman in the way!" With that
he grabbed her gun with blurring speed and
shoved her into Chris's arms. "Keep her out of

harm's way, dammit. Bully, when you hear me shooting behind them, you and a couple of the men come running like hell!"

The big muleskinner nodded and began to crawl under the wagon, then forward, using the mules for cover. Zeke, Jonas, and Chris joined his fire with a barrage of their own from beneath the wagon, pinning the road agents to the rocks. Steve lowered himself over the side of the road using a few stunted, prickly evergreens for hand holds. Then he crawled and climbed around the side of the mountain, just beneath the shelf of the road. Several times he felt his feet slipping out from under him as the dry, powdery soil and rocks gave way, but he scrambled and scratched forward to a more level space with somewhat surer footing. It seemed to take forever as he crouched and crawled until he was around the curve of the switchback, behind the men at the illegal toll station. Now if only he could climb up the steep precipice without losing his footing!

"You think he made it?" Bully asked Chris between shots.

"He was a skirmisher in the war. Rode with Palmer's Owls for two years. Reckon if anyone can do it, Steve Loring can," Chris replied before he fired off another several rounds.

Cass, who had reappropriated her gun from Chris, took a bead on a hat brim just shading the edge of a boulder. When she heard Chris's remark, she jerked and missed the shot. "How did you know about Steve and General Palmer?"

Chris grinned in spite of the noise and chaos of the gunfire. "I met the general last week at the freight office, when he come in to sign that contract."

Cass swore and began to reload her revolver. As desperately as she wanted that contract, she had bitterly hated getting it through Steve's largess.

Suddenly gunfire erupted from behind their enemies. Without waiting for her command, Bully, Dog Eating Jack, Jonas, and Zeke all raced past her and Chris, whose arthritic legs kept him from moving as fast. He held on to her with a strong right hand.

"Mr. Loring said for you to stay out of harm's way, Cass," he offered in explanation.

"Oh, he did, did he? Since when is he paying your wages, Chris Alders?" she snapped, trying to break free of the older man.

"Since he married you," came the quiet reply.

Then both of them realized the shooting had stopped. Jack came running back, yelling, "We got 'em, we got 'em!"

Cass jerked her arm free of Chris's restraining hand and ran toward the boulders, leaping nimbly as a doe over the huge log barricade. When she reached the cluster of men, Steve was standing coolly in the midst of them, issuing orders again.

Two road agents with raised hands were tied up by eager muleskinners. The dead body of the burly ringleader lay sprawled on the ground. A third leaned against a rock, badly wounded. Of the first two men Steve had hit when the fight began, one lay out in the road and the other was draped across a rock outcropping. The place looked like a battlefield.

"Never seen the likes of it," Bully was saying to Jonas. "He come up behind 'em from the side of the cliff and opened up with his Colt. Clean center hit on the big feller 'n nailed thet bastard there, both quicker 'n you cud blink. Then these two lily-

livered skunks threw down their guns 'n give up."
There was a touch of awe in his voice as he replayed the battle for the other muleskinners, all
men used to violence as an occupational hazard.

"Reckon you sure know how to shoot, Mr. Loring," Zeke, one of the youngest of the men, said to
Steve. "Near's good as Mr. Hunnicut."

Steve rubbed his cut and abraded palms against
his torn pantlegs as he surveyed the scene. "I had
to learn to shoot in the war. Only way to survive,"
he answered grimly.

"Too bad some Confederate didn't learn how to
shoot better," Cass snapped as she walked up to
him.

His grim face slashed into a hard smile. "They
never did. That's why they lost the war." With
that he turned to where two of the men were hauling the body of the ringleader away. "Wait. He
looks to be a little big, but I'll take his coat anyway."

"He sure won't need it where he's goin," Bully
said with a laugh.

Steve inspected the coat of heavy plaid wool.
The hideous body odor of the unbathed man clung
to it as permanently as the lines in the plaid de-
sign. A bullet hole punctured the side. Shrugging,
Steve donned the filthy but warm garment. "It'll
have to do till I can get one of my own. That blanket was getting to be a pain in the ass," he added
with a menacing glare at Cass.

They pulled into Fairplay that evening just
about dusk. It was a typical small mining camp
in the isolated wilds of the Rockies, comprised of
a few crude log cabins situated at odd angles, as
if dropped helter-skelter like dice from the hands
of a careless gambler. A sea of ragged, patched

canvas tents lay around them, mostly miners'
abodes. A few tents and cabins were fronted by
signs such as "Tangle Leg Saloon," "Feed Bin
Eats," "Beds—25 cents a week," and "Washing—
5 cents a shirt." One large tent near the edge of
the assemblage boasted, "Men taken in and Done
For."

Steve raised an eyebrow as he read the crude
sign, then observed the overripe brunette who was
looking him up and down like a she wolf trailing
a crippled mule deer. Her invitation was as bla-
tant as her sign. He smiled back in what he hoped
passed for a polite nod of regret.

When they pulled up at the largest log structure
with the sign "General Merchandise" across its
front porch, Steve climbed from the big wheeler's
saddle wearily.

Cass was already on the porch, pounding a fat
bald man heartily on the back. "You randy old
goat, Pepper, how the hell are you?" she said with
laughing affection in her voice.

"Just fine now that my tired old eyes seen you
again, gal. We been waitin' for you, Cass. Lord,
Zebulon nigh onto run outta whiskey! We'd have
us a regular riot if that happened. I already done
run out of yard goods, flour, 'n soap. Course—" he
scratched his head thoughtfully "—there ain't
much call for soap, leastways not since most folks
took their spring baths."

Steve stepped up onto the porch and waited for
Cass to introduce him, knowing how much she
would hate doing it.

The fat little man named Pepper looked at him
questioningly. "New man, Cass? He don't look like
no muleskinner. Where's Kyle?"

"He had business to attend to in Denver, Pepper.

We've been having trouble with Bennett Ames. This is Steve Loring . . . my husband," she added grudgingly.

His moon face split in a broad smile. "Whoopie, Cass! We gotta celebrate soon's we get them crates unloaded!" He pumped Steve's hand enthusiastically as he yelled for two heavyset young men, obviously his sons, to come out and help with the unloading.

"Not that wagon, Pike," Chris said to a boy as he headed for the first one in the caravan. "It's only got dynamite and mining gear for Gold Hill. You want the second wagon."

Steve turned to Cass incredulously. "You've been driving that wagon! Why the hell—"

"I never ask my men to take any job I wouldn't do myself. Hauling explosives included," she interrupted. "Besides, I'm the best damn driver in the Rockies!"

"Modest, too," he said with a grimace. "We'll discuss the driving assignments later, Cass. Now, where can a man get a bath, Pepper? I have three days of trail grit to chip off my body. I do trust we brought soap along?" he said, turning to Cass.

First Steve luxuriated in a big brass tub in the small room at the rear of Pepper's store, while Cass visited with old friends in the camp whom she had not seen in six months. Then Cass took her turn while Steve became acquainted with Pepper Jordan and his sons.

Eying the bullet hole and bloodstains in the filthy coat Steve had tossed in a corner of the large, crowded store, Pepper said in noncommittal inquiry, "You ain't been shot. 'Pears the feller wearing that coat was."

"Let's just say I had more need of it than he did," Steve replied grimly. Realizing that word of the shootout would doubtless be carried across town by the muleskinners, he explained, "We ran into a nest of road agents this afternoon. Tried to collect an illegal toll from our wagons. Cass took offense."

Pepper slapped his wide knee and his whole body jiggled with laughter. "I can just bet she did! Used her whip on 'em, too. She shoot that galoot?"

"No. After my wife, er, disarmed the leader with her whip, the other five opened fire. We were lucky none of our men were hit. Three of *them* are dead, though."

"And Steve here got all of 'em, including that big ornery bastard whose coat he's been wearing," Chris added, pulling up a chair near the glowing warmth of the stove in the back of the store.

Wanting to change the subject, Steve asked, "You have any warm clothes, coats that might fit me?"

Pepper looked at Steve's cotton shirt and denims with puzzlement. "You come up here without a coat? No heavy duds?"

Chris grinned. "He's a flatlander from back East. Didn't know how cold it gets up this high even in July."

Pepper again rocked his mountainous flesh with a burst of laughter. "I see. Tenderfoot been hornswaggled by them cussed freighters. Sorry, I'm plumb outta clothes, 'ceptin for a few pair of pants. No call for coats 'n such until fall." He paused to consider, then snapped his thick fingers. "But I know where you can get a good coat—feller was 'bout your size. Right fancy dresser, too. You seen Rena's tent when you come in? She 'n her gals is the only women in Fairplay right now."

Dawning understanding lit Steve's face. The buxom brunette with the rather explicit sign advertising her wares. "She have a man's coat for sale?"

Pepper slapped his knee. "Hell, she's got *everything* for sale! But a feller up 'n died real sudden like the other day—in her place. Too much excitement for a man his age, if you take my meaning," he said with a sly wink.

"And you think this Rena might be persuaded to part with the coat?" Steve's lips twitched, thinking of Cass's fury when she found out he'd bested her and how he'd done it. "I think I'll take a little stroll before the festivities begin here, Pepper."

Cass pulled a fresh pair of pants and clean white shirt from the small trunk she always carried in the wagon, then rejected them nervously. Damn, she might have known that bringing that man along would cause trouble! A party to celebrate their farcical marriage indeed! She suddenly felt insecure and angry with herself. She wanted to look pretty and frilly and feminine, something she had never considered on the trail before. Making deliveries to these isolated camps was strictly business. Fancy clothes were for city life, when she had to play a conventional role—as conventional as Cass ever was. She had learned over the years that using her looks and feminine charm could manipulate men in some situations better than her blacksnake.

But she didn't want to consider what her vanity might signify since Steve had entered her life. Doggedly she shoved the one pretty cotton dress she'd packed back into the trunk and again pulled out the trousers and shirt.

As she dressed, Cass thought about the night ahead. They would have to sleep together, in the privacy of one of the adjoining cabins, for appearances as newlyweds. Her pride required that she not explain to Pepper Jordan why she had married. And, in spite of her probable infertility now, Steve would demand his right to her body. Recalling the possessive way he had slept with her the previous night, she fidgeted with her brush, tangling it in her hair. Visions of his mocking face looming over hers, asking her to pay him for pleasuring her, flashed into her mind as she swore and ripped out a clump of coppery hair. To be humiliated that way again was unthinkable!

She would just have to get control of her stupid, animalistic cravings and subdue them, that was all. "He can't have that kind of control over me," she whispered. "I can't let him." Another part of her mind whispered painfully, *Yes, because once he's fulfilled his part of your bargain, you must pay his price and let him walk out of your life forever*. A tight aching squeezed her chest, and she doubled over to let it pass, then resumed brushing her hair with trembling hands.

Most of Fairplay crowded into Pepper's large log building that evening, the store owners, miners, the man who ran the local restaurant, even Rena Buford and her girls. In isolated mining camps where women were scarce, social hierarchies were luxuries the men could ill afford. Two fiddle players and a man with a banjo pounded raucous music for dancing. The food—corn bread, smoked ham, and beans—was not elegant, but it was plentiful. So were barrels of phlegm-cutter whiskey and strong German beer. Everyone laughed, talked, ate, and drank.

Poured into a gaudy rose satin dress, Rena Buford eyed up Steve from across the room, then sauntered over to where he stood talking with Chris and Bully. "I'll give you a deal on that coat you wanted if you dance with me," she said in a sultry voice, adding, "Your muleskinner wife isn't much for dancing, I bet."

Steve took her in his arms and they stepped to the lively foot-stomping music. The big pot-bellied stove was glowing and the crowded room was warm. It became quickly obvious to Steve that Rena was no more enamored of soap than the rest of the residents of Fairplay. But she did, after a good deal of cajoling, agree to sell him the coat for five dollars, more he suspected to spite Cass than for any other reason. They both knew the erroneous conclusion his wife would draw about how he obtained it.

"I'll stop by after things die down here and collect that coat, Rena."

"Sure that's all you want, sugar?"

He threw back his head and laughed. "Ah, Rena, you do tempt a man, but you know what a temper Cass has. I'd better just settle for the coat."

Cass stood in the doorway, scanning the motley press of people. Pepper had taken the crates of hardware and sacks of food staples and other items from the center of the floor to clear a space on the rough planks for dancing. With the shortage of women, the celebrants here were following a common Western custom, men dancing with men, taking turns reversing roles. The gaudily dressed whores in their satins and feathers stood out among the plaid shirts and denims of the miners like tropical birds among a flock of brown pigeons.

Cass had never disdained the "ladies of the line" who plied their trade across the West. After all, they were a part of reality, surviving the only way they could. Then she saw Rena Buford and Steve whirling around the floor with lusty vigor. Suddenly her whole perspective changed. She itched to take a whip to both of them for humiliating her publicly in front of her friends and business associates.

The dance ended, and Steve deserted Rena's charms to engage in a conversation with the owner of the Tangle Leg Saloon. Everyone in the room was impressed with Loring and pleased over Cass's choice of a husband. First her own men, now the men in the mining camps! Where was this going to end? she wondered. When he controlled everything?

Seething, she listened to Pepper blather on about what had happened to the road agents. Then, seeing her, he stopped short and said, "Been waitin for the right time, Cass. You 'n Steve gotta have a special dance while everybody drinks to your weddin'."

Before Cass could stop him, Pepper crossed the floor and threw a brotherly arm around Steve's much taller shoulder. "You 'n your new bride gotta dance." He left Steve half scowling and reached for Cass's hand, drawing the pair together.

Everyone in the house chorused in, urging the newlyweds to dance as they filled their cups and toasted fulsomely. Feeling self-conscious in her trousers, like one of the men who only played the part of a woman for the dance, she went unwillingly into Steve's arms. The music was slow, and his touch against her skin felt searing.

"You smell of cheap perfume," she muttered beneath her breath before she could stifle the jealous remark.

Steve looked down at Cass, her fat plait of hair gleaming in the lantern light. The severe shirt and trousers molded to her willowy curves, once again reminding him of the beautiful body she possessed. She smelled faintly of lilac soap, clean, soft, desirable, as different from Rena Buford as a sleek thoroughbred filly from a swaybacked plow horse.

He chuckled and drew her closer. "So you saw me dancing with her. You're not half as sorry about the smell as I am, believe me."

She looked into his eyes with disbelief etched on her face. "You mean you find her bountiful charms not to your liking? Of course," she paused thoughtfully, "*you'd* have to pay *her* instead of the other way around."

"Bitchy tonight, aren't we, love?" He whispered the question like an endearment, molding her tall, slim body indecently close to his. He could feel her stiffen in fury, but she made no attempt to break free. *Mustn't lose face in front of your men*, he thought in disgust as a sudden surge of desire swept through him. The dance ended abruptly and he quickly stepped back from her, bowing mockingly, lest his body betray any sign of his need.

Cass forced a smile, then turned on her heel to leave the floor amid the cheers of the revelers, now well on their way to being skunked. She considered joining in, but quickly rejected the idea. She wanted to be completely in control of her faculties when it came time for bed that night.

Observing Cass from across the room, Steve

brooded and sipped more of the potent tangle leg whiskey than he knew was prudent. What a wretched absurdity—to desire a woman who had forced him to marry her at gunpoint! Still, he knew he had awakened desire in her and could do so again. But after his last near brush with death by ceramic pitcher, he'd have to be very careful seducing her, and controlling his own fierce pride. He put down the tin cup and walked over to his wife.

"It's getting late, Cass. We have to leave for Gold Hill at dawn. Don't you think we should go to bed?" He smiled at the crimson staining her cheeks.

She fought down the urge to slap the arrogant smirk from his handsome face and nodded in agreement, willing her racing heartbeat to slow and her hot face to cool.

Steve stood in front of the small cabin Pepper had given them for the night, smoking a cigar. He had quickly picked up the coat at Rena's tent and then returned to wait while Cass readied herself for bed. Mercifully, all it had cost him was a fulsome kiss from the amazon before he was able to pay her and make his escape.

He turned over several scenarios in his mind. How should he approach Cass? Lord knew the last time had been disastrous. Whether he used patient explanations or impassioned declarations, he always ended up antagonizing her. Perhaps it would be best to proceed without saying anything at all. He'd just wait until she was half asleep, then slip into bed beside her and seduce her with actions, no words spoken.

The only flaw in the plan was that he had become considerably more foxed than his wife. Cass lay rigidly in the narrow bed, gritting her teeth as she waited for him, wondering if he had committed the ultimate humiliation against her and gone to Rena Buford's tent. She fought the urge to rise and search for her errant husband, knowing that if she found him with a whore she'd kill him.

After what seemed like hours, the door screeched open, letting in a shaft of silvery moonlight and a gust of cold air. Cass hunkered deeper into the thick comforter as Steve undressed in the dark. Hearing the rustle of his shirt being discarded, the click of his belt buckle, and the rasp of his denims being pulled down, she could picture in her imagination the splendid body that the darkness hid from her. Perversely, the more she imagined, the more she desired; the more she desired, the more she became angry.

Steve slipped quietly beneath the covers and reached for Cass, feeling the warm, soft curve of her hip beneath his hand as he turned her from her side to her back. His fingers splayed across her belly and he began to caress slowly, deliciously, working upward to cup one breast, then the other. He was rewarded when the nipples hardened and she gasped in pleasure that she was unable to conceal. Emboldened, he leaned over her and lowered his mouth to kiss her.

Cass had almost succumbed, letting her anger evaporate under his hypnotic caress, until his long, hard body covered hers and she could smell the distinctive cheap perfume of Rena Buford. On their walk to the cabin, she had noticed that the odious aroma was gone. Now he reeked of it again! She started to push him away, wanting to cry out her jealous fury, but pride and desperation stayed

her. She could never, never let him know that his
sordid liaison with a whore made her burn. She
had to become pregnant, and that meant letting
him use her body as he willed. Once she was with
child, she would send him away forever. Now, she
would simply have to endure.

Steve could sense the mercurial shift in her
mood, but decided against asking why. Every time
he tried to talk to the damnable woman it only
made matters worse. He brushed her lips with his,
then traced a silky outline around her mouth with
his tongue, forcing his way inside to ravage the
moist, hot cavity. Still she remained unresponsive.
Well, at least she wasn't biting him!

He left her mouth and rained soft nips and kisses
down her throat, over her breasts, down her belly
as his hand stroked her thighs, then insinuated
itself between them to test the hot core of her body.

Cass flinched in a spasm of involuntary pleasure, but did not give in any further as he continued the maddening assault on her senses. Heat
curled and uncurled in her belly, radiating down
her legs, up into the aching tips of her breasts.
Still, she lay rigid, running through her mind an
inventory of the freight they still had to deliver.

Feeling her brief but obviously repressed re-
sponses to his slow seduction, Steve's frustration
grew. She was making a bloody fool of him, lying
beneath him woodenly, fighting her own body's
urgings. *Hypocritical little bitch!* Without further
preamble he pulled her legs apart and plunged
inside her, his mind made up not to care if he hurt
her or not.

Far from hurting, his rhythmic thrusts created
a spiraling ecstasy in Cass's body. She could not
stop her fingers from digging into his shoulders as

she pulled him closer, closer, her body now wound tightly as a spring, flexing and surging with his as he increased their tempo.

"Finally you want it, do you?" he ground out, his voice muffled against her hair. With a few fast, hard thrusts he climaxed, releasing his seed deep within her in a white-hot surge of pleasure so intense it was painful. At once he withdrew from her and rolled away, turning his back on her and yanking the discarded blankets up to cover them.

Cass lay with her arms rigidly at her sides, fists clenched, refusing to give in to the misery that snaked through her belly like the lash of a whip. Tears overflowed her closed lashes and ran in silent, acid rivulets down her temples, soaking her hair, but she made no sound for him to hear in the still coldness of the night.

The next morning when Steve awakened, Cass was gone. He threw off the covers with an angry swish and dressed quickly in the chill air, glad of the warm new coat from Rena. After bathing last night he hated even the thought of touching the filthy coat of the dead outlaw.

Cass was already seated on the lead wagon's nigh wheeler when he walked over to where the men were gathering. He looked up at her chalky but composed face as she stared straight ahead. "Get down, Cass. I'm driving this rig."

"Go to hell," she said with a menacing flip of the blacksnake coiled at her side.

He reached up and wrenched the whip from her hand, then replied, "Get down or I'll drag you off that mule. That's the dynamite load and I'm driving it!" His eyes locked with hers, and he noticed her take in his new coat.

Ignoring the question that popped in her mind about the coat, she replied, "This is the most valuable wagon in the train, Steve. You're a greenhorn with mules. I can't afford the loss if you blow it to kingdom come."

He reached up none too gently and pulled her down, saying, "You can't afford to lose me either ...until I fulfill my side of the bargain."

Glowering, she stomped toward the next wagon without a word, after yanking her whip from his hand.

When they pulled out of Fairplay it was full daylight and Rena Buford was waving gaily at the train, along with the rest of the denizens of the rough camp. She blew a big kiss at Steve and called out, "Keep good 'n warm, sugar!"

Overhearing, Cass knew where his new coat had come from and how he had gotten it. She rode past the smirking, buxom whore with her head held regally high. The blacksnake itched in Cass's fingers.

They proceeded further into the Rockies toward Gold Hill, making camp for the noon rest on an open meadow. Just ahead of them lay a long, twisting road that dropped off at a sickening angle into a deep canyon below.

"Better use the drag logs, Bully," Cass said as she looked down the road. "We always need them on this stretch."

Bully Quint and several of the biggest muleskinners hitched a pair of mules to pull from one of the wagons several enormous logs a yard in diameter and ten feet in length. They hauled them to the lead wagon and began to fasten one log to the trailer, then the second and the third. Steve watched the intricate rope work with fascination.

"That supposed to slow me on the downgrade if my brakes fail?" he asked dubiously.

Chris, who was also observing, replied, "Considering the wagon's filled with dynamite, you'd better hope the brakes don't fail. I'll take it down. Been doing it for years, Steve."

Steve put his hand on the old man's arm and said quietly, "It's about time I took the most dangerous job, Chris, if I'm going to run this outfit. We stand here arguing and Cass'll be up there taking off in a trail of dust."

Alders shrugged and let the new boss man mount up when the wagon was readied.

"Think he can do it, Chris?" Cass asked worriedly. "He's only been driving a few weeks."

"Hell, he's made it this far all right. With the drag logs to steady him, he should be fine," Chris said heartily.

A sense of foreboding washed over her as she watched Steve release the heavy brake and crack the blacksnake over the mules' heads. She remembered his taunt to her about needing him for unfinished services.

Steve felt the creaking squeal of the flat wooden blocks as they ground against the rear wheels of the wagon when he pulled on the brake lever. The descent was becoming steeper and the wagon's momentum harder to control. He kept a steady hand on the jerk line, grateful for the lumbering pull of the heavy drag logs tied to the rear of the trailer wagon. They caught on every obstruction along the trail, and the men with him had to free them when they lodged tightly, but it kept the speed of the descent to a minimum.

The temperature was freezing cold, but still sweat soaked his body as he guided the team down the mountainside with laborious patience. Then at one sharp turn on the trail, he heard the new man, Jonas, call out, "Logs broke free!" Suddenly the wagon lurched forward, almost overrunning the plodding ten-span of mules as the drag weight of the massive logs was lost.

Steve let loose a volley of profanity as he eased up on the brake lever slightly, afraid that if he used it too hard the lines would snap. But now the wagon was in danger of crushing the mules, and him with the team! He could hear the men yelling as they ran down the trail behind him, but the team quickly began to outdistance them. Gently, as he alternately prayed and swore, he pulled on the brake lever and was rewarded with the sizzling hiss of hot wood grinding against iron tire rims.

Then another snap rent the air and the hiss ceased. The tension on the brake line was gone, broken like the drag logs. Steve gave the mules their head in order to keep them from being crushed, and the race was on as he cracked the whip over the leader's head. He could feel the powerful muscles of the wheeler beneath him bunching as he broke into a headlong gallop, one step ahead of sudden death.

The road before him took a sharp turn, but at the speed they were traveling, there was no way the two big wagons could negotiate it. Steve gave a long, steady pull on the jerk line to turn the mules left. The leaders responded and the span turned, but, as he expected, the wagons did not. The trailer tumbled to its side first, pulling the lead wagon with it. Cases of dynamite, mixed in with bolts of yard goods and crates of stove pipes, broke open, all the contents spilling across the mountainside. Sticks of loose dynamite bounced off his shoulders as he reined in the ten-span. Now on their sides, the wagons had become drag logs of a sort, slowing the runaway team until he could regain control. Miraculously, the mules stayed on their feet and the wagons did not fall over the precipice, pulling them all to certain death.

When Steve finally stopped the ten-span, he looked back at the debris littering the side of the mountain and the two overturned wagons. The first thought that struck him was that none of the explosives had detonated. He was still alive, and so were the twenty expensive pieces of livestock!

He could hear the shouts of the men as they raced on foot down the side of the mountain. Bully Quint was the first to reach him, just as he dismounted from the wheeler saddle.

"Damndest thing I ever seen! The shittin' dynamite didn't blow! You all right, boss?"

"Yeah, I'm all right," Steve replied, not at all as certain as he sounded. He walked to the side of the road and picked up a stick of dynamite. "It's frozen! That explains why it didn't explode, Bully!" He laughed, untensing as he stood surveying the chaos around him. "See if the wagons can be fixed," he ordered as his nervous laughter died away.

"Somehow those logs broke free and then my brakes snapped. Any ideas how that might have happened?" He looked from Quint to Jonas, who was very pale.

"I'll go get the others—"

"Wait here, Jonas. Bully can see to righting the wagons. Let's you and I go and look at those ropes," Steve said with an eye on the knife at the youth's belt.

Suddenly the boy bolted, but Steve caught him

with a quick left to the jaw, knocking him to the ground. He pulled out his gun and cocked it, then motioned to Jonas, "Get rid of the knife."

As the boy complied, he began to blubber and swear, sobbing out, "You were supposed to get blowed up! No one would'a knowed!"

"Bennett Ames would, I bet," Steve replied grimly.

Bully called out, "Boss, you're right! Look at the line for the drag. It's been cut! The bastard must've done it when we rounded that last turn before the logs broke. I was on the right side of the wagon and he fell behind me, got behind the wagon instead of staying clear. Any fool knows how dangerous it is to get between the drags and the trailer."

"Seems he had a reason for taking the chance," Steve replied. "Tie him up, Bully. I'll—"

"Steve!" Cass raced up to him and threw her arms around his neck with gusto, practically knocking them both to the ground. Quickly, she collected herself and jumped back to inspect him. "You're not hurt? What happened? I heard the men yelling that the drags broke."

"They were cut by our friend here, eh, Jonas?"

Steve explained about the attempt to blow up the wagons and why the dynamite had failed to go off.

"Ames is behind it! Thank God it didn't work," she said, looking at Jonas with menace.

Steve quirked an eyebrow at her and said softly, "Cassie, you never fail to surprise me. Can it be you would have cared if I was killed?"

She stomped over toward Jonas as she replied

snappishly, "Just remember, you haven't fulfilled your end of our deal yet. I need you alive and well until then. After that you can blow yourself straight through hell's gates!"

Chapter Ten

Cass stood in the spacious front foyer of their city house with a heavy cream-colored envelope in her hand. She knew it contained an invitation for Mr. & Mrs. Loring to attend the gala ball being given by the mayor and city council to celebrate the arrival of the Kansas Pacific Railroad on August fifteenth.

The summer was fast slipping away. Cass realized that with the weeks and months racing along as fast as a locomotive, her time was running out. She had scarcely a month left in which to get pregnant. It was not lack of Steve's husbandly attentions that had created the problem. Every night for the past two weeks since they returned from the mountains, he had performed in her bed. Each time was humiliating and joyless for her, so physically frustrating that she found herself tense as an overwound watch spring. But never, never again, she vowed, would she debase herself by asking him to give her release.

Once I'm fat and ugly with child, he'll never touch me again, she thought as she ripped at the gold-embossed invitation.

Just then the front door opened and Peggy admitted Kyle. Grinning a sunny good morning to her, he said, "Got yew an invite ta thet mayor's shindig?" His gaze swept from the elaborate envelope to her tense, haggard face.

"I don't know if I'll have time to go, Kyle. There's so much work to be done at the office—getting the crews hired and all the supplies ordered for General Palmer's railroad grading crews. And we have to take another delivery to Fort Union before winter." She massaged her temples after letting the invitation drop onto the polished mahogany table.

He surveyed her with shrewd eyes. "It'd do yew 'n Steve both good ta get all gussied up 'n dance 'stead o' workin' yoreselves like a span o' them oxen."

Her eyes turned cold and yellow with anger as she recalled the last dance she and Steve had attended, with such disastrous results. "I didn't have you drag him to me because I wanted for a dancing partner, Kyle!" she lashed out.

The little man remained calm. Such outbursts had become almost a constant pattern over the past weeks. " 'Pears ta me mebbe yew been workin' so much thet th' real job o' work yew had me 'drag Loring ta yew' fer ain't gittin' done. A little flirtin' and falderal with some o' them fancy fellers might be jist th' ticket."

"So he can dance all night with Selina Ames and then come home—" she stopped in mortification, realizing what she had almost blurted out. "Just let me handle Steve Loring my own way, Kyle," she said, daring him to open his mouth again.

Kyle shrugged helplessly as the front door slammed. Steve strode in with a furious scowl on his face. "Jonas is dead. Had his throat cut in his sleep in the city jail." He swore inventively.

"Body ain't safe nowheres nowadays," Kyle said with scant regret.

Cass's oaths made Steve's pale by comparison as she began to pace. "He hadn't confessed who paid him! Now we'll never be able to prove it was Ames."

"I got me a real easy solution ta thet pickle," Kyle offered, his hand resting lightly on the Colt in his holster.

"We can hardly walk up to Bennett Ames and shoot him, Kyle," Steve replied with a sardonic grin.

Cass's eyes narrowed. "Why should that bother you? With your insane blood feud from the war, you've already killed one man and plan to kill more."

"Only in self defense. Anyway, they weren't exactly pillars of the community like Ames. We'd raise a slight ruckus—I believe that's your Western word?—if we just shot our chief competitor," Steve replied drily.

"Thet snake needs killin'. I ain't partic'lar 'bout how we git it done, but if'n yew don't fancy takin' th' easy way..." Kyle let his words trail off with a shrug, looking from Steve to Cass.

"Oh, men! Don't any of you have the sense of half a brick? We'll just have to hit Ames where it hurts him most—in his pocketbook. We have the army contracts and now the railroad contract. We'll drive Ames Freighting bankrupt!'' With that pronouncement she stormed out the door, slamming it with a crash that made the beveled glass panes rattle.

"A mite tetchy lately. Yew wouldn't have no idee 'bout why, would yew?'' Kyle asked Steve guilelessly.

Steve's chiseled lips arched in a wintry smile. "The woman just doesn't seem to like men, especially when she's not in charge of the game she has to play.'' He looked at Hunnicut's deliberately expressionless face, sensing the protectiveness the Texan had always shown toward Cass. "Let's just say, Kyle, that Cassie needs a little more taming before I reward her.''

Putting together Steve's furious anger at the forced marriage and Cass's edgy tension during the weeks since it had been consummated, Kyle reached a startling conclusion. His eyes widened in amazement. "Here I been afearin' yew'd treat her rough. Thet ain't it atall, is it?'' he asked in dawning amazement.

"She's a selfish, high-handed ice princess who's used to treating men like she treats livestock. Well, Kyle, I may be her stallion, but I'll be damned if I let her use me without paying some price—and I don't just mean the stud fee I'll collect when I leave, either!'' Steve turned and stalked up the wide, carpeted staircase, taking the steps two at a time.

Kyle whistled low and scratched his head. "Whut a passel o' yeller-eyed devils them two's gonna have!'' He chuckled and ambled toward the kitchen, lured by the fragrance of freshly baked sweet rolls, mumbling beneath his breath, "Yep,

Steve Loring, yew jist may 'o cut a hawg in th'
ass! Cass ain't 'bout ta let yew go, whether either
one o' yew damn fools knows it yet.''

The giant ballroom was festooned with red,
white, and blue bunting. A huge picture of President Grant hung on the wall facing the main en-
tryway. Crystal chandeliers sent glittering prisms
of light beaming down on elegantly dressed men
in expensive dark suits and ladies in a rainbow
array of silks and laces. Huge sprays of red and
white roses gave off perfume from every table, and
an orchestra played.

Cass and Steve had been late for the mayor's
long-winded speech welcoming the Kansas Pacific
Railroad to the city. Now the dancing had begun,
to be followed by a midnight banquet.

Steve scanned the room for Will Palmer as Cass
stood by his side, her slipper unconsciously tap-
ping rhythm with the lilting waltz. "Want to
dance, Cassie?" he asked in an intimate voice.

She cocked her head at him with mock amazement. "You'd do me the honor? I'm under-
whelmed."

Steve looked at Cass. Her gleaming copper hair
was twisted in an elaborate coiffure of curls, and
her deep green silk gown was cut to reveal more
than it concealed. How well he knew the feel and
texture of those breasts, that slim, supple body.
"You'll be the belle of the ball, as they used to say
in Louisville." He swept her into the waltz. "I only
wanted to be first on your dance card."

"So you can stalk other prey later," she replied
in a brittle voice.

Selina Ames whirled past them in the arms of
Gordon Fisk, a visiting New York banker. "Jealous

again, Cassie," he chided. "I did nothing more than talk with Selina."

"And you just *talked* with that whore in Fairplay, too," she said acidly. Then, feigning a lover's endearment, she hissed, "If I catch you with another woman before you've performed your service for me, I'll geld you, my fine Yankee stallion."

The threat, spoken in such seductive tones, made him want to roar with bitter laughter. "I've created a Frankenstein monster, or more aptly, perhaps, a bride of Frankenstein."

"You said it, I didn't," she hissed back. Feeling his body stiffen, she looked up, surprised that her sally would register with him. But Steve was looking past her, across the room at Bennett Ames.

"I think I'll have a chat with Ames," he said softly.

"Now, Steve, you were the one warning Kyle off, remember?" As they danced nearer, Cass saw the gleaming black curls of Selina Ames. "Or, on second thought, is it the *other* Ames you want to *chat* with?" Her voice dripped venom and honey at the same time.

Steve smiled, perversely pleased with her jealous reaction. "Cassie, Cassie, always suspecting the worst," he chided mockingly.

When Cass and Steve stopped in front of the Ameses, they found brother and sister engaging one of the guests of honor in conversation.

"Good evening, Will," Steve said, taking two glasses of champagne from a passing waiter and handing one to Cass. "Please, let us drink to the completion of the Kansas Pacific and the beginnings of the Denver and Rio Grand Railroad."

Will laughed and raised his own glass in response, "To our long and mutually profitable ventures, Steve, and—" he turned to Cass "—to your wife, who is as beautiful as she is efficient. I've received your reports on the material estimates, Mrs. Loring, and they are most thorough."

Cass smiled blindingly. "Why, thank you, General. Clay—that is, Loring Freighting does pride itself on accuracy and fairness." She gave Bennett Ames a brief, scathing glance.

Ames bristled at her, but Selina put a placating hand on his arm and said sweetly, "Business is so dull for ladies, Bennett. Be a darling and refill our champagne glasses while I steal Mr. Loring for a dance?"

With a terse nod to General Palmer, Ames departed with their glasses. Selina glided toward Steve, who gave a smiling shrug to Will and took her in his arms. Cass stood beside the general, seething. "Well, at least she kept her brother and my husband from coming to blows."

Palmer chuckled. "It seemed you were the one more intent on doing battle with the unpleasant Mr. Ames, Mrs. Loring. Would you do me the honor of dancing with me?"

"Only if you call me Cass, General," she replied with her first genuine smile of the evening.

"Then, dear lady, Cass, you must call me Will. The military title does have its uses in business from time to time, but there is far more about the war I'd as leave forget."

Recalling that Palmer and Steve had been skirmishers, Cass well understood his wish to put the war behind him. Still, the man might hold the key to the enigma of her husband. "You and Steve have been friends since childhood, I'm given to understand, Will."

"Ah, yes. In Philadelphia. Our parents—at least

our fathers—were friends, too." Just as he was
about to launch into an explanation about the Loring banking family, Will caught himself, remembering that Steve wanted Cass to know as little as
possible about his background. "Now, if I might
risk boring a lady, I'd like to discuss business," he
said with a twinkle in his eye.

As the evening wore on, Cass watched Steve
dance with a succession of women, fat matrons
married to influential businessmen, flittering
young girls and the coldly beautiful Selina Ames,
who he seemed to partner more than any other.
He charmed them all, she fumed to herself, although she had certainly been giving as good as
she got, choosing from a long line of men cluster-
ing about her before each dance.

Cass had once dismissed the male adulation she
received with detached disdain, using men only
to further Clayton Freighting's interests. Then she
had tried to use them to make Steve jealous. That
certainly had proved a dismal failure! With an
ache deep in her chest, she thought of her earlier
conversation with Will Palmer. After his mapping
expedition south for his new railroad line, he was
off to Philadelphia to marry his beloved Queen
Mellon. Watching the way his eyes glowed when
he described her, Cass admitted for the first time
that genuine love between a man and a woman
was possible.

Looking about the crowded ballroom, she felt
as if scales were dropping from her eyes. She was
seeing for the first time, her vision no longer distorted by her parents' vitriolic relationship. Hus-
bands and wives laughed, danced, and talked
together with evident affection. *Kyle was right, I
should've tried to find a man who wanted to marry*

me, not forced one who didn't, she thought forlornly.

Almost against her will, her eyes sought Steve's tall, elegant figure. He stood out in the crowd with the chandelier lights catching his warm, sun-streaked hair in a golden aura as he threw back his head and laughed at some quip of Selina's. He was easily the most striking man in the room. And he belonged to her, by damn, not that Ames slut! Cass's weeks of pent-up sexual frustration came boiling up, almost choking her. She felt trapped and powerless.

Steve, who had also conversed at length with Will about his upcoming nuptials, was sharing a bit of Cass's self-pity as he indulged in some excellent bourbon. He looked over at Bill Byers, whose censuring expression caused him to lift his glass in a mock salute. "Here's to Blackie Drago. Pity a good Democrat wasn't invited into this den of Republican iniquity," he muttered beneath his breath. He turned his attention from the scowling editor to his beautiful copper-haired wife, who was standing by one of the big bouquets of roses. Pensively she pulled a white one from the mass and inhaled its delicate fragrance. He strolled unsteadily toward her.

"Enchanting picture, Cassie. You should wear white roses in your hair." He reached out and stroked the soft curls piled at the crown of her head.

"Don't, Steve," she almost pleaded.

"Why not, Cass? I'm supposed to touch you, to bed you, to do my husbandly duty, am I not? It's a husband's right, even a legal right, to gain pleasure from his wife, to appreciate her beauty . . . and you are beautiful, Cassie. There is that for me in this damnable arrangement."

His words were carefully articulated, almost as if he were—"Drunk! You're drunk, Steven Terrell Loring," she whispered in mortification, uncertain whether his inebriation or her longing created her anger.

He sketched a bow and winked. "Let's go home and I'll show you how drunk I am, madam."

"Yes, you do have your 'husbandly rights,' don't you, Steve?" she replied, suddenly smiling with a grim gleam lightening her eyes to pale cat yellow.

When they arrived at the city house, Cass accompanied Steve very solicitously into the study where she poured them each a generous snifter of brandy.

He arched a brow at her and concentrated on unthickening his speech. "I was under the impression you were distressed at intemperance."

"William Byers was. I bet he cuts you cold at the next social function," she replied with indulgent humor. "Drink up, darling." She lifted the tawny liquid to her lips, but swallowed very little. Steve rewarded her by draining his glass in a few grand flourishes.

Then she led him upstairs and put him to bed, swearing because hers was the only four-poster in the house. Well, there was a certain poetic justice in that.

Cass spent a very restless night, riven by nervous anticipation . . . or was it fear?

Steve awakened slowly. His eyes fluttered open, but he immediately shut them tightly. *Oh, Christ*, he thought fuzzily, *champagne and bourbon don't mix*. Still, his skull did not feel as though it were about to shatter. He vaguely remembered Cass giving him some brandy when they got home last night. *Great, just what I needed!*

His mind drifted, and then he became aware of a faint sound. He was not alone. Gingerly he turned his head and reopened his eyes. Cass was seated at her dressing table, running a brush through her long, copper hair. Her back was to him, giving him a delightful view of her beautifully rounded hips as they shifted provocatively under the sheer dressing gown while she vigorously plied her brush.

In seconds Steve felt himself become hard. The lack of resistance to his erection suddenly made him aware that he was totally naked. He smiled, thinking so much the better. But when he tried to roll quietly out of bed, he could not move! His eyes snapped completely open, and he turned quickly to the right, then the left. He raised his head to stare down at his nude body. He was tied spread-eagled to his wife's four-poster!

Still marinating in the residue of last night's generous liquor basting, Steve's brain slowly digested this fact as Cass became aware of his faint struggles. She swallowed nervously, then rose and walked to the side of the bed. She gazed at her husband's tousled hair, bloodshot eyes, and stubbled jaw. Even in this bedraggled condition he was a compellingly handsome male. She flushed ever so faintly at the mixture of cowardice and embarrassment that would not permit her to examine the long, lean-muscled body stretched out before her. She kept her eyes riveted on that striking but puzzled face.

Steve tried valiantly to focus his thoughts as he stared at Cass. Damn, she was beautiful! But what the hell was she up to? He closed his eyes and allowed his head to drop back onto the bed. "What's happening?" he asked thickly.

Cass swallowed, "It appears to me that you have been tie—ah, restrained on my bed."

"Restrained?" Steve frowned in concentration. Then his golden eyes opened and he jerked his head up to glare at her. "Restrained, my ass! I'm tied to your damn bed!" For emphasis, he gave a sharp, violent tug at the unyielding cords. "What the hell sort of game is this?"

Cass fought down the urge to avert her gaze. This could all be explained logically, and besides, he deserved everything she planned for him and then some!

"This is no game, my dear *husband*. I'm preparing to collect on a legal obligation. You gave me the idea yourself, last night." She was somewhat disconcerted by her captive's blank stare, but forged on doggedly. "You see, marriage isn't only a domestic arrangement; it's a legal contract."

Warming to her subject, Cass continued, "For example, as you so clearly put it, a husband has a legal right to expect certain..." she colored slightly as she searched for the word he had used "—pleasure from his wife. If she doesn't provide it, then he's within his rights to use, uh ... forceful persuasion. Now, if this is true for the husband, it must also hold true for the wife." Willing him to understand the absolute correctness of her logic, Cass stared intently at his handsome face. All she read there was dazed incomprehension.

Her courage was deserting her. Cass looked away and steeled herself to go on. "I mean, it holds true that a woman ought to be able to obtain her pleasure by forceful persuasion too—if she must."

Steve shook his head like a prizefighter attempting to throw off the effects of a punch. "Cass, what the hell are you babbling about? Jesus, I wake up buck-ass naked, with a hangover, tied to a bed, and you're reading me a goddamned lecture out of Blackstone? Are you crazy?"

Cass's color deepened under his scrutiny. Suddenly she was surprised by a low chuckle.

Steve's eyes were closed, his face puckering as the chuckle blossomed into laughter. "Oh, my God, now I understand." He almost choked. "Cassie, you are something! You're going to rape me, aren't you?"

Cass hissed furiously, "Keep your voice down! And I'm not raping you. I only intend to take what's legally mine!"

Although still vastly amused, Steve sobered slightly. "Yeah, I know, forceful persuasion. Well, I guess I can't complain. I've heard of men who pay whores for this sort of treatment."

Forcing back her anger at the implication of his comment, she smiled and inquired sweetly, "So men pay for this?" Her voice became brittle. "How much? Did Rena Buford tie you to the bed in her tent?"

His eyes narrowed as he stared up into that beautiful but determined face. "Damn you, Cass, let me loose!"

She shook her head slowly, her eyes taking on a disquieting gleam. "Not on your life," she ground out, emphasizing each word. "You took from me—now it's my turn."

Steve eyed her with growing uneasiness. He began placatingly, "Listen, Cass, you—"

"Be quiet," she snapped. "You took what you wanted from me, but when I tried to tell you—"

she paused, remembering her humiliation "—you degraded me. All right, now I'll take what I want."

Cass stared down at her husband with furious eyes. Steve's uneasiness grew as he desperately tried to think of some means of escape.

Watching him intently, she began to smile wickedly. "Don't even think it, Steve. If you try to yell, I'll stuff this in your mouth."

For the first time, he became aware of the balled-up scarf she had been nervously kneading. "As a matter of fact—" her smile broadened "—even though I doubt you'll yell—I don't think you'd want anyone to see you in this, er, condition—I might just stuff this in your mouth anyway if you don't shut it and keep it shut." She deliberately paused for effect. "Yes, breaking my stallion to the bit," she chuckled. "I'd enjoy that."

Steve believed her.

Cass sat on the edge of the bed, hoping her hesitancy was not reflected in her face. She bent slowly forward and planted a warm kiss on that beautiful mouth, then trailed light kisses down his chin to his throat.

Although Steve remained wisely silent, he was seething inwardly. So, she demanded her pleasuring, did she? Well, she might have gotten control of his arms and legs, but she sure as hell wouldn't get control of *that* part of him! He closed his eyes, the better to will indifference to her caresses and the better not to be distracted by the provocative sight of those beautiful breasts straining against the sheer fabric of her gown.

Cass lifted her head to study his face and was both pleased and emboldened to see that his eyes were closed. She leaned forward and slowly skimmed his lips with her tongue, a tactic he had often employed on her. He twitched slightly, but did not pull away. With her tongue she continued to trace a path down his chin to his throat and finally to his chest. Gently she licked and nibbled at his nipples, delighted as they puckered and hardened just as hers had always done under his erotic attentions. She ran her hands through the wiry hair covering his chest, across the rigid pectoral muscles, and then lightly raked her nails down his hard belly.

Silent, his eyes shut tightly, Steve was waging a losing battle.

Without daring to look, Cass slowly reached down to touch his half-flaccid flesh. Surprised at its heat, she quickly jerked her hand back, then glanced nervously at her husband's face. When she saw that his eyes were still closed, she gained the courage to turn her full attention to this mystery of male anatomy. She grasped his shaft, squeezing and kneading gently, not quite sure just exactly what she was supposed to do. However, her nervously tentative efforts were rewarded as he became stiffer and larger.

Cass was fascinated as she watched. Embarrassment now forgotten, she succumbed to other emotions, more powerful, more primal. Her eyes wide, her lips parted, she stroked the length of it, and was startled by a surprised gasp from Steve. Had she hurt him?

Cass saw that his face was turned slightly away from her. He seemed to be pressing his head hard against the mattress. From her own experience she well knew what that meant. In the past weeks, she had often reacted in the same desperate way. Smiling slightly, she returned her attention to his phallus, recalling some of the most intimate and embarrassing things she'd read in one of Dr. Elsner's books. With great care, she kissed and nibbled his swollen flesh. His hips twitched slightly and his breath became loud and ragged. Cass's smile grew, and so did her delight in her newfound power.

Without consciously intending it, she took him into her mouth, savoring the male flesh. Steve moaned softly as his hips betrayed him, thrusting upward slightly. She continued the sweet torture until her prisoner's moans grew to a throaty growl. His body writhed involuntarily against the cords that held him. Cass lifted her head and took the glistening shaft in her hand. Yes, he was ready, and to her amazement, she realized that she was too.

She quickly knelt on the bed next to him. She had read in Dr. Elsner's books that a woman could ride a man. Now she would see for herself! She hiked her gown about her hips, straddled him, and awkwardly lowered herself, gasping as she guided him into her with slick ease.

Steve groaned but kept his eyes closed tightly, partly out of rage and partly out of humiliation. He silently cursed his own lack of self-control and his wife's surprising skill. She was using his own body to betray him. He cursed his past cruelty in sexually tormenting her.

Cass began to raise and lower her hips carefully, experimentally. The sheer pleasure almost made her faint. Mindlessly, she began to thrust more rapidly. But almost as soon as she had lost control, Dr. Elsner's books flashed through her mind. She must go slow and watch Steve so that he did not cheat her again by "finishing" before she did. Her thrusts became almost languid, and she experimented with circular grinding movements.

With his head pressed back into the mattress,
Steve moaned softly and the tendons in his neck
began to knot. Recognizing the sign, Cass stopped
and leaned forward to thrust her tongue between
his lips. She had no idea how long she had spent
ravaging Steve's mouth when she became aware
that, of their own volition, her hips were once
again moving.

She pushed herself up, staring at the handsome
face beneath her. The idea flitted across her mind
that legal rights had nothing to do with this. Then,
all thought ceased as she continued to move, feeling Steve's body in perfect rhythm with her own.
She was out of control now, her hips moving
wildly as delicious contractions radiated upward,
downward, every which way until her entire body
was shaking, racked by the incredibly sweet con-
vulsions of orgasm.

Stunned and totally exhausted, Cass slumped
forward on Steve's chest. So this was what the
book meant! No wonder she hadn't understood.
She savored the last fluttering contractions of her
sheath upon her husband's still rigid shaft. For a
long time, she said nothing, her head pillowed on
the wiry hair.

Then, softly, she murmured in a thick voice, "I
didn't know. I couldn't even imagine this."

After a long pause, she whispered, "Steve, I
would never have kept this from you. You must
really hate me to do what you did." The sound of
tears caught in her voice.

Steve's mind churned. When Cass raised her
head to stare into his face, her tear-brimmed eyes
fanned his guilt into unreasoning anger.

"You play dirty, Cassie. You have me dragged

here, trussed up like a Christmas turkey to use as a stud. You expect me to come scratching at your bedroom door every night like a mangy cur. Now you tie me to a bed and rape me, and then *you're* hurt! Damn you, get off me!"

Cass sprang up as if she had been lying on a bed of burning coals. Forgetting modesty, she stripped off her gown, rushing to get into her clothes. She had to get away from him!

In spite of himself, Steve felt his unsated passion rekindle as he watched her beautifully curved young body. Cass twisted and wriggled into a pair of her tailored trousers, then yanked on a soft yellow shirt. When she turned back to him again, he used his helplessness and obvious sexual excitement as a weapon. He contracted his muscles and his shaft twitched and jerked, seemingly with a life of its own. She watched mesmerized.

"So you wouldn't do that to me, huh?" He laughed nastily. "Well, honey, what about me?"

Cass blanched, shaking her head. "No! You left me unsatisfied all those times. You had what you wanted. This was my turn."

Steve dropped his head back onto the bed, willing his body to relax, but his rage still flamed.

"What do you think, Cass, of a man like Rufus Clayton? He used your mother like a brood mare. He forced her. He earned your contempt, didn't he? Well, you are your father's daughter, sweetheart!"

Cass stood frozen in the middle of the room, her hands pressed protectively against her stomach. "You bastard! You enjoyed it, too. You did!"

Steve shook his head slowly, "That's what men like your father say. What if I did enjoy it? Lots of women enjoy making love, too. But they don't

want to be used . . . to be forced. You hypocrite!
You think because your father was an animal that
justifies whatever you do to me? You raping
bitch!''

Cass rushed forward and fumbled at the knot
on the cord binding Steve's right wrist to the bed-
post. When it came loose, she jumped back. But
he didn't move.

"I'm not like Rufus," she choked out.

He sneered, "Get the hell out of here."

Cass spun, yanked open the door, and stumbled
into the hall, blinded by tears.

When the door closed, Steve slumped against
the mattress choking back the bile of self-loathing.
He felt so sick to death of himself, of this entire
farcical "marriage" that he could vomit—or cry.

Chapter Eleven

Cass flew downstairs and rushed blindly from the house, not even taking time to tell Vera where she was going. She walked around back to the stables, knowing the place would be deserted. Not wanting to awaken the elderly stableman Red Curtis, she decided to saddle her own horse. She could not face anyone just yet.

Walking to the stall where her favorite mount, Angelface, was kept, she began to bridle and saddle the gleaming bay with the white face and sox. Large and intelligent, the stallion possessed a wicked temper on occasion. This morning his mood responded to hers as he skittered and snapped at her while she worked.

"Keep this up and I *will* geld *you!*" she growled low as she tightened the cinch. "I don't need to put up with your foul male temperament, even if I have to suffer his!"

She had a good many details to discuss with Kyle before their long journey to Fort Union with the winter army supplies. But on impulse she decided a long ride in the fresh air would work out some of her pent-up fury, not to mention her humiliation and pain. Of guilt she thought not at all ...consciously.

Steve sat at the dining-room table brooding over his third cup of spicy green tea. Although it was late in the morning, he was not up to fully appreciating the delectable meal in front of him.

He had taken a long, cooling bath after Cass left at daybreak, as much to calm his mind as to ease his raging sexual frustration. The bitch! The ruthless, unnatural, conniving, beautiful, desirable, maddening ...bitch! He set the cup down abruptly and stared at the fluffy omelette on the china plate, then ran his fingers through his hair, cradling his aching head.

That was how Kyle found him when he entered the room. *He looks nigh onta as bad as Cass*, the little gunman thought as he observed Steve's slumped posture and bloodshot eyes.

"Yew musta really tied one on last night at thet fancypants shindig," Kyle said as he gingerly pulled up a chair. Linen and china always made him nervous, so when Vera brought him his usual coffee, it was served black, in a tin cup, just as he'd always liked it.

"How kin yew stand thet stuff?" he sniffed, wrinkling his nose at the Oolong tea.

Steve managed a wobbly grin. "It goes down a lot easier than that ink you swill."

"Better git used ta it. We leave fer th' flatlands tamorrah. Real nice country—thousand miles from hay, seventy miles from wood, fifteen from water, 'n purely twelve inches from hell!"

"Sounds wonderful," Steve replied grimly. "I can hardly wait to see Fort Union."

Kyle paused, measuring his words now, uncertain of how to ask what he wanted to know. "It'll be a right long trip—hot winds, dust thick 'nough to swim through, even hail 'n brush fires."

"In other words," Steve interjected drily, "it's no place for a greenhorn. Don't think I relish going, but I'm certain my darling wife won't hear of anything else. She has need of 'my services,'" he added sarcastically.

Kyle's shrewd gaze measured the scowling man sitting across from him. "Yep, thet I reckon she does, like it or not, makes no never mind fer either one o' yew. But I told yew once't not ta treat her rough, Loring, an' I'm a man who purely hates ta repeat hisself."

Steve let out a bark of furious laughter. "Me hurt her! That's really rich, Hunnicut, really rich. Now why don't you just go to hell!"

"Whut did yew do ta her? She wouldn't say nothin' this mornin' but I never seen her so down, so..." Kyle struggled for the right words to describe Cass's demeanor. Gone was the brittle tension of simple sexual frustration. Although she had tried to conceal it, she was in real pain. "Whut kinda games yew playin' with her?" There was steel beneath the softly voiced question.

Steve sighted, guilt and anger all wrapped up in his frustration. Dejectedly he replied, "I didn't *do* anything, Kyle. She did it to me! Oh, hell, never mind. I'm not discussing what goes on in bed between me and my wife with you or anyone else. Let's just say I called a spade a spade."

"Whut's thet mean?"

"She acts like Rufus Clayton, so I told her she did," Steve said defensively, realizing how devastated Cass's reaction had been.

"Yew *whut*?" Kyle began to stand up, then regained control of himself and slowly sank down into the chair again. Knowing Cass and how she must've provoked Loring, he struggled to look at the matter objectively. In so many ways, this was the man for her, and he hoped she was the woman for the enigmatic Easterner, too.

"I got me some things ta tell yew. Mind, they's real personal—shared over a bottle o' tangle laig late one night. Cass don't drink much. Onliest reason she did thet time was 'cause she jist missed fallin' off th' side o' a mountain by a gnat's ass. I'm gonna tell yew 'bout Cass 'n her daddy, 'n yore gonna listen real good . . ."

The next morning at daybreak was a reenactment of Steve's first freighting trip into the Rockies, only this time the wagons were moving south to the hot desolation of Arizona. A widely spaced string of road ranches were the only hints of civilization along the trail.

Since Fort Union was the central location from which the army dispersed provisions to all its outposts in the Southwest, the train was far larger than the one to Fairplay and Gold Hill. Steve stood at the edge of the big loading corral behind the office, watching the colorful scene around him. Odd, how quickly he had begun to adapt to the raw frontier environment. His gaze scanned the livestock, oxen yoked restively in ten-spans to the lumbering Murphy wagons. The huge yellow and white animals bawled and swatted their tails while bullwhackers swore and popped their whips. The slow-moving but strong animals were best used for the long haul over mostly flat ground. Because this shipment was the last one before winter, the wagons were heavily laden.

Steve knew the trip would be brutal, but in a perverse way he looked forward to it. *Self-inflicted penance?* a voice inside him asked wryly. His eyes searched for Cass across the profane chaos of the freight yard. They had slept apart last night, a situation he planned to remedy soon on this trip. Since the bitter scene yesterday morning, she had been avoiding him, like a wounded animal hiding its pain.

When Kyle gave him the full story of Rufus and Eileen and their daughter, Steve realized the extent to which his cruelly cutting accusations must have hurt his wife. If only he'd realized how truly driven and desperate, how alone and frightened she had been, a seventeen-year-old-girl running a man's empire. The barriers she erected were like a suit of armor to protect herself, not the callous shell he'd imagined. Again he cursed himself for being a fool not to have intuited more of what Kyle had told him. He also cursed his dumb luck for being trapped in this impossible situation, but that was useless.

Satisfied she was not in the yard, he turned toward the office to give some last-minute instructions to Ossie. He entered the front door of the big brick building but went no further than three steps before he saw her. She was leaning over the counter, her back turned to him, conferring with the young clerk. Steve stopped for a moment as a wave of pure sensual enjoyment washed over him. He inspected her trimly clad little derriere, the revealing pants hugging her softly curved hips. Her hair fell in a fat, shiny plait to her waist, and he remembered the springy, vibrant texture of it, like spun copper, softly scented with lilacs as he'd buried his face in the luxuriant curls.

Steve's reverie was interrupted when Ossie saw him and called out a warm greeting. Cass spun sharply on her heel, the coiled whip lying on the counter now clenched unconsciously in one hand.

He gave her a lopsided smile and nodded to the boy, noticing how she stepped aside when he walked up to the counter.

"I'll be out back. We're ready to roll as soon as Kyle gets here," she said as she headed toward the back stockroom.

With terse instructions to Ossie, he quickly overtook her as she wended her way through the big store room, now mostly cleared of sacks, crates, and boxes. "Wait, Cass, please. We have to talk."

"What's there to say, Steve? You said it all yesterday morning, I believe." Her voice choked off, but she stood ramrod straight as she turned to face him.

"I'm sorry, Cass. I can say that," he replied simply. He tried to gauge her reaction as he walked slowly toward her, reaching out to clasp her cold, balled-up fists in his larger warm hands. He could feel the bite of the whip as its coils grazed his wrist. "You aren't going to use that on me, are you?"

He felt her tense in anger as she replied, "You've already illustrated the futility of using force against you, Steve."

"We were both wrong, Cass. I shouldn't have said what I did about you and Rufus. No matter what's happened between us, you didn't deserve that." He released her hand and reached to tilt her chin upward. Her eyes were round with confusion.

"Why . . . why are you saying this?" Her voice was scratchy, sounding far away in her own ears.

"Maybe because we have a bargain . . . because I—"

Just as Steve's hand caressed her cheek and he pulled her unresistingly into his arms, the back door slammed open and Bully Quint entered, halting in embarrassment. "I come for that last load of seed. We got room in one of the trailers . . ."

Cass wanted desperately to hear what Steve had been about to say, but the mood was broken as two bullwhackers barged in on Bully's heels and began to heft the grain sacks across their brawny shoulders.

"You riding that white-faced bay of yours?" Steve asked her as she turned toward the open door.

"Yes. I scarcely plan to walk alongside the oxen at twelve miles a day from here to Arizona. You'd better get a horse for yourself from the stables or you'll have awfully sore feet by the time we make camp tonight," she said with forced lightness.

He chuckled as they walked out onto the porch. "I've already bought a horse for myself."

Cass saw the magnificent gray stallion tied to the rail at the end of the building. The animal was easily as large as Angelface. He was a pale, solid pewter color, not the dappled shade more common among gray horses. His lines were clean and strong. Kyle stood admiring him as Steve and Cass stepped down from the porch and approached.

"His name's Rebel. I bought him yesterday from—"

"That's one of Blackie's prize race horses!" Cass

interrupted. "And his name's not Rebel," she added disdainfully.

"It is now," Steve replied with a grin.

"How the hell did you get Blackie to part—"

"Let's just say we made a deal," Steve replied smoothly.

"Shore is somethin' ta look at. Kindy skittish, though. Him 'n thet devil horse o' yourn gonna tangle, Cass," Kyle said.

She snorted. "Angelface isn't a devil horse."

"Let's just say he suits your personality. Maybe two wrangling horses reflect two wrangling owners?" Steve said with a wink as he stroked the big gray's muzzle.

Cass knew that her instincts regarding Steve's horsemanship had been correct. He was a natural because of his build as well as his training. Again she wondered why a Yankee from Philadelphia had been working on a stud farm in Kentucky. Obviously he was used to handling fine, spirited horseflesh. "Just see to your horse and I'll see to mine," she said waspishly and headed over to where her stallion was tied.

"This here's gonna be some trip, yessiree." Kyle's eyes narrowed as he looked from Cass to Steve and back.

"I think I can survive, Kyle. No more little surprises, like freezing my ass off in the mountains this time. I've come prepared," Steve said grimly.

Kyle chuckled. "Yew did right well 'nough from whut Chris 'n th' others told me. Yew got grit . . . even if'n yew are a bluebelly, but jist let me set yew straight 'bout th' Fort Union run. No freezin'. It's purely hot as hell from here on south. We take the flattest route through wide open prairie. Alkali dust'll crack yer lips till they bleed, 'n wind'll scorch th' shirt clean off'n yer back . . . thet is if'n yew don't drown in a sudden rainstorm er git yore skull cracked by hail. They got moskeeters so big down south a ways they thow rocks at th' bullwhackers passin' through."

Steve grinned good-naturedly, having shared the teamster's tall tales over the past weeks. "I know . . . the road ranches south of Pueblo are so bad the bedbugs sit up on the window sills and bark, and the grasshoppers are so big the farmers hitch them to plows. I'll survive, Kyle. I've been studying up . . . on lots of things," he finished cryptically as he swung up on Rebel's back.

That afternoon Kyle and Cass rode side by side in the gritty dust and heat, both watching Steve's progress on his first trek into the hot country. Until they passed Pueblo, the going would not really be that bad, except for the agonizingly slow pace of the oxen pulling heavily laden wagons.

Cass mulled over all the nights ahead of them on the trail. What had her husband meant to say to her that morning before they were interrupted? She knew time was fast running out. They could not waste these precious weeks sleeping separately. Somehow she would have to work up her courage and approach him that night. If they wanted privacy, they could have it. But after what she'd done to him, would Steve want her?

Kyle studied Cass quietly as her gaze sought out Steve over and over during the day. He'd noticed at the noon break that Steve had been busy seeing to several of their guard's horses. He was amazed at how naturally the dude worked with horses and how the tough and loyal employees of Clayton Freighting had given their respect and trust to Cass's husband. Steve was proving himself with the men and the business. As to his wife, now there was another matter all together. Kyle noticed her hands tense on the reins as Dog Eating Jack had a long conference with Steve.

"Th' men seem ta cotton real natr'l ta him, Cass," Kyle ventured innocently.

Deep in thought rehearsing her speech for that night, Cass colored and then snapped, "They used to come to me for directions."

"Wal, I reckon I cud sorta nudge him outta th' way fer yew..." he said consideringly, then scratched his head and continued. "Course, yew two had a bargain. He finished his part o' it yet?"

Her color deepened. "No!" With that she dug her heels into Angelface's sides and took off in a wild, angry gallop.

The summer had been hot and dry, unusually so for the high plains of northern Colorado. Dust hung thick in the air and coated men and animals with sticky, burning particles. Flies, always the bane of oxen, swarmed blackly, dispersed only momentarily by the twenty-foot bullwhips that cracked and popped, disturbing the oppressively still air.

Toward evening they passed one of Bennett Ames's freight caravans in the distance. They were returning to Denver with grain and produce from the agricultural valleys to the southwest. Although not as lucrative as Loring Freighting's army contract, it turned Ames a tidy profit.

Kyle and his heavily armed men watched warily as the other train vanished slowly over the flat horizon.

"How many days on the trail for them, Kyle?" Steve asked.

"Reckon 'bout two weeks, dependin' on weather 'n sech."

"No wonder the eggs are rotten when they finally get to Denver. The first time I had a Denver omelette I nearly singed the roof off my mouth," Steve said with a laugh.

"Onliest way ta eat them eggs is ta mix 'em up with chilis so's yew cain't taste th' eggs. Wheat's got weevils 'n th' vegetables is plumb wilted ta pus, but it's all folks kin git." Kyle shrugged philosophically.

"The railroad's changing all that, Kyle. Just wait until Will Palmer's narrow-gauge criss-crosses the territory."

"That'd put old Ames outta bizness right quick. He's got rich gougin' folks fer too long as is."

"I heard Blackie tell a crowd at the Bucket of Blood how Ames put flat stones between the bacon slabs and then sold them by the pound, not to mention siphoning off whiskey from barrels and substituting tobacco-colored water."

Kyle snorted. "Thet wuz the good stuff. In a pinch Ames's been knowed ta use gun powder 'n chili peppers when tabaccky's scarce!" They shared a laugh, and then Kyle looked at Steve and asked quietly, "Yew 'n Cass settle things yet?"

Steve shrugged in frustration. "I tried to talk to her this morning, but you've seen what a day it's been. I'll talk to her tonight. Where are we stopping?"

"Near a small fork on Cherry Creek. If'n th' drought ain't made it too muddy, there's a pool back a ways from th' road . . ." Kyle let his words trail off, planting a suggestion.

By the rakish grin on Steve's face, it was obvious he recognized the hint.

* * *

As Sour Mash banged the dinner iron that night, the men gathered for his obligatory prayer. Dusk was falling fast into night as he intoned, "Lord, send us a cooling breeze and some rain to whet our parched throats, we beseech you. But if you cannot or will not gift us with relief from this heat, please do not visit good weather on the Ames train either. Treat us all alike. Amen."

"Amen" was chorused from all across the huge circle of wagons as the men lined up to eat. Cass and Steve were nowhere in sight. Kyle smiled to himself as he bit into a chunk of hardtack.

Cass was hip deep in the water of the creek at that moment. Hearing the familiar clanging summons to eat, she ignored it and sank slowly into the cooling water of the pool. Isolated by a thick stand of brushy cattails and scrub willows far from where the men camped, it afforded her privacy to bathe and unwind. Kyle, Jack, and Bully knew to keep any of the men from spying on her. Feeling secure, she sudsed her hair and then dunked in the water to rinse off.

Just as her head broke the still surface of the pool, a low voice whispered softly, "You must've lost at least five pounds of trail dirt in the last ten minutes." Steve sat on a rock by the water's edge, obscured by the shadows of a willow in the deepening twilight.

Cass sputtered and splashed backward. Her carefully prepared speech fled from her mind as quickly as a stampeded herd of cattle. "What are you doing spying on me? Who let you by? My men always guard my privacy!" she gasped out indignantly, as he began methodically stripping off his boots and clothes.

"*My* men let me by, to join *my* wife for a leisurely bath," he replied as if it were the most natural thing in the world.

Cass watched him discard the last of his clothes. The hard-muscled length of his body gleamed dully in the waning light as he stepped into the water. Slowly he advanced on her. Cass stood her ground, feet firmly planted on the slippery mud bottom. Perhaps she would not have to make any painful speeches, only let nature take its course.

Steve stopped in front of her, feeling the first hint of the wind that had picked up at dusk as it ruffled his hair and caressed his body with cool night air. Cass shivered, whether from the wind or the nearness of him, he was not sure.

Slowly he reached his hand up to graze a hardened nipple. He could feel the silky slipperiness of the water on her skin as he hefted one high perfect breast in each hand, his thumbs teasing the puckered points until she gasped involuntarily. Still Cass did not pull away. He drew her to him for a kiss and she came into his arms warily.

His lips grazed her throat and he murmured, "Cassie, Cassie, so lovely, so soft . . ."

When he raised his mouth to hers, she found her own opening, responding, even as her arms curved around the sleek muscles of his shoulders. She could feel the scratchy texture of his chest hair against her sensitive breasts. Deep inside her, the heat of remembered pleasure began to rise and blossom, blotting out the pain and humiliation that had followed. They clung together and kissed fiercely. The world began to recede.

Suddenly the loud bawl of oxen and terrified whickering of horses blended with curses from the men. Steve raised his head to hear the cries.

"Smoke!" Cass cried out. "My God, Steve, brush fire!" At once they bolted for the shore and began to yank on their discarded clothes with frantic haste.

In summer, nothing was as deadly and dangerous on the high plains as a brush fire. It could spread, whipped by the rising wind until it became a solid wall of flame, destroying everything in its wake.

"We've got to start backfires." Cass yelled to him. "Thank God the creek's still high enough! We'll have to sacrifice some of the army blankets and feed grain for wetting our side of the backfire."

By the time they reached the camp, pandemonium reigned. Bright orange flames licked at the western horizon, casting an eerie glow over the twilight landscape. Kyle was on horseback, directing men to drive the frantic oxen and extra horses into the creek. At once Cass grabbed Bully's arm and pointed to a wagon filled with blankets. Soon he and two other men had the wool blankets unbundled and soaked in creek water.

Steve rushed over to Rebel, crooning calming words as he quickly bridled and saddled the horse, then took over direction of the men herding the livestock to the dubious safety of the low creek. Kyle gathered a dozen men armed with kindling torches to set backfires. By yelling and pointing he made his plans clear. The breeze was blowing flames toward them about a mile to the southwest. If it held steady and didn't shift, they might have time to set another line of backfires between the creek and the onrushing flames. Backed up by men with hastily uncrated picks and shovels as well as those with wet grain sacks and soaked blankets, they ran from the camp to meet the fire.

Once he had the livestock in the deepest part of the creek, Steve left them with a small group of men to hold them as best they could in the gathering darkness. Giving Rebel over to Quint, he raced back toward the wagons. The whole of the army's winter supplies for Arizona Territory, tens of thousands of dollars' worth, would be lost unless they could stop the fire. Even worse, their lives could be forfeited.

Like the others, he grabbed a blanket and drenched it, then swung a shovel over his shoulder and loped toward the southwest. As he ran, he searched frantically for Cass, wanting to get her into the creek near the horses. She was nowhere in sight. Knowing he'd find her wherever the danger was the greatest, he increased his pace.

They spent the night fighting the fire. Steve was covered with sweat and dirt as he swung the pick over and over, widening the trench and denuding it of all vegetation that could feed the hungry flames. At times it seemed hopeless, but Cass urged them on, racing from place to place along the backfire line with more wet sacking. Gradually the bare corridor of burned-off ground widened.

Steve watched her through the smoky haze of the night fires. She was soot-covered and exhausted, yet as calm and strong as any of the men who toiled for her. Suddenly a spurt of wind licked a flame near her pants. Racing to Cass, he threw her into the trench behind them, rolling her on the ground before the fire could ignite her clothing. As he smothered her smoldering clothes with the wet sacking in his hands, he found he was trembling with fear for her. "Go back to the creek and wait with the livestock and wagons, Cass."

"I can't, Steve! You know that," she cried, gasping for breath. Quickly she wriggled free of his embrace and rolled back to her feet.

She sprinted away, yelling for another bucket of water and more sacks of soaked grain to douse the western side of the backfire.

"Is it going to hold?" Steve yelled over the din at Kyle as he swung a pick into the hard, dry earth.

"Depends on th' wind. It's been dyin' down some. If'n it don't jump th' backfire clearin', we oughta make it." Kyle's eyes glowed an eerie pale blue in his soot-blackened face. Even his frizzy red hair, the color of flames, was now gray with ash and dirt.

Steve, too, was covered with filth, his hair singed, his hands bloody and blistered. Still, he swung the pick doggedly while watching out for Cass as she hauled water with the men.

Just before dawn the last of the crackling hiss died down and the prairie again grew deathly silent. Kyle trudged over to where Steve leaned on his pick handle. "Good thing th' wind stopped. Saved our hides, I reckon."

"How'd it start, Kyle? There was no summer lightning. Too far away for one of our men to have been careless with a match."

"I posted guards. Ernie 'n Lober. Ain't seen 'em since't this started," Kyle replied, scanning the eastern horizon where the sun's first feeble pinkish streaks were heralding daybreak. "Reckon I'll git my hoss 'n take a look-see."

"I'll go with you," Steve said quietly, regretting the way he'd treated the kindly Ernie at the Pueblo road ranch.

When they trudged into camp, Cass was waiting, an inventory list in her hands, several men already checking off their losses under her direction.

"It was Ames's men who set it," she said to Kyle, not even posing a question. "Ernie's horse was found a few minutes ago, up at the northernmost fork of the creek. There was blood on the saddle."

"I wuz fixin' ta ride out 'n take a look-see," Kyle said in resignation. He'd known Ernie Farrell since they were boys in Texas. He knew what he'd find. Turning to Steve, he said, "Best yew stay here 'n tend ta th' livestock." His eyes traveled to Cass, who swayed on her feet. Her right pant leg was badly singed where the fire had caught it and her face was blackened with ash and dirt.

Gently Steve put his arm around her shoulders. "You know how to handle it best, Kyle."

"The hell with proving Ames did it. I want that son-of-a-bitch dead," Cass ground out when two of her older bullwhackers were carried in, dead of burns and smoke inhalation.

The inventory went on until nearly noon. Most of their shipment and the livestock were unharmed, saved by the dying wind and the unstinting efforts of the men. The two dead teamsters were to be buried that afternoon. When Kyle rode in with Ernie and Lober over the saddle of an extra horse, Charlie Filbert knew he'd be reading over four burials. Both of Kyle's sentries had been murdered.

Tight-lipped and exhausted, Kyle unsaddled his horse and considered going after the Ames train. With a fresh mount he could catch them by dark.

Reading his thoughts, Steve walked over to Kyle, who was sipping bitter coffee and staring at the northern horizon. "All you'd find is a freight caravan of valley produce. Whoever set the fires and killed your men is long gone back to Denver. Probably to report to Ames, Kyle. Chasing after those freighters won't settle anything."

"Reckon not, ceptin' fer one thang. Recomember whut Cass said 'bout a man like Ames—he bleeds real bad through his pocketbook. I figger ta take me a few volunteers 'n hit thet train at night. Ever try ta cook wheat 'n apples soaked in kerosene?" His smile was a slashed parody of humor.

Steve returned it. "I don't imagine you'll have a lot of trouble raising your volunteers from among the dead men's friends."

"They won't be one wagon left ta roll on thet train by sunup tomorrah."

Cass watched the exchange between Steve and Kyle, angry to be left out, yet so exhausted she could only trudge slowly to where they stood. By the time Steve explained Kyle's plan to her, the little Texan had already recruited more than enough men to help him.

Charlie Filbert, in his most solemn demeanor, read from the Bible as the sullen heat of noon beat down on the assembly. No sooner were prayers finished and the dead men lowered into the earth than Kyle and six men rode north.

Steve looked at Cass and then said quietly, "The rest of this can wait. I'm giving the men the afternoon to sleep. Everyone's so exhausted they'll do more damage than good if they try to work now. And you—" he reached for a sooty lock of hair "—are heading back to that pond for a soak, then a good, long rest, too."

She started to protest, then shrugged. He was right about letting the men rest, but she wanted to be the one giving the commands. "I'll tell the men. Then I want you to come with me to the pond." She hesitated until he nodded.

The water was heavenly as they both languidly sudsed and rinsed off. Steve had brought their bedrolls and laid them beneath the shade of a willow on the far bank. When she emerged, dripping from the water, he was waiting with a clean linen towel and a jar of burn ointment.

Too exhausted to protest, she let him gently dry her. "That must be the only unburned linen left in the whole train," she murmured as his strong hands enveloped her with the snowy towel. The soft massaging felt wonderful to her aching muscles. Then he drew her to sit in the shade as he checked the superficial burns on her thigh and arm.

As he delicately brushed ointment over the red flesh with his fingertips, he realized how easily she could've been disfigured or even killed. "I'm going to kill Bennett Ames," he muttered, more to himself than to her, unaware he'd said it aloud.

Recalling how he'd leaped into the flames and pulled her out, risking his own life to save her, Cass touched his face softly. "Thank you, Steve, for what you did this morning . . . for everything."

Nodding wordlessly, he lay her back in the shade and draped a thin cotton sheet over her naked body. She was asleep before her head touched the ground.

The cool fingers of night reached out, stirring Cass to wakefulness. Slowly she opened her eyes, staring up at the stars gleaming across the vault of late summer sky. The air was chilly now, but Steve's body heat enveloped her, radiating warmth as he lay with an arm and leg draped possessively across her. Gently she stirred beneath the covers, lifting his arm from her breasts so she could sit up.

She studied his face by starlight. He was still the most heart-stoppingly handsome man she had ever seen, but with those accusing golden eyes closed in sleep, he looked younger, almost vulnerable, not at all the angry stranger she had forced into marriage. Recalling his tender ministrations to her that afternoon, Cass felt her pulse quicken. Could he forgive what had gone before? Was there a chance that he might care for her, want to stay with her?

Mentally she shook herself. He was usurping her place as head of the freight line, arrogantly issuing orders to her men. He had even cruelly mocked her needs as a woman after teaching her desire. She could not afford to love him.

Love him! The idea jolted Cass, and she flinched in panic. Steve stirred restively as his arm once again reached out to fall across her hips. Carefully, praying she did not awaken him, Cass lay the arm back, then disengaged his leg from hers and slipped from beneath the sheets.

Clean clothes were laid out near her bedroll. He had thought of everything that afternoon. Quickly she slipped the blouse and pants on, then the soft buckskin moccasins she reserved for wear in the evenings around the campfire.

Steve watched her slip away through slitted eyes, wondering if she'd return or remain with the men at the big campfire. He could smell food and coffee. After twenty-four hours without nourishment, even Sour Mash's cooking would taste like ambrosia.

By the time he slipped on a fresh pair of pants and rummaged through his bedroll for clean sox,

Cass had returned with two plates heaped high with stew. Nervously she set the steaming tins down on the blanket and then stood up quickly, saying, "I'll be right back with coffee."

"Wait," he called after her. "We don't need coffee. There's water in my canteen." He motioned to where it hung on a willow branch near the pool.

Almost reluctantly she sat down and reached for a plate. They ate voraciously in silence, both starved and uncertain of what to say. When they had finished, Cass picked up the plates and spoons and walked to the pool, where she quickly rinsed them clean.

"You look almost domestic, Cass," he said in a caressing voice. She turned to meet his warm gaze. Steve could hear the tins rattle as her hands shook for an instant. Then she regained control and stood up regally. Her hair was tangled, falling in a blaze of copper glory around her shoulders. The sheer white shirt revealed as much as it concealed in the now bright moonlight. He could feel her shiver. In fear? Or was it desire?

"Come here, Cass. Please," he added softly as he stood up, too, his arms reaching out to her.

"I'm not domestic, Steve. I never have been and I don't want to be. I'm who I am and you're who you are ..." She paused, the words, the question lodged in her throat.

He could sense the apology as well as the defiance in her voice. "It's all right, Cass," he said soothingly, taking a step toward her, his arms still open.

"I don't know, Steve," she whispered painfully as he willed her to enter his embrace. He was bare-chested in the cool night air, but when she touched him, his flesh was warm, burning as hot as the fire the preceding night. Her fingers laced through the thick tan pelt of hair on his chest, and she could feel his heartbeat accelerate.

Steve held Cass lightly. His hands stroked her wildly tangled clean hair, then ran down lower, to cup her buttocks, lifting her gently to rock against his pelvis. When his lips began to trail soft, wet kisses across her bare skin where the shirt lay open, she arched against him and her arms slid up to encircle his neck. They moved into a seeking, exploring kiss that grew in intensity as it ground on. Slowly, unwittingly, they knelt, still fused in the kiss, tongues dueling, breathing ragged as their hands sought, caressed, held fast.

He unbuttoned her shirt with practiced ease, freeing her breasts to the cool air. Her nipples rewarded him, puckering to hard points. He suckled one, then the other as he reclined, holding Cass above him. She lay across his long, lean body, feeling the insistent hardness that strained for freedom from his denims.

She shifted to the side, then reached down and began to unbutton his fly with less practiced fingers. When she took the hard length of him in her hands, he gasped out a muffled oath that sounded for all the world like an endearment. He let her stroke and explore for a few moments, then realized he was on the brink of losing control. This woman, so untutored, excited him in a way the most practiced European courtesans had never been able to do.

He began to peel her shirt off, easing her busy fingers away from his aching staff to give it respite. Then he rolled her beneath him and began to rain kisses over her breasts, lowering his mouth to her navel as he unbuttoned her pants and slid them over her satiny hips, careful not to rub the tender burned area on her right thigh. Slipping her moccasins off and tossing her pants aside, he knelt up and surveyed her beautiful body, so slim and pale in the moonlight.

Cass was awash in a haze of pleasure so intense she could not feel the night's chill when the heat of his body left hers. She stared transfixed as he slid his denims off and knelt beside her once more. Her arms reached up to welcome him as if it were the most natural thing in the world.

He eased one knee between her thighs and slowly parted them as his lips met hers for another breath-stealing kiss. When he slid inside the wet heat of her sheath, she arched up and clamped onto his hips with her long legs, riding fiercely with him. Cass wrapped her arms around his shoulders, feeling the muscles tense and flex as he strained over her. She muffled her cries of pleasure in the tendons of his neck, biting and kissing him, feeling the wanting, the ache low in her belly spreading out once again. Now it was so painfully familiar.

Steve could sense her need. All his desire to punish her, to withhold the release she so desperately craved had evaporated. He slowed their frantic rhythm, struggling to control his crest until she could join him. One hand caressed her breast while he murmured indistinct love words into the fragrance of her hair. When he flicked his tongue into her ear and softly bit the lobe, he could feel her nails dig into his back. She let out a gasping, joyful cry of ecstasy as she gained release, her whole body bathed in perspiration, quivering. His body answered by pouring his seed into her in long, shuddering thrusts. Then he collapsed onto her, cradling her in his arms as he rolled them to lie on their sides.

Cass buried her head against his chest, feeling the pounding of his heartbeat, knowing her own answered in like tempo. "This is the first time we both..." Her whispered words halted, and she was aghast to realize that she had spoken aloud.

"Yes, together at last, Cassie. That's how it's meant to be...how it will be from now on," he murmured into her hair as he held her fast.

As the chill night air dried their sweat-sheened bodies, Cass's own personal devil taunted her, asking, *How long is 'from now on'?*

Chapter Twelve

Denver

"I'm so delighted that you've decided to join our group, Abel. Your investment will be richly rewarded. The future lies in your magnificent Colorado, and who better to profit from the expansion of the territory but one of its original settlers?"

Abel Barlow smiled at Will Palmer's words and raised his glass in salute. "To the Denver and Rio Grande Railroad, General."

Thurston Smith began to rustle the papers he held. Both men turned to the lawyer, who cleared his throat gravely and said, "Gentlemen, I have some documents here for you to sign, confirming the terms of Mr. Barlow's investment in General Palmer's railroad venture."

The three men were seated in a private corner of the dining room at the American House, one of the poshest hotels in the city. While conducting business in Denver, General Palmer always used it as his headquarters. Its quiet elegance and unobtrusive staff perfectly suited his needs.

Smiling, Will took the proffered pen and signed his name on all the documents, then handed them across the table to Abel Barlow.

As Barlow signed, Will watched the intent old man. Hailing from Ohio, he was one of the territory's first Anglo settlers. Abel had come west in 1859 and built one of the earliest cattle empires in southern Colorado. Now he wanted to expand his considerable wealth. The rails coming south would allow him to ship his beef to Denver and other lucrative Eastern markets, as well as bring staples and manufactured goods cheaply and quickly to his ranching valleys.

"I trust that settles the matter. Here is the check." He handed it to Will Palmer who gave it to his secretary. The young man had been waiting patiently for the formalities of the signing to conclude. He took the documents and the check and departed with a polite nod.

Will turned to Attorney Smith and said, "We do appreciate your services in drawing up the papers, Thurston."

"Not at all, General. I'm honored. I've represented the Barlow family's interests for many years," he said with a note of pride as he nodded to the solidly built man with graying blond hair who sat across from him.

"Yes, Thurston and I go back to the early days in the territory." Abel Barlow's light gray eyes moved from the beaming old attorney to study Will Palmer attentively. He raised his glass in another toast. "To the opening of southern Colorado."

When they finished their toast, several waiters began serving food from heavily laden silver trays. The men had barely tasted the richly sauced tornedos of beef when their culinary pleasure was rudely interrupted.

Bennett Ames, his face black as a thundercloud, stormed across the room to Palmer's private table. "General, I just wanted you to know the sort of people you're doing business with!" His florid complexion was mottled with rage. "I've been burned out! An entire train of fresh produce from the San Luis Valley, wagons and all, reduced to ashes. My teamsters were fortunate to escape with their lives."

Will Palmer dabbed a napkin at his lips with seeming aplomb and then asked quietly, "Do you mean to imply that your competitors, the Lorings, were responsible for wrecking one of your caravans?"

Thurston Smith interrupted, "Knowing the reputation of that dastardly gunman Cassandra hired, I would scarcely be surprised at anything he or she might do. Rufus Clayton would never have dealt with such a ruffian."

Palmer's blue eyes were calm and shrewd as he addressed the livid man towering over him, twitching in obvious frustration. "I've known Steve Loring all my life, and I can vouch for his integrity. Since he is now the man in charge of the freight company, I sincerely doubt the veracity of your rash remarks, Mr. Ames. Can you prove who burned your wagons?"

Abel Barlow sat back and listened to the exchange in silence, his hand clenching and unclenching until the dinner napkin he clutched was reduced to a mass of wrinkles. He kept the telltale gesture concealed beneath the table. Only the unnatural sheen in his icy gray eyes would have been noticeable to an observer, but both Will and Thurston were busily engaged in discussing Ames's disaster with the infuriated freighter.

"Have you notified the marshal, Bennett?" Smith inquired.

Ames let out a snort of profanity, then looked uneasily about the large dining room, now beginning to fill with patrons. Lowering his voice, he replied, "Of course, but he assures me it happened so far away that the trail would be cold if he sent out any men. I'll just have to handle it my way, but you must understand, General, that, friend or not, Steve Loring is in with a pack of vipers. They'll steal you blind on that grading contract!" With that he turned and stalked from the room, nearly overturning a heavy silver candelabra as he bumped an empty table in his path.

"You've already let the contracts for the railroad grading crews to this Loring fellow?" Barlow asked Will.

"Yes. I assure you Mr. Ames's accusations are groundless, or else there is more here than a simple act of sabotage," Will replied evenly.

"The two freight lines have been in bitter competition for well over a decade. However, matters have changed since Cassandra's father passed on," Smith added with obvious disapproval of Cass in his voice.

"I've heard of Clayton Freighting, of course, but Ames mentioned a Loring as the contractor," Barlow said in confusion.

Will smiled and replied, "One and the same

now. My old comrade in arms Captain Steven Terrell Loring married Cassandra Clayton this summer. Loring Freighting's bid was by far the better offer, I assure you, Abel. Steve may be new to Colorado, but he's an astute businessman with a bright future in the West."

"As you say, of course, General, as you say," Abel Barlow murmured as they resumed their interrupted meal.

"You irresponsible young fool! You assured me your past was buried, as dead as our cause in the war," Abel Barlow thundered, slamming his hand down on the heavy walnut bureau in his hotel suite.

"I'm known as a solid Republican, a Union man here in the territory," he continued. "If our Southern sympathies were ever disclosed, not to mention your little spying forays against the Federals during the war, I'd be ruined politically in Colorado!" Abel glared at the younger blond man who reclined calmly on a large leather chair in one corner of the spacious room.

"It was your idea, Father, to invest in Palmer's damnable railroad. I told you he could identify me if he ever saw me," Vince Barlow replied defensively as he rubbed the bridge of his nose in consideration.

"And I told you we need that railroad for our business, even if that accursed Yankee general is the one building it. You can easily enough stay clear of Palmer. Thank God you used your mother's maiden name when you enlisted in the blasted federal army. But that doesn't relieve us of the problem of this Loring fellow who seems bent on searching you out. I thought you'd lost his agents before you left St. Louis three years ago."

Vince Tanner Barlow grimaced. "I made two unfortunate oversights, I'm afraid—no, three. I left O'Brien and Wortman to snivel everything they knew about me to Loring, but most of all, I left Lieutenant Loring alive after I killed his white-trash cousin. Still, whoever would have dreamed he'd be so persistent? Tracking me for five years, over eight hundred miles . . ."

"I trust you can remedy the problem now before our whole life in Colorado comes unraveled?" Abel asked with a steel glint in his cold gray eyes.

"Since the lieutenant has already taken care of my old Copperhead connections, all I need do is deal with my single-minded pursuer himself. One lone Yankee at an isolated post like Fort Union can easily fall victim to an unfortunate accident, Father," Vince replied with an identical glint in his eyes.

"Then see to it at once!" the old man thundered.

Arizona Territory

The days seemed endless, with the blustery winds lashing them and the sun parching the life from men and animals. The oxen's hooves split and bled from the corrosive alkali dust. Midway, one of the sudden hailstorms Kyle had warned Steve about hit the train, bombarding them with hard white stones over an inch in diameter. Steve huddled with Cass beneath a wagon, protecting her from the worst of the battering with his own body. Then just as abruptly as it had begun, the freak storm ended and they rode on into shimmering heat by afternoon.

Cass studied her husband's alkali-blasted face. In spite of the rigors of the trail, they had shared a bedroll each night beneath the stars, as far from the rest of the men as they could safely sleep. When the campsite allowed them sufficient privacy, they made love, neither one caring that they were filthy and exhausted from the grueling days on the road.

A subtle change had taken place in their relationship after the prairie fire. As she had said, for the first time they were truly lovers. At least the physical part of their marriage was resolved to their mutual satisfaction. Still, Cass was uncertain about many other things that confused and angered her. Steve was sometimes teasing and often solicitous of her, as he had been during the hailstorm. But he was also the boss, the man the teamsters looked to for orders and decisions. Cass found herself in the once unthinkable position of adviser. Yet she could not make herself openly oppose her husband, at least not on the trail in front of the men.

Reining in Angelface to keep pace with the crawling slowness of the oxen, Cass watched her husband's stoic endurance. Back in July when he'd had his first disastrous confrontation with the mule, she never would have dreamed he would become the man riding beside her, tough and trail-hardened, threatening to take her business away from her. *Is it only the business you're afraid of losing? Or are you afraid of losing him?*

Steve looked up and caught her studying him with troubled eyes. He smiled in spite of the pain from his cracked lips. "Kyle says we'll be in Fort Union tonight. A real bed for us, Cass, even a bath first."

His voice, low and suggestive, brought color

stealing to her cheeks. "I could certainly use the bath. So could you," she rejoined tartly.

Steve watched her lope Angelface ahead, realizing how exhausted and dispirited she must feel. Although he fought to hide his misery beneath a tough facade, he, too, was weary and eager for trail's end.

As Rebel plodded along, Steve thought about their arrangement. Both were being drawn far deeper into this relationship than they had intended. Instinctively he knew that Cass had changed and so had he, but did that mean she wanted him to stay? Once she was great with his child, would she resent her physical limitations and blame him for usurping her place? Even now, when one of the men came to him with a question, he knew it infuriated her.

At first he had enjoyed putting her in her place and taking command. Then he learned from Kyle, Blackie, and others how bitterly a lone girl had struggled to build Rufus Clayton's empire. It was unfair to shove her aside, no matter that she had forced him into the marriage. She had earned her position of leadership among the men.

Steve turned the prickly issue over and over in his mind. He could keep to their original bargain and leave her the freight empire if a son was born. Yet he knew he could never desert his own child.

Could you desert Cass? Do you love her? Those exceedingly disquieting questions kept recurring. Steve Loring had never thought to fall in love, certainly not in any storybook romantic way. He'd seen what such a quixotic notion had cost his otherwise practical father.

He'd had no such illusions even when he'd entered into an engagement with Marcia Coleman.

She was shallow and childish, but she was also passionate and biddable. He'd been willing to settle for that, until her real personality became evident that day in the stable. Lord, he'd had a bellyful of scheming women!

Steve swore at his own ambivalent feelings for Cass, wondering if she, too, felt torn and uncertain. Or did she only yearn for the physical delights he had taught her? After all, making love was still a means to her original end—to own the line free and clear. Still, there was a chance she cared for him and wanted their child for its own sake. If so, they could make a life together, a real marriage, not the travesty of a bargain with which they had begun. Cass had not declared herself, other than by surrendering in the heat of passion. *Neither have you*, his conscience countered.

"What yew chawin' on?" Kyle interrupted as he reined in beside Steve. The little Texan and his volunteers had caught up with them three days back after accomplishing their mission at the Ames train.

His reverie interrupted, Steve turned to Hunnicut and scowled. "I'm wondering how it'll feel to chisel this alkali off my body—that is, if I *can* chisel it off."

"It'll come clean with a good soak. Ain't as easy ta git some other thangs ta come clean, though," Kyle added shrewdly.

Ignoring the invitation to discuss his feelings for Cass, Steve reached for the canteen on his saddle and grimaced as he took a drink of the brackish, alkaline water. "Tolerable drink, if we'd pitch it out and fill our canteens with whiskey," he groused.

"It's whut folks back on th' Texas border usta

call water yew kin chew. They got them a well at th' fort that's passable."

"Christ, I hope so," Steve answered, wiping the sweat from his forehead and then replacing his soaked hat. "Dare I hope any of the settlements in Arizona Territory are big enough to have a civilized bathhouse?"

Kyle snorted. "Shit, the cemeteries er bigger 'n th' towns. Got them a sign outside o' Taos I seen once't. Said, 'Smile. Yore jist passin' through. We gotta live here.' We're goin' ta th' biggest army post in this here hellhole. Fort Union's got nigh onta three hunnert men, not countin' camp followers, whiskey peddlers 'n sech. Yew kin git a bath 'n a bed. If'n yew'n Cass er lucky, mebbe one o' them officers' cabins might even be empty." Then he added guilelessly, "Apache seem ta put a real dent in th' ranks o' junior officers."

Steve's first view of the army outpost was not one to inspire awe. A bleak adobe wall loomed low across the flat, brushy ground, the efforts of weather and Apache depredations being equally detrimental to its upkeep. Just in front of the perimeter lay a cluster of cabins and tents, the desert version of a mining town, serving the fort with a saloon, a whorehouse, and a general store. Near the meandering sluggish waters of a creek sat a large wooden structure. The bell atop its roof indicated it was the army hospital. Across from it, a straight line of crude adobe cabins were set aside for married enlisted men and their families.

Kyle hailed the sentry at the gate, who signaled for the crawling train to proceed into the main compound. The wide-open expanse of the parade ground was the focal point of the frontier army post. Ramshackle barracks and cook shacks lined one side, while somewhat more habitable looking officers' cottages and the post commander's house were situated on the other.

They rode slowly past the guard house where two ragged, unshaven men carrying carbines stood their duty, looking every inch as hard and dangerous as their prisoners. The warehouses and stables were at the far end of the parade ground. Long used to the routine, Cass rode ahead quickly and ordered the lead bullwhacker to pull the wagons in a double line in front of the sheds.

Everything looked sun-bleached and sand-blasted. Too weary to observe more, Steve simply dismounted close to where Kyle and Cass were talking with the garrison commander.

"I'll send my quartermaster to begin logging in the supplies, Miss Clayton," Steve overheard the colonel say. She murmured something to him, doubtless about her marriage. The big, craggy-looking officer's tired eyes locked on Steve.

They exchanged amenities, and Colonel Shaker offered them a cottage recently vacated by one of his captains. All Steve could think of at that point was a soothing soak in a large tub. When he frankly expressed that wish to the commander, the old man's jowls shook with laughter.

"That can be easily arranged, Mr. Loring. After you and your wife refresh yourselves, you must be my guests for dinner tonight."

Steve's eyes strayed to Kyle who was busy talking with the quartermaster. "Mr. Hunnicut is welcome, too, if he chooses to break tradition," the colonel added in embarrassed afterthought.

Cass interrupted with a chuckle. "Colonel, you know Kyle always declines hospitality if it involves a clean tablecloth or breakable dishes. He and Sam have a lot of catching up to do over a bottle of whiskey at the saloon.''

Cass soaked in the tub, blissfully dozing in scented bath salts until her relaxed reverie was interrupted. Her eyes flew open as Steve walked in and shoved the creaking door closed. Sputtering, she sank beneath the bubbles. "The least you could do is knock!"

He grinned as he started to strip. "I'm the only one who'd dare come in while my lady was bathing, Cassie. But you need to get that delectable little ass out of the tub. I've got two men coming with fresh water for me.'' He continued stripping off his sweat-soaked shirt and then unbuckled his belt, knowing her eyes were riveted to his body.

Cass couldn't look away as the muscles of his shoulders flexed and rippled while he tugged off his boots. She could smell the musky, salty aroma of man sweat and it aroused her, just as it had all the past nights on the trail when they had come together, savagely and silently. Her nipples were hard as she submerged her breasts beneath the water, trying to hide her reaction.

Watching her, Steve chuckled and picked up a towel, waiting to dry her when she stood up. Laughter danced in his golden eyes. "Water's getting cold, Cass. You don't want those men bursting in while you're mother naked, do you?''

She muttered a muffled oath and stood up, yanking the towel from him and wrapping it about her body. So hasty was her reaction, her foot slipped on the bottom of the tub and she tumbled against his chest, and found herself enfolded in his arms. "Let me go or I'll be as filthy as you are all over again!"

After sweeping her up in his arms, Steve released her abruptly and set her on the bare wooden floor. "You've been awfully irritable lately, Cass. I'd say uneven temper is a sign of breeding, but since you've always been such a termagant, it's hard to tell." His eyes bore into hers, waiting for a reply.

Cass began to rub herself dry with fast, furious strokes, struggling to ignore her husband's piercing stare. In fact, her courses were late as he well knew from their nightly lovemaking, but she had never been regular, so it proved nothing. "I seriously doubt that I'm pregnant, but even if I am, it's too soon to tell. What makes you such an expert, anyway?" she asked with a sudden stab of jealous curiosity.

Her face was so transparent at times that it amused as well as touched him. "I don't have another wife or mistress with a passel of kiddies tucked away somewhere, Cass," he said with a wink and that infuriating grin.

A loud banging on the door interrupted them. It was Colonel Shaker's orderly with bathwater. Cass scooted behind the large dressing screen in the corner as Steve answered the summons. Now she would be forced to endure the torture of watching him bathe while she dried her hair and dressed.

Steve's offhand mention of a possible pregnancy had upset Cass. He was so casual about it. Would he just collect his "fee" and walk away? She plied the towel to her hair with vigorous, angry motions, trying to subdue the strange ache that clogged her throat.

* * *

"It is so nice to have you visiting us from Denver, Mrs. Loring. I must hear all the latest news. Is that dress the latest style? I do declare I've not seen anything cut quite that way without hoops." Abigail Shaker babbled on through the long, tedious dinner, leaving little opportunity for anyone else to join in the conversation.

Steve took it in patient stride as the dumpy little woman chattered, imagining how bleak and lonely her existence on an isolated post must be. She certainly seemed friendly enough to Cass, which surprised him, considering the strong antipathy Cass had indicated toward poor Abigail. Of course, the Denver social scene and the latest fashions were scarcely Cass's favorite topics of conversation.

And it was hot. The commander's house was the largest and most imposing one on the post, but it was frame. Unlike adobe that held the sun's rays at bay, the wood seemed to soak up the blistering heat and store it, only to release it at dusk, thwarting the blessed cool of night. The dining room was sweltering.

As he was shoving a fork full of greasy roast mutton across his plate, Steve realized Mrs. Shaker was addressing him. Her crimped girlish hairdo and protuberant lead gray eyes gave her the appearance of a quizzical sheep.

"Whatever made you come west, Mr. Loring? You're obviously a man of refinement who lived a cultured life back in civilization."

Steve debated rehashing the tired story of his whirlwind courtship of Cass in Chicago, but rejected it. "I find life in Colorado a great challenge, Mrs. Shaker. The West is where my future lies." Although he addressed the older woman, Steve's eyes moved to Cass, almost in a dare.

"Yes, I can imagine how much of a challenge it must've been, taking over this dangerous freight business and dealing with all those awful men who drive the wagons. A gentleman would be hard-pressed to keep them in line. I do so admire a man who can uphold his principles in the face of the adversities in this wilderness," Abigail replied primly, her eyes darting to Cass, then returning to Steve.

He used his napkin to good advantage, covering the smile that hovered on his lips and said only, "I've done my best, under adversity, to uphold my principles, dear lady, I assure you."

"You are so fortunate, Mrs. Loring, to have found such a gentleman," the colonel's lady gushed.

Cass struggled to keep her fork under control. She felt an almost irresistible urge to plunge it into that smirking potato face, right through Abigail's pudgy nostrils. "You can't imagine how I searched to find the man I needed, Mrs. Shaker," Cass replied in a dulcet voice as she sipped at her tepid water. To add to all else, Abigail Shaker was temperance, and there was not even the civility of wine to mitigate the abominable food and company.

By the time they had made their farewells to the colonel and his lady, Cass was seething. "The unmitigated gall of that whey-faced bitch!" Cass muttered beneath her breath as they walked across the parade ground. "'I do so admire a man who can uphold his principles!'" Cass mimicked the older woman's voice with scathing fury. "Do you know she's scarcely said a dozen words to me in the past four years. Last time I was here, the colonel and I dined with two of his unmarried officers. Abigail had the most dreadful migraine."

Suddenly Steve understood the reason for Cass's anger. Mrs. Shaker wasn't just eager for company from civilization or curious about Cass's sudden marriage. "She thought you were a shameless hussy consorting with all those vulgar bullwhackers, didn't she?"

"And now that I'm all properly married—wonder of wonders—to a real gentleman, I'm back within the pale. Just to ruin your image, I should have told her I fished you out of a tumbleweed wagon," she said spitefully.

"Temper, temper. That wouldn't serve either of us, would it, Cass? Forget the old bag. She's scarcely worth your scorn," Steve replied wearily. "Let's get a good night's sleep in that heavenly-looking bed."

Cass laughed in spite of herself. "If that lumpy old army mattress looks heavenly to you, you've really lowered your standards. Of course," she snapped pettishly, "you already did that when you married me! Go to sleep, Steve. I'm going to walk over to the wagons and check on how much has been unloaded."

"We can do that in the morning, Cass. It's too dark, and everyone's either asleep or drinking at the saloon outside the post."

She shook her head stubbornly. She was too agitated to sleep. She needed to walk in the cool night air and get the stale smell of Abigail Shaker's perfume and fried mutton out of her clothes. "If we want to leave tomorrow by noon, we need to have everything in order," she said doggedly.

"This post at night is no place for a woman alone." Steve looked at her delicate face and enticing curves bathed in moonlight and felt an irritating blend of desire and exasperation warring within him.

"I've been taking care of myself on this post and in far worse places for years, Steve." She turned with a swish of her skirt and headed toward the storage sheds.

Other than throwing her kicking and screaming over his shoulder, Steve could see no way to stop his stubborn wife. Angrily he caught up with her, and they walked quickly across the parade grounds to the dark cluster of half-empty wagons.

"There should be a guard posted, dammit," Cass muttered, half to herself. "Ever since Shaker came here, the discipline on this post has been abysmal, but Kyle should've seen to it."

Steve, too, had noticed the slovenly way the fort was manned. The men's uniforms were ill-kempt, even the officers', and the enlisted personnel seemed insolent and lazy. The place reeked of neglect. If the Apache ever decided to make a concerted push, the place would be an easy target.

"It's a thankless job, Cass. I expect the wind and the heat just plain sap an officer's will," he said. He felt a bit of Martin Shaker's bone weariness himself at the moment.

The wagons cast distorted black shadows in the moonlight. Sitting in a double line in front of the long warehouse, they looked like a cluster of black and gray blocks, some giant's toys aligned and ready for play. Cass walked briskly toward them and vanished between the rows. A prickle of apprehension washed over Steve with a sudden draft of cool night air. It was odd that Kyle hadn't posted one of their men before leaving the fort for the saloon, Steve thought suddenly. Then he smelled smoke, the odor of hand-rolled cigarettes. Who would be smoking out here where no sentry appeared to be posted? "Cass? Cass, where are you—"

Steve's question was cut short when a muffled scream erupted several wagons down. He could hear the sounds of a scuffle as he raced to find Cass. She was struggling with a shadowy figure, who was trying with no measurable success to subdue her. Just as he closed on the man and grabbed him by the collar, another man materialized from the wagons to his left.

Steve connected with Cass's assailant, landing a thumping blow to the man's midsection as he yanked him around. Then he shoved the gasping fellow against his companion, who had advanced toward them with an upraised knife glinting wickedly in the moonlight. The knife wielder barely missed slashing his friend as he staggered backward with the dead weight of the coughing man crushing him against a wagon.

Cass watched the two men go down in a heap, but the one with the knife rolled free of his companion and again headed toward her unarmed husband. Then a third figure appeared behind Steve. As she yelled out a warning, Cass leaped nimbly over the wagon tongue behind her. Her hands clawed at the coiled bullwhip hanging on the wagon's left side. Thank God some bullwhacker eager for Taos lightning had left his gear behind!

Used to the lighter, more flexible blacksnake, Cass found the four-foot hickory stock of the bullwhip ungainly, but she was desperate. With a quick shake she had its twenty-foot length uncoiled. Stepping clear of the wagons for freedom to wield the whip, she watched Steve dodge the man coming at him from behind. With scarcely time to aim the blow, she let the whip arc with a lightning hiss.

It cracked across the shoulders of the man with the knife, wrapping its heavy lead-shot poppers across his face and neck. With bone-crunching impact the splayed rawhide thongs at the end of the whip cut into the man's skin, shredding a cheek and nearly tearing out an eye. He let out a scream of agony and dropped the knife, reaching up to claw at the whistling whip as it released him. Cass again drew it back to aim at the second figure, who was reaching inside his coat for what looked like a small pistol.

Steve took advantage of the diversion she created by landing a hard blow to the jaw of the man who had attacked him from the rear, knocking him to the ground. The fellow went down, but before Steve could finish him off, the first man fired his small-caliber pistol. Steve felt a searing burn slice up his right arm as the bullet grazed him.

Instantly the report of the gun was followed by the sharp crack of Cass's bullwhip. The pistol went flying out of the gunman's hands as he, too, clawed at the slashing poppers that kissed him so brutally.

Steve saw the gun land beneath a wagon and dove after it as Cass continued to ply her whip. Grabbing the Remington pocket revolver, he rolled up and fired at one of the two who were closing on Cass. The fellow went down with a cry, and one of his companion yelled, "I've had enough, Billie!" He fled down the line of wagons, ducking between them for cover as Steve fired after him. The other two melted into the darkness amid the wagons, leaving behind the discarded knife and the gun Steve had appropriated.

Cass looked around, whip still in hand, searching the shadows for their attackers. The yelling, whip-cracking, and gunshots finally stirred an outcry from a sentry on the far wall across the parade ground. Half a dozen men came running toward Steve as he took the whip from Cass's hands and tossed it to the ground.

"Are you all right, Cass?" He held her tightly for a moment, breathing in the silky texture of her hair with its lilac perfume.

"I'm fine, but you're bleeding all over my best summer dress," she replied crossly, breaking free to examine his arm. Gritting her teeth to stop the trembling, she forced herself to pull the ripped coat sleeve back and examine the deep, bloody furrow the bullet had cut down his arm. "Damn, that's deep," she said in alarm.

"I've had worse. Anyway it's my right arm. I'm left-handed, remember, Cassie?" He smiled as she searched his coat pocket for a linen handkerchief and began to bind up the wound.

"Let's get you to the hospital," she said as the tardy soldiers reached them.

"Forget it. We've got whiskey and clean linen in our cabin. But first I want to know why there was no guard posted on our wagons."

By the time Colonel Shaker came puffing up with his paunchy belly heaving, Steve had his answer. The soldiers found Lew Ford, one of their fiercest bullwhackers, lying unconscious behind a wagon. "So much for the guard Kyle posted," Steve said as the soldiers took the bludgeoned man to the post hospital.

Steve quickly outlined what had happened for

the colonel, disavowing any knowledge of who the men were or who might have sent them. He and Cass described what little they had been able to see in the moonlight. The colonel assured them the men were not soldiers under his command. Nevertheless, there would be a roll call and inspection the next morning to see if the Lorings could identify them from among the fort's personnel.

Dismissing that unlikely possibility for turning up the asassins, Steve sent down to the saloon for Kyle, who could check for any signs. Given the darkness and the dusty dry ground, it was not likely to do any good, but he knew Hunnicut would want to check it out.

"You ought to have the surgeon look at that wound," Cass repeated as they entered their cabin, with his good arm around her shoulder for support.

"Why? You hoping he'd amputate? This place is so filthy I might just contract blood poisoning if I let the army surgeon tend me," Steve said as she lit the lamp in their cabin. The sudden blood loss had made him light-headed with shock.

"So you're willing to chance me over a Yankee doctor. We must be making progress, Steve," Cass murmured cryptically as she picked up a pitcher and poured fresh water into the basin on the dry sink.

He looked at her back for a moment in puzzlement, then began to struggle with the coat. The blood had begun to dry and crust, fusing cloth to skin. He picked and cursed.

"Here, let me, before you—damnation, you've started it bleeding again!" Cass untied the hankie tourniquet and then carefully finished the separation of coat from arm.

Steve studied her in the lamplight as she worked. Her elaborate hairdo had come unpinned during the fight. He reached up with his good arm and tucked a stray curl behind her ear, then stroked her cheek. "I haven't said thank you for wielding that whip so well, Cassie. You probably saved our lives. I didn't know the men left them hanging on the wagons like that. They always seem to wear them like parts of their clothes."

She laughed wryly. "I didn't know either, I only hoped one of the men might have left a spare behind." Her clear amber eyes searched his face for a moment. "You didn't exactly need rescuing yourself. For a Yankee, you'll do to ride the trail with," she said honestly.

"Such a compliment from you, little reb." His eyes met hers and he lowered his mouth to kiss her, but she pulled the coat from his arm at that moment. Tossing the ruined garment onto a wooden chair, she led him to the dry sink and motioned for him to sit down.

"Let me wash this off so I can see if you need stitches," she said with a calmness she didn't feel when he gazed at her that way. "Who do you think they were, Steve?"

He shrugged his good shoulder. "Not army issue, that's pretty sure. Too easy to identify with Shaker's little inspection at reveille. I'm afraid they'll blend into the riffraff drinking and whoring at the camp. Kyle won't be able to trace them. Too many men come and go from Fort Union every day."

"Whoever they were, someone hired them to kill us," she said, deep in concentration as she gently bathed the wound free of dried blood.

"Kill us? Or kill me? Don't forget I have some old enemies. I may be endangering you by staying near you, Cass."

She snorted. "You aren't getting away from me that easily, Loring. Don't forget Ames. He's wanted me dead for at least six years. Maybe when the brush fire failed, he sent someone else to finish the job."

Steve shook his head thoughtfully. "Doubtful. Kyle would likely have run across them when he and the men caught up with us on the open trail. Anyway, there wasn't time for Ames to send killers from Denver after he heard about his burned-out train."

"He might have sent someone even before the fire—to shoot us during the confusion of fighting it." She inspected the wound, then rummaged through the bag of medicines she had taken from Sour Mash's wagon. Approaching him with a vial of ointment and some linen strips, she began to rub the evil-smelling concoction into the long, ugly furrow.

He felt her deft touch and the cool soothing of the medication. "You're a natural as a nurse. See why I wanted you to tend me instead of the surgeon?"

She stiffened for an instant, then sighed. "Yes, Steve, I have a woman's soft touch, don't I? This is woman's work. Cracking that bullwhip wasn't."

"But you do both equally well," he replied, surprising himself and her.

"Not well enough to please my father . . . or my mother. I was never the lady she wanted for a daughter, any more than I was the son Rufus wanted.

"I fought to protect her from his temper for years after my brothers died. But she only sided with him when I tried to take their place. She was so . . . so weak, almost as if she wanted his abuse, or at least expected it. I got tired of fighting her battles and my own. Then I stopped," she said coldly. "I swore I'd never beg or try to please either of them, ever again!"

That was more than she had ever volunteered to him about her earlier life. Most of what he knew, Kyle and Blackie had told him. He felt compelled to make a confession of his own.

"Your parents weren't the only ones who found fault with their child, Cass. My father and mother agreed on nothing except how hopeless I was. Robert Loring expected perfection and self-discipline in a son. My mother was a lady who wanted all the courtly flourishes performed for her."

"I'd think you excelled at that," she couldn't resist snapping back. "You charm every woman you meet."

He chuckled mirthlessly. "You don't say that like a compliment, somehow. Oh, I suppose I did learn the facade of manners from my mother, but I also learned that a great lady can hide ruthlessness behind a fluttering fan. Let's just say my parents' marriage wasn't made in heaven either." He looked up at Cass as she wrapped his arm, and realized that he, too, had revealed more than he intended.

"Did he abuse her?" She had to ask. Had Steve lived through the same ugly scenes she had?

"Lord, no! My father never touched a woman in anger in his life. He just looked elsewhere for comfort. My mother was frigid. A woman whose only passion—" He stopped abruptly, realizing he was about to reveal the existence of Graham Hall and his family's wealth. "Let's just say she had no passions, no real warmth, Cass." He reached up and stroked her cheek, then pulled her down onto his lap with his good arm. "Now you, on the other hand, have a great deal of natural warmth."

"And you have suffered a great deal of blood loss. This isn't the time," she remonstrated as his warm lips trailed magical kisses along her throat and collarbone. She knew her heart was thudding in her chest like some wild thing's. "Are your parents still alive?" she asked, pulling free of his embrace.

"Let's not talk about our parents' ill-fated lives anymore, Cass. You know I desire you, and you, my hot-blooded little witch, desire me." Even with one arm out of commission, he was amazingly agile as he pulled her back to claim her mouth in a deep, probing kiss.

We desire each other, yes. But do you love me? Will you stay with me once our bargain is met? She burned to voice the words aloud, but then all thoughts fled as another kind of burning consumed her.

Late that night, as Steve slept fitfully beside her in the large bed, Cass lay awake, satiated in body but not in soul. They could come together so easily, so splendidly now. Each time he kissed her, or even looked at her with those hot golden eyes, she melted and wanted him, fiercely, desperately. Cass thought bitterly of how neatly she had fallen into the very trap she'd created the marriage to avoid.

He desired her but did not love her. Apparently his parents had such a terrible marriage he would never trust any woman with his love, least of all her—the cold, manipulative female who had degraded him by dragging him to the altar at gun-point, the woman who had literally violated him.

"What will happen when I'm no longer able to return your passion, Steve? When I'm swollen with child, fat and ugly?" She was alarmed when she realized she'd whispered the words aloud. One quick glance at his moon-bathed face convinced her that the laudanum she'd given him earlier had done its work.

He just looked elsewhere for comfort. Her heart froze as she recalled the words he'd used to describe Robert Loring. Of course, Steve could simply walk away, collect his due and leave her once she was pregnant. He didn't even need to stay and maintain the facade of a marriage as his father had done. Once, Cass would have rejoiced to have the deed accomplished and Steve safely erased from her life.

Painful, choking laughter bubbled up inside her. With each passing day she was more and more certain that she carried his child, but now she didn't want its father to leave her . . . ever.

Chapter Thirteen

Denver

"Dr. Elsner will see you now, Mrs. Loring." Gerta, John's quiet German nurse, stood in the doorway, motioning her inside the treatment room that adjoined his office. Cass walked stiffly in and greeted her old friend with a tremulous smile.

Welcoming her with a fatherly hug, John said, "And what is it today, Cassandra? You look in the bloom of health."

Cass replied, "Ever since we began the trip down to Fort Union, I suspected I might be pregnant. Now that we've returned and I'm back to all the creature comforts of my city house, I still have the same symptoms."

Dr. Elsner's eyes were grave as he asked, "What symptoms, Cassandra?"

"I've missed my second month's courses, and foods that I normally love make me biliously ill—Vera's hot and sour soup, green chilis, raw oysters. And even after a week back home in my own comfortable bed, I'm tired all the time."

He nodded. "This sounds as if you most certainly are expecting a child. I'm going to have Gerta help you disrobe and cover you with a sheet. Then I'll examine you and ask a few more questions, ya?" He patted her hand as she nodded, then called for the nurse.

The examination confirmed Cass's suspicion. As she dressed, she turned over in her mind the question she had to ask John. But how to ask such an unseemly thing! Her cheeks were pink with more than the bloom of pregnancy when she walked back into his office.

John's face was solemn as he rose from behind his cluttered desk and ushered her to a seat. "Well, Cassandra, you will fulfill your papa's will, ya?"

"Only if the child is a boy," she murmured.

"Does this pregnancy make you happy—or do you endure just for the sake of the will?"

Her head shot up. "Oh, yes! Yes, I want the baby—I don't even care if it's a boy or a girl . . ." Her voice faded away in misery.

"Something is troubling you, Cassandra. You are in excellent health. The tiredness, the indisposition, all that will pass in a month or two. You will have a fine, strong child—this I promise you. So, what is the matter?"

She looked into his kind, earnest face. Taking a deep breath, she said, "I told you about the terms under which I married—that Steve and I . . . well, we didn't . . . that is . . ."

His face broke into a gentle smile as he replied,

"It seems you used the fertility schedules to fine advantage—or did you adhere only to those times?"

Her face reddened anew, but she returned his frank appraisal. "No. Steve disliked your schedule rather vehemently, I'm afraid. That's part of the problem. You see...after I read the books you gave me, well, let's just say everything changed between my husband and me. Now I need to know..."

"Yes, Cassandra?" He sat patiently in the chair beside her, waiting.

This was much more difficult than her first angry confession to him last summer. "How long will it be until my pregnancy will show—to my husband, that is?"

Elsner considered, beginning to get an inkling of what she was skirting. "Another month, I would think. You are tall, but on one so slim, little padding you have to hide the baby under, ya?"

She returned his smile with a wobbly one. "That's all? Oh, damn! Oh, I'm sorry, John, but you see...well, will it harm the baby if we—if I..."

His intuition confirmed, John smiled and reached over to pat her arm in reassurance. "No, Cassandra. You and your husband may continue to make love. Until a week or so before the birth, it is normally quite safe. For many women, even the day before it does no harm! Not to worry about that. I will watch your progress. I am very pleased that you want this child for the sake of the child, not for the sake of your father's will."

"Oh, John, I want the baby because it's Steve's! I've never told anyone that," she blurted out in amazement.

His smile was beatific now. "Not even Steve?"
At her quick denial, he added gently, "Do you not
think it is time for you to tell him a great many
things? Things, I think, he has a right to know?"

"It's complicated, John. Very complicated, but
you're right. I'll have to tell him soon."

Dr. Elsner's office was crowded that morning,
but that was scarcely unusual. An Irish "terrier,"
his face bloody and swollen from a brawl the night
before, sat on a narrow bench in the waiting room
alongside an elderly Chinese man whose dilated
eyes betrayed his frequent trips to a "hop joint"
to smoke opium. A pregnant woman in ragged calico shared a worn sofa with an immaculately
dressed German shopkeeper's Frau. As Cass
wended her way out of the crowded waiting room,
Bully Quint's bulk suddenly loomed in front of her.

"Howdy, Miz Cass," he croaked, sheltering his
left arm carefully. "Damn fool mule got away from
me. One of them unbroke ones. Guess I got careless
ta let him get his business end in the way of my
arm." He displayed the odd angle at which his
forearm was bent, obviously broken.

Distracted by her discussion with John, Cass
was surprised to see him. Recovering, she said,
"That looks bad, Bully. You be sure and follow
Doctor Elsner's orders to the letter and tell him
to send his bill to the freight office."

She departed with Quint's profuse thanks, still
preoccupied with the problem of how to tell Steve
about the success of their "bargain."

Only a month and he'll know.

Steve sat at a secluded corner table in the
Bucket of Blood, sipping a whiskey and rereading
the letter from his Uncle Lucas for the third time.

Seeing his young friend drinking at such an unlikely hour of the day, Blackie Drago strolled over.

"You're lookin' for all the world like a man expectin' ta be hanged at first light," the little Irishman said as he pulled up a chair.

Steve snorted. "Closer to the truth than you'd ever guess, my friend." He looked at Drago with measuring eyes, then sighed and showed the papers to him. "We've become pretty good friends in the past months, Blackie. I figure you have quite a few contacts on the odd side of the law. Time may come when I need your help." He waited as Drago skimmed through the letter, a report on his uncle's search for evidence to clear Steve's name at Fort Smith.

Blackie took a sip of thick black coffee laced with cream. No liquor till sundown was his maxim as a saloon owner. When he finished reading, he let out a low whistle. "It's a peck of trouble you're in, boyo, and that's no foolin'. This here Lucas Loring—" he thumbed the elaborately embossed letterhead "—he a swell back in Philly?"

Steve smiled. "He runs the largest bank in the city."

Blackie took another swallow. "He runs it for you, don't he? Always knew you were a gent, but such a rich one! Cass don't know, does she?"

"No. And until things are settled between us, I don't want her to. As far as my wife is concerned, she had Kyle pick a hard case out of a tumbleweed wagon down in the Nations so she could drag him to the altar."

Dawning understanding filled Drago's eyes, making them glint with pinpoints of ebony light. "So, she has a man under her thumb—or *thinks* she has," he added with a wicked chuckle.

They raised cup and glass and shared a toast and a laugh.

"You better be lookin' over your shoulder until your uncle's men clear your name back in the Nations. It's sure and certain I am that Cass would never be goin' back on her word, mind, but lots of men would cut their mither's own dear heart out for less than this reward."

"That's my worry—oh, not that I'll hang in Fort Smith, but that someone is trying to kill me here in Colorado." Steve quickly outlined the series of disasters culminating in his and Cass's brush with death at Fort Union.

Blackie stroked his moustache consideringly. "Ames it likely is, the bastardy rascal."

"It could be someone else . . . the man I came west to find," Steve said cautiously. Blackie's eyes narrowed as he listened to Steve narrate the story of his five-year-long odyssey in search of Abner Henderson's murderer.

"So it could be Ames or this Tanner fellow, and you not knowin' which. Describe Tanner to me," Blackie commanded. But when Steve complied, Drago's exceptional memory of faces could come up with no match for the verbal picture. "I'll spread the word I'm lookin' for the bastard. Say he owes me money on a gamblin' debt 'n see what my sources can turn up."

"I owe you, Blackie," Steve said simply.

"Never fear, laddie. I'll be collectin' some day. Maybe have you name your first child after me."

Steve looked worried for an instant. "What's your real name, Blackie?"

Drago's laughter boomed. "Oh, I'll not be tellin' you that till I can collect!"

* * *

"Whut's thet skinny weasel doin' here? I thought yew throwed him out once't 'n fer all," Kyle said peevishly as he looked across the parlor at Clark Matthews, who was engaged in conversation with Will Palmer.

"Oh, Kyle, Clark is harmless enough, even if he is a pompous ass. It seems since his arrival he's been ingratiating himself with all the town's leading citizens . . . just like someone else I know," Cass added beneath her breath as her eyes strayed to Steve. "Anyway, I found out he has a widowed mother and two younger sisters back in Kansas City. The family is pretty hard against bad luck, and he stupidly spent the last of their cash coming to Denver to entice me to marry him. It seems my father's concerned attorney moved heaven and earth searching for him after the will was settled."

Kyle snorted. "Always did wonder how he turned up jist then. Thet polecat Smith dug him up, fer all the good it done him! 'N now yew er fixin' ta feel sorry fer th' poor Matthews clan 'n give 'em some cash money, I betcha, ain't yew?"

"Well, I can scarcely marry him now, can I?" she snapped back. "I simply offered him a job tallying livestock at the road stations. Neither you nor Chris has the time, and it's a simple enough task."

Cass knew she was unreasonably defensive and angry, but her stomach had been queasy ever since the smells of Vera's cooking floated upstairs while she was dressing for the business dinner she and Steve were hosting that evening. Now even roast lamb made her nauseous!

A week had passed since her visit to John Elsner, and Cass still fretted about when to tell Steve his bargain was completed. She had struggled to con-

ceal her bouts of exhaustion and loss of appetite
from everyone, but several times she noticed
Steve's speculative eyes on her when she felt particularly green. She had gained little or no weight
yet, but her body seemed to be redistributing the
pounds with vengeful intent. What her hips, legs,
and arms lost, her breasts and lower abdomen had
begun to take on. No matter his passion, Steve
was going to recognize the signs soon.

Smoothing her brown silk skirts, Cass nodded
to Kyle, who had stopped by to report to her about
the rail shipments that arrived that evening. "I'll
see you at the office in the morning. We'll need to
plan a trip to Pueblo by next week at the latest."

"Thet winter stock'll wait, Cass. Don't push so
hard. Talk it over with Steve." The minute he ut-
tered the words, Kyle wanted to call them back.
She stiffened momentarily, but said nothing.
Would Cass's fool jealousy of her husband never
end? Tipping his hat, he left her to her guests, with
one parting glare in Clark Matthews's direction.

Steve watched his wife walk across the crowded
parlor, greeting guests and making small talk. Her
burnished coppery hair was set off by the rich
chocolate hue of her gown. Few women could wear
brown to advantage, but on Cass, with her golden
complexion and tawny eyes, what might have
been drab became vibrant. She looked breathtak-
ingly lovely, and worried. Ever since the arduous
trek to Arizona, Steve had noticed the signs of
strain. Of course, given the life-threatening situations she had survived, it was small wonder she
was tense and irritable.

The very thought of endangering her made his
guts clench. If Tanner had inadvertently found

him, or if it was Ames who was trying to kill him, he didn't want his wife in the line of fire. Striding purposefully over to her, he took her arm and gave her waist a proprietary squeeze. "Let's get this social farce over with and retire early," he whispered in her ear.

Dinner was superb and everyone commented on Vera Lee's talent. Sitting next to Clark Matthews, Cass watched him devour copious amounts of roast lamb and sauteed potatoes, followed by a rich almond pastry dessert. Several appetizer and soup courses had preceded the main dish. Each course was accompanied by wine. Cass pushed the flaky pastry around on her plate and sipped sparingly at a sweet German ice wine.

After the men returned from their brandy and cigars in the study, Steve murmured to Cass in disgust, "Your dear cousin is foxed."

Cass smiled sweetly and said, "Being an expert on overindulgence, you ought to know. Put him up in the green room for the night. He can repent in the morning. You always have."

"If I didn't on my own, you found ways to make me." His barb brought angry color to her face, and he chuckled.

After all the guests had departed, a very unsteady Clark Matthews was put to bed by the butler who Cass had hired as extra help for the party. She decided to offer Bentley Everett a permanent job after seeing the way the wiry little man hefted the crumpled, lanky Matthews and virtually carried him upstairs single-handed.

"Poor Clark," she giggled, realizing that even the small amount of wine she'd imbibed with virtually no food was making her giddy.

Steve scowled. "He's scarcely a laughing matter. The stupid oaf dumped a glass of my best brandy on Will's jacket and then overturned a chair. Would've broken Gabe Waters's leg if it had landed on him. Your cousin is a walking disaster!''

"Well, we'll send him off to the San Luis Valley after tomorrow. You said yourself he could at least count and record livestock tallies," Cass replied wearily.

"At least it'll get him away from Denver before he accidentally burns the city to ashes. Forget Cousin Clark and let's go to bed, Cass."

She put her hand on his arm. "There's something I want to discuss with you, Steve—in the study," she said when he would have ushered her upstairs.

Shrugging, he followed her into the study. While she reclined in one of the big leather chairs, he walked to the liquor closet and poured himself a shot of brandy. "For the one I didn't get to drink courtesy of Cousin Clark. Want a sherry, Cass?"

"No, thanks."

"Awfully abstemious here lately, aren't you, Cassie?" He cocked a brow quizzically.

Ignoring his question, she said, "I heard indirectly from a couple of Blackie's street boys that you received a letter from back East . . . about Fort Smith. It was bad news, but they didn't know anything else."

Steve's face froze. "What did you have to do to wring that out of them?"

"I scarcely bullwhipped them!" she shot back.

"No, but I can bet you used every feminine wile in the book and some others of your own invention. Never fear, Cassie, your wanted man is still wanted. I'm not going to ride off and leave you. I just received a letter from an agency I hired back

East. They traced the Copperheads for me earlier. Now they're trying to clear me of the killing in Sweetwater, but so far, nothing's turned up on the witness, and Judge Parker won't relent. Seems he was infuriated by my 'escape.'"

"So why is Blackie involved?" Her eyes bored into him. More was going on here than she knew, and Cass didn't like being kept in ignorance.

"After all the recent attempts on my life, it occurred to me that Blackie's expertise just might be very useful. He knows the whole Denver underground and has contacts from St. Louis to San Francisco. He's trying to help me, Cass. I trust him. Surely you do—but then, you don't want me cleared, do you?"

Unwittingly, she flew into his arms with a sob. "Don't say that! My God, don't ever say that! Oh, Steve, I don't want you hanged!"

He held her, stroking her thick, springy curls and murmuring, "You just want to keep me under your control, eh?"

Her head shot up and she glared at his cynical expression. "As if I've ever been able to control you since the day we were married! Not even tied to a bed!" She flushed and lowered her gaze.

He chuckled, then held her chin up with one hand, looking deeply into her amber eyes. "Cass, is there something you want to tell me?" He could feel her stiffen for an instant, then she hugged him fiercely, burrowing her face against his chest.

"Yes," she replied in a muffled voice. "I want to tell you that all I've been able to think about all evening when I was supposed to be talking railroads and freight contracts with Will Palmer and Gabe Waters was . . . how gorgeous you looked in this white silk shirt and how much . . . I . . . wanted

... to ... do ... this." Her busy fingers flicked out the studs with amazing dexterity and she ran her hand inside, exploring his warm, furry chest, feeling his heartbeat accelerate furiously as she kissed and nipped where her hands had pulled the shirt open.

"Oh, Cassie, damn!" He bent down to catch her under the knees and lifted her in his arms, all thoughts fleeing his mind but making love. As he carried her from the study, he left the door ajar. They kissed fiercely while he climbed the carpeted stairs.

Clark Matthews skulked behind the open door, clinging weakly to the knob for support. He fought down the waves of dizziness and nausea that swept over him. Damn, he'd just puked up a seven-course dinner, probably his lunch and breakfast, too!

After the servant had undressed him and doused the light, he'd rolled over on the wide, soft bed and felt the world spin crazily. He never made it to the chamber pot. Rather than humiliate himself by letting the servants see the mess and report it to Cass, he'd cleaned it up himself. But all that exertion had brought on a fierce thirst, and he'd used up every drop of water in the pitcher scouring his filth from the floor. He'd been on his way to the kitchen for a drink when the angry voices of his cousin and her husband drew him to hide behind the closed doors to the study.

Steve awakened early the next morning, but Cass was not beside him. Since they had begun the trek to Fort Union well over a month earlier, they had slept together every night. He was growing accustomed to awakening each day with Cass

n his arms. Now for the past several days she
ad slipped from their bed early. When he would
ouse himself to search, he would find her drinking
'era's herbal tea and munching on toast in the
ining room.

"I wonder, Cassie, I wonder . . ." he muttered to
imself, his mind turning over the possibility that
he was pregnant. Morning indisposition might
xplain her sudden spate of early rising and the
dd diet she had been following the past weeks.
'ass used to hate tea and always ate a hearty
reakfast.

He pictured her naked body in his mind. Her
ace looked a little pinched and pale, but her
reasts were, if anything, fuller. She had been so
oncerned about the deadline in Rufus's will that
he had bitterly castigated him the first time her
ourses came after their marriage. But as he re-
iewed the last two months, he was almost certain
he had not had a recurrence. Surely Cass knew
vhat that meant. But then again, remembering
er innocence and fright on their wedding night,
erhaps she would not be certain. With Cass any-
ning was possible.

As he dressed, Steve debated confronting her.
ast night after she had become so emotional,
rying to him that she didn't want to see him
anged, he had started to ask her if there was
nything she wanted to tell him. At the time he
ad not been certain exactly what he expected her
o confess. That she wanted him to stay with her?
hat she loved me? He paused suddenly, his shirt
alf buttoned. God, did he expect her to admit she
oved him when all he did was tease and taunt her
bout how she had blackmailed him into mar-
.age?

The reciprocal question asked itself as he resumed buttoning his shirt with unsteady fingers. Did he love her? Would he stay with her and build a real marriage after his name was cleared and he was free to leave? From the start of the bargain, he had planned to assume full responsibility for the child, but what of Cass? She was his wife, and he desired her as he had never before desired a woman. She was perverse and domineering, openly manipulative, scarcely the kind of woman his mother would approve.

Steve chuckled at that. Lordy, was Cass Clayton ever the opposite of Marcia Coleman! He was glad of that contrast. He now realized that marriage with a coy, simpering bit of fluff like Marcia would have been pure hell. Of course, there were days when marriage to Cass had been pure hell, too, he considered wryly.

"I've given as good as I've gotten, I suppose," he muttered to himself, still ambivalent about his feelings for his wife. Whether she knew it or not, he strongly suspected she was pregnant. Just what that would mean for the continuation of the marriage was uncertain. But one thing was certain. If he expected Cass to express her true feelings for him, he would first have to express his for her. The only problem was that Steve honestly did not know what he felt!

"Soon, soon, Loring, you're going to have to decide because I have a feeling you're going to be a father in fairly short order," he whispered as he stood in the dining room doorway, looking at Cass's wan face as she concentrated on sipping Vera's herbal tea. She did not see him as he observed her. With shoulders slumped and fingers tightly clenched around the cup, she looked so frail and vulnerable it tore at him. Making a vow to think the whole thing through within a day or two, he ambled into the dining room.

"I see Vera's made a convert," he said, looking at her teacup

"Oh, it just seemed to sit better after all the wine last evening."

"Speaking of wine, I imagine your cousin is sleeping off one beaut of a hangover," he rejoined cheerfully.

"Oddly enough, no," Cass replied, putting down her cup with a puzzled expression on her face. "Vera said he was up and gone when she came down this morning. Probably embarrassed at making such a spectacle of himself last night. He left me a note saying he was leaving to begin the stock inventory. Maybe he was afraid you'd fire him," she added with the first hint of a smile tugging at her lips.

Steve shrugged. "I expected he'd be abed for at least a day, but I can't say I'm sorry to see him gone while there are still dishes in the house left unbroken."

Looking up from a ledger, Steve rubbed his eyes and shook his head to clear it. He'd spent two days going over the summer's records. Profits had been good. With the approach of winter, when the shipping rates into the snowfast mountains doubled, the money should virtually roll in.

"Ossie, have the seed grain shipments from the railhead been stored in the warehouse yet?"

The boy looked worried. "Don't rightly know, Mr. Loring. I can run down there and check. That's usually Mr. Quint's job, but what with him out

with that busted arm, I ain't—I'm not sure he finished the tally."

Steve smiled at the youth's thin, earnest face
with its generous splash of freckles and wide-set
hazel eyes. "Never mind, Ossie. I need the fresh
air to clear my head. I'll walk over and see. I meant
to check in on Bully in any case and see if he needs
anything. I wonder what the doctor said about the
recovery of his arm," he added absently as he
headed past the counter.

An hour later a very perplexed and uneasy Steve
walked into Dr. Elsner's office. He hesitated in the
crowded reception area, wondering whether he
wanted to know what John Elsner would tell him.

Bully Quint's broken arm was recovering nicely.
With it tightly splinted up, he had supervised the
unloading of an entire boxcar of seed grain. He
had also told Steve about meeting Cass in the doctor's office a week earlier.

A tight knot of fear began to form deep in Steve's
guts. Was she ill? Or if she was pregnant, was there
some problem about her carrying a child that she
was too afraid or too ashamed to share with him?

The doctor set his mind to rest about illness or
a problem pregnancy at once. Yes, Cass was definitely pregnant, and no, she was in no danger.
Her symptoms were temporary and quite normal.
If the kindly older man wondered why Cass had
chosen not to tell her husband about his impending fatherhood, he kept it to himself.

Thanking Elsner, Steve left the office with a
great deal to ponder. Why hadn't she told him?
Did she think confessing her condition would be
the final admission of what her father had led her
to believe was her natural female "weakness"?
That he would take advantage of her pregnancy

to wrest final and complete control of the business from her?

That she might fear he would simply collect his "stud fee" and walk away never entered his mind. Steve Loring would never desert his own child, and in knowing something so intrinsic about himself, he overlooked the obvious: Cass did not know that he felt that way.

They had never discussed their child's future, only the need to have a son to fulfill the conditions of the will. He had on more than one occasion worried about what kind of mother she would make. Would she love her son, or see him as a means to an end, consigned to nurses and governesses? Or, worse yet, if they had a daughter and lost the freight business, would she resent or neglect their child?

But the weeks had sped into months, and their stormy and embittered relationship had turned into one of grudging cooperation and mutual desire, if not one of avowed love. Knowing Cass as he did now, Steve found it difficult to believe that she would be a neglectful mother.

Why didn't she tell him of her pregnancy? Again, like a tongue worrying a sore tooth, his mind turned to her fears of him as the usurper, the man who was slowly taking over her hard-won empire. In subverting her men's loyalties and playing political games here in Denver, Steve had to admit he had given her reason to suspect the worst. He'd exacted some pretty cruel penalties from her for the forced marriage. And she had no inkling that he was wealthy and did not need her business.

"We've been playing games too long, Cass," Steve said as he walked into the storeroom behind the freight office. Before his resolution deserted him, he decided to face her and tell her everything about his background, that he planned to stay with her and their child, even, God help him, that he loved her!

It was after office hours, and Cass had sent Ossie home. She stood alone in the center of the storage room, an inventory list in one hand and a pencil in the other. Seeing him standing in the door, scowling at her, she felt a twinge of surprise and fear. Suddenly she remembered Ossie had mentioned that her husband had gone to talk to Bully Quint, who had seen her in John's office last week.

"Steve, I—" Before she could say anything more, he interrupted, stalking her as he had that first night at the Pueblo ranch house.

"You're pregnant, Cass," he said in a determined voice, "and you didn't tell me. Don't you think I'm a concerned party?"

She moistened her lips with her tongue, but her throat suddenly went dry. "I was going to tell you, Steve," she whispered.

"When, Cass?" He stopped in front of her and took the pencil and paper from her limp fingers, laying them on a nearby barrel.

She fought for breath when he cupped her shoulders with his long, strong fingers. "Soon, Steve, as soon as I..." Her voice trembled and she stopped, realizing that she wanted to say *as soon as I knew you loved me*.

"As soon as you had to—when your body betrayed you? When you couldn't hide the truth? Oh, Cassie, you're not the only one who's kept secrets." He put his arm around her shoulders and led her toward the back door, out into the cool fall air.

"What secrets, Steve?" she asked warily.

The evening was clear with the promise of a

starry night ahead. "I never told you about my family, where I—"

"You Steve Loring?" The tall, thin man wore a marshal's badge that glinted dully in the twilight. He stood at the end of the long wooden porch that backed the brick building and overlooked the corrals. The .44 caliber Remington in his hand was cocked and aimed dead center at Steve's belly as he walked steadily toward them.

"What if I am?" Steve replied easily, giving Cass a nudge toward the office door, out of the line of fire.

"I have a warrant for your arrest, Mr. Loring. You're wanted for murder by the Fort Smith bench. Just raise your hands and come along quietly."

Steve heard Cass gasp as his eyes pierced hers with a blazing glare. "Well, *Mrs*. Loring, I guess this answers my question, doesn't it? You had to keep me here until you were positive my job was done. Now you've set me up so I'd be disposed of all quiet and legal!"

"No! I didn't! I could never turn you over to the law. Oh, Steve, you must believe—"

"I was a fool to trust you! You love your empire—" he gestured around him with a furious chop of his arm "—too much to risk my taking over! Nothing else matters to you—me, our baby, nothing! Damn you to hell, you betraying, lying bitch!"

"I didn't send for him." She looked at the marshal, then back at Steve's furious face.

"Who the hell else knew about me? Who but you and Kyle and Blackie? They had nothing to gain, Cass. Only you did."

"Save it, Loring. You and your missus can argue

tomorrow. Now I have to lock you up for the night and wire Fort Smith that I have you in custody." He glanced behind Steve at the Denver police officer who had cautiously slipped up with his gun leveled at Steve.

"Marshal, this is all a terrible mistake. My husband is one of the most influential merchants in the city." Cass walked toward the lawman, getting between him and Steve, frantic in her entreaty.

Gently but firmly, the thin man shoved her aside, nodding to the policeman, "Get our horses."

Cass stood riveted to the porch floor, frantically looking around. If only she had her blacksnake! Steve was unarmed, too. Or was he? No gun was visible, but he had taken to carrying a .31 caliber pocket revolver in his jacket as a precaution against any more assassins. Did he have it now? The vision of her husband lying on the porch with his lifeblood pouring into the rough planks made her knees weak. Kyle would know just what to do, but he was long gone for the night, as were Chris and all the other men.

Cass watched Steve, hoping for a sign from him, but she knew that he mistrusted her too much to rely on her help. She would just have to chance it and act alone. She quietly followed the local officer, whom she knew was a quiet youth with little experience as a lawman. "Officer Cummings, you have to help me," she called out as she approached him at the bottom of the porch steps. He had one hand occupied untieing the horses from the rail when she appeared to slip and fall, colliding with him and knocking him to the ground.

Her plan was to wrest the gun from him and back off the marshal, but before she could do anything, Steve took advantage of the diversion.

When Cass had followed Cummings, the marshal kept his gun steady on Loring. But when she fell off the steps and knocked the boy down, his eyes wavered for a split second. Steve lunged at him, and the gun exploded as the two men went down. The marshal was a raw-boned, strong man who struggled mightily as Steve rolled on top of him, reaching with his left hand to get a hold on the lawman's wrist before he fired the lethal weapon at him point-blank. Steve's right hand moved lightning fast, grabbing a handful of long, shaggy hair and using it for leverage to pound the marshal's head against the bottom of the brick wall. As he slammed the lawman's head onto the masonry, he was rewarded with a sickening thunk. Steve wrenched the marshal's gun free and leaped up, looking toward Cass and the young policeman.

A bullet whined past his head and splintered into the brick behind him as he dove from the porch and took off in a run toward the nearest corral. It was full of half-broken mules, the ones that had accounted for Bully's injury.

"Better a broken arm than a broken neck," he muttered as he climbed the fence and dropped into the midst of the milling, restless animals. Cummings was close on his heels, firing several shots. Then Steve heard the marshal's voice as he, too, joined the chase. That man must have a skull denser than brick, Steve thought as he slipped the latch on the corral gate. As it creaked open, he started to yell and flail, stampeding the wild, frightened animals to freedom.

The two lawmen in the path of thirty onrushing mules dove for cover. At last he'd found the best use for mules, Steve thought with grim humor.

The herd fanned out in a cacophony of chaos, racing in circles, kicking at each other and any obstacle in their way. By the time the lawmen were able to work their way past the braying barricade to the front of the building, Steve had vanished.

Cass, bruised and sore from her tussle with the young officer, found the two men standing in the street in front of the office. The marshal was issuing orders in fast, furious sentences. The policeman, with a sullen angry glare her way, took off around the building to retrieve the horses. He returned a scant minute later to inform the marshal that their horses had been stampeded by the mules.

"I suppose you'd have no idea where your husband might be, Mrs. Loring?" the tall, angry man barked, seeing her standing in the front door of the freight office.

"None whatsoever, Marshal," she replied in a tear-thickened voice. She struggled to stop her trembling. Oh, God, had either of them shot Steve? Was he safe or bleeding to death in some back alley?

She knew he would never come to her for help. How could he think for an instant that she was capable of so monstrous a thing as betraying him? Yet, by not telling him that she was pregnant and not admitting that she wanted him to stay with her, Cass had sealed her fate. She was the only one in Denver, except for Kyle and Blackie, who knew he was wanted in Fort Smith. After her jealousy and anger when he had assumed control of the line, she knew how it must appear to him.

Her chest constricted with pain as she stood in

the doorway of the freight office, hugging her arms tightly around herself. Silent, acid tears ran down her face like a river. "Oh, please, please, God, let him live. He's innocent." Taking a deep breath, she began to run toward Kyle's hotel, heedless of the cold night air.

Chapter Fourteen

Laboring for breath, Steve crouched in the alleyway, the marshal's gun clutched in his left hand. His leg burned like a prairie fire where Cummings's bullet had grazed him. Thankfully it was just a flesh wound or he'd never have been able to make the circuitous run to Will's hotel, cutting across back streets and dodging the full-scale manhunt his pursuers had instigated. There seemed to be men with badges and guns on every corner, looking for Denver's freighting king, now a wanted murderer set to hang at Fort Smith.

Steve would have preferred going to Blackie Drago for help, knowing full well that the chief of the Denver underground would be far better equipped to hide him. But the Bucket of Blood was too distant to chance, while Will's hotel was nearby. Also, he had a suspicion that the law would be watching Blackie's place since he was known to be a frequent customer. It was also common knowledge that he and Will were business associates, but Steve gambled that the lawmen would never dream that General William Jackson Palmer might harbor a fugitive. The only person in Denver who knew they'd been childhood friends was Cass. That gave Steve pause, but he would have to chance it. Will was his only hope.

All his options were poor and growing worse with each passing hour. He had been hiding behind a rain barrel since dusk. It was nearly midnight. He must wait until the city slept, then sneak into the American House before dawn when the halls were devoid of guests and servants. Stealthily, he watched for his chance to slip in the delivery entrance, praying everyone was asleep.

Will Palmer was asleep also. When the bleary-eyed man opened the door, Steve hissed, "It took you long enough, damn! I was sure someone would've opened their door to complain about the noise at this hour." He limped inside the room and collapsed on the sofa.

After checking the corridor, Will Palmer closed the door. "Lucky for you my suite is isolated at the end of the hall, else that would probably have been the case. What the hell's happened?"

Steve winced as he eased his bloodstained leg away from the velvet sofa cushion. "I'm a wanted man, remember? My past has finally caught up to me—with a little help from my beloved wife," he said grimly. His mouth was a tight, angry slash set in a face grown pale from blood loss.

Will gaped in amazement at Steve's words. "I can't believe Cass would turn you over to the law. Why on earth?" As he asked the question, he walked quickly to an inlaid rosewood cabinet and poured a stiff shot of brandy.

Steve took the drink gratefully and downed it in a couple of swift swallows. Grimacing at the invigorating burn of the liquor, he answered. "Why? Because I've fulfilled my end of our bargain. She's pregnant, Will. She doesn't need me anymore—and obviously, in spite of what I know you're about to say, she doesn't want me around interfering in her business."

Will studied Steve's grimly set face and knew it was useless to argue. Still, now that he knew Cass Loring, he felt positive his friend was mistaken about her. "Why in heaven's name would she turn you over to the law and create a monumental scandal?"

Steve watched Will refill his glass as he replied, "Cass has always created scandals. You mentioned that very fact to me when you first heard I'd married her. No, Will. Alive I'd always be a threat. She knows about my agents back in the Nations. What if they clear me? Then, if I was the bastard she takes most men to be, I could really control her business. I guess she decided not to take that chance. No one else but Kyle, Blackie, and you know I'm wanted. Who stood to gain, Will?"

The raw anguish in Steve's quiet voice cut Palmer to the quick. Gone was the flint-eyed youth vowing vengeance for his cousin's murder. Steve had fallen in love with his wife and was eaten up by what he believed to be her treachery. For now, Will must see to his friend's safety. "You need a doctor. Then we'll have to get you out of Denver."

Managing a crooked grin that was part grimace, Steve said, "You know I had worse than this in the war. Hell, so did you. Just get me a bottle of whiskey and some linens to bind it up. I haven't got time for a doctor." Then a sudden thought occurred to him. "That federal marshal or any Denver law come around here asking for me earlier?"

"No. Do you think I'd have been sleeping if I knew half of the city was out gunning for you? Cass didn't betray you. What more proof do you need?"

Steve winced as he unwrapped the makeshift bandage from his leg. "She probably mentioned it, but you're too important a man to disturb at midnight. They'll be here come morning. Give me that bottle."

Will's face quirked in an unwilling grin as he replied, "I've doctored lots of gunshot wounds, remember? Hold still."

"I'll try not to bleed on your fancy upholstery," Steve replied with asperity, then swore when the burning surge hit his raw flesh.

As Will bandaged the long, ugly gash, they discussed how to get Steve out of Denver.

"I'll need Rebel. I know he'll be hard to steal from under Cass's nose, but he's the fastest thing in the territory."

"How do you propose to get the horse, then? I can smuggle you out of the city in my personal carriage. I have an idea for a safe hiding place, too, but that horse is simply too easily remembered, Steve."

"Blackie!" Steve exclaimed. "I bought Rebel from Blackie. He can steal him from under the nose of the entire Denver police force. Right now I need to get out of your room before you're sucked into this mess, Will. Can you get your carriage here in the middle of the night? With a change of clothes I can slip out the back and ride in the carriage to a prearranged place outside the city to meet Drago."

Steve quickly penned a note to Blackie, which Will asked his most trusted clerk to deliver.

"Just like old times. I owe you my life again," Steve said as his friend helped him into the Palmer carriage. The predawn streets were deserted and silent.

The two men clasped hands fiercely, each fearing it might be their last meeting. "You've saved my life a time or two, Captain, as I recall," Will answered gruffly. "I'll wire your uncle and inform him that the investigation in Sweetwater had better be expedited, lest the Loring family lose its scion. Have a safe journey to Abel Barlow's ranch. Just show him my note and he'll give you refuge. As soon as I get word from your uncle about the charges at Fort Smith, I'll be in touch. Take care, Steve."

Unlike Will Palmer, Kyle Hunnicut was wide awake when the pounding began on his hotel door. Being situated in a far less prestigious section of town, his hotel was not peopled by discreet residents. As Cass waited for the Texan to answer her knock, several speculative pairs of eyes fastened on the disheveled, hysterical woman.

"Kyle, a federal marshal came to the office and tried to arrest Steve!" she blurted breathlessly, collapsing in the room's lone chair.

Kneeling beside her, he asked, "How in hellfire did th' law ketch up ta him?"

She shook her head in misery. "I don't know, I don't know, but he thinks it was me."

"Thet's plumb loco! Whut happened? He git clear o' thet marshal?"

"I think so—oh, Kyle, I pray he did, but they shot at him as he ran. What if he was hit?"

She quickly described Steve's escape, ending with a sob. "He could be hidden somewhere alone, bleeding to death, thinking I betrayed him."

"Now, now, Cass, don't . . . don't." Kyle held her shaking shoulders awkwardly. He was always uncomfortable when a female cried, but now when that female was Cass, he was at a total loss. She had never cried once since he'd known her, and they'd been through many a hard time together.

"Oh, Kyle, I love him, even if he is mule-stubborn. I can't live if anything happens to him!" Her eyes were filled with crystalline tears as she clenched her fists and fought to control her outburst.

"Why in hell would he think yew'd put th' law on him?"

"I'm pregnant, Kyle. He doesn't think I need him anymore," she said softly.

"Wall then, stop talkin' crazy 'bout dyin' 'n all. We'll git him safe, but yew got his baby ta think o'. I bet he'll go ta Blackie fer help. He afoot?"

"Rebel was tied out front of the office. He wouldn't let the marshal ride him, but they took him with them so Steve couldn't get to him."

"I'll go ta Blackie's place. Thet feller knows ever' time a gnat pisses in Denver. He'll find Steve, don't fret yerself, Cass." He started to pull on his boots.

"I'm going with you, Kyle."

"Now, thet purely ain't smart, Cass. Them badges'll be watchin' yew. Best ta go back ta th' house 'n wait there. I'm used ta workin' outside th' law. Yew ain't," he added with a reassuring grin that he was far from feeling. Who had found out about Loring's past? Grimly he remembered the attempts on Steve's and Cass's lives at Fort Union as well as the near miss with the brush fire. Could Ames have somehow stumbled onto their desperate secret and be using it to get rid of at least one competitor, after his previous attempts to kill them both had failed?

After hiring a hack to take Cass home, Kyle rode quickly to the Bucket of Blood. He and Drago would find some answers sure as he was born in Texas.

When he reached the saloon, Kyle was met with blank looks and evasions about Blackie Drago. Finally, a Colt pressed savagely into the throat of Gus the bartender got him the information he needed. Drago was headed to a rendezvous with some mysterious person. On pain of death the big bartender swore that he didn't know who or where.

Putting the pieces together, Kyle knew the rendezvous had somehow been arranged between the saloon owner and Steve. All he could do now was wait until Blackie returned and then persuade him one way or the other to divulge where Steve was hidden. Kyle Hunnicut was a very persuasive man.

In spite of his throbbing leg, Steve was glad to be free of the carriage and mounted on Rebel. At least he stood a chance of outdistancing any pursuers on the big gray. The sun was well over the eastern horizon now, sending its hot golden light to dispel the darkness. He was glad of the dry, trackless weather as he headed south toward the isolated Barlow ranch near the Arizona border. By late afternoon he rode into rain, but forced himself to consider how unlikely it was that anyone could pick up his trail this far from Denver.

With every mile he traveled, Steve felt the pain in his heart growing. How could she have done it after all the months they'd spent together? The loving they'd shared? The child they'd created? He could still see Blackie's grim face, hard and unbelieving, when Steve told him what had happened.

Will was chivalrous and visionary, but Steve had expected the shrewd old Irishman to understand Cass's motives and face the truth. He concluded that beneath the facade of a machine politician lay the heart of an incurable romantic. Then Steve recalled Blackie's distant love of Cass's mother. He swore aloud. What was it about the Clayton women that led men to act so blindly?

"Hell, I'm as big a fool as either of them. After the way we began, I should've known the real Cass Clayton!" He rode south, intent on banishing the dream of a new life in Colorado. That was dead now, as dead as the love between him and his wife.

Taking a less traveled route and hiding from other riders made the journey stretch longer than it should have. He half expected to see Kyle at his back each night when he fell into a feverish, exhausted sleep. Although Blackie didn't know his destination, Will did, and both the fools believed in Cass. But Hunnicut did not come.

On the fourth day he reached the Purgatoire River. His eyes scanned the vast, rolling grasslands to the southeast where Abel Barlow's cattle empire stretched. Patting the introductory letter from Will in his vest pocket, Steve kneed Rebel into an easy lope along the riverbank. By noon he should reach his haven. The law could never find him in this lonely wilderness.

"Rider comin', Mr. Abel," a banty-legged young wrangler called out. "No one I ever seen afore."

Abel Barlow observed the tall, heavily armed man mounted on a superb gray stallion. His face was grizzled with several days' beard, and his eyes glinted with a hard, dangerous light. Yet he did not have the look of a gunman or drifter about him. Barlow waited while the stranger dismounted, noting the way he favored his right leg.

"Afternoon," Steve said evenly. "I'm looking for Abel Barlow."

"You've found him. What do you want?" Barlow stood several feet away, hands hooked casually in his belt. Several young cowhands wearing guns hovered nearby.

Something about Barlow's stance and his strange grayish eyes seemed vaguely familiar to Steve. A sense of foreboding prickled up his neck, but he dismissed it, certain he had never before laid eyes on Will's wealthy backer for the Denver and Rio Grande. Keeping an eye on the hired help, he reached carefully into his vest pocket and handed Barlow the note from Will.

Abel Barlow read it, recognizing General Palmer's handwriting. Long a poker player, his hand never wavered as he held the paper. Looking at Loring with a carefully schooled expression of welcome on his face, Barlow said, "You're welcome to the hospitality of the Double B for as long as you need to stay, son."

Late that night Abel Barlow dispatched a rider for Denver. As the hoofbeats thudded dully into the distance, Abel marveled at the luck that had brought his son's nemesis to him. "Whoever in hell would've imagined that damn bluebelly captain would end up on a wanted poster?" he chuckled to himself. The hunter had become the hunted.

Of course, wanting to remain in General Palmer's good graces, Barlow could scarcely have Loring killed on the Double B. But if the law tracked him here from Denver and arrested him, well, Will Palmer surely couldn't fault Abel Barlow. It should take no more than three days after the wire reached his contacts in Denver for the federal marshal to arrive.

Vince wasn't due back from the cattle drive to Fort Lyon for at least a week. If the captain had seen his son, shooting would've been inevitable and the resulting questions very difficult to answer, regardless of who emerged the victor. No, it was much neater this way. He had cursed the bungled attempt by Vince's amateurish hirelings at Fort Union. Now, without him or his son turning a hand, Loring would be disposed of legally. Abel settled in to play the role of genial host for the next couple of days.

Kyle Hunnicut was saddle sore. He'd ridden for two days and still had not caught up with Steve. He cursed Blackie Drago's tardiness in returning to the Bucket of Blood, and then the time it took to convince the Irishman that he was on Steve's side.

Blackie finally agreed to take him to the stand of alders south of town where he had met Steve that daybreak. Drago had "liberated" Rebel from the law and had brought along weapons, clothes, money, and other necessities supplied by Will Palmer.

Drago did not know Loring's destination, but Hunnicut's boast about tracking fly sign over cracked pepper was not an idle one. The muddy trail helped too. By the time the rain stopped, he had found a woman at a small way station who remembered a wounded stranger on a gray stallion. Now he was nearing the Purgatoire. If no one in Trinidad had seen Steve, he'd make a sweep of the neighboring spreads, beginning with the largest.

Something niggled in the back of his mind about Will Palmer having a backer for his railroad from the southeast—some big cattle baron. No name came to mind, but if he heard it, Kyle knew his memory would take hold. He was patient and he was relentless.

The next day his quest was rewarded when the name of Abel Barlow came up in a Trinidad saloon. Directions to the Double B were easy to obtain, and Kyle was off. It was simply too much of a coincidence to follow Steve's trail this far south, so close to one of Will Palmer's business associates, for there not to be a connection.

Vince Barlow rode up to the corral at the Double B, tired and dispirited. How was he going to tell pa? Two hundred head of cattle lost on the turn of a card. He'd only gone into Mesa Verde that first night for a little fun. How was he to know he'd get suckered into a poker game by some slick sharpie with two gunmen backing him?

What was done was done. The beef contract with the army was piddling anyway. The Fort Lyon shipment could be made up easily next week. Still, he knew his father would be furious, just as he'd been furious when Loring had escaped Vince's killers at Fort Union. He'd have to consider how to handle that problem, too. Damn, life had become complicated in the past five years!

Steve watched the man ride in, greeted familiarly by the hands at the corral. Again, that same eerie instinct he'd had about Abel hit him, as if he *knew* a total stranger. He could not see the man's face, but there was something about the walk, the way he carried the Henry rifle in his hand.

A .44 caliber rimfire! Vince Tanner's expensive rifle! It was he. Abel Barlow was some sort of kin—and here he was, sitting in a nest of rattlesnakes. Casually he slid from the shadows of the porch and slipped inside, heading for his room.

Barlow had made no attempt to disarm him, but then Steve's own natural wariness and some subliminal mistrust about the rancher had led him to act with extreme caution in spite of Will's assurances and Abel's apparent hospitality. He wanted his rifle and Rebel, knowing he'd have to fight his way off Double B land—he laughed— Double B for two Barlows, of course! Tanner must have been a phony name Vince had assumed during the war.

Steve checked his weapons, while his mind furiously improvised a plan. Abel was at a roundup camp that morning and would likely not be back for several hours. Time enough for Steve to confront his long-sought enemy and ride off. Of course, he had no way of knowing what Abel had told the rest of his hands about his visitor.

The housekeeper seemed friendly, and the men at the bunkhouse were the usual collection of cowhands, a motley assortment of slick-eared boys, stoved-up old wranglers, and a smattering of hard cases. Lord, he was beginning to think like Kyle Hunnicut! Right now he could use the Texas gunman's backing. "Hell, he'd likely join them and shoot me," he muttered as he slung a cartridge belt over his shoulder and checked the action on his rifle again.

The front door slammed and Steve heard footsteps walking toward the parlor. Had the men at the corral told Vince that Abel had a visitor, or even cautioned him about who the visitor was? Not knowing, Steve decided to take no chances. He moved stealthily to the window at the front of the upstairs hall. As far as he could tell, the hands were going about their chores as if nothing out of the ordinary had happened.

The big ranch house had only one set of stairs. Deciding he might be a sitting duck if he used the long, narrow corridor, Steve quietly walked to the back end of the hall and slid the window open. He climbed out and inched his way down the steeply slanting roof to a trellis attached to the side of the house. By the time he reached the bottom of the rickety ladder, his clothes were torn and his hands full of abrasions from rose thorns. But at least no one had seen him.

Steve entered the kitchen soundlessly and stopped to listen. The fat housekeeper, Marabelle, was out in the orchard picking apples for tonight's dinner. When he heard the clink of glass and then the splash of a drink being poured, he knew it was young Vince. Smiling evilly, Steve glided through the dining room and stopped in the doorway to the parlor. The Henry rifle was standing carelessly in the corner by the arched front door, well out of reach.

Strangely, the rush of icy rage that he'd felt when he confronted O'Brien and Wortman did not come as he watched the unshaven, dirty young man upend his glass, then reach for a refill. Suddenly Steve realized that his need for revenge was gone. He was tired of the hunt and the killing. Still, seeing the Colt strapped to Vince Tanner's hip, he knew he had to deal with him if he did not want to live the rest of his life with the threat of assassination hanging over his head.

"Hello, Sergeant Tanner, or is it Barlow now?" he asked, his rifle leveled on Tanner.

Vince Barlow dropped his glass, choking as he whirled on Loring. "You! How the hell did you find me?"

"Stupid luck—as stupid as those men you sent after me at Union?" Steve asked conversationally, his eyes never leaving Barlow's gunhand.

Barlow twitched but admitted nothing. "Where's Pa? What'd you do with him?"

"Oh, he's been entertaining me royally the past couple of days, waiting for the marshal from Denver to collect me, I expect," Steve replied drily, realizing that Vince Barlow knew nothing about his being wanted by the law. "Your father's off checking on a roundup crew, but before he returns—"

"Too late, Loring. I'm back," Abel interrupted. The unmistakable click of a gun being cocked echoed in the quiet room. "My Winchester is aimed at your back. I'd hate to put a hole in you and cheat the hangman. Drop your gun." Steve did as he was ordered, his mind racing furiously. "Now move forward," Abel commanded.

Steve realized he had only one chance, a lousy

one at that. He had to maneuver the old man between himself and the son. But first he had to get Abel to press the muzzle of that Winchester against his back.

"I told you to move all the way into the room, Loring," the man behind him growled.

Steve did not move.

"Move, goddamit!" Abel jammed the rifle barrel into Steve's back. Feeling the pressure against his spine, Loring stepped forward on his right foot, but no sooner had it touched the floor than he pivoted, twisting his body so that his left side was turned suddenly to the man who had been prodding him. The fluid move caused the rifle barrel to slide along the flat of his back as Barlow pulled the trigger.

Inside the room, the shot seemed as deafening as a dynamite blast. The slug thudded harmlessly into the opposite wall, but the muzzle blast felt like a torch against Steve's back. Ignoring the searing pain, he grabbed the older man in a bear hug, spinning him around to form a shield in front of him.

Startled by Steve's blurring attack, Vince was slow in freeing his pistol from its holster. He fired, but the bullet meant to rid him of his hated enemy smashed into his father instead. Steve staggered back as Abel's lifeless body was propelled into him. For a moment the room was still. Pinned against the wall, Steve clutched Abel's limp form as the rifle slipped from the dead man's fingers. Vince stared in disbelief at the widening red stain centered precisely between his father's shoulder blades.

Kyle had approached the ranch house from the rear. Now, as he moved stealthily into the kitchen, he mulled over what he would say to Steve. "Damn," he muttered to himself, "whut a pickle! A feller on th' run's bound ta be a mite spooky. Don't want to have him let daylight through me 'fore—" His ruminations were shattered by the sound of two gunshots in the next room. For a fraction of a second, the Texan froze, then pulled his Colt and slipped into the dining room.

Instantly the little gunman read the scene before him. When Vince stared at the intruder, Kyle recognized the unreasoning animal terror in his eyes. He would have to kill this one.

Young Barlow never even got off a shot. Kyle's slug hit him squarely in the chest, tumbling him backward until his legs seemed to dissolve beneath him. Vince Tanner Barlow was dead before he hit the floor.

"Damn fool. He thet Copperhead yew been chasin all this time?"

"Yeah, Kyle. He was the one," Steve replied wearily, letting Abel's body fall to the floor.

"They're daid," Kyle pronounced with the assurance of a mortician. "We got us another problem, though. We gotta git—pronto!"

They left the ranch house by the back door and cut through the orchard, then doubled back toward the stable. Responding to the shots, the housekeeper, apron laden with apples, dashed past them as they hid in a thicket. Kyle retrieved his buckskin, which he'd left tied in the trees near the creek. By the time Steve had slipped into the stable and led Rebel out, they could hear Marabelle screaming and several men yelling. They rode at breakneck speed, but after about twenty minutes, it seemed apparent no one was giving chase.

Steve reined in, getting his bearings. As Kyle followed suit, they sat looking at each other for a moment.

"What now, bluebelly?" the Texan asked, uncertain of just what to do about Loring.

"You can get clear of shooting Vince Barlow. Will Palmer can identify him as a deserter and Copperhead spy. With his influence, you'll be fine. Just get back to Denver and have Will handle it before he leaves for his wedding in New York."

"An' whut er yew gonna do?"

"You know I'll hang if I go back, Kyle. Did she send you to bring me in?" Obviously the Texan did not intend to kill him.

"Never fixed on seein' yew hang, Steve. Cass come ta me th' night she helped yew git free o' thet marshal—"

"Helped me!" Steve interrupted furiously. "She sent for him with his warrant, and that damn kid shot me, thanks to her."

"Yore wrong, Loring. She tried ta git his gun so's yew cud git free o' th' marshal."

"I don't buy it, Kyle. Did she tell you my part of our bargain's been fulfilled? She doesn't need me anymore. Now I'm a liability."

Kyle swore as he looked into the intent golden eyes narrowed on him. "Ain't gonna do me no good ta tell yew she sent me ta see if'n yew wuz hurt, ta help yew get clear o' Denver?"

"Will Palmer and Blackie Drago already saw to that, but I owe you for saving my life at Barlow's ranch. Now I have to go back to Sweetwater and try to clear my name, Kyle. This won't end until I do."

"Whut then, if'n yew do git shut o' th' law? Cass loves yew, 'n I got me a feelin' yew love her. Yew got a youngun' a comin' in th' spring, too." He waited, watching the pain in Loring's carefully set face.

"I don't know, Kyle. Everyone defends her, but I can't believe she didn't wire that marshal. I need some time after I'm through dodging the law. As to the baby—" he paused and his voice took on a rough edge of emotion—"you take care of Cass until it's born. I'll be back after that to settle things between us . . . if I can."

Kyle nodded. It was the best he could do for the present. "Watch your backside in th' Nations. Yew ain't the greenhorn yew wuz last spring, but don't go gettin' cocky neither. Yew bluebellies mighta won th' war back East, but this here's a whole new game o' cards."

Steve managed a grim smile. "I'll remember that, Kyle. Thanks." He turned the big gray and headed southeast.

Kyle watched the lone rider vanish over the horizon, then rode north, wondering if Cass would ever see her husband again.

Chapter Fifteen

Graham Hall
January 1871

Steve folded the telegram and held it in his hands. Freedom. Final, irrevocable freedom after all the months of waiting. He walked around the corral, watching Rebel with his harem of mares. The big gray snorted and a cloud of frosty air came from his nostrils. The chill winter weather made the stallion want to run more after being confined in the stable.

"I know how you feel, old boy," Steve murmured softly as his fingers creased and recreased the telegram unconsciously. He headed to the tack room for his saddle. It was a good brisk day for riding and thinking.

Technically he'd been a free man since last October, but the wire he just received assured him that his agents had retrieved all the wanted posters and spread the word among the lawmen and bounty hunters in the far-flung Oklahoma Territory that he had been exonerated.

When he'd arrived at Sweetwater, the town newspaper was already circulating word that Bessie Lannaman, the paramour of the man he'd killed, had been found by some Eastern detectives. Bessie confessed her part in the scheme to rob and murder the rich dude.

Steve had wired his Uncle Lucas at once. The elder Loring was much relieved that his fugitive nephew had finally surfaced. After Will had contacted Lucas last September, telling him Steve was headed to south Colorado, young Loring seemed to drop off the face of the earth. When the truth about Tanner being Abel Barlow's son had been revealed, Will and Lucas had both feared that Steve would go so far into hiding that they would never be able to find him, even after their agents cleared him of the charges in Sweetwater.

While the Fort Smith court attempted to rectify the miscarriage of justice, Steve quietly rode east, back to Graham Hall. He spent the early months of winter waiting restlessly for word that he was indeed completely safe from the erratic arms of the law.

He told his mother nothing of what had tranpired during his long absence. Overjoyed that her only son was at last returned to her, Amelia had questioned him little once he angrily told her that his life as a wanted man had not been pleasant. She desisted, biding her time, greatly relieved that his wartime vendetta was now over.

Steve, too, was happy to have the weight of his oath of vengeance lifted from his shoulders. Vince

Tanner was dead. "No more ghosts from the war," he said aloud as he cantered Rebel across the frosty grass. Will would soon be docking in New York after his extended tour of Europe. While honeymooning, Will had gathered more funding for the Denver and Rio Grande. Steve knew that his friend would head for the Rockies come spring. Will's crews had already begun grading for the rails south to his utopia, Colorado Springs.

Cass's freight wagons were supplying the work crews. With every passing month his thoughts turned more often to his wife. He was free now to return to the Rockies with Will Palmer. But unlike Will, Steve had no loving wife to stand beside him. His face twisted with anguish as he remembered the circumstances of his parting with Cass. She had betrayed him, set him up to hang.

Will, Blackie, and Kyle had all protested her innocence, but no one had seen Cass's inner demons the way he had. *None of them love her the way I do*. He cursed himself for using the present tense. He could not love her still, not after what she had done. But with every passing month the time of her delivery drew nearer. Would he return—take their child from her? Did he want to confront her again and risk revealing how much her deception had hurt?

"I could probably send an attorney with a nurse, and she'd gladly give over the baby after she's met the conditions of Rufus's will," he said bitterly. But some deeply buried, utterly perverse part of him refused to believe what his rational mind accepted as the truth—that Cass was guilty.

Steve had spent the fall trying to resume his old life as a gentleman horse breeder. Graham Hall flourished. His business manager and capable staf.

had run the place well in his absence, requiring only the most cursory oversight. At first he had thrown himself back into the work, putting his new prize gray to stud with a number of his best fillies. The spring would bring Rebel's first foals.

"My life is settled and prosperous," he said as if to reaffirm the conviction. But the parallel between Rebel's impending fatherhood and his own was a painful reminder. April hung like a promise, waiting for his decision.

"Miz Amelia, he's just had a little too much to drink," the maid whispered, twisting her hands in frustration as she watched her husband, one of Steve's grooms, guide their weaving employer up the stairs to bed.

Amelia Loring stood at the top of the wide, curving fan of steps, clenching her satin robe lapels with whitened fists as she watched Hal Pryor haul her son to bed.

"It's that disgraceful hussy from Denver who's the cause of this," she whispered tightly, not aware that Anne overheard her.

For months Steve had drunk, gambled, and in general led a wastrel's life. It was almost April now and the spring foaling was about to begin. He had far more important things to occupy his time than consorting with that woman. Amelia vowed to have a long talk with Steve in the morning. He must have a suitable wife. She had paid a social call on the Colemans last week. Marcia still was not married, although several of the most eligible bachelors from Louisville pursued her.

The next morning after a breakfast of dry toast and a gallon of unsweetened strong tea, Steve was on his way to the stables hoping to avoid his late-rising mother. After the debacle last evening, he did not need another lecture. His skull already throbbed enough.

A couple of hours of riding helped clear his head and settle his stomach. By noon Steve felt almost human as he reined in the big gray on the rise overlooking Graham Hall. Lush green grass covered the open meadows and swelling hills like a thick, soft carpet patterned with precise white fences and tall clusters of oaks. The three-story house gleamed in the sunlight, fronted by wide Doric columns and a double-tiered porch. Manicured shrubbery and swaying willow trees added to the fairytale aura.

Perfect symmetry, beauty, tranquility. He had always felt Graham Hall was his birthright, far more so than the stone mansion in Philadelphia. Now neither place held his heart. He was bored and restless, drawn inexorably to the very untranquil, asymmetrical beauty of the Rockies.

His musings were cut short as the sound of hoofbeats echoed on the soft, muddy trail behind him.

"So deep a frown, darling. Don't tell me you still have that dreadful hangover? But then you did tie one on last night. I thought I'd find you out riding it off." Selina Ames gave a low, wicked chuckle as she reined in beside him. The sunlight bounced off her gleaming ebony curls as she tossed them carelessly back. Dressed in a deep rose riding habit, she did look alluring.

After swinging effortlessly off Rebel, Steve helped her dismount from the stupid sidesaddle. Odd, how his opinions on so many things had been altered during the time he'd spent in Colorado. Once, the idea of a woman astride a horse would have appalled him. Now it seemed the only sensible way to ride. But in genteel Louisville, ladies always used sidesaddles, and Selina was playing her role to the hilt.

Last November she had taken Louisville by storm, an elegant belle from Denver by way of New York. Steve knew she had plied Will and Queen Palmer with questions about him when she had met them in New York. There was no other reason for her to have detoured through Kentucky on her way home. She had broken her engagement to Gordon Fisk, a prominent New York banker she'd met in Denver last year.

Mirthlessly he realized how his transformation from impoverished outlaw to wealthy landowner had influenced her decision to dump her paunchy middle-aged suitor and pursue him instead. Unwisely perhaps, he'd dallied with her over the tedious winter months, more to infuriate Amelia than anything else. That the affair was also a slap at his wife he never consciously considered.

He removed his hands slowly from her waist, but she did not take her arms from his shoulders. Rather she pulled him closer and nuzzled his neck where his shirt collar lay open. "You smell good, darling," she murmured.

Steve snorted in derision. "I smell like horse and sweat and the leftover bourbon whiskey that's finally worked itself through my pores."

"I don't mind . . . at all," she whispered, tightening her embrace.

Carefully Steve removed her arms and turned away, staring down at Graham Hall. "Well, I mind."

"You're drowning your pain in whiskey, Steve, hiding from the truth. Why don't you face it? Divorce her," she said with flat finality.

He whipped his head around and stared at her. "Don't presume, Selina, that just because we've slept together you can tell me how to run my life," he said in a clipped, cold accent.

Her large dark eyes became lustrous with tears. "That's cruel, Steve. I don't want you to destroy yourself over a woman who tried to kill you. She doesn't love you. I do!" She turned and dabbed a lacy kerchief at her eyes.

Steve walked over to her and cupped her shaking shoulders in his hands. "It was a rotten thing to say. I apologize, Selina." He paused and then admitted, "You are right about my behavior. I've been drowning myself in self-pity. I've had nothing to do here—not really. The hall runs itself. My stockmen handle the breeding and sales. Lord knows my mother rules the household with her steel-in-velvet touch."

He laughed softly as he thought of Amelia, then began to pace, running his fingers through his hair. "I have to go back to Colorado and face Cass. Not for the sake of the marriage—it was doomed from the start—but for my child. Cass wants her empire, not the encumbrance of a baby," he said bitterly.

Selina watched his agitated, angry gestures through narrowed eyes. *He still loves her.* "She's an unnatural woman. Everyone in Denver always said so. You can arrange a divorce easily, Steve— and get custody of your child," she added quickly, then paused. "How will you raise it—I mean, if you have a daughter—or even if it's a son, a child needs a mother."

"You sound like my mother, Selina, and believe me, that is no compliment!" he said with a grim slash of a smile.

"You've told her about your marriage? About the baby?" she asked in amazement.

"No, of course not. I just meant you're pushing me toward a matrimonial net I want to avoid at all costs now."

"Just because Cass was a poor wife doesn't mean all women are like her," she said placatingly.

He barked a harsh laugh. "That is one masterpiece of understatement, Selina. No woman on earth is like Cass Clayton. But I'll give her one thing. She was direct and to the point, no pouting or crying and wheedling to get what she wanted."

"Is that what you think I'm doing—wheedling you into marriage?" she asked, a hot tinge of anger flushing her cheeks.

"Save the indignation, Selina. I never led you on when we began this thing. You knew I was married," he said with weary resignation. It had to end, but damn if he liked having it unravel in so ugly a fashion.

"Yes, you were married—to a woman who doesn't want you or your child!" she lashed back. "What are you going to do after you reclaim the baby—bring it to your dear mama to raise?"

His eyes narrowed to golden slits. "Hardly. But my plans for my child, whatever they are, don't include a marriage to give him a mother."

Selina's features calmed and a smile bowed up the corners of her full lips. "So it would seem we're both bound for Colorado, Steve. Pity it's to be on separate trains. I'll see you in Denver, darling. Who knows, maybe by the time I arrive my brother will have run Loring Freighting out of business," she added spitefully.

* * *

As he seated himself across the dining room table from his mother, Steve knew she had something to spring on him. Smiling inwardly, he thought of the surprise he had in store for her. Over the months since he'd returned from Colorado, Amelia had pursued her goal with single-minded devotion, trying every tack imaginable to throw him and Marcia Coleman together again. As he ruminated about his return to Denver, he sipped from his wineglass, not really tasting the excellent claret.

"I ran into Priscilla Coleman yesterday at the dressmakers. She and Marcia were being fitted for the most exquisite ball gowns. Marcia's was of a deep turquoise shade that matched her lovely eyes. Her mother's—"

"Please spare me a recitation about the Coleman women's taste in clothes, Mother," Steve interrupted dryly.

"Don't be rude, Steven. What I was attempting to say is that Beau Snodgrass was to be Marcia's escort, but it seems he's taken a fall from a horse and broken his leg. Poor Marcia is without an escort for the Tremonts' spring gala. You simply must ask her."

Carefully swallowing a chunk of roast lamb, Steve paused and then looked at his mother in resignation. "You never give up, do you? I have no intention of squiring Marcia to the Tremonts ball," he said flatly.

"I suppose you plan to escort that Ames hussy just to spite me," Amelia said with a voice threatening tears.

He wiped at his mouth with a linen napkin after taking a generous drink of claret. "As a matter of fact, your dislike of Selina has rather tended t

goad me into seeing her. You might take a lesson
from that and back away from your machinations
with the Colemans. I'm not going to marry Marcia."

She stood up abruptly, all thoughts of the lavish
meal before her forgotten. "I suppose you'd marry
that Denver slattern who jilted her fiancé in New
York and then came to Louisville quite improperly
chaperoned! Why, the rumors I've heard about
her—"

Steve interrupted her with a sharp laugh. "Believe me, madam, when I assure you that what
you've heard in Louisville about Selina Ames isn't
the half of it! You should meet her brother. A nice
pair of vipers they make."

She put her elegant white fingers to her throat
with one hand and clutched the chair with the
other. "You plan to marry a woman like that?"

"No, I do not. Nor do I plan to marry Marcia.
You see, Mother, I am already married." He
paused for effect and then reached over and assisted her back into her seat. "Do sit down. We
have a few matters to discuss."

For once in her self-controlled life Amelia Loring
was speechless. "Married? But...but who?
Where?"

Steve told her. He also told her his plans for the
future.

*Pueblo, Colorado
April 1871*

The weather was unseasonably warm for early
spring. But for weeks Cass had been so plagued
by fevers and wracked with misery that she

scarcely noticed. Holding on to the rail for support, she eased herself along the porch in search of a breeze, then sank down onto a big chair in a shady corner near the morning glory vines.

Getting up and down from furniture had become a real problem in the latter stages of her pregnancy. She had become so large and swollen that any movement was difficult. Remembering Eileen's troubled pregnancies, Cass feared for her unborn baby. Never had she dreamed that carrying a child would make her frail and ill like her mother.

For the first six or seven months she had been fine, as strong and resilient as ever in spite of the gradual weight gain, but toward spring her stomach had again become queasy. She had anticipated lower back aches as her pregnancy advanced, but not the blinding headaches that had virtually incapacitated her of late.

She sat on the porch rubbing her abdomen unconsciously in a protective gesture. With her eyes closed, she laid her head against the back of the chair.

"Here, missus, I brung you a cold cloth for tha headache," Bettie said as she bustled across the creaking porch floor. "There, that feel better?" she asked as she placed a wet compress to Cass's fore head.

"Mmm, yes, thank you, Bettie. I don't know what I'd do without you," Cass replied honestly

Bettie Wade's thin, homely face split in a gap toothed grin. The young serving girl had come t Cass's city house in Denver last fall. The tearft maid had just been dismissed in a fit of pique b Selina Ames. Her mistress left for the East to mee her fiancé without giving a thought to how Bett would survive without references. When Cass took her in, the girl was slavishly grateful.

"It was such a good idea comin' down here to the ranch. Nothin' like fresh air after all that city smell," Bettie said, patting Cass's wrist solicitously.

Removing the compress from her pounding head, Cass said quietly, "What you mean, Bettie, is that the isolation of Pueblo was better for me than spending the holidays in Denver. With Steve gone, I scarcely felt up to Christmas balls and callers on New Year's Day."

"Now, don't you go takin' on about *him* again," Bettie scolded. Shortly after joining the household staff in Denver, Bettie had made it clear that any man who would desert a wife like Cass was beneath contempt. "Is that young rascal kickin'?" she asked as Cass's hand flew to her left side suddenly.

"Yes, he is!" For a moment, Cass's eyes glowed like sunlight on amber, giving animation and color to her pale, drawn features, but then the look of joy faded as the headache bore down again. "I've been so worried about the baby lately, Bettie. For months he was so active, but since this nausea and the headaches began, I scarcely feel him move anymore. Maybe I should start for Denver tomorrow and have Dr. Elsner check me," Cass said uncertainly.

"Nonsense! What can a man—a foreigner like him anyways—do for you that a good midwife can't?" Bettie said dismissively.

"I promised John I'd come back before the baby is due. I want him to deliver my child, Bettie. He is the best doctor in the territory even if he is a man," she said, trying desperately for a humorous tone in her voice.

"You got weeks yet. First babies is always late. Just you rest and I'll bring you some of my special herbal tea for that headache," the maid said soothingly.

Cass settled back in her chair. Never in her life had she felt so utterly spent and incapable of making decisions. "Maybe it's a good thing Steve left me," she whispered without conviction, thinking she might be as ill-suited to bearing children as her mother had been. Tears welled up in her eyes as she remembered their bitter parting and Kyle's disheartening report to her when he returned from the Barlow ranch. At least the baby would be a small part of her love to keep and cherish. If only it was healthy and strong, she no longer cared if it was a boy or a girl. Damn Rufus and the business. All it had brought her was heartache.

At that low moment, Kyle Hunnicut came striding across the yard. Seeing the tear stains on Cass's wan face, he hopped up the steps and knelt beside her chair. Awkwardly he took her hand and patted it saying, "Now, Cass, don't take on so. Yew feelin' poorly agin? I been fixin' ta talk ta yew 'bout headin' ta Denver. Thet doc feller might cud help—"

"She don't need no doctor," Bettie interrupted vehemently with a murderous glance at the little Texan. Shooing him away from Cass, she offered the tea. "You just drink this and then have a good, long nap."

Ever since she'd come to work for Cass, Bettie and Kyle had been antagonists. The tall, gaunt woman particularly disliked the way the Texan drew Cass into discussions of the freight business.

She tried at every juncture to keep him away from her mistress. At first Cass had been amused by Bettie Wade's protective jealousy, but when it became apparent that Kyle was mistrustful of the girl, she became genuinely upset over the situation. Now, like everything else, the matter had slipped from her control during the past weeks of fatigue and illness.

Cass looked up at Kyle as Bettie helped her rise. "Maybe tomorrow, Kyle," she answered faintly. "Maybe I should go to see Dr. Elsner. I wanted to feel stronger before making the trip back to Denver, but now . . ." She shrugged in resignation.

"You just rest and forget about Denver. Bouncin' that baby around in a wagon—the idea's crazy," Bettie said, giving Kyle a look that dared him to refute her logic as she helped Cass toward the door.

"I gotta check some things in th' city, Cass. Reckon yew'll be all right if'n I'm gone fer a day er so?" he asked quietly, ignoring Bettie.

"Yes, Kyle. Just keep an eye on Bennett Ames for me. I'll manage here." Cass paused and turned to add, "Oh, Clark stopped by last week on his way to the San Luis road station. How's he working out, Kyle? He seems to be trying hard enough."

Kyle scratched his head. "Wal, we ain't had no thievin' down thataways fer a while. Whut's Chris say 'bout him? It's purely his job o' work ta keep tally on th' stock."

Cass looked perplexed. "Chris dislikes him almost as much as—" She broke off abruptly, but the Texan knew she had meant to say "as much as Steve did."

"Enough of this business talk. Can't you see you're upsettin' the missus?" Bettie asked crossly.

"Take keer o' yerself, Cass. I'll be back quicker 'n a muleskinner kin bust open a barrel o' tangle laig."

The pain was excruciating, roaring down on her as she twisted the wet sheets in her clenched fingers. All the bedclothes were drenched with her own perspiration. "Water, Bettie, give me water," she cried between the contractions that robbed her of breath.

"Now, just drink this good, warm tea. It's full of herbs to help with the pain," Bettie said in a soft, calm voice.

Cass tried to sip the hot, bitter fluid and felt her bile rise. "No, no more, please. Bring me water—cold ... plain ... water," she gritted out, shoving the cup aside as another wave of agony spread through her.

"But the pains—" Bettie said.

"The pains have been coming for nearly a day now and I'm no nearer to delivering this baby than I was last night," Cass replied when the contractions subsided. "Maybe I need the pain." She turned from the girl and looked over at Rosario, who stood by the other side of the bed wringing her hands.

The old cook was not a midwife as Bettie Wade claimed to be, but she had seen many births and knew that this one was not proceeding normally. "Senora, it will be all right. First *niños* always take longer. I will get you some water from the well. Nice and cool." She left the room, waddling as fast as her considerable bulk allowed.

Rosario was hauling up the bucket when she heard riders. Crossing herself in gratitude when she saw Kyle Hunnicut dismount, she called out to him. Another man, a stranger in a city suit carrying a leather bag, rode with him.

"Oh, Senor Kyle, I am so happy to see you! The senora is having her *niño*, but it is not going well."

Kyle's face whitened beneath his freckles as he looked over at his companion. "Plumb glad I brung yew, doc."

John Elsner began to walk briskly toward the house, "How long ago did the labor begin?" he asked Rosario as she shambled along beside the small man.

"Last evening, Senor." She looked at his instrument case and asked with hope in her eyes, "You are *el medico*?"

"Yes, I am a physician," Elsner said quickly as he opened the front door. When he neared Cass's room at the rear of the long hall, he could hear her faint, panting cry, feeble and weak with exhaustion.

"Who are you?" Bettie Wade asked as Elsner walked toward the bed, eyes fixed on Cass.

"Oh, John, thank God you've come," Cass gasped. "I'm afraid for the baby, so afraid."

"Not to worry, Cassandra. Just breathe in short, shallow pants, ya, lightly, like that. Now, relax. I am very glad your friend Kyle came to me when he did. I told you to return to Denver sooner," he remonstrated gently as he began to examine her.

Bettie stood transfixed in horror for a moment, then yanked at the sheets in outrage. "You put that down. I'm tendin' the missus!"

Kyle eased into the room with Rosario behind him and reached for Bettie. "Th' doc's here now 'n he kin tend Cass. Yew ain't got no diploma from no fancy school in England—"

"Austria," Elsner interrupted with a chuckle as he leaned over Cass.

"Wall, alls I knowed 'bout ferrigners from Europe is them thet comes from England." Kyle clamped his hands on the maid in a grip that quelled her protest in spite of the fact that she was a good four inches taller than he. "Now git whilst the doc does his work. Rosario kin help him."

With that he shoved her none too gently through the door. Dr. Elsner continued his examination of Cass, a frown creasing his brow. "How close together are the pains?" he asked. Between the lengthening contractions, he continued to question Cass about how she had been feeling over the past month since he'd last seen her.

Kyle kept his vigil in the parlor as Rosario shuffled back and forth from the kitchen to the bedroom. The expression on her face did little to reassure him. Toward midnight, his pacing was interrupted by a low moaning cry, the first he'd heard from Cass in all the long hours since he had arrived with the doctor.

With leaden feet he walked down the long hallway to her bedroom door. Now the sounds of exhausted weeping were clearly discernible, intermingled with the low, accented voice of Dr. Elsner. An icy dread squeezed at his heart as he stood frozen in the hallway.

Just as he reached up to tap on the door, Rosario opened it. Her tear-streaked face almost made the tough little gunman's knees buckle.

"Is Cass—" he croaked

"*La senora vive, todavía, pero el niño es muerto.*" The old Mexicana's words were spoken rapidly in a choked voice, but Kyle knew enough border Spanish to understand.

The infant boy was dead. Cass was still alive. Alive for how long? He stood awkwardly in the open door as Rosario hurried to the kitchen to fetch something for the doctor. Kyle could see a small, still bundle, carefully swathed in linen lying on the bureau across from Cass's bed. Dr. Elsner was bathing her chalky, sweat-soaked face with a cloth. She was barely conscious but still sobbing brokenly, murmuring words he could not decipher. Kyle knew what she was saying, nonetheless.

In a moment Rosario returned with a fresh glass of water and the doctor quickly stirred something into it. While Rosario held Cass's head up, he cajoled her into swallowing the medication, then gently lowered her to the bed. She was blessedly unconscious in a few moments.

Seeing the stricken little Texan rooted in the doorway, John Elsner gave Rosario instructions about sponging Cass off and changing the bed linens, then carefully picked up the small bundle from the bureau and walked out the door.

"Do you have here on this ranch a burial place?" he asked softly.

Averting his eyes from the tiny shroud, Kyle nodded. "I'll git Henry ta make a coffin. He's good with carpenterin'. Whut 'bout Cass? Is she gonna be all right?" He couldn't get the air into his lungs as he waited for Elsner's reply.

"I think so, but—" he paused for a moment, his thin face wreathed in very nonprofessional pain "—the labor was unnaturally long, and she is very weak. I do not know," he finished helplessly.

"*Por favor*, take the *niño* to the first room at the end of the hall until morning," Rosario said from the doorway. She crossed herself and added, "I will pray for his soul until the padre comes." She turned back into Cass's room to finish tending her mistress.

"Thet Wade woman wuz always stickin' her nose in when nobody wanted her, now where in tarnation is she?" Kyle growled as the doctor carried his small burden to the place Rosario had specified.

While Elsner put the baby in the empty bedroom, Kyle checked Bettie's room. It was empty. A brief search of the house yielded nothing. She was gone. He returned to the parlor where the doctor was pouring a glass of whiskey.

"She's plumb skeedaddled," Kyle said in astonishment. He accepted the drink and tossed it off while Elsner sipped thoughtfully on a glass of sherry.

"Perhaps she had reason to flee," the doctor said quietly. "Come with me."

They walked into the kitchen and Elsner picked up a cup filled with the bitter herbal concoction Bettie had been pouring down Cass for the past weeks since she'd begun feeling poorly.

"Yew said somethin' earlier 'bout Cass laborin' unnaturally long . . ." Kyle said with a flint edge to his voice.

"I've talked with Rosario, who described Cassandra's symptoms. I myself questioned her and observed her condition when I delivered the child. It was dead before it was born. This—" he held up the cup "—is a very slow acting poison. Foxglove taken over many weeks in increasingly larger doses will kill. Also it explains the premature birth."

"Thet bitch killed Cass's baby 'n tried ta do fer her, too," Kyle said in a quiet, deadly voice.

Elsner looked at the little Texan's eyes, hard and cold as agates. He almost pitied Bettie Wade.

At first light, Henry Longtree began to make a small coffin from fine oak wood. Kyle rode out to check the trails from the ranch for sign of the Wade woman. As he suspected, she had stolen a fast horse and headed up the main road to Denver. To Bennett Ames, he'd bet his life on it. By endangering Cass and killing her child, Ames had already bet his—and lost.

But vengeance must wait, for Cass lay unconscious, tossing and crying out for Steve. Kyle kept a vigil by her bedside. Dr. Elsner and Rosario spooned a few mouthfuls of broth into her and sponged her feverish body.

Rosario's priest from Pueblo said a simple burial service for the infant whose mother fought for her life even as his small body was committed to the earth on a green hill beyond the ranch house. Chris, Kyle, Rosario, and Dr. Elsner were joined by the men who worked on the place.

The plain wooden marker was carved with the words "Steven Terrell Loring, Jr., April 10, 1871." Cass had chosen the name months earlier, after Steve had left her in anger. Kyle devoutly hoped that Cass would live to replace the wooden monument with one of fine marble.

By the third day her fever broke and Cass settled into her first night of restful sleep in months.

When she awakened the next morning, a very rumpled, red-eyed Texan lay collapsed in a chair across the room. Hearing her move, he bolted up and moved quickly to the bed. "Yer gonna be all right, Cass," he said, as much to reassure himself as her.

Cass's eyes were wide and her face haggard as she frantically searched the room, hoping against hope that her memories of that night were mistaken.

"He's gone, Cass," Kyle whispered in a choked voice. "Rosario's padre come out and said th' words over him." As she wept in agony, he held her.

"He was all I had left ... of Steve ... his child," Cass cried out through her tears. After a few moments, she subsided. In a voice so low he could barely hear it, almost as much to herself as to him, she said, "After everything, all the schemes, the blackmail, the jealousy, I loved him. I loved him so much I didn't care if the baby was a boy or a girl. Rufus Clayton's freight line be damned! I only wanted a part of Steve."

"He'll come back, Cass," Kyle said with all the conviction he could muster, praying it was true.

Later that evening Cass inquired about Bettie. She had slept through most of the day after eating some soup. Now once more awake and aware of her surroundings, she missed the overly attentive maid.

It was John Elsner who told her about the poison and the serving girl's role in her child's death. Cass took the catastrophic news altogether too calmly for the physician's liking. She appeared numbed by the enormity of the tragedy.

"I do not like it," Elsner said to Kyle later after giving Cass a sleeping draught. The two men sat at the kitchen table as Rosario served them a simple meal. "She has lost too much. First the husband, now the child. Should I not have told her about the poison?" he asked reflectively.

"How'd yew 'spect she'd a acted if'n we tried some made-up story 'bout Bettie up 'n takin' off?" Kyle countered.

The doctor sighed. "Ya, you are right, my friend. What will happen now, I wonder. Cassandra needs her husband. Can you locate him?"

Kyle scratched his head in confusion, torn between wanting to search for Steve and to face down Bennett Ames. He considered, then replied, "Don't know. Steve knowed 'bout the young un. I got me a feelin' he'll come back. Them charges agin him down in th' Nations been dropped. I think he'll come ta collect his young un even if he blamed Cass fer whut happened last fall."

"What will happen now that the terms of her papa's will have not been fulfilled?" Elsner asked quietly.

"I know whut won't happen. Thet varmint Ames won't see a dime o' profit from Cass's misery!"

Just as they were finishing their meal, Rosario admitted a lone traveler through the front door.

Blackie Drago walked into the kitchen, his wizened face as somber as his name. "I received word this mornin', gentlemen. Is Cass all right?"

"Physically, ya," Elsner replied carefully as Kyle motioned Drago to take a chair.

Rosario poured him a cup of coffee and began to fix him a bowl of stew and a slab of buttered bread.

"What would you be meanin' by 'physically'?" the Irishman asked shrewdly. "Her spirit's been done in, is it?"

Elsner nodded. "So much tragedy." He and Kyle quickly explained to Blackie about Cass's poisoning and her bereft, listless attitude now that her child, the last link to her husband, was dead.

"I hate bein' the bearer of more evil news." With an oath, Blackie opened the April 13 issue of the *Rocky Mountain News*. The first-page story detailed the passing of a freighting dynasty. Thurston Smith was interviewed at length, explaining how the death of Cass's son meant Loring Freighting would revert to her cousin by marriage, Clark Matthews.

"I wanted to beat that son-of-a-bitch shyster lawyer here with the news. I expect himself'll be arrivin' with an eviction notice by tomorrow."

Bennett Ames crumpled the telegram in a ball and threw it across the thickly carpeted floor of his San Francisco hotel room. It skittered and landed beneath a claw-footed table by the window.

Swearing virulently, he stomped after it. Taking the fat cigar from his mouth, he applied its glowing tip to the paper's edge. Once it caught, he laid the smoldering mess in a large ashtray and watched it burn. Although not directly incriminating, the wire could link him to the Wade woman's death.

"Damn that idiot! I've never kept a tight enough control over our plans. Now this, this dangerous, stupid, bungled complication—and all for nothing!"

He paced and swore, his mind racing. Kyle Hunnicut was a man to be reckoned with, and Ames knew that when he returned to Denver the deadly gunman would be out for his blood. He snorted, wondering if the Texan had already throttled his worthless sister.

"If only she'd married Gordon and stayed in New York."

But that was a useless thing to worry about now.

Selina had always done exactly what her spoiled whims dictated. His immediate problem was his own safety. He knew that Hunnicut would blame him for the Wade woman's work. He could scarcely face down a deadly gunman. No one in his employ had displayed any remote ability to compare with the crafty Texan's.

"I need a couple of men who no one in Denver knows. Experts." He began to smile coldly.

Last evening he'd made another deal with a man who might well be able to help him. Wexler had sold him a sizable shipment of opium. The "hop joints" of the Chinese and other addicts in Denver were very profitable customers of Ames Freighting.

The pub where Ames agreed to meet Wexler's "friends" was on the waterfront in a district known as Sydneytown. The smell of salt air and the refuse from the wharves spilled into the vile interior, mixing with the odor of grimy, unwashed bodies. Rotting floorboards creaked beneath Ames's feet as he wended his way past drunken customers clanking their ale mugs together and gulping their foul liquor.

He watched a drunken sailor being shanghaied by three "ducks," penal colony refugees from Australia. A smell of death pervaded the stale air.

A waitress, the fat old inkeep's wife, waddled up to him and looked him over, noting his fancy clothes. "You th' toff what Wexler sent?" she asked sullenly.

At his nod, she motioned for him to follow her to the rear of the pub where two "ducks" sat at a corner table. One was tall and beefy with the map of Ireland stamped across his broad, pale face. He was built like a pugilist, and his numerous scars attested to the fact. His companion, obviously the man in charge, was a slight, wiry fellow with dark yellow stringy hair and beady little gray eyes.

"Jackie they calls me, mate. Jackie the Weasel," he said as he plucked a long, wickedly gleaming stiletto seemingly from out of nowhere and flipped it onto the table top where it vibrated, imbedded in the scarred wood. "This 'ere's Al. I unnerstan' you wants ta 'ire me 'n me mate."

Chapter Sixteen

"I think you better come down and handle this, Mr. Drago," the bartender said gravely.

Blackie Drago set down the ledger he'd been perusing in his office at the Bucket of Blood and looked at the giant man who filled the doorway. Gus's handlebar moustache and slicked-down hair added to his fearsome appearance. "What is it that you can't be handlin' the matter?"

The burly barkeep shuffled awkwardly. "That feller you helped last fall, the one Hunnicut came asking about—he's back, sitting in the corner with a newspaper. Been drinkin' for about an hour steady."

"Steve Loring's back?" Blackie asked as he jumped up from behind his desk. Quickly he headed for the barroom. Lord, the answer to his prayers.

When he saw Steve in a travel-stained Eastern

suit hunched over a whiskey glass, he paused in his headlong rush. The newspaper was an old one, no doubt the one from a month ago with the story about his son's death and Cass's disinheritance. Judging from the haggard look on Steve's face and the half-empty bottle on the table, he was hit hard by the tragedy.

"You just get off the morning train, Steve?" Blackie asked as he eased into the chair across from Loring.

Steve didn't even look up to greet his old friend. Taking a swallow from his glass, he stared at the headline in mute misery. Finally, he whispered, "I came back for him . . . now it's too late . . . all for nothing."

"I'd scarce be callin' it nothing. You still have a wife, Steve. She's been needin' you somethin' awful, lad," Blackie replied.

Steve raised his bloodshot eyes and stared at Drago in disgust. "So she does, now that her precious freight business is gone. I just came from the office. Thurston Smith was there going over the books."

"You're wrong, Steve, wrong about everythin', but it's grievin' you are, so I'll let it pass," Blackie said quietly. He reached over and took the whiskey bottle in his hand. "You need some sleep, a hot bath, and a good meal. Then we'll talk. Come."

Something in the little Irishman's tone caused Loring to rise unsteadily to his feet and follow Drago toward the stairs.

Blackie was right about his need for sleep and a long, hot soak. Since boarding the train in St Louis, he hadn't had a decent night's rest. He had arrived in Denver to be greeted by that punctilious bastard Smith and his smarmy weasel of a client

Matthews, both hypocritically offering their condolences. Everyone was so sorry, as much for his loss of the business as the death of his child. His son, the boy that would've insured Cass her dream. How monstrous an irony! She saw the baby as a means to that end. He'd returned to Denver only for his child. Now they both lost.

Damn her! She was the one who should have been punished, not the baby! As he dressed in Blackie's private apartment after resting and bathing, he felt clear-headed, but still hollow inside, numbed by a pain so intense it bordered on rage. He was like a lighted match downwind of a powder keg. Yanking on his clothes, Steve wanted to face Drago and get the confrontation behind him. He knew all too well the blindness that afflicted men where his conniving wife was concerned. He opened the door and walked down the hall, his footsteps muted by the thick Turkish carpet.

Blackie sensed rather than heard his entry through the open door of the office. "You look some better. Junie'll be bringin' you up a tray," he said, ignoring Steve's attempt to deny his need for sustenance. When the redhead had departed for the kitchen, Blackie observed the hard, cold set of Steve's features. "You even care to hear how your son died?"

Steve's head wrenched up, his face contorted with pain. "I can imagine how! Her mother suffered from stillbirths. Cass was probably so busy riding from camp to camp she killed my son with her own carelessness."

Drago's knuckles whitened on the arms of his chair as he fought down the urge to pistol whip Loring. Only Steve's obvious agony kept his own temper in check. "Your wife and son were poisoned. You nearly lost Cass as well as the boy."

Steve stared blankly at Blackie, waiting for him to elaborate. "She wanted that babe with all her heart. If anythin' caused her hardship, it wasn't overworkin', it was grievin' for the likes of you! When Kyle came back with word that you'd gone east to clear your name, she waited for word. Not a line did you send, not even when you were free and clear. She went to Pueblo, heartbroken, to wait for the child. It was all she had left of you."

"You said she was poisoned," Steve interrupted impatiently.

"And that she was, by a maid she took in out of her own soft heart—a woman fired by Selina Ames."

Steve's eyes flashed in amazement. "Selina?"

"Aye, Selina, Bennett's darlin' sister."

"How do you know the maid did it?"

"John Elsner it was who saved Cass's life. Kyle brought him to the ranch just in time to stop that divil woman, her and her herbal tea! The babe was dead before he was born, Steve," Blackie's face was pale and strained as he waited for Steve's reaction.

Junie tapped lightly on the office door and then opened it, interrupting the two haggard-looking men. "I brought the food, Mr. Drago," she said uncertainly.

He waved her to deposit the tray on the desk and leave. "Eat even if you don't feel like downin' anything," Blackie said with compassion.

Steve stared at the steak and eggs and felt his bile rise. He shoved the tray away and put his head in his hands. "You think it was Ames?" he asked. Surely Selina couldn't have been involved. Thinking of his tawdry affair with her, he felt doubly sick. Had she come after him in Louisville thinking she'd marry him and hand over Cass's freight line to Bennett?

"We'll niver know the truth of it from Bettie Wade. She was found murdered outside the city a few days after she fled the ranch. Kyle it was who found her, strangled."

"It isn't like Cass to take this without fighting back. She stands to lose everything," Steve said, turning over the bleak possibilities in his mind.

"She's been holed up at the ranch. Won't do a thing. Even Kyle can't get through to her. Doc Elsner says her body'll recover right enough, but her spirit's broken."

"And she needs me, I suppose," Steve said sarcastically.

"And you need her, lad." At the look of intransigence stamped on Loring's face, Blackie added quietly, "Don't you even want to see his grave?"

At dusk the next evening Steve rode up to the long, low outbuildings at the Pueblo road ranch. Strangely, his thoughts returned to when he had been brought here at gunpoint last year. *The ranch looks the same. But there is a new grave on the hillside out back of the house.*

He felt his courage desert him. He had to know if there was a grain of truth to what Blackie Drago had told him. She was his wife no matter what the circumstances of their parting last fall. He had an obligation to support her now that she had lost everything.

Reining in the livery horse he'd rented yesterday in Denver, he dismounted and walked slowly toward the front porch. It seemed only yesterday that a tall, slim woman in tan pants had stepped off those stairs, calmly inspecting him with cool amber eyes.

Rosario opened the front door, her eyes widening in surprise and joy. "Oh, Senor Steve, I am so happy you have returned. The senora, she grieves so, she does not eat, even Senor Kyle can do nothing with her." She ushered him inside as she continued her rapid chatter. "*El pobrecito niño*, oh, Senor, I am so sorry for you both," she said, crossing herself quickly as they walked down the hall.

"Where is Cass, Rosario?"

"Where she is all days now, in her room. She sleeps so much—too much now, *el medico* says. But now that you have returned, it will be better, *sí*?"

Before he could reply to that arguable point, the old cook had tapped on the bedroom door. Steve felt a queer tightening in his throat when a muffled voice said, "Come in, Rosario. Who is—"

Cass's voice failed her when she saw him standing behind the cook. He looked so tall and strong, so forbidding, she thought bleakly.

"Hello, Cass." Before he could say more, Rosario practically shoved him in the door and closed it as she left. Steve could barely see Cass in the dim light. Without a word he walked to the bedside table and lit the coal oil lamp, then turned to her.

Cass sat mutely, not knowing what to say. She blinked at the bright light, unused to having even the curtains open during daylight hours. She had existed in a twilight world of silence and misery ever since the baby died.

He stared at her in amazement. Blackie was right about one thing—she must have been near death. Her face was waxen and her eyes were ringed with grayish circles. She had obviously not brushed that glorious mane of copper hair in weeks. It hung in a ratty braid that was half unplaited. But far worse than her disheveled, haggard physical appearance was the lifeless look in her eyes as she stared at him, not saying a word, almost looking through him as if he were a ghost.

"Blackie told me you'd been ill," he said awkwardly, looking down at her.

"I'm alive," she whispered, almost as if she felt guilty about the fact.

This Cass, beaten and cowed, was not the woman he was used to dealing with, the woman he had married at gunpoint, the woman who always gave as good as she got. "I arrived in Denver yesterday morning and went to the office," he began hesitantly, uncertain of how to explain why he'd returned or what he wanted, uncertain if he knew any longer.

"Why did you come back, Steve?" She didn't look at him, and her voice had the same leaden, defeated quality that her face reflected.

"I always intended to return, Cass," he said as he paced across the floor to the window. Shoving open the curtains, he could see the sun setting. "I wanted to see my child. And . . ." He paused as the pain squeezed his chest again. "If you didn't want the baby, I was going to take him—or her."

He heard a strangled noise, a sob, a cry of outrage, he was not sure which.

Before he could turn to face her, she gathered a deep breath and said, "Get out! Get the hell out of here!"

Swinging her legs over the side of the bed, Cass came at him with her hands stretched out in claws. She stumbled against him in a tear-blinded rage.

His strong, familiar hands closed around her arms as he crushed her against him.

She felt wraith-thin and as fragile as porcelain. "Cass, Cass, please, I'm sorry."

She struggled with the dizziness that threatened to buckle her knees as she cried out against his chest, "You think I didn't want my own child? That you could just walk in and take my baby away from me?"

"You sold me off quick enough after my job was done, Cass," he said softly, oddly without rancor. Did he still believe she'd turned him in?

"And if I'd betray you, I'd desert my own child," she echoed woodenly, pushing feebly away from him and sitting down on the edge of the bed. Nothing had changed. Nothing ever would change between them. "Why don't you just go, Steve."

His shoulders slumped as he looked down at her. "What will you do now, Cass? Matthews and that weasel lawyer of his will be serving eviction papers on you."

"Do you still believe I give a damn about the business?" She gave him a withering look that crumbled into bleak despair. "Let them have it and welcome."

Recalling his belief that Cass wanted only her empire and would have consigned her son to a nursemaid or hated a daughter, he cringed in remorse. Whatever demons had driven Cass Clayton, they were gone now. He paused, then said simply, "You're my wife and I want to provide for you."

"I don't want your charity, Steve. Just go and leave me in peace." She rolled back onto the bed and curled up in a small ball with her back to him.

Everything that had happened in the past forty-eight hours began to whirl about in his head. He needed time to think. Nothing would be served by arguing with his fragile wife. He closed the door quietly as he let himself out. He did not see the silent tears that poured from her eyes as she listened to him retreat.

Steve walked up the hill to the small knoll crested by a copse of softly whispering aspens. Blackie said he and Kyle had ordered a fine marble marker. He could see the small oak cross, even in the gathering darkness. He knelt by the grave and his fingers traced the name, Steven Terrell Loring, Jr.

"She planned ta name th' baby fer yew if'n it wuz a boy," Kyle said quietly. He saw the shiny tears glimmering dimly on Steve's face when he looked up.

"I thank you, Kyle, for all you've done. Blackie told me she'd have died, too, if you hadn't brought the doctor when you did."

"Onliest thing wrong wuz I let thet Wade woman hoodwink me. Never trusted her, but I let her tend Cass. Now I know Ames hired her, him 'n thet bitch sister o' his'n. But real convenient like he's gone ta San Francisco on bizness. He'll hafta come back someday, 'n I got me a real long memry." He paused and watched Steve as his hands stroked the marker's smooth contours. "I'll be in th' kitchen, Steve. Take all th' time yew need."

When Steve finally composed himself enough to return to the house, Rosario was dishing up plates of roasted chicken and fresh garden greens. Only Kyle sat at the table.

"Where's Cass?" Steve asked with concern. Was he so sickened by him she wouldn't come to the table to eat?

"She don't leave thet room much. Never eats at th' table, Steve. Scarce a day Rosario kin git her outta bed. I jist 'bout plumb give up, too."

"We have to do something, Kyle. Smith will serve eviction papers from the new heir."

Kyle snorted and cut into a chicken breast without much enthusiasm. "Thet numbskulled fool come out here last week. Said his 'dear cousin' cud stay on here fer a spell and recuperate! He'll take keer o' her, her bein' kin 'n all!"

"*Pobrecita!* She will lose everything. If only the *niño* had lived. He was *perfecto, bello*," Rosario said in a wistful, sad voice.

"I'll take care of Cass . . . if she'll let me," Steve said quietly. "I'm a rich man. My family owns a bank in Philadelphia and a stud farm in Kentucky." Rosario looked astonished. Even Kyle paused with a glimmer of surprise etched on his face.

"Thet gal's got pride. Always made her own way," Kyle said. He knew that Steve and Cass had not settled matters between themselves. "Yew still think she wired thet marshal?" His shrewd gaze measured Loring.

Steve shrugged helplessly as he shoved a chicken leg around on his plate. "Hell, I don't know. I was wrong about other things." He could still see Cass's wounded fury when he'd accused her of not wanting her child.

"This here place 'n ever'thin' in Denver city, too it all belongs ta her, not thet snot-nosed little shit He'll lose it all ta Bennett Ames in a couple o months."

"Yeah, I know. Kid's dumb," Steve said in disgust. "If only there were some way to get that wil overturned."

Kyle snorted. "Cain't git her ta fight. She's plumb give up, Steve. I never thought I'd see th' day when Cass Clayton'd let a shyster lawyer 'n a damn fool boy run her over. She needs this here place, Steve." *She needs yew, too.*

Steve nodded as something niggled at the back of his mind. A perfect boy, beautiful, Rosario had said. Grimly Steve shoved his plate away. "Cass have a copy of that will here at the ranch?" he asked Kyle.

Denver

"Morning, Thurston," Steve said conversationally. He watched the attorney's pinched face tighten even more than usual as he strolled into the law office.

"Well, good day, Mr. Loring," Smith replied stiffly. "I'd heard you went to Pueblo to see your wife. Dreadfully sorry state of affairs, but I must serve eviction notices on her for the ranch and the city house here in Denver. I'm afraid everything, including the furnishings, reverts to my client. Of course," he added placatingly, "Mr. Matthews won't ask for any of your wife's personal effects or wardrobe."

"Awfully decent of him," Steve said without rancor as he took a seat on the edge of Smith's large mahogany desk, swinging his leg carelessly. He waited until the scrawny lawyer began to twitch in impatience before he said, "As a matter of fact, Thurston, the disposition of the will is precisely why I'm here."

Smith shuffled papers, always his way of stalling for time while he ordered his thoughts. "I fear the courts were quite adamant about the fulfillment of the will. Tragic as the death of your son was, the will is an unalterable fact."

He watched Steve's composure crack just a hair, but the tall Easterner again relaxed and said, "I've just talked with Cass's attorneys—they work for Will Palmer now, representing the railroad."

That barb struck Smith. After the disaster with Abel Barlow the preceding year, all hopes he entertained for the prestige and profit of representing the Denver and Rio Grande had faded. "I fail to see what any other law firm can do to change the will," he replied in obvious affront.

Steve's eyes were like shards of gold glass now. "You misunderstand. We don't plan to change the will or contest it in any way. We merely plan to see it fulfilled—to the letter of the law. Attorney Melchior will be in touch in a day or so..." He paused as he swung his leg off the desk, then turned to stare down at the pompous little man. "Oh, Thurston, tell Cousin Clark not to be in too big a rush moving into the city house."

When he walked out the door, Smith's jaw still hung slackly. What the hell was the arrogant Easterner up to? He'd had R. G. Dunn run a check on Steven Loring last fall when the shocking story about his wanted status was disclosed. The credit investigation had found that the unlikely outlaw was the scion of one of the wealthiest banking families in Pennsylvania! It explained much, including how Loring knew General Palmer so well.

Thurston Smith realized that a man with Loring's brains and connections wasn't bluffing or making idle threats about his wife's inheritance. But what in hell was he up to?

*　*　*

After a busy morning spent going over Rufus Clayton's will and then conferring with Cass's attorneys and bearding Thurston Smith, Steve knew he had put off an unpleasant task long enough. Attorney Melchoir had volunteered to handle it, but if he was going to go through a court fight, Steve knew he must talk about the key question with John Elsner immediately.

"You are certain Cassandra will not be asked to testify?" Elsner asked worriedly.

Sitting across from the doctor in his cluttered office, Steve leaned forward. "No, she won't, John. As much as I want her to keep her birthright, there's no way I'd put her through it. If you and Rosario will do it, that should be sufficient."

"And what of you, my young friend?" The doctor's warm brown eyes were kind. "You will testify, ya?"

"I...I have to do it, and I learned in the war that what you have to do isn't very often what you'd choose. I can handle it. I must." He stood up and shook hands with the slight physician. "Shalom, John. I'll see you in court."

As Steve left, John Elsner watched the sure stride of Cassandra's troubled young husband. "You are the one who needs peace, Steven. May God grant it to you and to Cassandra. It is a very brave thing you do."

"I do not know if I can do this thing you ask, Senor Steve," Rosario said with her chocolate brown eyes wide and dark with fear.

Steve put his arm around her, comforting himself as well as her. "It's not easy for any of us, but you can do it, it may save Cass's inheritance for her, Rosario."

Swallowing, she straightened up and smoothed her purple taffeta dress, her finest gown, set aside for special occasions. Testifying in court was the most special occasion since Rosario Maria Dolores Santiago de Vasquez's marriage thirty-five years ago.

While Steve reassured Rosario, Thurston Smith attempted to do the same for his client Clark Matthews. The thin, nervous young man's clumsy gait and mannerisms seemed even more pronounced as he paced in the antechamber. "How could you have let this come before the judge, Thurston?" he accused. "What can Loring possibly hope to gain by reopening the case? When they failed to produce the male child, the judge ruled in our favor."

Smith stroked his chin and said very carefully, "The three-year time limit is over now, yes. And the boy is dead."

"But what could that foreign doctor or the greaser woman tell the judge to make him change his mind?" Like a frustrated child, Matthews banged his hand on the oak table beside him and let out a shriek of pain followed by a volley of oaths. He had caught his bony wrist on the sharp edge of the table. He muffled his swearing, sucking on the painfully reddening welt on the wrist.

"Young buffoon," Smith muttered beneath his breath as he spied William Byers advancing on him, pencil and pad in hand. Sighing, the attorney knew it was going to be a very long day. "Calm yourself, Clark. And, please, let me speak for you with the good editor," he admonished sternly.

When the crowded courtroom was finally quieted, Judge Wilfred Bromley requested Attorney Smith and Melchoir to approach the bench

"Gentlemen, in view of the very sensitive nature of this evidence, I feel the interests of all parties concerned would be best served if the spectators were asked to leave."

William Byers paced furiously, making short, fast notations for himself every few moments. "They've been in that courtroom for nearly three hours. It's bad enough excluding the public, but to have the temerity to keep me waiting past my deadline is unconscionable," he fumed. Like everyone else in the city, Byers was eaten up with curiosity. What could the reason be for reopening the clear-cut case disposing of Rufus Clayton's estate?

Finally the heavy mahogany doors of Judge Bromley's chambers were opened by the bailiff. Now Byers would have his story! He approached the officious and usually knowledgeable Thurston Smith, who was first to leave the room. Smith's expression was one of barely suppressed wrath. Behind him came the gangly Matthews boy who had inherited the Clayton wealth, looking rather like a badly beaten blue tick hound. The silent youth shuffled past Byers with eyes fixed straight ahead, practically trampling on his hapless attorney's heels.

"Thurston, I say, what was the decision?" It took no profound newsman's instinct to tell that the ruling had gone against Smith and his client.

Pueblo

Cass sat on the front porch rocking quietly in the big chair Kyle had bought for her before the baby was born. Everything else in the nursery had been packed away, but she insisted on keeping the rocking chair as a tangible reminder of her loss.

The baby had been her only link to Steve, who had left her in such bitterness. But now after his son had died, Steve had returned. "To take his child away from an unfit mother," she whispered aloud on the still evening air. The ranch had been even more lonely than usual the past several days. Kyle and Rosario had gone with Steve to Denver. No one had explained the reasons to her, and she had not asked.

Chris Alders remained behind, staying at the house, with several younger men posted as guards each night. Now that she had lost everything, she doubted that her life was any longer in danger, but let them do as they wished. In any event, Cass didn't care if she lived or died—unless Steve loved her. Only that would heal her. But he had made his continuing mistrust abundantly clear that first night after he returned. Now he was off in Denver doing heaven only knew what.

When Kyle's familiar gelding came loping up and he swung down, Cass looked puzzled. Where was Rosario? *Where is Steve?* For the first time in the five weeks since her son had been born, Cass felt a genuine stirring of curiosity. Perhaps that's why she'd taken to sitting on the porch the past two days, waiting.

"Evenin', Cass. Yew look some better," Kyle said as he mounted the stairs. At least her hair had been brushed, even if her simple cotton frock did hang loosely on her thin body.

"Where is everyone else?" she asked with a hint of impatience lacing her voice.

He chuckled. "Yew tired o' yore own cookin' already? Rosario's on th' spring wagon. Be along soon. I rode ahead." He deliberately did not mention Steve, waiting to see if she would ask.

Cass fought an inner battle for several minutes while Kyle went to the kitchen to wash up. Finally she rose from the rocker and walked slowly into the house. Kyle sat calmly at the kitchen table rolling a cigarette. "Somethin' on yore mind, Cass?" he asked innocently.

"Yes, you know damn well there is," she said with some of the piss and vinegar of the old Cass. "Why did you all go to Denver ... and where's Steve?" She held her breath. *What if he's left me again?*

"Oh, Steve, wal, he had ta stay on in town. Someone's got ta run th' freight office. He said ta tell yew Miz Vera'll be real put out if'n yew don't come home fer her fancy cookin'."

"What do you mean, 'run the freight office'? We don't own it anymore," she said in bewilderment, sitting down on a chair across the table from him.

"Since't day afore yesterday, we do. Steve, yew see, he got him this idee from readin' ole Rufus's will. Went 'n talked ta them fancy lawyers o' yourn and then th' doc. He didn't figger on tellin' yew 'bout it jist in case we lost in court." He paused and then took her hands gently in his, finding it painful to explain what he must. "Cass, it wuz real hard on Steve, doin' whut he done, 'n him bein' a rich dude, wal, he didn't do it fer yore money neither. He done it fer yew."

"What? What did you and John Elsner and Rosario ..." Suddenly a dawning comprehension hit her. "The will," she said in a choked voice. "It said I had to bear 'a male child' within three years of my father's death. It didn't say that my baby had to live for me to meet the terms of the will, did it?" Her eyes were flooded with tears, and a metallic taste filled her mouth.

Kyle nodded, patting her hand awkwardly. "Thet's whut th' doc 'n Rosario had ta say fer thet lawyer feller. Steve got ever'thin' back, Cass."

She stood up numbly. It was all too much, the memories pouring back over her in a hot, painful avalanche. "So he's running the office in Denver again," she whispered.

"He had ta stay 'n fix a lot o' messes thet fool cousin o' yourn made. He damn near give the bizness ta Ames in a couple o' weeks! Cass . . ." He paused and stood up, sensing her pain and confusion. "He's hurtin' bad, too. He done this fer yew 'n he wants yew ta come ta Denver."

"Why, Kyle? He owns Loring Freighting now, free and clear by the terms of my father's will. He's not a wanted man any longer. He can do whatever he wants. I can't control him."

"Thet whut yew want—ta control him? Never did work, 'n yew knowed it even back afore he got hisself cleared. Cass, he owns thet stud farm back in Kentuck 'n his pa left him a whole bank in Philadelphy. He don't need yore money. He's waitin' fer yew in Denver. Don't make him wait too long."

Cass couldn't sleep that night. She rolled across the wide soft bed, caught in the throes of painful memories. Was Kyle right? Had Steve reclaimed her inheritance for her because he cared for her? Did he still think she'd betrayed him? If he was as rich as Kyle said, he obviously did not need her money. That also explained a great deal about his educated ways, his passing references to travel and study in Europe, his lifetime friendship with Will Palmer.

Did she dare to hope that a man like Steve, whom she had humiliated, threatened, and blackmailed into marriage, could love her? Cass had fought loving him for so long before she relented and admitted it to herself. Could he have done the same? Or was it only his noblesse oblige, that damn driven sense of duty that had sent him west in the first place, searching for Vince Barlow? She was his wife, therefore his obligation. He couldn't love her, he couldn't! Cass knew with bitter certainty that she would hate a man who treated her the way she had treated Steve. But Kyle's words tore at her. *He's hurtin' bad, too.* What if it were true? He'd lost the child he'd come all this way to reclaim, a child he had obviously wanted as much as she.

"You're a coward, Cass Loring," she said to her mirror the next morning as she inspected herself with a grimace of distaste. How could any man desire her the way she looked now? Her hair was filthy and lank, her bones practically protruding from her skin.

"I stink and I'm starving," Cass announced to a startled Rosario as she marched into the kitchen.

The cook almost dropped her rolling pin in amazement. The old fire was back in her mistress's eyes. "I have a fresh batch of sweet rolls baked up for Senor Kyle and eggs for a fine omelette. I'll get one of the men to heat water for a bath while you eat, Senora."

As she scuttled off, Cass called after her, "Heat lots of water. I have to wash a month's grime out of all this hair."

* * *

Steve spent the days in frenetic activity at the freight office and stock yards. A week had passed since his victory in court and no word had come from Cass. The picture of her all alone, haggard and forlorn, frightened him, but he had to give her time. That was why he had sent Kyle. She would accept the news about how they won the case from her old friend better than from him. Anyway, it was still too raw and painful a wound for him. Testifying in that court had been the hardest thing he'd ever done, but it was behind him now. If only Cass could put it behind her, too.

Until she rallied—or until he had to ride south and drag her to Denver—Steve had to straighten the mess the incredibly inept Matthews boy had made. After he'd fired Ossie Wilkers, whom Steve quickly rehired, Cousin Clark had proceeded to alienate virtually every muleskinner, bull-whacker, and freight yard worker in their employ. Odd, when he'd been an errand boy counting stock he had seemed a sensible, if not overly bright, employee. As an employer, he was utterly incapable of making a rational decision.

For the first day or so Steve had wondered if he'd come crawling back in search of his old job, but when Matthews failed to appear, he had far more pressing matters to consider. He rehired all the men who had left and worked from dawn to late into the nights on account books. Loring Freight was now busily hauling supplies south from Denver for Will's grading crews. Work on the Denver and Rio Grande's first rails had begun this spring, and the crews needed everything from food staples and whiskey to dynamite and pickaxes. By the time Will returned from his mapping expedition into New Mexico, everything had to be running smoothly.

So much for his days, but each night when he dropped exhausted into bed—that big four-poster bed with its erotic and frustrating memories—he found his thoughts centered on his wife. If only they could recapture what they'd lost.

For a long time he'd tried to convince himself that he merely desired Cass, then subtly and gradually his feelings had become far more complicated. That evening when the marshal had come to arrest him, he'd been on the brink of confessing his family background. He'd wanted her to confess, too, that she wanted their child . . . that she loved him.

If he still desired her now as he had before he thought she'd betrayed him, then he must love her. Only a fool would believe against all evidence that she was innocent. He sighed, guessing that he was a fool.

With each passing day, Steve became more worried. What if she had fallen ill again? Lord, she'd been so fragile when he left her last week. Perhaps he should send the doctor down to the ranch to check on her. He mulled over the possibility that evening as he sat at the dinner table. "Tomorrow I'll get John and we'll—"

"You'll what, Loring?" Cass stood in the dining room archway, dressed most fetchingly in one of her white blouses and form-fitting tan pants. Her hair was shiny, tied loosely with a brown ribbon at the nape of her neck, curling loosely around her shoulders. The gray hollows were gone from beneath her glowing amber eyes. His old Cass was back!

Chapter Seventeen

Steve stared speechlessly at her for a second, then carefully put his fork down and stood up.

"You'll do what with John?" she repeated as she walked slowly into the dining room.

He pulled out a chair and motioned for her to sit down. "I was worried about your health...I was going to have John go to the ranch and check on you," he replied.

"Just send him or bring him yourself?" she asked coolly as she sat down, glad to have her shaky knees relieved of their burden.

He sighed. "You heard me, Cass. I was coming, too," he admitted. "It's been nearly a week since Kyle went to Pueblo to tell you the news..." His voice trailed off as he grasped for a way to explain his very confused feelings.

"Why did you do it, Steve?" Her question cut

to the heart of the matter. "You don't need my money. You're rich."

His face strained toward a lopsided smile. "Cassie, I wanted you to have what was rightfully yours. It was the least I could do—"

She jumped up from the chair in pained fury. "You were obligated to rescue your poor, penniless, ill wife! Duty again, Steve? Well, I thank you. And I guess I have my answer."

She turned to leave but he quickly overtook her and his strong hands on her shoulders stopped her flight.

"Cass, wait, please." He stopped, uncertain of what she wanted, uncertain of how to explain his feelings. She trembled when he touched her. Before he realized it, his face was buried in the fragrant hair falling over her shoulder. "This has nothing to do with duty," he whispered.

She whirled, freeing herself from his mesmerizing embrace. "It has nothing to do with love either—or trust, or anything lasting. You came back to claim your child out of a sense of duty. Now you've provided for me. You don't have any further obligations, Steve."

"This isn't an obligation, Cassie—it's what I want!" He reached for her with a fast, desperate grip, pulling her against his body and molding her to him. Steve felt a surge of desire mixed with anger as he lowered his mouth and kissed her.

Cass was lost in his fierce, hard embrace, opening her mouth to his invading tongue, returning his harsh caresses with a fiery desperation that matched his own. But all the while her mind cried out that this settled nothing between them. Still, she could not break free. When he picked her up

in his arms and walked from the dining room
toward the stairs in the foyer, she clung to him,
returning his kisses in breathless abandon.

Steve reached the top of the stairs in a few swift
strides, then headed toward the bedroom, shoving
the door open with his foot and closing it behind
him with a kick. Only when he began to set her
down did he realize how feather-light and fragile
she still was. He gentled his caresses, nuzzling her
throat softly and holding her carefully as he asked,
"Cass, are you all right? I mean, can I? Can we . . ."
He paused and just held her, stroking her hair as
he took a deep breath. "I don't want to hurt you,
Cassie. You were so ill."

She could feel him trembling with desire held
in check. His tenderness touched her deeply. "You
won't hurt me, Steve. I'm recovered, just a little
on the skinny side," she whispered against his
chest.

Her softly muffled reply led him to begin kissing
her again, this time more slowly. He began to unfasten her shirt, his lips following his hands, button by button, until he peeled the soft white cotton
from her shoulders. God, she was thin, her skin
pale and almost translucent. He lowered his head,
and his warm mouth brushed the tips of her
breasts through her thin camisole.

Cass reached up to the first shirt stud on his
chest, quickly pulling it out, then working her way
downward until she could pull the shirt tails free
of his pants. She ran her hands through the thick
tawny hair on his chest, then wrapped her arms
around his lean waist, clinging to him as they
blended their mouths in a long, exploring kiss.
While his tongue wove its magic with hers, his
fingers unhooked her camisole and then did mad

dening things to her breasts.

Cass arched instinctively into his hands, clinging to him and moaning out her need as he caressed her. When he left her aching nipples and unfastened her belt, her mind began to function again as she whispered breathlessly, "My boots."

Understanding, he scooped her up and turned to the bed where he lay her down carefully. Then he tugged off the soft leather riding boots and began to peel away her fitted tan trousers. She helped him with a wiggle of her hips as he yanked them free.

For a moment he stood over her, looking at her nearly naked body, clad only in lacy pantalets and the opened camisole. Cass felt suddenly uneasy. She was wraith-thin and sallow. Perhaps she was no longer beautiful to him.

As if sensing her doubt, he knelt by the side of the bed and began to run his hands across her breasts, hardening the nipples into aching points. Slowly, reverently, he moved lower over her silky abdomen, now concave. He stroked her hip bones and ran his hands down her thighs to her knees. When he retraced his warm, sensuous examination, he punctuated it with kisses that burned through the sheer batiste undergarments. "You are so lovely," he breathed as he began to unfasten the pantalets.

Cass forget her fears and everything else as his warm, deft hands and lips caressed her now naked flesh. When he pulled away, she watched him quickly take off his boots and shed his pants. His splendid body was still bronzed and corded with lean, sinewy muscles. She ached to run her fingers through the thick tan pelt on his chest and feel her palms curve over the rounded biceps of his arms.

Wordlessly he knelt on the bed and came into her arms, very carefully supporting his weight on his elbows and knees as he began to kiss her again. She ran her hands greedily all over his body as she returned the kiss, then reached down between them and grasped his hard, pulsing shaft, stroking it until he gasped and shuddered with pleasure.

"Cassie, go slow, I don't want to hurt—"

His words were cut off when she guided him into her with a smooth, gliding arch of her hips. The ecstatic writhing of her hips convinced him of her recovery. With gradually building ardor, he thrust into her, blinded by an intense need to absorb her, to be absorbed into her.

Cass felt the old familiar hunger, aching for release. After so long an abstinence, her response was fast and fierce as her nails dug into his shoulders and she began to shudder in climax, crying out his name over and over in hoarse, breathy little whispers. When he surged in a final explosive thrust and joined her, his words were muffled into her tangled hair. Had he said, "I love you?"

They were both sweat-soaked and breathless. Cass felt utterly exhausted and shaky as a newborn foal. She had far from regained her old stamina. Steve rolled gently off her and pulled her to him, then ran his hand softly across her cheek. "I'm afraid I've overtaxed you," he murmured.

"I'm not," she answered, snuggling against him, too weary to examine her fears or his motives.

He held her for a few moments, then pulled cover over her and slipped from the bed. "I'm going to have a bath drawn and ask Vera to make a tray for you. I'll be right back. Rest now." H bent down and kissed the tip of her nose lightly.

Through leaden eyes Cass watched him don a heavy velvet robe and silently walk from the room. She dozed until the splashing of hot water awakened her. Kate was emptying a large bucket into the tub in her dressing room. Just then Steve came through the hall door carrying a tray laden with food. The heavenly aroma of roast beef and apple pie emanated from beneath the linen napkin.

Several more splashes of water sounded next door. The tittering whispers of the two housemaids made Cass's cheeks pinken as she sat up in the big four-poster bed, realizing that Kate and Peggy knew exactly how she and Steve had just spent the early evening.

"I never did get to finish my supper either. Let's eat together," he suggested genially as he spread the feast on the small bedside table and began to dish out a generous portion for her.

She sat up after reaching to the floor for her camisole, which she slipped on and fastened. Eyeing the enormous slab of pink meat and mound of mashed potatoes, she looked at him with a faint smile. "Trying to fatten me up?"

He quirked one brow. "You're the one who said you were too skinny. I just want you to regain all your strength," he said suggestively as he poured two glasses of ruby-colored claret.

Handing her one, he touched his glass to hers in a toast. "To the future, Cass."

Uncertain of what to say and unwilling to break the warmth of the moment, she nodded and drank. They ate in silence for several moments, both famished after a long, arduous day.

When he handed her a slab of Vera's flaky apple

pie, she groaned. "I don't know if I can eat all of this."

"Then have your bath first," he suggested helpfully, taking the plate from her and depositing it on the tray.

As she soaked and luxuriated in the scented water, Cass's mind was not nearly as placid as her body. She was tired and satiated, mellow with wine and good food, but the things she'd come to Denver to discuss were still as unsettled as ever.

Do you love me, Steve? He had toasted to their future, told her he desired her, and confessed that he had not stayed in Denver from a sense of duty. But he had not said he believed her innocent of betraying him to the law. She worried her lip with her teeth and pondered what to do. If not duty, was it merely lust? Considering her skeletal condition and how terrible she'd looked when he last saw her at the ranch, she doubted that. He had been tender and gentle, desiring her but holding back until he was certain not to harm her. Her husband simply had to hold deeper feelings for her in spite of his hateful accusations when he'd first arrived.

Cass knew she could not bear to lose him now, but it was best to wait. She would let things sort themselves out gradually. Before that marshal had shown up last fall, they had been on the brink of establishing a real marriage. There was still time, all the time in the world. Closing her eyes, she began to hum softly as she lathered her body with scented soap.

Steve awakened gradually as the first light of dawn filtered into the room. He felt rested, at peace, satiated as he had not been in years, maybe never before in his life, he realized as his mind became fully alert. Cass lay snuggled securely against his side, in a soft, warm cocoon. He looked at her delicately lovely face, so serene and youthful in sleep.

She was too thin and pale, but she had never seemed more beautiful to him than at that moment. *You love her, you fool.* He smiled ruefully as his fingertips played with a bouncy copper curl. His arm lay possessively across her waist, and her long hair spilled over his upper body like a gleaming cloak.

For several moments he lay very still, studying her sleeping face while he considered his own confused emotions.

She had come back to him, not because of the business, not out of any hope to control him. She had returned simply as a woman seeking her husband, wanting him to understand that she shared with him the loss of their child. Their marriage was more important than their bargain. It was a delicate thing, this building of trust and love between two such volatile people.

"We have a long way to go, Cassie. I hope we make it," he whispered softly as he kissed the tip of her nose. Carefully he extricated himself from the tangling strands of her hair, recalling how it had become so mussed last night. She was still weak from her ordeal, but when they had finished dinner and returned to bed, it had been a long time before they slept. He wanted her to rest now, while he left for his early morning appointment with Will Palmer. After slowly slipping from the bed, he tucked the covers securely around her. Gathering up his robe, he left the room and his sleeping wife.

After a quick bath and shave, Steve departed without benefit of Vera Lee's restorative oolong tea. He was already late for his breakfast with Will. Grinning to himself, he was certain his old friend would forgive his tardiness.

As he strolled into the hotel dining room, he immediately spotted Palmer's meticulously attired figure seated at his usual table. The slim, shorter man rose and greeted him warmly.

"At last, after all those weeks surveying in the south, it's good to have the amenities restored," Will said as they clasped hands.

As if on cue, a waiter appeared with a silver pot and a china cup for Steve. His face lit up as the waiter poured steaming, fragrantly steeped tea. "You do think of every amenity. Sorry I'm late, but I had a surprise visitor last evening. Cass is back in Denver, Will."

The warm gleam in Steve's amber eyes told Palmer that having Cass back was a good thing, a very good thing indeed. After the tragedy with their child, perhaps things would work out for the star-crossed couple after all.

"I take it your wife is recovered from her ordeal," he said with a smile. "We must have her meet my wife as soon as Queen arrives. I'll arrange for a visit to our new homesite in Colorado Springs. It is really the Garden of the Gods, you know."

Steve sipped his tea and smiled at his visionary friend. "I'm sure Cass and Queen will become friends, Will. They're both strong, unconventional women." He paused, then asked, "Are your grading crews being adequately supplied? You've been south for quite a while. Any problems?" A worried frown crossed his brow.

"If you mean any sabotage from your ill-mannered competitor, none to date. We post guards, and your Mr. Hunnicut's been very thorough with security on the supply trains. Until Ames comes back from the West Coast I think things will remain quiet."

Steve's expression blackened. Clenching his fist, he let it rest on the white linen tablecloth. "When Ames arrives in Denver he won't live long enough to cause your railroad or our freight line any trouble," he said quietly.

"You have no proof, Steve, that he hired that woman," Will said very carefully, then added quickly, "I understand he was the one with the motive, and Lord knows, he has a vile enough reputation to do such a perfidious thing, but I don't want you in trouble with the law again."

"You and I both know what Ames is capable of doing, Will. I won't give him another chance at my wife." Steve paused, and his eyes took on a cold golden glow. "Don't worry, I'll handle it so the law can't touch me."

Will cleared his throat, uncertain of how to deal with this coolly dangerous side of his boyhood friend. Odd, the war had hardened them both, but his own natural optimism had sent him on a visionary quest, while Steve's bloody and tragic past seemed destined to lead him into a series of vendettas. "One avenue you might explore is Ames's sister. I understand the Wade woman worked for Selina before your wife hired her. Perhaps she could be convinced to tell the law what she knows."

Steve's face reddened. "That bitch is too smart to betray Bennett, but if she ever returns to Denver, I'll gladly wring her lily white neck." His guilt over Selina had intensified when he learned it was her former maid who poisoned Cass. Steve swore an oath that the Ames family would pay dearly for their crimes.

"You have a lot to live for now, Steve. Think of your wife before you act rashly," Palmer advised.

"I am thinking of Cass, Will, believe me I am."

Wanting to change the subject, Will reached into his jacket and extracted a list of the proposed camp sites on the southward route where the grading crews were preparing the roadbed for the rails.

After they discussed timetables and materials to be shipped, Will said laughingly, "When I rode into Watson's Livery yesterday, I was startled at his new assistant. Your wife's cousin has certainly come down in the world."

"Matthews is working for Watson?" Steve considered, then laughed. "I guess after the mess he made at the freight yard no one else would give him a job, so his lawyer took pity on him. Or maybe old Thurston's making the fool work off his legal fees." At Will's puzzled look, Steve added, "Thurston Smith owns Watson's Livery."

"How do you find out all these things?" Will asked in amazement.

"Blackie Drago knows even more than Bill Byers. You really ought to rub elbows with a few Democrats, Will," Steve added with a wink.

Will stiffened in mock affront. "I'll have you know, sir, that my father once had a perfectly respectable friend who was a Democrat. I was too young to be allowed to mix with him, of course."

Both men chuckled, then Steve scolded, "Such pomposity, Will. Shame on you."

Wiping his mouth with his napkin, Will scooted back his chair. "Speaking of pompous, our youthful livery hand had his ego sadly pricked while I was paying for my horses' upkeep. This most incredible woman of amazonian proportions came storming up to him, dressed rather, er, immodestly in feed sack clothing."

"Lots of the miners' women use feed sacks instead of yard goods to make clothes," Steve said.

"Yes," Will responded drily, "but do they usually have 'Pride of the Family' flour with the label displayed like a banner across their more than ample bosom?"

Steve threw back his head and laughed, and Palmer continued. "The 'lady' in question gave him the verbal thrashing of his life about a spavined horse he'd sold her. As your muleskinners would say, 'She burned the grass black for thirty yards around her' cussing him."

Steve envisioned the priggish braggart who'd had the asinine nerve to court Cass reduced to such a humiliating pass and roared again with laughter. "I only wish Thurston had been there, too."

"Perhaps he was summoned to handle the amazon's refund if he is indeed the real owner of the livery. One could hope," Will said, wiping the tears of mirth from his eyes.

If anyone in Denver possessed less of a sense of humor than Clark Matthews, it was Attorney Smith. This sent them both into another fit of laughter.

While Steve and Will discussed the railroad supply route and local gossip, Selina Ames made her morning toilette. Arriving on the train the previous evening, she had been filthy and exhausted, then furious when she had reached her brother's city house to find him still not back from San Fran-

cisco. "The wretched coward is afraid of Steve
Loring," she murmured to herself as she critically
inspected a new bonnet.

Having lost all hope of seducing Steve into marrying her, she was again taking up her pursuit of
Gordon Fisk. Although paunchy and balding, he
was every bit as rich as Loring, and possessed of
a far more malleable nature. While she had dallied
with Steve in Louisville, Gordon had returned to
Denver to check on one of his banks. She planned
to run into him "accidentally" that morning. She
already had a heart-wrenching story made up
about why she'd fled from him back in New York
last fall.

The day was glorious, a perfect cool and sunny
morning in May with Colorado's azure sky graced
by fluffy bits of white clouds, whipped about by a
brisk, playful breeze. Cass decided to walk to the
office and surprise her husband. She'd slept scandalously late, then eaten an enormous breakfast
while Vera fussed over her, urging second and
third helpings of griddle cakes and maple syrup
on her. Now it was time to digest that mountain
of food by taking a leisurely stroll across town.
After her long months of absence, Cass felt the
need to reacquaint herself with the city. So much
of life had passed her by during her confinement
and the subsequent weeks of grieving.

"I grieved for Steve even before the baby died,"
she whispered wistfully. Perhaps everything
would work out. They could have more children,
now because they wanted them as proof of their
love, not to seal a bargain and meet the terms of
her father's hateful will.

Cass strolled toward her Cherry Street office,

stopping to talk with a wide assortment of people, muleskinners in dirty denims, women in fancy linen dresses, shopkeepers and saloon owners. The city was booming with freight wagons clogging the muddy streets and large stagecoaches crammed with newly arriving passengers. Some would make their way to the gold camps, but many would stay in Denver, opening every kind of business from barber shops to banks.

A sense of exhilaration surged through Cass after she left the elegant Victorian residences behind and turned down Larimer Street. One of the newest banks, owned by the illustrious New York firm of Fisk and Kellog, had only this week opened its etched-glass doors for business. As she neared Mr. Fisk's bank, her mood suddenly shifted. Walking directly her way after disembarking from a carriage was Selina Ames.

The beautiful black-haired woman was dressed in deep purple with an elaborate feathered bonnet protecting her perfectly coiffed hairdo. In her plain white blouse and brown skirt, Cass felt drab and pale by comparison. Then remembering what she had so painfully blocked for weeks, she itched to rip Selina's hair from her head and strangle her with those satin bonnet strings. It was Selina's former servant who had murdered little Steven!

Catching sight of Cass Loring's pale, blazingly angry face, Selina slowed. She had plenty of time before Gordon arrived. So this emaciated, gutter-mouthed hoyden was the woman for whom Steve had spurned her! Smiling coldly, she greeted Cass, ignoring the redhead's quivering anger.

"I see you aren't carrying your blacksnake, Cass. Pity. You look as though you'd enjoy plying it on me," she said with a scathing inspection of her rival.

"I'd rather use it on your brother. A cowardly slut like you isn't worth the effort it would take to peel the cheap paint off your face." Cass stared at Selina with the loathing she usually reserved for particularly repellent species of warehouse cockroaches.

"You may think I'm beneath touching, Mrs. Loring, but after your beloved husband escaped from you, he touched me often." She studied Cass's reaction, which was clearly one of disbelief. She paused casually and inspected her gloved fingers, smoothing the kidskin leather. "His stud farm, Graham Hall, is exquisitely beautiful. Doubtless if it weren't for his benighted sense of obligation to his child, he never would have returned to Denver."

Cass watched Selina's eyes as an icy hand squeezed her heart with certain dread. "Steve detested you. You're Bennett's sister," she said as if that were tantamount to being a leper.

The brunette laughed. "But I do possess certain social graces and recall, dear Cass, that neither I nor my brother betrayed Steve to the law. He blames you. Besides, I was accepted in Louisville society, something a swearing, sweating female in muleskinner's clothes could never be." She waited a beat, then added with a vicious smirk, "Ah yes, Steven is as magnificent a stallion as the ones he breeds—except for that one scar. He received it during the war. It cuts across his right thigh just above—"

Cass hit her squarely in the mouth. Selina stumbled against the rough brick of the mercantile wall, snagging her taffeta dress. Her bonnet flew back and was crushed between the bricks and her shoulder as her hair came flying from its pins.

In a low, deadly voice Cass rasped out, "I changed my mind. If I had my blacksnake with me I'd peel every inch of skin off your fat, whorish body!" She turned and walked stiffly down the street, leaving the voluptuous brunette rubbing her bruised lips and smoothing her torn dress. The feathered hat was beyond repair.

When Cass stormed into the freight office she already had dried her tears. A cold, killing rage replaced the tearing hurt. Selina couldn't have lied about Steve. That scar was not visible, and he never discussed how he'd received it, other than to say it happened while he was skirmishing during the war. Her husband had had a tawdry affair while she carried his child—an affair with the woman whose brother was responsible for their child's death! And she knew he had done it out of spite, because he despised her for forcing him into marriage, for being an unnatural woman who he believed couldn't even love her own baby. Suddenly the tears threatened to engulf her again. She choked them back as she nodded to Ozzie.

"Mrs. Loring!" the boy said in joyous amazement. "Gee, I'm glad you're back." He hesitated awkwardly, sensing that something was amiss. "Er, Mr. Loring's not here yet. He was having breakfast with General Palmer. If you want, I can go to the American House—"

"No—no thank you, Ozzie," she interrupted. "Is Kyle back from the south yet?"

"No, ma'm. We expect him any day. Mr. Chris is here, though. He's out back getting ready to leave with a shipment of heavy machinery."

Nodding her thanks, Cass walked past the boy

and headed for the rear door. As she wended her way past crates and boxes in the crowded storeroom, she recalled bittersweet memories from the past. Angrily she considered what she'd say to Steve. The pain was so raw! Then she heard the wheezing voice of Sour Mash Charlie Filbert as he lectured one of the young muleskinners.

"Always treat your mules like women, with affection and caresses, my boy, and you'll be repaid with docility and ease of management."

Bristling, she stood on the porch and glared down at the tomato-nosed old preacher. "That's true, Reverend Filbert, only if the mules happen to be as old and feeble as those relics that pull your cook wagon. As for my freighting mules—like any woman worth her salt, they'd kick you to your just reward in the next life if you tried to soft-soap them."

"Now, Miz Cass, you know—"

"Where's Chris?" she asked without further discussion.

The young muleskinner Amos motioned toward the cluster of big heavy crates across the yard. "Loading boilers and pipes for Caribou," he explained.

Cass strode across the yard to where Chris Alders and Bully Quint were checking a particularly heavy load to see that it was balanced properly.

"Hold up until I get back, Chris. I'm going home to change into my trail gear and saddle up Angelface."

"Cass," Chris said dumbly, staring at her. Her words barely registered. "When did you get back to Denver? Where's Steve?"

She turned impatiently, saying only, "It's a long story, Chris. I'll tell you on the way to Caribou.

feel a real need for some fresh mountain air to clear my head."

When Steve arrived at the office that afternoon he half expected to see Cass at her desk. He'd planned to return before the noon hour and take her to lunch, but there had been an auction and he had made an excellent deal for over a hundred mules of prime quality. Before he realized it, the afternoon was almost gone.

The office was empty but for Ozzie, who knew only that Mrs. Loring had come in that morning for a moment, then headed back to talk with Chris. Sighing, Steve thought she must've returned to the house. He knew that Chris's shipment for Caribou had been scheduled to leave that morning.

When he walked into the front foyer, Bentley Everett was waiting with an envelope in his hand. The wiry little butler looked very unhappy. "Mr. Loring, your wife left this for me to give you this evening. I'm really glad you returned sooner."

With a knot of dread tightening his guts, Steve tore open the envelope and read the brief note.

Steve:

I ran into Selina Ames this morning. Your former mistress was very graphic about certain parts of your anatomy, so you need not waste time devising lies about your relationship with her in Louisville.

I need time to think before we discuss the divorce. The trip to Caribou will take two or three weeks. Kyle can handle things if you decide to return east before then. He'll be back in a day or two.

Cass

Steve crumpled it into a ball and swore until the little butler winced in mortification.

"Tell Vera to serve our dinner to the staff, Bent. I'm going after my wife. We'll return in a few days!"

Chapter Eighteen

Kyle Hunnicut wanted nothing so much as a hot
bath, a cold beer and a soft bed. He had been on
the trail for several grueling days, riding from
camp to camp. Loring Freighting had undertaken
a massive job supplying the grading and building
crews for General Palmer's railroad.

As the grading parties blasted and hacked a level
roadbed south, the supply wagons followed with
everything from pickaxes and dynamite to flour
and beans. Whiskey came, too, in fifty-gallon barrels along with women in cheap portable tents.
Building railroads was a profitable business for
many people besides the barons of industry who
set the process in motion.

Kyle's job was to see that the building and the
supplying went smoothly, without interference
from hostile Indians, road agents, or Bennett
Jones's saboteurs. Outside of one minor run-in

with an overly ambitious bunch of illegal "toll collectors," nothing worthy of his concern had occurred. The toll was not collected. Two of the collectors were at the undertakers in Pueblo. It was all a "job o' work" for Hunnicut.

Feeling much refreshed after his bath, he headed for the Bucket of Blood and the second item on his agenda, a cold beer to wash the hot alkali trail dust from his parched throat. A bit of news from the best source of gossip in the city was always helpful to a man in Kyle's profession. Blackie would know how Steve was faring at the office and perhaps a bit about his and Cass's meeting in Denver.

When he'd stopped by the Pueblo road ranch yesterday, Rosario had described the change in Cass, saying she had gone to Denver. Everything looked encouraging. If only those two hot-headed fools would wake up.

"I'm startin' ta think like one o' them damn fool mushy dime book writers," he muttered to himself as he stepped into the smoky saloon. The big crystal chandelier reflected dully on the polished oak floor. Kyle could hear raucous cawing over the plinking of the piano as a brightly plumed bird in a gilded cage competed for attention and whiskey soaked crackers.

The usual crowd drank at the long bar. Some men played cards and billiards, while others enjoyed the ladies of the line in lively dancing. Most were teamsters, some miners, and the rest an assortment of local merchants, clerks, and hard cases.

Kyle returned greetings and motioned to Gus the bartender to send a beer to his usual table. Since their unfortunate altercation over Blackie, whereabouts the previous year when Steve had fled, the fat man and the little Texan had become friends.

Thoroughly weary, Kyle hunched over the table and swallowed down the cold ambrosial brew in a few foamy gulps, then ordered a second. When he reached for the mug, a voice cut into his absorption with his thirst.

"It's glad I am to see you at last, bucko." Blackie sat down across from Kyle with no preamble and leaned forward, his dark eyes gleaming with intense concern.

"Whut's wrong?" Instinctive unease gripped the Texan.

"Ames is back." At Kyle's immediate stiffening, Blackie continued quickly, "He's gone into hiding, cowardly scum that he is. I've my grapevine at work on locatin' him, but in the meanwhile I learned somethin' more. It's two of the worst blackguard cutthroats from the Sydneytown waterfront he's hired and brought back with him to Colorado. Jackie the Weasel's known as a snake from Frisco to Panama."

"I kilt me plenty o' rattler's in my time, Blackie," Kyle said with narrowed eyes.

"More like the bastard is an asp—little, fast, and deadly poisonous. His specialty is knives, front or back makes no mind to the likes of him. His partner Alf is a big, mean divil, crushes men's skulls like me boyo at the bar there cracks walnuts at Christmas time. I sent a man to warn Steve and Cass."

"Ta warn 'em? Where are they?"

Blackie cleared his throat, then sighed. "It seems it's another feud, laddie. Cass took off with Chris for Caribou early this mornin'. Now mind,

I'm not knowin' the details, but when Steve found out this afternoon, he lit out after her mad as a scalded bobcat, sayin' he'd be draggin' her back.''

Kyle swore and shoved his hat back on his head in disgust. "Thet's jist great! We got us Ames 'n a whole pack o' his rattlers out who knows where, 'n them two er off feudin' while'st thet son-of-a-bitch picks 'em off!" He stood up and tossed a coin on the table for his beer. "So much fer thet soft bed. Whut time'd yew send thet feller after Steve?"

"Only a couple of hours ago, it was, when I got word of the doin's. Steve can take care of himself, Kyle. It's only fair warnin' I'm sending him.''

"Yep, if'n he ain't so cross-eyed mad at Cass thet he shoots his own laig off. Watch fer Ames ta come up fer air hereabouts. Even a water snake's gotta breathe sometime. I'll be back with them two fools soon's I kin git ta 'em.''

Steve saw the glow of the campfire just as he crested the hill. Scuddering clouds had swept the moon behind a thick veil, obscuring the trail before him, but the wagon ruts were well worn on this first leg of the journey into the mountains. He'd had no trouble following them in spite of the cloudy night. When no sentry challenged him, Steve's anger grew. Chris Alders should know better. This was placing Cass and her wagons in danger.

Just then, as if awakened from a doze, a squeaky-voiced boy called out. Recognizing the boss, Amos Priddy quickly apologized and motioned him toward the encampment.

"Amos, in the war we shot boys younger than you for falling asleep on guard.''

"Yessir, Mr. Steve. It's been real quiet the last half-dozen trips. Guess I got careless."

"See that you don't stay that way. It could get you dead real fast." With that admonition Steve rode toward the circle of wagons and the fire.

Reining in Rebel, he swung down as Bully Quint and Dog Eating Jack eyed him in nervous expectation. When Chris Alders rounded one of the wagons and saw Loring's harsh expression in the flickering firelight, he froze in his tracks. "Howdy, Steve. Sorta been expectin' you," he said in a clear voice. The sudden silence around the fire magnified the hum of insects and the distant howl of a coyote. Even the pop and hiss of the fire seemed to intensify as Steve walked silently toward it.

"Where is she, Chris?"

"I'm not hiding from you, Steve Loring." Cass's voice rang out contemptuously as she stepped into the firelight. Her blacksnake hung casually across her shoulder, but she clenched the handle fiercely.

"Let's go somewhere private, Cass. We have to talk," he said quietly.

"I have nothing to say to you. Go back to Denver. Your whore's waiting for you there!" Her eyes glowed like the hottest coals of the campfire, a deep, clear reddish gold.

Steve advanced on her like a patient hunter about to ensnare a wounded quail. "Cassie, let me explain," he said in a voice so low the onlookers had to strain to hear it.

"Stay away from me, Steve. I'm not bluffing." She uncoiled the whip in one smooth, lightning-fast movement. The lash lay at her feet like a pet snake.

Still he kept walking toward her in slow, measured steps, never breaking stride. "Put it down,

Cass. This isn't the way."

"There is no way, not for us. You whoremonger! Go back to Selina—if you can forget that she and her brother are murderers!"

"I'm sorry, Cass. You must believe that. I didn't know what Bennett did—her part in it, anything. I was angry because I thought you'd betrayed me. I was wrong. I know that now."

He reached out for her just as she raised the whip. "You believe I didn't betray you—so you betrayed me!" she cried as the blacksnake lashed out with a sharp crack, whistling around his high leather boots.

"Dammit, Cass, it happened before I came back, before I knew—"

Again the whip cracked, this time higher, cutting into the back of his hand as he reached for her. He grabbed for the whip, but she was too fast for him, whirling toward the open fire, now quickly cleared of men. She took her stand and raised the blacksnake.

Goaded to furious anger by her mulish stubbornness and the sharp, burning cut she'd administered to his hand, he lunged at her with an oath. She let the whip crack again. This time his sudden move caused Cass to miss her mark. The tip of the whip hit his face, sending his hat flying and leaving a wicked red slash across one cheek. He stopped and touched his fingers to the wound. They came away bloody.

Cass stood transfixed in horror at Steve, her husband, his beautiful face scarred by her hand! What had she done? She could have blinded him!

Still he stalked her, now with a feral light of cold rage ignited in his golden eyes. He was forewarned when she raised the whip again, her reflexes slowed by her tear-blurred eyes. He caught the whip and yanked it away from her, catapulting her into his arms.

Cass felt the breath squeezed from her lungs as one arm tightened like a vise around her waist. His other hand threw the whip with a crash into the licking flames behind them.

"I ought to turn your backside up and use that blacksnake on your pink little ass," he grated hoarsely as he dragged her away from the prying eyes of the men, toward the darkness beyond the fire.

Cass struggled to breathe when he released her, shoving her roughly against a wagon. "Steve, I—"

"You're going to listen to me, Cassie, and listen good," he hissed. "I've ridden Rebel half to death to reach you. This was a fool, dangerous thing, tearing off with Chris into the mountains."

"I've grown up riding wagons into these mountains," she shot back defiantly.

Only his eyes glowed in the dark of the moon. His face was shadowed as he spoke. "You ran away, Cass. The woman I married isn't a coward. You should've stayed to face me."

Her head shot up furiously. "Face you with the fact you slept with the woman who murdered your own baby? What was to be gained, Steve?"

He reached out and grasped her arms in his hands. "I didn't know, Cass. With God as my witness, I didn't know about any of it. How could I? Elina came to Louisville. I was alone, miserable, drinking too much, squandering my life." He released her and stepped back, running his hands through his hair in nervous misery. "I admit I used her to spite you. I knew you hated her and I blamed you for sending the marshal...aw, hell, Cass, it was a rotten, stupid thing to do. I realized that and ended it long before I came west. I am sorry for it, Cass. When Blackie told me what happened, I felt gut sick to think I'd touched her." He looked into her eyes, just as the moon came out from behind its cloud cover.

Cass let out a soft gasp of pain as she saw the blood oozing from the slash she'd inflicted. Instinctively she reached out, touching his cheek gently. Taking a linen kerchief from her pocket, she carefully dabbed at the wound with trembling fingers. "I'm sorry, too. I didn't mean to do this It was an accident."

"You didn't want me touching you, Cassie, did you?" His grin softened the harsh planes of his face.

"I was afraid," she admitted unwillingly "Every time you come near me, I do things I neve thought I would...or could."

"I love you, Cassie," he said simply. "Maybe you love me, too, and that's why you're afraid."

She stopped in her ministrations to his cut chee and looked into his face with wide golden eye filled with uncertainty. "I don't know—no, that a lie. I do know. I've loved you for so long, but didn't think..."

"That you could trust me?" he supplied.

She nodded. "And I didn't think you loved m not after the way we started. You didn't trust m Steve. When that marshal came, you turned me in a flash."

He pulled her into his arms and stroked h back. "I know. It took me so long to accept t truth, to quit fighting it. You're right, you kno After the way we started, I was bitter. A m doesn't like being forced." He felt her stiffen and drew her nearer, kissing her neck softly, nibbling at her earlobe as he wound his hand in the fat plait of hair hanging down her back. "But I couldn't help myself. I fell in love with my wife. It's just taken me a while—"

A horse thundered into camp and a hubbub of voices arose as Kyle's distinctive twang rang out. Steve and Cass broke apart and quickly walked around the wagon.

"Been lookin' ta ketch up with yew fer quite a spell. We got us a gallon jug full o' trouble, Steve." Hunnicut looked uneasily at the slash on Loring's cheek, but then observed the way Cass held on to him and decided that at least one matter had been settled properly.

"What's going on, Kyle?" Steve asked.

"First off I come ridin' after a feller Blackie sent ta warn yew 'bout Ames bein' back. Found him daid by th' side o' th' road jist outside o' town. Then when I rode in here, thet Priddy boy wuz done fer, too."

"Amos!" Cass gasped.

"Throat cut on both o' em. Real quiet like. Seems Bennett Ames got him some new hired help. Some fellers from Australey. Call 'em ducks n San Fran. Blackie Drago calls this here Jackie ist plain onery. Dangerous as a poked rattler, only aster."

"Get out there and look around, Bully, Jack. ou, Seth, bring the boy's body in." Steve turned o Kyle after issuing the orders. "Just what do you 1ink is going on?"

"Dunno," Kyle said consideringly. "Mebbe th' oy stumbled on 'em while'st they's watchin' th' amp. Too dark ta see much sign. Cain't be 'nough o' them ta try 'n take a train this size."

"All they wanted was to stop Blackie's man from warning us and then try sabotage when an opportunity presented itself," Cass reasoned aloud.

"Or they wanted to kill either or both of us. If we were careless and, er, wandered off, Cass, we'd be easy targets." Steve watched her eyes widen in mortified understanding.

"And we almost—"

"Exactly."

"Come first light, I'll check thet place where th' boy wuz kilt. Till then yew two might's well git yew some sleep." Kyle paused and looked up at the gathering clouds again blocking out the moon. "Damn! If'n it ain't fixin ta rain, Vera Lee ain't a better cook 'n Sour Mash Charlie!"

"I'll see to the guards. You scoot into that wagon over there where you're out of the line of fire," Steve said to Cass.

"In case you've forgotten, boss man, I've run these trains and fought with Ames long before you came on the scene. I can stand watch the same as any man. And besides, Kyle's had less sleep than anyone."

Kyle looked from Steve to Cass and scratched his head. "Now lookee. This here's my job o' work 'n I'm good at it. I kin last me a night er two without sleep, leastways till I check ever'thin' out. Th' two o' yew jist settle up betwixt yerselves." He scooted strategically away, calling out orders to several muleskinners.

"Into the wagon, Cass. Anyone out there can take a pot shot at you silhouetted in the firelight."

"They can do the same with you. Are you sure Abel Barlow and his son are both dead?" she asked, abruptly changing the subject.

"Yes, reasonably so. I had to leave in rather a hurry, but Kyle had Will check on Abel and Vince Barlow. Two headstones in the family plot. No charges against either of us." As he talked, he ushered her toward the wagon. Then, seeing the worried look in her eyes, he considered for a moment. "I'd bet on Ames and his San Francisco thugs, but when we get back to Denver, I'll run a check, just to be certain. Now, in with you."

He lifted her up into the open rear end of one of the wagons, which served as cramped sleeping quarters on inclement nights. "Kyle's right. We're blowing up one hell of a storm. I'll be back as soon as I check the camp, Cass. Wait here for me?"

His eyes glowed even in the gathering darkness as he held her hands, softly rubbing his thumbs across her knuckles. She sighed in capitulation, knowing he was right about the weather. "Hurry back. I think it's going to be a gullywhopper." Her face heated up as she remembered the last time they'd shared a bedroll in a hailstorm.

Steve carefully made the rounds of the twenty-wagon perimeter. By the time he climbed into the wagon, fat drops of rain pelted down, soaking his clothes. The rain quickly turned to large icy stones as he shivered beneath the crude canvas roof lashed above him. As he crouched in the crowded quarters, Cass helped him strip off his wet clothing. The flickering lamplight revealed that she had already changed into a simple cotton nightshirt. It was worn thin and softened by age, revealing the slim contours of her body as the coal oil lamp glowed against the fabric.

"You used to sleep in denims and boots when we first went on the road together," he said in a desire-roughened voice as he reached up to catch her flowing hair, now unplaited and brushed.

"I only wear this when I have the privacy of a wagon. It's more comfortable," she added primly, feeling suddenly vulnerable. She looked into his face and touched the dried cut on his cheek. "I have some salve from Sour Mash's medicine chest. Maybe it won't scar if . . . oh, Steve, I'm sorry." She threw herself against his chest, kneeling between his legs as he sat on a packing crate.

Steve caressed the copper cascade of hair falling down her back and soothed her sobbing. "Cassie, Cassie, it's all right. Anyway, a 'dueling' scar will make me look rakish." He held her tightly and lifted her chin with one hand. The beauty of her golden, tear-streaked face took his breath away.

"I'm cold, woman. Come, warm me," he whispered as he slid to the floor where a bedroll was spread between the crates. Cass held on to him, running her hands up his chest, over his biceps, circling his neck with her arms as they reclined in the close quarters.

He buried his face in the spill of her hair, then rained kisses on her eyelids, drying her tears with his soft, warm lips. She tasted salty and sweet and he groaned with desire. "Cassie, I love you. I need you. I was so lost without you," he murmured against her face.

She ran her fingers through his shaggy bronzed hair, then framed his face between her hands and said softly, "I'll never leave you, Steve. I love you too desperately."

The thudding of the hail on the heavy canvas was matched by the sounds of their hearts as they kissed fiercely and clung together in the wonder of love, newly discovered and newly confessed. Slowly Steve slid the soft folds of her nightshir up until he could work it over her shoulders. She helped him, pulling it free of her long, tangled hair.

At once his hands were on her breasts, cupping and caressing as she arched and moaned. When he took one hard pale pink nipple in his mouth, she clasped his head to her and kneaded her fingers into his scalp. The flickering light turned his sun-streaked hair brown, then gold as she tousled it. She watched in wonder for a moment, then closed her eyes tightly as sensations swamped her.

Slowly he trailed his hot, moist mouth down her belly, laying her back against the bedroll as he moved lower. When his fingers grazed the copper curls between her thighs, she parted them for him willingly.

"Easy, Cassie, just let me . . ." he breathed into her softness. When his lips moved lower and his eager mouth tasted her feminine wetness, she gasped in shock, then fell back in exquisite ecstasy, quivering, powerless and mindless in pleasure.

Steve could feel the response of her whole body as he caressed her softly and intimately, nuzzling, licking, and kissing. When her fingers dug into his hair and held tightly, he intensified his loving until he could feel the rhythmic contractions against his mouth. Cass thrashed her head as waves of pleasure, so keen they were almost painful, washed over her.

When the lovestorm gradually subsided, she looked down at him, her eyes wide with amazement. "I didn't know it could be done like this . . . I mean . . . not all the way . . ." Her voice trailed off in embarrassment as he grinned and slid up the bedroll between the crates to be beside her.

"Men and women can make love many ways,

Cass. We have the rest of our lives to discover them." He paused a beat, then couldn't resist saying, "I can't believe that John Elsner was so remiss as to omit the books that talked about—"

She clubbed him playfully with a pillow. "I didn't read *everything* in those books." She paused thoughtfully. "But come to think of it, there were some outrageous drawings . . ." She reached down to assure herself of what she felt. His pulsing phallus was rigidly hard in her hand, probing into her belly. She stroked it tentatively once, then again as he gasped and sank back on the makeshift bed. "You'll have to help me if I forget what I read," she whispered over the noise of the storm and his loud, rasping breathing.

Cass slipped downward to the end of the bedroll, while her hands experimented with her glorious new toy. She had been so in his power. Now he was obviously in hers. An interesting way of loving, she decided as she lowered her lips and was rewarded by his ragged gasp of pleasure. He guided her head gently as she took the sleek male flesh in her mouth.

He was so big, but the heat and hardness seemed an enticement, as did the way his body involuntarily bucked and arched, raising his shaft as she took him deeper, deeper. The storm raged on outside, a steady torrential rain now as they established this new kind of sexual rhythm. She raised, then lowered her head, practicing what she knew, improvising what she did not. Judging by his response, she was doing all right. When she felt him stiffen and cry out in climax, Cass felt a thrill of pleasure as he exploded, pouring his life-giving fluids into her as the rain poured onto the parched Colorado soil.

Steve labored to breathe in the warm confines of the wagon. Sweat sheened his body as he reached down and drew Cass up to lie against him. The sweet, musky aroma of sex blended with the smells of wet canvas and soaked earth. He kissed her lips, then her eyes and cheeks as he threaded his fingers in her hair. "Cassie, you never cease to amaze me, girl. Never."

"Think you should write John a note of thanks?" she asked with a puckish grin, amazed at her own boldness with this man she had long adored, but not until now really trusted.

A chuckle rumbled in his chest as he enfolded her in a tight embrace. "John's a perceptive man. I think the glow on both our faces will convince him of how apt a pupil you've proven." He reached for the edge of the bedroll and pulled it over them. "Let's get a little sleep, darling, before tomorrow's long trip back."

"I love you, Steve," she murmured against his chest.

"And I love you, Cassie, my wife," he said softly as they both drifted off to sleep.

Neither noticed that the rain had slowed to a soft misting in the early morning hours.

"Damnation, I knowed it!" Kyle stood by the crest of the ridge between two shale outcroppings, the place where he had found Amos Priddy's body the previous night. Hail and torrential rain had obliterated all traces of any trail the stealthy killers might have left.

Steve watched Hunnicut's careful exploration as he walked on foot around the entire perimeter of the wagons in concentric circles. Finally, when was clear that no clue remained, he said, "Kyle, you and I know who sent them. You scared them off, probably—no, more than probably—back to wherever Ames is hiding. They'll have to report their failure and get new orders."

"Yeah, I reckon thet's th' way it'll be," the Texan admitted in disgust. "Blackie's got hisself a real good bunch o' boys back in Denver. Might cud be he'll turn over a rock 'n find Ames fer us."

"Then let's go back to Denver right now," Cass interrupted as she climbed quietly up the rocks to where the two men conferred.

Steve turned and looked at her with undisguised affection and exasperation. She glowed with energy and fierce determination, standing there in her muddy boots and those delectably fitted trousers. Her hair had worked its way loose from its plait and curled in the humid air, giving her a wistful, young appeal. Always unconventional, always lovely. "Kyle will go to Blackie and see what he's learned. I have another idea for getting information about Ames—one you definitely aren't going to have any part of."

"Now you see here, Steve Loring, it's my life too. I was Ames's target for years before Kyle dragged you in here. You're not fighting my battles for me!"

"No one's fighting any battle yet, Cass. We're just going to do some reconnaissance, as we used to say in the army."

"Cass," Kyle said apprehensively, "I'm bein paid ta tangle with rattlers like them 'n yore footin' th' bill. Let me nose 'round th' city 'n see whut I kin turn up."

She seemed to relent at his suggestion, bu turned to Steve with a wary yet curious look i her eyes. "Just what do you plan to reconnoiter that I can't come along?"

Steve's face darkened and his eyes were hard as he looked past her, staring at the trail north to Denver. "You said Selina Ames is back. If I have to, I'll beat the truth out of her—"

"I can do a better job than you and I'd relish it," she interrupted.

"That's just it," he snapped more sharply than he intended, then sighed. "Look, you can't barge in and threaten to peel her painted face off with your blacksnake," he remonstrated.

Cass reddened as she said, "I already told her exactly that. And I'll do it. You can't stop me, Steve. If Bennett is back, she can lead us to him. Anyway, you owe me the chance to confront her."

"I don't like it, Cass," he said, feeling guilty and afraid for her all at once. "You're too . . . well, too involved."

"And I suppose you're not," she parried with tightly leashed anger. "We're wasting time. Let's ride for Denver!"

The trio of tired, muddy riders reached Denver by late afternoon. Kyle headed to the Bucket of Blood in search of Blackie while Steve and Cass headed for the Ames city house, agreeing to meet Kyle at the saloon after they'd seen Selina.

"I only hope our quarry is at home. Now remember, Cass, stay calm and let me handle her." He stopped before they dismounted and put his hand softly over hers as it rested on the pommel of her saddle. "Are you sure you want to do this?" His voice was filled with concern. "It'll be ugly, Cass."

She placed her other hand over his and squeezed. "I'm sure, Steve. I'll be fine. 'Jist yore backup.'" She mimicked Kyle's accent. But she

slung her whip casually across her shoulder befo[re]
dismounting and gave Steve a wicked grin. "S[e]-
lina has lots of fancy breakables in her house."

The Lorings' quarry was indeed at home,
though preparing for afternoon tea with her "rea[c]-
tivated" fiancé, Gordon Fisk—or at least he wou[ld]
be very shortly. It had been childishly easy to fa[ke]
an accidental encounter with him yesterday a[nd]
tearfully give him her creative version of w[hy]
she'd gone to Louisville and left him at the alt[ar].

Hearing the front door open and the butler a[d]-
mit someone, Selina smoothed her silk gown a[nd]
puffed up one ebony curl. Passing inspection [in]
her mirror, she turned to the door. Perhaps G[or]-
don was a bit early. When she walked to the t[op]
of the long, winding stairs and looked down in[to]
the foyer, her heart caught in her throat.

Steve and Cass Loring stood there, having [ob]-
viously dismissed her spineless butler and se[nt]
him scurrying to the pantry. Steve's face was da[rk]-
ened by a day's growth of beard, making him lo[ok]
decidedly dangerous. Cass was pacing with th[e]
whip in her hands. Both were tracking mud acro[ss]
her cream and royal blue carpeting.

"I usually have my servants receive freight [or]
liveries at the rear door. You're ruining my ca[r]-
pets," she said, haughtily, staring down on the[m].

Steve looked up at her with a wolfish grin. "[We]
aren't delivering anything, Selina. You are. Yo[ur]
brother's worthless carcass."

"Don't be absurd. Bennett's in San Francisc[o],"
she said, stepping back from the top of the stai[rs].

Cass uncoiled her whip and let it shinny acro[ss]
the floor like a living thing. "You have a lot [of]
pretties in this entry hall. More in the library a[nd]
parlor." With no further preamble the wh[ip]

cracked with blurring speed. A large cut-crystal vase shattered on the floor, spilling water and smashed red roses across the expensive carpet.

"No! Stop it, you, you, filthy animal! I'll call the law, I'll have you—"

"Not before Cass wrecks your house, you won't, Selina," Steve interrupted her diatribe conversationally.

"And after I finish with the crockery and doodads, I'll start on you," Cass said, flicking the whip again.

Selina stood poised at the edge of the stairs. A long hallway stretched to her right and left with servants' stairs down the back offering her only chance of escape. Even as her eyes darted down the hallway, she could see Steve's long legs taking the stairs in front of her two at a time as effortlessly as a mountain cat jumping from rock to rock. In her long skirts and high-heeled slippers, before she could even reach the first door he'd be on her.

She put her hand to her throat and pleaded faintly, "What do you want, please?" Steve reached for her elbow, clamping it in a viselike grip and dragging her downstairs. She cringed as she faced the golden-eyed fury of Cass Loring and her whip.

"We want to know where Bennett is, Selina. We know he's back in Denver. Blackie's underground found out yesterday. Bennett sent his new lackeys to kill us, but they only succeeded in killing one of Blackie Drago's men and a boy who works for us," Cass said with withering contempt.

"You're trying Cass's patience, Selina," Steve whispered silkily in her ear. "That isn't healthy."

"I didn't have anything to do with this! I don't

know what Bennett does. He comes and goes at all hours. Please, you have to believe me." She turned beseeching eyes on Steve.

A crash of glass brought a rain of crystal and gold pelting down on them as Cass's whip pulled the elaborate chandelier in the foyer from its plaster mooring. The whip twisted and shattered the crystal prisms even before the dainty Italian light fixture hit the floor.

Selina cringed, covering her face and head protectively. Cass waved the whip in her face as Steve held her.

"Selina, there are things a man won't do to a woman...but another woman, a woman who's got a very personal score to settle..." The whip skittered across the floor. "Stand back, Steve."

Selina clung to Steve with iron strength in her whitened fingers. "Wait, please, she's insane!"

"As insane as Bettie Wade was when she poisoned my wife and son? That bitch worked for you, Selina." Steve's voice was as hard as the jagged glass that surrounded them.

Selina forced her words out between hiccupped sobs. "I didn't know anything about Bettie, except that she'd been killed! I never sent her to work for Cass. I fired her before I left for New York. The stupid ugly chit was incompetent...having an affair with some man...mooning over him night and day...neglecting her work. I swear, Steve! Why would I send someone you could trace back to me?"

"No, you wouldn't. But Bennett might not give a damn about you. If she'd succeeded, my wife would've been dead, too, and that moronic Matthews boy would've inherited. Bennett was making short work of him when I got back to Denver."

Steve shook Selina. "Where's Bennett, Selina? Tell me or I'll leave you alone with Cass, I swear it."

Selina crumpled, trapped and desperate. "He came in earlier today with two horrible men. They talked in a funny accent. I couldn't understand half of what they said. I never mix with Bennett's business, Steve. I only know he was taking them with him to meet some Chinese—at one of the opium dens on Hop Alley."

"Making a delivery, no doubt," Cass said in disgust. "Bennett's traded in opium ever since the first Chinese came here from the railroad camps. That's why he goes to San Francisco. Blackie says he has 'investments' there, too."

"Where is this place, Selina?" Steve asked.

"I don't know—I swear, I don't know. Surely you don't think I'd go to places like that?" She shuddered in horror.

Steve turned to Cass. "I believe her. She wouldn't want to dirty her silk skirts with her brother's filthy deals, and she for sure wouldn't set foot on Hop Alley."

Cass's eyes narrowed as she looked scathingly at the puffy-eyed, disheveled woman whimpering in front of them. "I suppose you're right. Blackie'll know who Bennett deals with. Kyle may be one step ahead of us already." Cass paused and looked at Selina again, a deadly, cutting glare that froze the brunette's blood. "You stay clear of this fight—don't even think of trying to reach your brother and maybe, just maybe, you'll live. But if Bennett escapes, I'll come after you and flay you to death!"

Her gown wrinkled and torn, Selina crumpled in a heap, on the floor, sobbing, oblivious of the broken glass and smashed furniture surrounding her.

That was how a very shocked Gordon Fisk found her a scant half-hour later.

Chapter Nineteen

The Bucket of Blood was having a slow afternoon as Kyle and Blackie sat at a secluded table in the back of the room. They could see down the length of the bar stretching to the front door. When Steve and Cass came rushing in, Kyle said to Blackie, " 'Pears ta me they might jist've found out somethin'."

"About time someone did," the little Irishman said in disgust. "Niver had me boys come up this empty before. Arrivin' in town today, vanishin' again in a twinklin'. As if that slimy bastard oozed off the face of good Mither Earth."

"We know where Ames has gone," Cass reported breathlessly.

"That is, if you know who he sells opium to, we can find him," Steve added, looking at Drago.

With relish Cass described their encounter with Selina to Blackie and Kyle. The Texan guffawed

413

and Drago roared with laughter. "Maybe now she'll be marryin' her banker and headin' east with him, the poor dumb sod." Blackie paused, then said, "I thought of Hop Alley, but me boys came up empty this mornin'." He grinned ruefully. "A difficult thing it is, gettin' a Chinaman to trust a good Irish lad. But I do know who Ames sells his poison to. Name's Sing. At least, that's all he's been callin' himself since he set up shop on the Alley."

Blackie made a hand signal to two grizzled-looking toughs, who came over to the table. If a pants-wearing, blacksnake-toting woman struck them as odd, they seemed unconcerned as they tipped their hats in perfunctory courtesy.

"Ace, Chaney, you'll be showin' these gentlemen the way to Sing's place in Hop Alley. Do assist them in any way they ask." He turned back to Steve. "I am presumin' you and Kyle don't want the law brought in on this little incident till the dust clears?"

Steve nodded as Cass interrupted impatiently, "Let's go before Ames disappears again."

Steve grinned crookedly at Blackie and said, "I guess you can see the, er, impasse we have here, Drago?"

Blackie reached for Cass, and before she realized it, he'd taken the whip from her shoulder. "Now, lass, Hop Alley is no place for the likes of a lovely woman like yerself." He reached down and slid the Navy revolver from her holster and tossed it to Steve. "Let them handle it." His tone of voice left no doubt as to his implacability.

Cass felt his hand on her arm. For a small man he possessed incredible strength. Cass turned furiously on Steve. "You can't do this to me!"

"Yes, I can. You handled Selina, and God knows, you've risked that beautiful little neck on wagons from here to Fort Union, but Hop Alley is where I draw the line, Cass. Keep her here till we get back, Blackie."

"That I will, lad," Drago replied as he carefully tossed the whip to the busy barkeep and then began to escort Cass upstairs to his private apartments. She shrieked several remarkable oaths that caused the hardened barman to wince, but Steve and Kyle departed with their guides, ignoring her outburst.

Once in the apartment, Blackie locked the door and pocketed the key, then released her with a sigh. "It's sorry I am, girl, and well you know it, but you're not leavin' here to go traipsin' into an opium den."

He pulled out a chair and Cass grudgingly sat down.

"Have you eaten? You're still as thin as a gallows ghost."

"Nothing since breakfast," Cass replied distractedly.

"I'll have Junie bring us an early dinner. Don't fret. They'll deal with Ames 'n be back in time for dessert with us."

Finally he coaxed a reluctant smile from her. "You win, Blackie . . . for now."

The street would have been ominous looking even on a sunny morning. At the end of a rain-laden day in foggy twilight its appearance was enough to make even Drago's toughs edgy. Kyle kept one hand on his Colt. The gaslights, newly installed on most Denver streets, were an amenity not brought to the detested Chinese who resided

in the alley. Since the 1864 flood, most of the city
had been rebuilt of substantial brick, but the
dwellings here made gold camp shanties seem
handsome edifices by comparison. Quiet Chinese
men in dark cotton jackets and baggy trousers
scuttled noiselessly on slippered feet, seemingly
impervious to the mud that sucked at the
strangers' horses.

No one looked at them or acknowledged their
presence in the twilight world of Hop Alley. Amer-
icans and other foreigners with the price of a pipe
often found their way to Sing's place. No one questioned the lord of the Oriental underground.

"That's it," Ace said, pointing to one particularly large two-story frame structure in a dark corner where an unnamed street turned off from the
main alley concourse.

"Now, how do we git in without Ames gittin'
out?" Kyle puzzled, scratching his head as he
thought.

Steve inspected the building, noting the narrow
gangway between it and the adjacent building.
"Ace, Chaney, I assume the locals know you?"

"We busted a few heads here once when a girl
from Blackie's place ended up at Sing's—pretty
little China gal from Canton," Ace said.

"You know where the back door is?" At the
men's nod of understanding, Steve said, "Go to
the back and wait. Kyle and I'll try the front door.
Feel free to come busting in any time you hear
sounds of a scuffle."

As the two men rode quietly around to the rear
of the hop joint, Steve checked his Army Colt.

"Yew ready ta storm in, bluebelly? Reckon I'm
glad ta have a winner backin' me agin this here
kind o' place. Plumb gives a feller th' shivers,

yle said as he dismounted.

Steve grinned. "No scarier than you rebs in the
g of the Smokies, Hunnicut. Let's go see if we
an buy us a pipe." They left their horses standing
the shadows and moved toward Sing's place.

Kyle snorted as they approached the front door.
Why is it I got me a feelin' it ain't gonna be a
eace pipe they's smokin' inside thet place."

A sharp rap brought no immediate response, so
teve tried the door. It opened on surprisingly well
led hinges, and the sickly sweet odor of opium
rifted into the fog-drenched air. When they
epped into the deserted hallway, the smell in-
nsified, compounded with dank wood, filthy bed-
ing, and stale urine.

"I don't like this, Steve. I don't like this one
etle bit," Hunnicut averred beneath his breath
his eyes darted from side to side, watching for
ny flicker of movement.

Suddenly a man materialized from the darkness
the end of the hall. His face was very pale and
s long wispy beard glowed silvery, but the rest
his form was obscured by the long, shapeless
lack robe he wore. Even his hands were tucked
the voluminous sleeves, hidden.

Heavy-lidded eyes pierced the gloom with long-
racticed precision as he inspected the two heav-
y armed foreign devils. "Good evening, sirs. I am
ing. How may this humble one serve you?"

Cass was chewing on a piece of roast pork with
esultory interest when a shot rang out, followed
y the splintering of glass and several loud oaths.
he noise carried up from the saloon, even through
e heavy door of Blackie's apartment.

Blackie put down his knife with a sigh. "Might

be knowin' a man couldn't have a meal with
lovely woman in peace." He reached into h
pocket and extracted a key, then turned to Cas
with his black eyes narrowed. "Think I'll be letti
Gus handle this one," he reconsidered calmly an
pocketed the key.

The mayhem continued unabated for sever;
minutes. Finally Cass said, "You'd better se
what's going on, Blackie. I can't very well fin
Steve and Kyle all the way across town in som
opium den I don't even know the name of. I'll b
good. Promise." She looked him straight in th
eye.

Sighing, he stood up. "I'll send Junie in to kee
you company." He unlocked the heavy door an
called down the hallway.

Almost immediately the tall redhead appeare
"You want me, Mr. Drago? Awful racket dow
there." She walked toward the open door as sł
belted her violet silk robe rather carelessly. A lor
stretch of fishnet-clad leg was still revealed as sł
sauntered past the little Irishman and entered h
apartment.

"Stay with Cass—and don't be turnin' you
backside to her. She's not to leave here, no matte
what." He directed his stern gaze at Junie, wł
nodded with narrowed eyes at Cass, whom she ha
never liked.

"Blackie, I don't need a keeper," Cass shot bac
in asperity, but he had already closed the do
and headed downstairs.

Junie was not quite Cass's height, but she wou
have outweighed her considerably even when Ca
was up to her normal weight, not ravaged by il
ness. Cass considered her options; a stand-up slu
fest was not one of them.

"How'd you get on Blackie's bad side, freighter lady?" the whore asked contemptuously as she leaned against the door, eying Cass's muddy, disheveled appearance.

Cass walked over to the mantel, her mind whirling. "I'm not on Blackie's bad side, Junie. He's just suffering from the common male delusion that women have to be saved from themselves. He's 'protecting' me."

Her mind was whirling as she strolled across the floor of the spacious parlor, apparently aimlessly. Often over the years since Rufus's death, Cass had spent pleasant evenings here, laughing and joking with the wily little Irishman. She knew he was fond of a very expensive French cognac that he kept in the carved walnut liquor cabinet beside the mantel. She'd tasted it once and found it fiery and bitter. She had swallowed it in a gulp the way the muleskinners drank their wicked Taos lightning and had fallen into a paroxysm of coughing. Blackie had laughed and explained to her that one was to take tiny sips after savoring the pleasant but powerful brandy fumes.

She eyed Junie calculatingly, wondering how she held her liquor. Cass knew she drank heavily, but somehow doubted that Blackie had ever shared his imported treasure with the woman. A "muleskinner's cocktail" of barrel whiskey and blackberry cordial was more her style. The sounds downstairs were beginning to abate. Obviously Cass had no time to get Junie drunk. A plan quickly formed as she knelt by the cabinet and extracted the expensive brandy.

"While the men are off being brave fools, we women might as well enjoy ourselves," she said with a flourish as she pulled the cork from the half-empty bottle.

"Say, that's Mr. Drago's good stuff. You can't—"

"I always drink it with him, Junie," Cass protested innocently, then asked with wide-eyed astonishment, "You mean you've never been invited to share his cognac with him?" She waited a beat.

Junie straightened up and marched across the room toward the mantel. "Just pour me a snort. Might as well finish the bottle," she added brazenly.

Cass reached for two of the good snifters and poured each half full. Making a flourish of heating the brandy over a candle, she handed a snifter to Junie. Once warmed, the potent fumes would rise up in an unwary imbiber's nose. "Bottoms up," Cass said cheerfully, raising the glass to her lips, careful not to inhale.

The prostitute was not so prudent. She took a deep breath of cognac vapor along with a giant gulp of the fiery liquor.

Immediately Cass was rewarded when tears began to gush from Junie's eyes and she wheezed for fresh air. In her coughing frenzy she didn't notice Cass pick up the fireplace poker from beside the mantel and swing, right on target.

As the big redhead crumpled to the floor in an unconscious heap, Cass knelt to pull a derringer from the woman's robe pocket and a knife from her garter belt. Junie was always armed.

"Hope I didn't brain you too hard," Cass said by way of apology, then reconsidered. "But then you'd have to have brains for it to hurt, I guess." With that she slipped stealthily through the doo and headed for the back stairs of the Bucket of Blood.

The night air was cool and damp, laden with fog as she ran down the dark alley after depositing Junie's stiletto in her boot. The pea shooter gun she carried in her hand. "It's not worth much, but I haven't got time to get another," she muttered as she edged between two buildings, intent on reaching the front of the street where she prayed Angelface remained tethered.

Suddenly a figure loomed out of the darkness with a gun gleaming dully in his hand. "And here I was wondering how to extract you from the protective custody of the second floor while my men created their little diversion. I should have known you're a resourceful bitch!"

"You!" Cass stood rooted to the ground in amazement as he removed the gun from her hand.

"We're going for a ride in the country, my darling," he said brightly, as if discussing the weather at a Sunday school picnic.

Cass shivered in revulsion. Then he prodded her with his Colt and she stumbled from the alley with him behind her.

"This situation is most distressing, esteemed sirs, most distressing, indeed," Sing said in his precisely articulated English as he led Kyle and Steve down the long, grimy hallway to his private quarters. Once inside the heavy door, it was as if they'd entered another world, certainly another building. Gone was the stench and filth of the outside corridor. The air was not fogged with opium smoke nor fouled by the stench of human excrement, but lightly perfumed with sandalwood. Plush satin pillows were piled in one corner of the thickly carpeted room. An intricately carved black lacquered desk stood in the center with two high-backed crimson chairs. Sing motioned for them to be seated.

"This is some surprise, Mr. Sing," Steve said casually as he sat down.

Kyle gingerly followed suit, but scooted his chair so as to have a clear view of the door behind them as well as the one across the room.

Sing noted the little Texan's caution and smiled in understanding. "You are a man who understands power, Mr. Loring." It was not a question, but a simple statement of fact. "I, too, am such a one. And like you, I have much to lose." He paused and gestured around the lavishly appointed room. The rings on his fingers gleamed and winked like playful stars on a clear night.

"I can see that, but it doesn't concern us. We're not here to put you out of business—only one of your suppliers—Bennett Ames. I know he's here," Steve said in a steely voice, hoping his bluff would work. God knew how many goons this wily peacock had waiting in the wings!

"Just so. Mr. Ames is the root of both our difficulties at present." At Steve's impatient look Sing cleared his throat and continued bluntly "The Chinese community is not well regarded in Denver, and this unworthy one's business is exceptionally repellent to the city fathers."

Steve nodded. "I know the Chinese have been unjustly persecuted, Sing, but somehow you don' exactly fit the image of a poor, hard-working la borer who'll fall prey to a pack of drunks from Cherry Street saloon," he said in a voice laced wit irony.

"If what has happened here is blamed on thi

innocent one, I stand to lose everything," Sing said. "I had a most profitable business arrangement with your competitor. I would now like to offer such to you."

Steve stood up, suddenly feeling a surge of apprehension wash over him. "In the first place, Sing, I don't want your business. It stinks—literally and figuratively. Secondly, I do want Ames—and the longer you stall, the messier this is going to get."

"As you wish," Sing said with a regretful sigh. He would just have to dispose of his problem without Loring's help. Perhaps the other one? But first he must get rid of these dangerous men before even more misfortune befell him. "Follow me, please."

Sing glided out of the room through the door behind his desk. The hallway was clean if spartan, quite unlike the opium rooms in the front of the premises. He unlocked a door and stepped inside. This was how he was discovered only a few hours ago."

"Son-of-a-bitch!" Kyle breathed as he knelt and examined the dead body of Bennett Ames. "His head's been stove in, Steve."

"So I see," Loring replied, rolling Ames's bulk onto his back with the toe of his boot. Neither man took his eyes off Sing. Kyle stood up and placed his hand over the handle of his gun with practiced casualness.

"What happened?" Steve asked levelly, his eyes boring into the expressionless face of the opium lord.

Sing bowed slightly, almost as if in apology, an odd gesture for a man Steve instinctively took to an arrogant bastard. "A falling out among thieves is, I believe, your quaint Western expression. Two men accompanied Mr. Ames here to discuss the new shipment of merchandise. I was to pay him after we agreed upon terms, but I was delayed, regrettably, for over an hour. When I arrived, my servants informed me that Mr. Ames and his associates awaited me in this room. When I entered..." He let his beringed hand sweep to Ames's crumpled, bloodied body.

"Whut's ta make us think yew didn't have yore bully boys do this?" Kyle asked reasonably.

"And cut my source of supply? That would have been very unwise," Sing replied, also reasonably.

"He's right, Kyle...unless Ames got greedy or pushy. Maybe you hoped to find another source—like us?" Steve studied Sing.

"If I wished to do this, would I be so foolish as to have the deed performed on my own premises? You know the risk when a white man dies anywhere in the Chinese neighborhoods, most especially one as influential as Bennett Ames."

"But who in tarnation—"

"You said Ames came with two other men?" Steve interrupted.

"From San Francisco. From even farther awa' originally. Across the same sea that this unworth' one traversed on the long journey to America."

"Them 'duck' fellers?" Kyle said with narrowe' eyes.

Sing nodded silently.

As they talked, Steve's mind was racing. "Am' hired them, but like the man here said, Kyl' there's no honor among thieves. Someone el' must've upped the ante."

"But who?"

Steve's eyes narrowed in calculation, and ' swore. "Who had the most to gain by my deat'

By Cass's?" He gestured to Ames's body and said to Sing, "He's all yours. I'd suggest dumping him in a ditch outside town late tonight." With that he motioned to Kyle and they quit the room in haste.

"Yew thinkin whut I think yore thinkin'?" Kyle asked incredulously as his short legs churned to keep up with Steve's long strides.

By the time they reached the Bucket of Blood with Ace and Chaney on their heels, Steve and Kyle had decided on a course of action. But first they needed to reassure themselves that Cass was safe.

The minute they hit the door of the saloon the wreckage gave Steve's guts a sharp twist. The elaborate room, with all its gaudy Victorian glass and furniture, was in shambles. Gus, the huge, mustachioed barkeep, was sweeping up the debris while a few men stood quietly drinking in one corner.

Blackie came through the back door, his coat wet from the foggy night air, his face ashen as he approached them. "I heard you comin' back and had to be here to tell you. She's gone! The little devil of a minx brained Junie, took her gun and knife, and vanished. I've been prayin' she went after you and you found her." He could see that this was not the case. "Me boys and meself have been combin' every back alley between here and the Chinese section for the past hour. Nothing!"

"No one's seen her?" Kyle asked in a tight voice, knowing how good Blackie's grapevine was.

"I take it this was a diversion?" Steve said, gesturing to the wreckage about them. He felt numb with terror.

"And bein' the fool that I am, I fell for it!" Blackie said in anguish.

"We gotta git out there 'n find her." Frustration was etched on every feature of Hunnicut's face. Cities were not places where his tracking skills could help.

"I'll start with the most dangerous place she could be," Steve said as he walked toward the door. "You check Ames's place and our house. Meet you back here in half an hour!"

When Kyle explained their suspicions to Blackie, the Irishman swore furiously. "It was them that started the fight in here! Australians run out of their own country, the whoresons. God help them if they've harmed Cass!"

"God ain't gonna have nothin' ta do with this," Kyle said grimly.

"You're mad!" Cass said contemptuously, trying desperately to hide her revulsion.

Clark Matthews chuckled, a grating, irritating habit of his when things were going his way. "My dearest cousin, scarcely that. I'm quite in command of all my faculties. In fact, considering how well I've deceived everyone in this miserable excuse for a city, I believe I've been positively brilliant." He paused to consider, congratulating himself. "Yes, Bennett Ames is eliminated, and soon your beloved spouse will join him. Also that distasteful little ruffian you hired," he added with spite.

Cass looked around the room surreptitiously praying for an idea to occur to her. They were seated in the parlor of Bennett Ames's ranch house outside Denver. After abducting her at the Bucket of Blood, Clark had joined a fearful-looking thug at the edge of town and they'd ridden here. The man, who she knew by his accent to be one of Ames's San Francisco "ducks," was standing guard outside. Cass knew that Matthews must plan to use her as bait to lure Steve and Kyle. She had to escape and warn them. No one had ever suspected her bumbling, pompous stepcousin of being a murderer in league with Bennett Ames!

Her hands were bound in front of her, making it difficult to work on loosening the rope. How could she divert him? "Why did you kill Bennett if he was your partner?" she asked, stalling for time.

Matthews sneered. "I *used* him, the stupid oaf. Oh, I know he thought he'd run me out of business after I took over your freight line. That was his only reason for helping me. Like you and your husband, he saw only what I chose to reveal—a simpering boy."

"Not the scorpion you really are," she couldn't resist saying.

His eyes flashed for a second, then he reached over and stroked her cheek, trailing his long, bony fingers down her throat to where her blouse buttoned. She pulled back in disgust as he stroked the swell of her breast. "I really must do something about your execrable taste in clothes, my dear. That is, if you see reason and choose to save yourself a great deal of unpleasantness by marrying me."

"Marry you!" Cass nearly leaped from her chair.

"Tut, forget your present husband. He'll soon be only a memory."

"I'd rather marry a Texas rattler," she gritted.

He looked at her with faint annoyance, as if she were a particularly dense child. "Pity. I'll inherit regardless, you know ... if you die with Loring, everything will go to me. But it will take more time that way. The courts, you know. You could really expedite matters and save yourself in the process if you consented to wed me."

"You really are mad," Cass whispered, realizing his monstrous intentions. If she married him, making his claim legally impeachable, he could kill her as easily as he now planned to kill Steve and Kyle.

He chuckled malevolently once more. "Consider your options, love. You haven't but an hour or so. I had Jackie deliver a note for me before we left town. I rather suspect your heroic rescuers won't let you down."

I can't be bait, luring them to their deaths! "You were scared spitless of Kyle back in Denver, Clark. Who's going to help you take on him and Steve?" Find out the odds. Think, think of a plan!

His eyes narrowed consideringly. "Those two fools will come alone. Besides my somewhat inept man from the livery stable, I was able to persuade two formidable professionals of Bennett's to work for me. All I had to do was promise them one insignificant shipment of opium in return for disposing of him."

Cass's eyes narrowed. "Sing's opium? To use one of our crude Rocky Mountain expressions, Clark, you've cut a hog in the ass now. Even Blackie Drago doesn't mess with Sing."

He waved his hand in dismissal as he pulled back the heavy velvet drapery and peered into the faint gray light of dawn. "I've already made plan Mr. Sing and I will reach amicable terms, I'm certain."

* * *

"Th' way I figger, they's all holed up in th' house." Kyle knelt by the barn door examining tracks in the soft mud.

They'd ridden at breakneck speed through the darkness after one of Blackie's boys had come to the saloon to give a sealed note to Steve. The instructions were succinct. He and Kyle were to come to Ames's ranch alone and unarmed, telling no one anything. Otherwise Cass was dead. The note included a lock of her copper hair. Although it was not signed, both men knew who had sent it. By taking a shortcut over the foothills with which Matthews was unfamiliar, they'd gained a scant hour to study the lay of the land.

"He's got more help than just the two ducks?" Steve asked.

"Extry horse in th' barn. Been ridden tonight. Yeah. I reckon he's got him one other gun. Way I figger, Matthews 'ud have one man at an upstairs winder, 'nother on th' front door, an' mebbe th' third feller coverin' th' rear. If only we knowed where they got Cass," he said in frustration.

"They won't hurt her until they have us," Steve said with an assurance he was far from feeling. He rubbed his head, exhausted and aching, wracking his brains for an answer. "There's only one way, Kyle. The way we did it at Barlow's ranch—only this time we'll each know the other one's there. I'll go in the front after you get in place in the back. Matthews will know you're out here someplace, but he won't want to do anything until he can get us both together. The bastard probably doesn't want to shoot us anyway—too obvious. I imagine he plans some sort of 'accident.' Apparently he had Ames send all his ranch employees off to work away from the house. The only witnesses left now that he's killed Ames are his own thugs."

Kyle snorted in disgruntled agreement.

"Once I'm inside I'll see if I can find Cass and then stall. You'll have to create a diversion to smoke the others out."

"Smoke!" Kyle grinned and looked back at the rolled bales of dry straw mounded crudely in one corner of the barn. "Reckon I kin carry enough makin's if'n I use my rain slicker fer a sack. Give me a couple o' minutes ta reach th' back. Got yew any extry matches? I'd purely hate to run out."

Steve fished through his pockets and came up with a handful of wooden matches in the flat case with his slim cigars. "I'll stall and wait for the smoke to start," he said as he watched the little Texan slip out of the barn.

If Kyle could get around to the back of the house undetected, they might have a chance. He had Steve's Colt. To appear unarmed, Loring had concealed a small sleeve gun of Blackie's in his shirt and left his holster empty. Several minutes passed as he slipped back to where Rebel was tied. Hearing no shots or sounds of a struggle, he assumed that Kyle had made it.

Slowly Steve mounted up and began to ride toward the front of Ames's deserted ranch house. It was a big gamble, assuming that Matthews wouldn't shoot him on sight, but it was their only chance. Cass's only chance. Thinking of that lock of copper hair made his gut twist.

Matthews smirked as he saw Loring riding up alone and unarmed. The man smart enough to outfox Bennett Ames was not so foolish as to expect Loring and Hunnicut to simply walk into his web. He had anticipated a trick. He knew the little

Texan was lurking somewhere, but once he had two hostages, they'd make quick work of Kyle. Matthews had boundless confidence in himself and his men. He turned to smile at Cass. "It's all working splendidly at last. Now I can kill that bastard. He should've hanged when I called in that marshal last year."

Cass gasped. "It was you!"

He smiled. "I've been working this out for over a year, ever since that pompous old lawyer located me in Kansas City and informed me about the lamentable fate of my rich Uncle Rufus. When I finally succeeded in getting rid of Loring, you had the bad grace to turn up pregnant. Of course, I could scarcely have that. The Wade bitch was such a hag, it was quite an acting feat to woo her. But I managed to convince her of the need to, er, dispose of you and your brat."

Cass saw black spots before her eyes, then red, blinding red rage. "You . . . you." Her voice shook. His flat, pompous mask of assurance slipped as the hate radiated from her, hitting him like a slap.

"You took Steve away! You killed my baby! It was you—you, not Bennett!" She lunged at him, head down, butting him in the stomach before he could dodge.

Matthews crashed against a library table. Cass barely stopped to reach down with her tied wrists and yank the stiletto from her boot.

"Alf, stop her!" Clark screamed to the big thug in the next room, but before Alf could shamble into the parlor, Cass raised the knife with incredible speed and strength, aiming it in blind rage at Matthews's hateful face, now a taut mask of terror. Just as she plunged the blade forward, he instinctively jerked his head back, baring his throat as he fell against the heavy table. Junie's long, razor-sharp stiletto slashed through his jugular and imbedded itself against the bones of his neck, lodged tightly, permanently.

Alf was on her then, grabbing her like a stick doll, while Clark Matthews fell with a gurgle to the floor.

It seemed she wrestled in the uneven contest for moments, but they were only seconds. Then Steve burst in the room and grabbed the big duck from behind. He yanked Alf's arm free and Cass fell gasping to the floor, nearly landing on her dead "cousin." She rolled up, dazed but looking for a weapon, knowing that Alf was twice her husband's size. She tugged at Clark's holster, trying to extricate his gun, but her bound wrists made her fumble.

Steve had fought with heavy cavalry sabers and his bare hands against some fearful opponents, but this brute beat anything he'd ever imagined in his worst nightmare, including a grizzly bear! He landed a knuckle-breakingly hard punch, which seemed scarcely to phase the bastard, but had no time to free the small gun strapped to his forearm. Alf grabbed a hold of him in a grip not unlike a bear would employ. *Damn, he'll snap my spine!*

Just as Alf tightened and Steve began to see explosions of light behind his eyes, the big man lifted his opponent off the ground to shake him. As Alf reared back, Steve's foot, kicking at his tormentor's shins, caught the wall behind him. Using it to push off, he caused Alf to lose his balance and topple forward.

Thick smoke began to billow into the room, choking Cass and the two struggling men. Then the little greasy man Clark had called Jackie came bounding on cat feet down the stairs, a deadly knife in his hand. Cass raised the big revolver she had freed as he tried to slip behind Steve. The two men locked in brutal combat stumbled into her line of fire.

She struggled to get up and move in for a clean shot when Kyle yelled from the hall. Jackie turned in time to meet his fate, his blade only inches from Steve's neck when Hunnicut's bullet knocked him sideways into the hallway doorframe.

Alf's merciless bear hug had been broken as he and Steve fell to the floor, with the duck landing on the bottom. As air rushed into Steve's lungs, it was knocked out of Alf's. Steve grabbed an ear on each side of Alf's bald head and jerked it up, then smashed it down against the hardwood floor. "One good turn deserves another," he grunted out as he continued the pounding until the giant lay with his arms spread-eagled and his eyes rolled up in his skull.

"I think yew kin quit now," Kyle said drily as he holstered his gun.

Cass walked shakily over to them, letting Matthews's revolver drop onto the sofa.

Kyle was at her side quickly, cutting the ropes that abraded her wrists. Steve stood up and reached out to her.

"Cass, oh, Cassie, you all right?" His voice was hoarse as he held her chin up and looked into her face.

"I'm fine," she said uncertainly, coughing in the thickening smoke.

"Thet's more'n I kin say fer this here varmint." Kyle kicked Clark Matthews's body over to hide the bloody neck wound from Cass. She buried her face against Steve's chest.

Loring turned to Hunnicut as he held her, saying, "There was a third one—"

Kyle grinned through the smoke. "Not any more, they ain't. He kindly come in at the wrong time, when I wuz settin' a fire."

Cass coughed and Steve, too, felt the sting of the smoke as the whole back of the house blazed.

"Let's get the hell out of here!" Steve swept Cass up into his arms and they dashed for the front door, leaving Clark Matthews and his henchmen to their funeral pyre.

"What the hell did you do?" Steve choked out through the billowing smoke.

Kyle grinned. "Soaked thet dried straw with cookin' grease 'n lit it. Then stuffed it in th' stovepipe in th' kitchin."

Just as they reached the front door, the ceiling in the dining room began to cave in, quickly followed by a whooshing rush of thick black smoke that obliterated the living room and its grisly contents.

The three survivors stood in the yard, gulping in the clear morning air. Pink and orange streaks began to show on the eastern horizon as the dark of night gave way to a glorious new day.

Kyle returned to his hotel after they had stopped at Blackie's place to assure him all was well. The Texan announced that not having slept in two days entitled a body to a few hours of shuteye.

Steve and Cass, muddy, sooty and sorely exhausted, agreed and went home to Vera Lee's ministrations. After her bath, Cass was too tired to chew, but the cook was adamant, saying she wa already too thin. She and Steve shared a light mea of fresh strawberries and poached trout with crusty bread and butter, then trudged upstairs to sleep the clock around.

It was late morning when Cass opened her eyes to look at her husband. He was already awake, his head propped up on one hand while the other lay possessively across her waist just below her breasts. Gleaming dark gold eyes studied her with undisguised love.

He stroked her temple and plucked a curl from the pillow, holding it to his lips. "When I saw that lock of your hair in the note . . ." He groaned and buried his face in her neck, holding her tightly.

Cass stroked his back and clung to him, murmuring, "I was so afraid he was going to kill you and Kyle—I knew you'd come." She hesitated, then continued as he held her, "He said he sent the marshal after you last year, Steve." She looked up into his eyes.

He kissed her eyelids and cheek softly. "I know, Cass. I know everything now. But I should have trusted you, I should have known you couldn't turn me in. And I should have come back sooner, when I was cleared. Maybe I could have stopped that woman. Cass, so much of this is my fault."

She shook her head in sorrow. "No, you couldn't have known. None of us suspected Bettie Wade and Clark. He killed our baby, Steve. He sent her to poison me." Tears clogged her voice.

"Shh, don't cry. It's all over now. He can't ever hurt you again. No one will."

"I wanted the baby so much. I'd lost you. He was all I had left of you. That's when I knew the business didn't matter anymore—only you and I, being a family."

He held her and stroked her hair as his throat

thickened with tears for the child they'd lost, for all the wasted, bitter time they'd been torn apart. "We *are* a family, Cass, and I'll never leave you again. I swear it."

She stopped crying, feeling oddly purged at last, cleansed from all the ugly, twisted hates of the past, her father's, Bennett Ames's, even Clark Matthews's. It was over, and she held the man she loved more than life itself. Cass looked up at him and confessed, "I was afraid. From that first day on the porch when Kyle rode in with you, I sensed something..." She groped for the right words to make him understand.

He did. "I felt it, too, Cass." He chuckled. "You were intimidating, beautiful, bitchy, and arrogant. But I wanted you. It took a while longer to realize I loved you. Even when I failed you and thought you'd betrayed me, I still couldn't stop loving you, Cassie."

She put her fingers gently on the healing cut on his cheek. "I've scarred you. My temper has always been awful." She paused for a moment, then said thoughtfully, "I've always felt so insecure. I thought that to be a woman meant to be weak." She laughed ruefully. "So I guess I set out to turn myself into a man...what I thought all men were ...ruthless, cruel, bullying..." As she averted her eyes, Steve could feel her shudder.

He pulled her closer as if to protect her from a chill. "Cass, you were trying to survive the only way you'd ever been taught how. Rufus Claytor couldn't crush you, not Ames, not me. God, whatever made me think centuries ago that I wanted a simpering, biddable female for a wife? No, Cass you're what a real woman should be—honest, courageous, intelligent." Steve tucked a hand unde her chin and raised her head. With utmost tenderness, he gazed into her eyes. "Just promise me one thing, wife."

Cass nodded, "Anything, husband."

His voice caressed her. "Don't bring that goddamned blacksnake to bed with you!"

Stunned, Cass watched the grin spread across Steve's handsome face, and the surprised laughter that bubbled up in her washed away the last of her regrets and self-recriminations. He kissed her lightly and sat up against the headboard, pulling her with him.

"The freight business is yours, Cass. You earned it—not because of inheriting it from Rufus, but because of what you did with it after he was gone. You won, Cass, in spite of him. You beat him at his own game—without becoming like him."

She lay her hand on his chest and felt the steady thud of his heart. "Not without your help. You saved it all for me—for us. Now it's ours, Steve, and I want it that way."

He shook his head. "No, Cass, sooner or later you'd resent me if I kept coming between you and your men." When she began a denial, he shushed her with a light kiss, then continued. "The line is yours to do with as you see fit—Loring Freighting, Cass Loring, proprietor. That's what the new sign will say, the one I ordered yesterday while you were soaking all the grime off that delectable little body." His hand grazed a breast through her thin silk gown, but she ignored the thrill of pleasure.

"If I run the line, what are you going to do?" she asked apprehensively.

"Well, darling, Blackie's been talking to me about investing with him in a really classy whorehouse," Steve replied in a tone of innocent enthusiasm.

Cass's eyes widened in shock. "Steven Terrell Loring!"

Her protest was cut short by her husband's laughter. "I'm sorry, but you were so worried that I'd waste away for want of a job."

She surpressed an oath. "Stop teasing!"

"Yes, I know. Business is very serious." He smiled. "You do remember the Loring banking interests back in Philadelphia? Well, with that backing, I'm going into railroading with Will. Oh, not building them. But with the money my Uncle Lucas is wiring, I'll start that series of forwarding houses we've discussed."

Her eyes lit up in understanding and relief. "You would be the link between the Denver and Rio Grande and my wagons that can take goods where the trains can't go!" she finished excitedly.

"For now, yes. I'll start that way, investing in good inventories and selling them at a healthy profit—giving your freight business its fair cut," he added with a wink. "But by the end of this century, the rails will be taking over, Cass. Precious few places will be without a railhead."

She smiled and looped her arms around his neck. "By that time we'll have grandchildren to worry about diversifying our investments. That is, if you'll consider starting a family now."

"I might consider it," he murmured into her mouth as they slid down into the bed, kicking back the covers. He peeled her silky gown up and slipped it over her head. She ran her fingers through his chest hair, then up to his neck, pulling him down to kiss her again. Their tongues entwined as their bodies writhed, softly gliding a rubbing, promising each other. They rolled in the heated embrace until she was atop him. With his long, strong fingers he gripped her hips and raised her over his aching shaft.

Cass arched up and impaled herself joyfully, welcoming his sleek, hard flesh inside her body, joined as one with her. This was so different than that first time she'd ridden him. Then she had been a frustrated, vengeful woman, afraid of her own sexual awakening and her love for this man. Then she had been seeking to dominate, to take. Now, she wished only to give. She gloried in it.

Steve thrust up, in perfect rhythm with her, looking up into her beautiful face, willing her eyes to meet his. His thought communicated itself to her and her eyes opened wide, overflowing with love. He could feel her cresting, feel the delicious, rhythmic contractions radiating outward from the center of her like shock waves.

Cass felt him swell and stiffen as he spilled his seed deep inside her. She gazed down on him in speechless wonder. His arms released her hips, gliding up to her shoulders, pulling her down so she reclined on his chest. Her hair curtained them like pale flames as they both panted in satiated exhaustion.

Cass chuckled lazily and nibbled on his lip. "I take it that you like my proposal about starting a family?"

Steve cocked an eyebrow at her. "Not so fast, Mrs. Loring. Although I've found your past proposals absolutely impossible to refuse, you do realize—" he pinched her rump "—that I drive a hard bargain? What's the price?"

"The only price is love," she murmured as she covered his lips with a long, sealing kiss.

Epilogue

Denver, 1872

Blackie Drago and Kyle Hunnicut were pacin
holes in the carpet of the upstairs parlor. Finall
unable to stand it any longer, Vera Lee abandone
the coffee and sweet rolls that she had been a
tempting to get them to consume. She brought i
another tray. A large bottle of good Irish whiske
and two glasses filled with ice were the on
things, other than a stout club, that the harrie
woman could think of to make them cease the
pacing. She poured two generous shots and jabb
them at the men, daring them not to sit down a
drink.

"You would think a woman never had a ba
before in all history," she said with asperi
"Everything is going fine. Dr. Elsner and Rosa
both assured me. Now drink."

Her tiny stature hid a will of iron. Both men complied, sipping the soothing libation.

"Steve's th' lucky galoot. Leastaways he's got hisself somethin' ta do whil'st we jist stew," Kyle groused.

Blackie winked devilishly at Kyle and said, "And would you be wantin' to take the father's place at Cass's bedside?"

The little Texan paled and spilled his drink down his shirtfront. "Lordy, no! Thet bluebelly's got more guts 'n a five-hunnert-pound hawg!"

Just then John Elsner stepped into the room, beaming. "Gentlemen, the Lorings have a beautiful daughter!"

Blackie silently crossed himself and tossed down the last of his drink in one gulp. Kyle threw his hat, which he had refused to part with all day, up into the air with a loud rebel yell of glee.

Inside the bedroom, Steve looked tenderly at his exhausted wife. Her hair was matted and her eyes ringed with dark circles, but she had never looked more beautiful to him. She was watching Rosario bathe their daughter as Steve sat on the edge of the bed, squeezing her hand softly.

Cass shifted her gaze to her husband. He looked like a brigand, not a prosperous merchant. His face was grizzled by a day's growth of beard and his eyes were red-rimmed. She'd awakened him early that morning to calmly announce that it was time to get John Elsner. He'd thrown on his clothes and raced across town in their best carriage to pound on John's door.

She reached up and touched the scar on his cheek. It had healed to a thin white line that made his perfect masculine beauty seem somehow more dramatic. Still, she regretted the mark. He smiled and took her hand, kissing each fingertip in turn.

"She's beautiful as her mother," he said softly.

Rosario brought the squalling bundle to the bed and gave her to the proud father. "She is *muy hermosa*. What will you name her?"

Steve held his daughter, and a twinkle came into his eye as he looked at Cass. "Since I'd promised Blackie we'd name a boy after him, I guess we'll have to compromise."

"Blackie loved my mother, Rosario, so part of her name will be Eileen," Cass explained.

"But that scrawny little Texan out there saved my life twice, so in gratitude he's getting his share, too. What do you think of Kylie Eileen Loring?"

"I think they will both be pleased. I will go tell them now," Rosario replied as Steve gently placed little Kylie at her mother's side.

Steve looked down at the quieted child who was tugging eagerly at Cass's breast. She stroked the soft pale gold curls on her daughter's head and said, "We have a daughter. Next we should have a son." She looked up at him with a gleam in her eye.

"Kyle said we'd have a passel of 'yeller-eyed devils,'" Steve replied with a laugh. "A girl is one job o' work. A boy is another.... How much?" he asked with a grin of pure love.

Cass reached up and pulled him into her arms next to their contented child. "I'll think of a price," she replied serenely.

Author's Note

In writing a story about a Colorado freighting empire in 1870, I was faced with a research challenge that was fascinating and colorful, yet for the layman, frightfully technical. There is a thin line between entertainment that edifies and edification that bores, as my associate Carol always reminds me. Once I was immersed in books about Murphy wagons and ten-span mule teams, I realized I was in grave danger of crossing that line if I used half of what I learned. In most instances, Carol cajoled me to simplify the descriptions of freighter's equipment without sacrificing accuracy. For those interested in more detailed accounts of men and women who hauled life-sustaining goods across the Great American Desert, I can recommend a number of superb sources.

The most colorful firsthand account, as retold by his daughters based on his own correspondence, is David Wood's "*I Hauled These Mountains in Here!*" by Frances and Dorothy Wood. The anecdotal materials give the real flavor of the mountain freighting business in all its diversity. Another excellent anecdotal source that provides a good scholarly overview of the industry is *The Transportation Frontier: The Trans-Mississippi West, 1865–1890* by Oscar Osburn Winther.

Three unpublished scholarly dissertations were particularly useful in helping a "greenhorn" to understand the intricacies of livestock, wagons, and the way they traveled the trails: "Wagon Roads in Colorado, 1858–1876" by Clifford Hill, University of Colorado M.A. Thesis, 1949, and "The Rise and Decline of High Plains Wagon Freighting 1822–1880" by Henry Pickering Walker, University of Colorado Ph.D. Thesis, 1965. "The Western Army Frontier 1860–1870," by Raymond Leo Welty, State University of Iowa Ph.D. Thesis, 1924, gave a good picture of how the army worked with (and sometimes against) the freighters.

Colorado Territory during the era when Steve Loring and Cass Clayton collided was truly a land of chaos and promise, the perfect backdrop for their outrageous relationship. Lyle W. Dorsett's *Queen City, A History of Denver* gives an excellent account of the building of a brash gold town that against all odds, became the leading city in the Rockies. For further general background on Colorado, solid standard references are Robert G. Athearn's *The Coloradans* and Marshall Sprague's *Colorado*. For some more colorful and anecdotal information on urban life and the vices of the muleskinners, see *The City and the Saloon: Denver 1858–1916* by Thomas J. Noel and *The Saloon o* the Mining Frontier by Elliott West.

Terms of Love is peopled by a cast of characters larger than life, except that a number of them actually lived. Steve's old army companion and later builder of the Denver and Rio Grande was William Jackson Palmer, a man of vision and tenacity. *Rebel of the Rockies* by Robert G. Athearn and *A Builder of the West, The Life of General William Jackson Palmer* by John S. Fisher tell his story as a man of many talents living in an extraordinary era on which he left an indelible mark. Fisher also details Palmer's remarkable career during the Civil War. He led "Palmer's Owls," Union skirmishers whose exploits not only provided him with a general's star at the age of twenty-eight, but also provided me with the story of a Union sympathizer ambushed by Confederates after aiding the Owls.

Dr. John Elsner, the selfless Jewish physician, and William Newton Byers, the priggish publisher of the *Rocky Mountain News*, are portrayed much as history reveals them. Some of the fictional characters, such as Blackie Drago, the king of the Denver underground, and Rena Buford, the gold camp whore, are based on composites of people who really lived in the rough-and-tumble territory. The Reverend "Sour Mash" Charlie Filbert was a joy to create from drawings and old photos. I know he lived, at least in the spirit of many an itinerant preacher who went west to seek the salvation of souls and ended up in an unlikely occupation. Kyle Hunnicut, of course, appeared in *Capture the Sun*, and the little Texan was so beloved of our readers that Carol and I decided to bring him back a decade earlier as Cass's "security officer" in *Terms of Love*.

For one liberty with history, I must beg indulgence. The fabled Hanging Judge, with whose fearful reputation Kyle was to threaten Steve, did not come onto the federal bench in Fort Smith until May 2, 1875, after which he served for twenty-one years. Isaac Parker became such a legend that I felt compelled to use him in my story in spite of the four-year time discrepancy. The preceding judge, who held court in Van Buren until March 3, 1871, did not have the recognition that Judge Parker evoked. For a detailed account of Parker's life and the experiences of his federal deputy marshals in the Nations during the 1870s, see *Law West of Fort Smith* by Glenn Shirley.

Acknowledgments

As always I must express my indebtedness to my associate, Carol J. Reynard, who reads my reptilian syntax and translates it into cleanly printed out copy on our word processor. I know that machine is black magic, but computer illiterate that I am, I am slavishly grateful.

As the author's note on sources indicates, a great deal of research was involved in *Terms*. Securing unpublished graduate theses and the wide variety of other materials I requested was not an easy task, but Hildegard Schnuttgen, head of reference at Youngstown State University's Maag Library, performed it with her usual expertise and efficiency.

Terms has a formidable and varied group of villains in its cast. Both they and the good guys came to the shootouts properly armed, courtesy of our meticulous weapons expert, Dr. Carmine V. DelliQuadri, Jr., D.O.

My husband, Jim Henke, helped us with several knotty plot problems as well as choreographing the fight scenes and keeping us from coming unraveled under pressure of deadlines. Even more importantly, he has tried his hand as a romance author and written a wonderful love scene in *Terms*. He's eagerly waiting to see how many readers can pick it out this time!

Please send your guess to:

P.O. Box 72
Adrian, MI
49221

POP STOOD OVER ME,

the gun pressed against
the side of my face.

Was the first time I had
ever had one to my head.
First time I had been that
close to death. To the end.

And at the hand of
Pop. Pop? Pop!

YOU WOULD THINK

I would be thinking
about whether or not
he could actually do it
since he wasn't real.

But the hugs were real.
And the gun was real.

Weren't no ghost bullets
in that clip.

Those were real bullets.

Fifteen total.
One for every year
of my life.

MY STOMACH

was aching,
the quaking world
in the bottom of it,
and it wasn't long
before I could feel

myself splitting
apart.

A WARM SENSATION

ran through the lower
half of my body,
seeping
down my leg
into my sneakers.

Cigarette smoke
cut once again,
this time by the smell
of my own piss.

09:08:40 a.m.

THEN POP UNCOCKED THE GUN,

wrapped his arms around me
again,

squeezed tight like
I was some rag doll,
stuffed

the gun back into
my waistband.

I SCREAMED,

pushed him away,
yelled until my throat
stripped,
until my words became
sizzle.

Weak.
Wet.
Worried
about looking like
a punk-ass kid.

And my father
leaned against the wall,
staring,
chin up,
cocky,
quiet,

while I exploded.

AND LIKE OLD TIMES

Uncle Mark
came to his side
like a brother,

pulled the extra cig,
the one tucked
behind his ear,

handed it to
my father,
chest heaving.

Eyes on me,
he threw the cig
in his mouth.

Buck took his cue.
I backed into
a corner,

wished this
stupid elevator
would get to L,

for this whole
thing to hurry up
and be done.

Buck struck
a match and the
elevator came

to a stop.

A STRANGER,

chubby,
light skin,
almost white,
the type that
turns red,
that burns,
dirty brown hair
curled up
on his head,

got in the elevator
like a normal guy.

Didn't acknowledge
nobody.

No dead body.
No live body.
No smoke.

Normal.

SO I FIGURED

he was real.

Which
made me real

embarrassed
about the pee

but
made me real

happy
I wasn't all

the way gone.

THE THICK PALE DUDE

stood staring at his
blurry reflection in
the metal door

when Buck started
trying to get his
attention.

Yo,

Buck said.

Psst.

The guy didn't
budge.

Yo, dude,

Buck called,
reaching
for his
shoulder.

THE MAN TURNED AROUND.

I know you.

Buck flashed his
big choppy grin.

*Your name
Frick, right?*

> Only to people who
> know me
> know me,

the guy said,
reluctantly reaching
for Buck's hand.

Remember me?

Buck said,
like a distant
relative at a
reunion.

Buck,

he said,
showing the back
of his T-shirt again.

Oh shit,
Buck?

Head cocked.

Buck?

Arms wide.

What's good, man?

Nothing.
Is good.
At all.

THIS IS

Dani,
Mark,
Mikey,
and

you remember
Shawn?

This his little brother,

Will.

BEFORE FRICK COULD ANSWER,

I asked Buck
how he knew
him,

what his connection
was to me,

what he was doing
in this spooky-ass

elevator.

09:08:50 a.m.

HOW DO I KNOW HIM?

    Buck scoffed,
      shaking his head.

This is the man
who murdered me.

WAIT.

Wait.

Wait . . . wait.

Hold up.

Hold

up.

Hold the hell

on.

On my brother,

on Shawn's name,

You serious?

Wait . . .
Wha?

Wait, wait, wait.

. . .

What?

YOU HEARD ME RIGHT.

See, Frick here—

    Buck paused.

Why they call you that, anyway?

    he asked,
    sidetracked.

        It's really Frank. Twin sister,
        Frances. Frick and Frack
        came from my uncle.
        Stupid shit old men call you
        stick in the hood,

    Frick explained.

Who you tellin'.
Matter fact because
of you—

    Buck paused again,
    turned back to me.

Because
of him, Will,

the only reason
people 'round here
know my government name
is from reading it on
my damn tombstone.

BUCK'S REAL NAME

was James.

I've only heard it one time.

Buck better
than James.

Buck short
for young-buck.

Nickname given
by stepfather as a joke

because Buck
couldn't grow no facial hair.

Smooth baby face,
nothing rough

about it.

BUCK WAS TWO-SIDED.

Two dads,
step and real.

Step raised him:
        a preacher,
        a real preacher,
        not scared of no one,
        praying for anyone,
        helping everyone.

Real run through him:
        a bank robber,
        would steal air from the world
        if he could get his hands on it.

PEOPLE ALWAYS SAID

he was taught to do good
but doing bad
was in his blood.

And there's that nighttime
Mom always be talking about.

It'll snatch your teaching
from you,

put a gun in your hand,
a grumble in your gut,
and some sharp in your teeth.

BUT HE DIDN'T START THAT WAY.

At first Buck was
a small-time hustler,
dime bags on the corner.

Same old story
until my pop got popped
at the pay phone that night.

Then he became a big brother
to Shawn
and a robber to a bunch of
suburban neighborhoods
every morning
      (he knew better than to
        jack people around here)

and come back with
money (the most)
sneakers (the best)
and jewelry (which he loved to show off).

BACK TO FRICK.

I was shocked
when I heard that
this dude killed Buck.

       Yeah,

Buck said,
hand on
Frick's shoulder
all buddy-buddy.

       This the guy.

He glanced
at me.

       Shawn never
       told you that story?

HE NEVER REALLY TALKED ABOUT IT,

I said.

Shawn just said
you were shot
and that he knew
who did it,

I explained,
remembering that time.
Shawn's face a candle,
melted wax,
flame flickering out.

I remember the cops
banging on our door
to question him,

to tell him they heard
he was close to James—

that was the one time
I heard Buck's real name—

and to ask him
if he knew who might've

done it,
killed him,
shot him
twice

in the stomach,
in the street.

SHAWN AIN'T SAY NOTHING

to the cops,
to no one,

just locked
himself

in his room
for hours

and the next
day I caught him

sitting on his
bed pushing

bullets into
gun clip.

09:08:54 a.m.

WELL, LET ME TELL YOU,

Buck said.

We were hanging out at the court
sharing a bottle of something cheap
and strong just before it went down,

Buck said.

Shawn was telling me how he had
gotten into a little scuffle, nothing
major, with one of the dudes from
the Dark Suns,

Buck said.

Said he had to get your mother
some kind of soap she uses that
he could only get from the store
down by where they hang out.

A DUMB THING TO SAY

would've been to
tell Buck how important
that soap was

that it stopped Mom from
scraping loose a river
of wounds.

But instead
I just said,

Riggs.

I'M NOT SURE WHAT HIS NAME IS,

Buck said.

Said Shawn
said he was
going to the
store when
the dude   *Riggs*
ran up on
him talking
all this shit.

Said it was
nothing
serious, just
poppin' off
at the mouth
about how he
was a Dark Sun
and how Shawn
ain't belong
around there.

Said Shawn
was in his
feelings
all huff-huff
explaining to
Buck how he
had grown up
with the kid   *Riggs*
and how the
kid was brand-new.

Buck said
he told Shawn
to let it roll off,
but he couldn't
because that's
just how he was.

All emotional
all the time,

Buck said.

WHILE HE'S GOING ON ABOUT THIS DUDE,

I'm trying to show him this chain
I just got from some kid out in
the burbs. Didn't even snatch it.
I just growled a little bit and asked
for it and the sucka just took it
right off and handed it to me.
Ain't even snatch it,

Buck said,
thinking back on that day
like he still couldn't
believe it.

But what does that have to with
my brother and this guy?

I said,
pointing to Frick.

Hold on.
I'm gettin' to that.

SO BECAUSE SHAWN WAS

tripping so hard about this dude,
I gave him the gold chain,

Buck said,
proud.

A gift.
His first one.
Then Shawn left
the basketball court.

And that's when I came,

Frick chimed in,
a big smile
on his face
like he had just
won some
kind of award.

HOW TO BECOME A DARK SUN

1 TURF:

    nine blocks from where I live.

2 THE SHINING:

    a cigarette burn under the right eye.

3 DARK DEED:

    robbing someone,
    beating someone

    or the worst,
    killing someone.

Note: Apparently, you also gotta be corny.

I WAS ASSIGNED

my Dark Deed
for initiation,

Frick explained.

And it was to kill Buck?

No,

he said.

Funny thing is,
I was just supposed
to rob him.

I didn't think it was
a *funny thing* at all.

Everybody knew
Buck was always flossin',
always flashy. But nobody
would touch him because
of his pops. Both of them.

Real and step.

GANGSTAS

always respect
older
        (original)
gangstas
          (OGs)
and preachers
who act like

gangstas.

FRICK SAID

his plan was to
jack the jack-boy.

Said he knew Buck
would be at the court

so he ran up on him,
pulled the hammer,

and got laughed at.

BUCK SAID

he couldn't get got
by a dude who he could
tell was as soft as the
suburban joker he'd
just jacked.

Everybody in the
elevator laughed.

Except me.

09:08:58 a.m.

WHATEVER, MAN,

Frick said.

I was just trying to
earn my stripes.

Can't knock me for that.

He turned around,
caught eyes with
Pop and Uncle Mark.
They nodded in agreement.

No judgment over here,

Uncle Mark said,
throwing his hands up.

Anyway, this crazy fool,
Buck, swings at me.
Just tries to take me
even though I had a boom stick!

Frick looked
at Buck, shook
his head, then cut
his eyes to me.

I got scared.

So I pulled
the trigger.

BUCK BENT

his pinky and ring
finger back,
turned his
hand into
a gun.

Bang-
bang.

AGAIN

What does this have to do
with Shawn?

     I asked.

          Shawn stuck to The Rules,

     Frick replied.

You mean.

     I swallowed.

You mean he . . . he . . .

     I struggled
     to get it out.

     Now Buck put
     the finger gun
     against Frick's
     chest and repeated,

Bang-bang.

ACTUALLY,

he only pulled the
trigger once, so it
was more like,
Bang,

Frick corrected.

Fifteen
bullets.

TOOK ME OUT

before I ever even
got my Shining,

Frick said.

Rubbed just under
his right eye
like it still
rubbed him
the wrong way.

FRICK YANKED HIS COLLAR DOWN.

See this?

he asked,
exposing a hole
in his chest,
dime-sized,
disgusting,
bloody
but not
bleeding.

*Your brother's
fingerprints are in
there somewhere.*

Buck *Ha*'d!
Replied
before I had
a chance.

*And I bet
it's his
middle finger!*

WHEN THE JOKE WAS OVER

I asked how Shawn
could've known Frick
was the guy who killed Buck.

Buck said there was only
one other person at the
court that night,
always there
all the time,

a young kid
running back and forth
trying to dunk.
Not shoot.

Said he thinks
I might've known him.

Tony.

And he wasn't trying to dunk.
He was trying to
                    fly.

TONY TALKING

ain't the same as snitching.

Snitching is bumping gums
to badges, but
Tony ain't run to no cops
or cry to no cameras,
nothing like that.

Tony talking
was laying claim,
loyalty,
an allegiance to
the asphalt around
here, an attempt
to grow taller
       get bigger
one way or another.

NOW LET ME ASK YOU

> *how you know*
> *this kid Riggs got your brother?*

> Buck fired back.

Because he clearly got revenge
for Shawn taking out this guy,

> I pointed
> to Frick.

> > *Frick, you know*
> > *a kid named Riggs?*

> Dani asked
> out of nowhere,
> her voice
> floating over
> my shoulder.

Little dude.
Big mouth.
Dark Sun.

I figured
the description
might help.

Frick looked at me,
confused.

Who?

ANAGRAM NO. 5

I wish I knew
an anagram

for POSER.

FRICK LOOKED

at me like I was crazy,
shrugged his shoulders,
and turned around
and faced the door.

Couldn't see
his reflection.

Couldn't see
any of their
reflections.

Just mine,
blurred.

FRICK HAD

his own cigarettes
and
his own matches.

Finally
Finally
Finally

the elevator came to a stop.

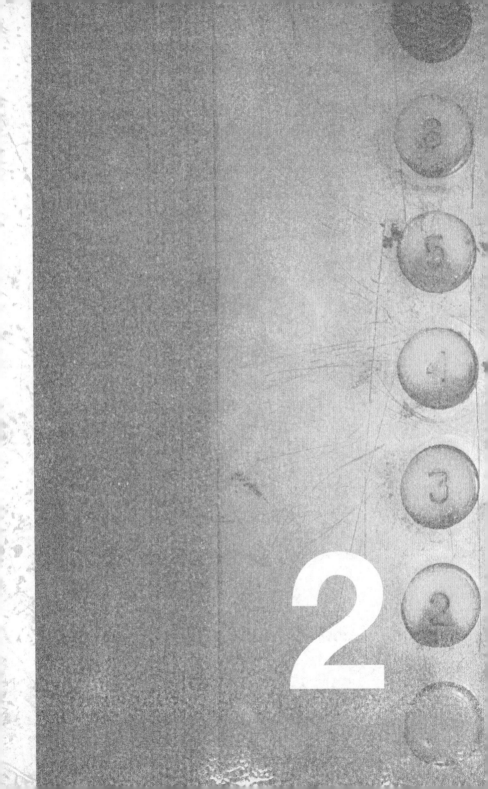

WHEN THE ELEVATOR DOOR OPENED

no one was there.
So I reached over and pushed
the *L* button
again and again and
again and again.

Because that's what you do
when you want the door
to close faster.

Another one of those
elevator rules.

COME ON,

I huffed
under my breath,

impatient,
pissy,
pissed off,
scared,
scarred,
and straight-up
uncomfortable being
crammed in this
stupid
steel
box,

this vertical coffin,

another second.

UNCLE MARK CHUCKLED.

You would never survive
in prison, nephew.

FINALLY

the elevator door
began closing.

I exhaled,
happy we were
almost there.

One floor to go.

And just before
it was shut,
before the door clicked
in place,
four fingers slipped in
just barely catching it.

The elevator door
began opening

again.

09:09:07 a.m.

HIM.

Shawn.

Stepped into the smoky box
wearing exactly what he wore
the night before:
      blue jeans,
      T-shirt,
      gold chain.

But not his alive outfit.
His dead one.

The one that came
with bloodstains.

EVERYBODY

was so happy
to see him.

Shawn!

Buck yelped,
reaching out
for him.

They slapped hands.
Buck fiddled with
the gold chain around
Shawn's neck.
Moved the clasp
to the back.

Shawn looked at Dani.

Look at you!

he said,
taking her hand,
spinning her around.

Uncle Mark
gave him a light
tap in the ribs.

Big man!

he said
proudly.

Shawn turned,
gave him a hug,
caught a glimpse
of our father.

Pop!

he said,
natural,
his face
beaming.

Our father
wrapped his arms
around Shawn,
cocooning him.

Then pulled away,
shook hands
like men,

like partners.

ALL

the un-alive/un-dead
lined up along the wall
puffing their cigs,
smiling

as Shawn
finally
          finally
faced
me.

WHEN WE WERE KIDS

I would follow Shawn
around the apartment
making the strangest
noise with my mouth.

Hard to explain the sound.
Burpy but not a burp.

Like burp mixed
with yawn mixed
with hum.

Something like that.

For twenty minutes straight.
From bedroom
to kitchen
to living room
back to bedroom.

To punish me,
he would wait for me to finish,
to run out of steam,
to let it go,
to get tired

of being immature.

And then,
to my surprise,
he wouldn't say a word to me
for the rest
of the day.

I LOOKED AT SHAWN.

He looked at me.

Shawn,

I said.

But he said
nothing.

I repeated,

Shawn?

Nothing.

I STEPPED TOWARD HIM,

hugged him.
He didn't hug back.

Just stood there,
awkward,

a middle drawer
of a man.

I ASKED HIM

why he wouldn't say nothing,
why he was ignoring me,

but still,
nothing,
not a word,

not even a smile.

I TOLD HIM

about the
drawer,
the gun,

that I did
like he told me,
like Buck told him,
like our grandfather told
our uncle, like our uncle
told our dad.

I followed The Rules.
At least the first two.

I hadn't cried.
I hadn't snitched.

EXPLAINED

that I was on my way to take
care of his killer,

follow through
with Rule Number Three.

Told him I knew it was Riggs.
Told him I thought it was Riggs,
then told him I knew it was Riggs
again.

CONFESSED

that I was scared,
that I needed
to know I was
doing the right thing.

THE RULES ARE THE RULES

Right? Right? Right?
Right? Right? Right? Right? Right?
Right?   Right?
Right?   Right?
Right?   Right?
Right?   Right?
Right?   Right?
Right?   Right?
Right?   Right?
Right?   Right?
Right?   Right?
Right?   Right?
Right?   Right?
                    Right?
                    Right?
                Right?
                Right?
            Right?
            Right?
            Right?
        Right?
        Right?
        Right?
        Right?
        Right?
        Right?
        Right?
        Right?
        Right?
        Right?

Shawn?

I WAS BREAKING DOWN.

The tears were coming
and I did what I could
to hold them back.

Took my eyes off Shawn,
hoping to fight the crying
feeling by not looking.

But everywhere else
was everyone else,
cigarettes glowing

like a bunch of
L buttons.

09:09:08 a.m.

I LOOKED BACK AT SHAWN,

tears now pouring from his eyes
as he softly snotted and hiccuped
like a little kid,

tears pouring from his eyes
tears pouring from his eyes
tears pouring from his eyes.

I thought you said
no crying,
Shawn,

I said,
voice cracking,
one of my tears
bursting
free.

But only one
so it didn't count.

No crying.

No crying.
No crying.
No crying.

AND EVEN THOUGH

his face was wet
with tears he wasn't
supposed to cry
when he was alive,

I couldn't see him
as anything less
than my brother,

my favorite,
my only.

AND THERE WAS A SOUND

like whatever makes
elevators work,

cables and cogs,
or whatever,

grinding,
rubbing metal on metal

like a machine moaning
but coming

from the mouth
from the belly

of Shawn.
He never said nothing to me.

Just made that painful
piercing sound,

as suddenly the
elevator came to a stop.

JASON REYNOLDS

RANDOM THOUGHT NO. 5

The sound you hear
in your head,

the one people call
ears ringing,

sounds less like a bell,
and more like a flatline.

THERE WAS A MOMENT

before the door opened
when we all just stood there,
sickening
smoke thickening,

crowded in

this cell
this coffin
this elevator

quiet.

I LOOKED AROUND

only seeing the orange glow

of five cigarettes puncturing
the sheet of smoke
like headlights in
heavy fog.

Only five cigarettes.

Shawn hadn't lit one,
became invisible
in the cloud.

And I felt like
the cigarette meant for him
was burning in
my stomach,

filling me with
stinging fire.

09:09:09 a.m.

I WANT OUT.

The door opened slowly,
the cloud of smoke
rushing out of the elevator,
rushing out of me
like an angry wave.

I caught my breath as

Buck,
Dani,
Uncle Mark,
Pop,
Frick,
and
Shawn

chased behind it.

The *L* button
no longer lit.

I stood alone
in the empty box,
face tight from
dried tears,
jeans soggy,
a loaded gun
still tucked in my
waistband.

Shawn
turned back toward me,
eyes dull from death
but shining from tears,

finally spoke
to me.

Just two words,
like a joke he'd
been saving.

YOU COMING?

JASON REYNOLDS

Acknowledgments

I'd like to give special thanks to my agent,
Elena Giovinazzo, who saw this work first and
suggested I write it in verse; and to my editor,
Caitlyn Dlouhy, who took it and helped me
shape it into what it is now. The unwavering
belief you both have shown me is nothing short
of remarkable. Thank you. To my family, but
more importantly, for this book, my friends,
who have been with me in precarious situations
where our humanity curdles and our ethics
are put to the test. I couldn't have written this
without our childhoods. To the young men and
women serving time in detention facilities: your
stories, your testimonies matter. Your lives are
often sacrificed by the failures of people twice
your age. But you will make it. You will make it.
Also, to the poets. Without poetry, especially
when I was younger, being a writer would've
seemed like a futile attempt. The poets taught
me the functionality and power of language.
And lastly, to my dear friend, Randell Duncan.
We miss you. Rest easy, brother.

A Reading Group Guide to
Long Way Down
By Jason Reynolds

Discussion Questions

1. Using details revealed in the text, create a character sketch or character collage of the book's protagonist.

2. Unlike a traditional prose novel, *Long Way Down* is written in verse. Poets are known for using language intentionally and with precision, often choosing words with connotative and denotative meaning. Reflect on the significance of the protagonist's name. The word Will can be used as a proper name, but also as a verb and a noun. In what ways does the protagonist encompass multiple meanings of his name?

3. What are "The Rules"? Do you agree that these three rules exist? If so, can you remember how you learned about them? If not, are there other unspoken rules that you follow instead? What do you think Will means when he writes: "They weren't meant to be broken./They were meant for the broken/to follow."

4. When we analyze poems, we pay attention to the poem's format. This includes things like length, shape, line breaks (including the use of enjambment and caesura), and spacing on the page. Identify a section of the novel where you think the format adds meaning to a passage and explain how the poem's format impacts the meaning.

5. Will enjoys finding anagrams, especially when the anagram illuminates or comments on the meaning of the original word. Explain the connections between the anagrams that he creates. Why are they significant to the story?

6. When Shawn turned eighteen, what did his mother worry about? What do you think she meant in saying that when Shawn walked in the nighttime, he needed to make sure that the nighttime wasn't walking in him? Do you think Shawn tried to heed his mother's warning?

7. Will includes a list of nicknames for a gun. Are there any other nicknames that you know of that he did not include? What are the different connotations of each name? When Will puts the gun in the back of his pants, what nickname does he use for it? What does his choice suggest about his feelings toward carrying the gun?

8. Who does Will believe killed his brother? What are his reasons for believing this? Do you think he's right?

9. Throughout the novel, Will uses figurative language (simile, metaphor) to describe things or feelings. For example, when he holds Shawn's gun for the first time, he notes that it is, "Heavier than/I expected/like holding/a newborn." In this example, the juxtaposition of the image of a newborn baby with the weight of the gun highlights the deadliness of the gun and loss of Will's innocence. Find an example of figurative language that you think is especially effective and explain why it is significant.

10. How does Will plan to avenge his brother's death? In this moment, do you think he is doing the right thing?

11. Through flashbacks, Will shares memories of his brother. What do each of these memories reveal about their relationship?

12. When the first ghost enters the elevator, Reynolds includes a time stamp at the top of the page. How much time elapsed between the first stop and the bottom floor? Why do you think Reynolds includes these indications of the passage of time? Do they inform or complicate your understanding of the text?

13. How does Will recognize the first ghost that enters the elevator? What was the ghost's relationship to Shawn and Will? What message do you think he is trying to convey with his words and actions?

14. Why doesn't Will recognize Dani at first? What questions does she have for Will? What message do you think she is trying to share with him?

15. Why did Uncle Mark start dealing drugs? Why did he keep dealing? How did he die? Why do you think Uncle Mark wants Will to act out what will happen when he follows the rules? What message is he trying to convey with his words and actions?

16. How did Will's father die? How does the relationship between Uncle Mark and Will's father parallel the relationship between Will and Shawn? Why do you think Will's

father pulls the gun on Will? Does Will understand what his father is trying to show him?

17. Frick is the only ghost to enter the elevator whom Will does not know. How is he related to the story? Why do you think he visits Will?

18. The last person who enters the elevator is Shawn. What does Will tell his brother? How does Shawn respond? What rule do both brothers break? Do you think Shawn wants Will to avenge his death by shooting Riggs? Explain your answer.

19. The last words in the book are a question. How do you think Will answers this question? Where do you think Will will be five years after the end of the book?

Guide prepared by Amy Jurskis, English Department Chair at Oxbridge Academy in Florida.

This guide has been provided by Simon & Schuster for classroom, library, and reading group use. It may be reproduced in its entirety or excerpted for these purposes.

Turn the page for a sneak peek at *All American Boys*.

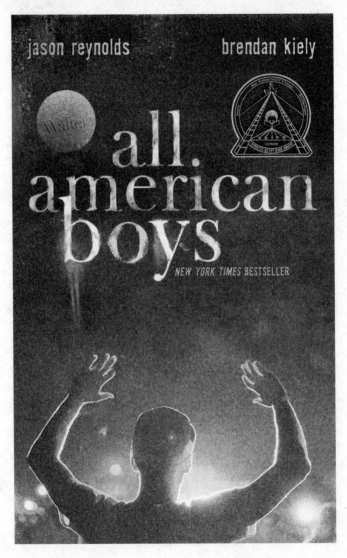

Your left! Your left! Your left-right-left! Your left! Your left! Your left-right-left!

Yeah, yeah, yeah.

I left. I left. I left-left-left that wack school and that even more wack ROTC drill team because it was Friday, which to me, and basically every other person on Earth, meant it was time to party. Okay, maybe not everybody on Earth. I'm sure there was a monk somewhere on a mountain who might've been thinking of something else. But I wasn't no monk. Thank God. So for me and my friends, Friday was just another word for party. Monday, Tuesday, Hump Day (because who can resist the word "hump"?), Thursday, and Party. Or as my brother, Spoony, used to say, "Poorty." And that's all I was thinking about as I crammed into a bathroom stall after school—partying, and how I wasn't wanting to be in that stiff-ass uniform another minute.

Thankfully, we didn't have to wear it every day. Only on Fridays, which was what they called "uniform days." Fridays. Of all days. Whose dumb idea was that? Anyway, I'd been wearing it since that morning—first bell is at 8:50 a.m.—for drill practice, which is pretty much just a whole bunch of yelling and marching, which is always a great experience right before sitting in class with thirty other students and a teacher either on the verge of tears or yelling for some other kid to head down to the principal's office. Fun.

Let me make something clear: I didn't need ROTC. I didn't want to be part of no military club. Not like it was terrible or anything. As a matter of fact, it was actually just like any other class, except it was Chief Killabrew—funniest last name ever—teaching us all about life skills and being a good person and stuff like that. Better than math, and if it wasn't for the drill crap and the uniform, it really would've just been an easy *A* to offset some of my *C*s, even though I know my pop was trying to use it as some sort of gateway into the military. Not gonna happen. I didn't need ROTC. But I did it, and I did it good, because my dad was pretty much making me. He's one of those dudes who feels like there's no better opportunity for a black boy in this country than to join the army. That's literally how he always put it. Word for word.

"Let me tell you something, son," he'd say, leaning in the doorway of my room. I'd be lying on my bed, doodling in my sketch pad, doing everything physically possible to not just stop drawing and jam the pencils into my ears. He'd continue, "Two weeks after I graduated from high school, my father came to me and said, 'The only people who are going to live in this house are people I'm making love to.'"

"I know, Dad," I'd moan, fully aware of what was coming next because he said it at least once a month. My father was the president of predictability, probably something he learned when he was in the army. Or a police officer. Yep, the old man went from a green uniform, which he wore only for four years—though he talks about the military like he put in twenty—to a blue uniform, which he also only wore for four years before quitting the force to work in an office doing whatever people do in offices: get paid to be bored.

"And I knew what he was trying to tell me: to get out," Dad would drone. "But I didn't know where I was going to go or what I was going to do. I didn't really do that well in school, and well, college just wasn't in the cards."

"And so you joined the army, and it saved your life," I'd finish the story for him, trying to water down my voice, take some of the sting out of it.

"Don't be smart," he'd say, pointing at me with the finger of fury. I never managed to take enough bite out of my tone.

And trust me, I knew not to push it too far. I was just so tired of hearing the same thing over and over again.

"I'm not trying to be smart," I'd reply, calming him down. "I'm just saying."

"Just saying what? You don't need discipline? You don't need to travel the world?"

"Dad—" I'd start, but he would shut me down and barrel on.

"You don't need a free education? You don't need to fight for your country? Huh?"

"Dad, I—" Again, he'd cut me off.

"What is it, Rashad? You don't wanna take after your father? Look around." His voice would lift way higher than necessary and he'd fling his arms all over the place temper-tantrum style, pointing to the walls and windows and pretty much everything else in my room. "I don't think I've done that bad. You and your brother have never had a care in the world!" Then came his favorite saying; it wouldn't have surprised me if he had it tattooed across his chest. "Listen to me. There's no better opportunity for a black boy in this country than to join the army."

"David." My mother's voice would come sweeping down the hallway with just enough spice in it to let the old man know that once again, he'd pushed too hard. "Leave him alone. He stays out of trouble and he's a decent student." *A decent student.* I could've had straight *As* if I wasn't always so busy sketching and doodling. Some call it a distraction. I call it dedication. But hey, decent was . . . decent.

Then my father's face would soften, made mush by my mother's tone. "Look, can you just try it for me, Rashad? Just in high school. That's all I ask. I begged your brother to do it, and he needed it even more than you do. But he wouldn't listen, and now he's stuck working down at UPS." The way he said it was as if the lack of ROTC had a direct connection to why my older brother worked at UPS. As if only green and blue uniforms were okay, but brown ones meant failure.

"That's a good job. The boy takes care of himself, and him and his girlfriend have their own apartment. Plus he's got all that volunteer work he does with the boys at the rec center. So Spoony's fine," my mother argued. She pushed my father out of the way so she could share the space in the doorway. So I could see her. "And Rashad will be too." Dad shook his head and left the room.

That exact same conversation happened at least twenty times, just like that. So when I got to high school, I just did it. I joined ROTC. Really it's called JROTC, but nobody says the *J*. It stands for the Junior Reserve Officer Training Corps. I joined to get my dad off my back. To make him happy. Whatever.

The point is, it was Friday, "uniform day," and right after

the final bell rang I ran to the bathroom with my duffel bag full of clothes to change out of everything green.

Springfield Central High School bathrooms were never empty. There was always somebody in there at the mirror studying whatever facial hair was finally coming in, or sitting on a sink checking their cell phone, skipping class. And after school, especially on a Friday, everybody popped in to make sure plans hadn't been made without them knowing. The bathroom was pretty much like an extension of the locker room, where even the students like me, the ones with no athletic skill whatsoever, could come and talk about the same thing athletes talked about, without all the ass slapping— which, to me, made it an even better place to be.

"Whaddup, 'Shad?" said English Jones, making a way-too-romantic face in the mirror. Model face to the left. Model face to the right. Brush hairline with hand, then come down the face and trace the space where hopefully, one day, a mustache and beard will be. That's how you do it. Mirror-Looking 101, and English was a master at it. English was pretty much a master at everything. He was the stereotypical green-eyed pretty boy with parents who spoiled him, so he had fly clothes and tattoos. Plus his name—his real name—was English, so he pretty much had his pick when it came to the girls. It was like he was born to be the man. Like his parents planned it that way. But, unstereotypically, he wasn't cocky about it like you would think, which of course made the ladies and the teachers and the principal and the parents and even the basketball coach even more crazy about him. That's right, English was also on the basketball team. The captain. The best player. Because why the hell wouldn't he be?

"What's good, E?" I said, giving him the chin-up nod while pushing my way into a stall. English and I have been close since we were kids, even though he was a year older than me. We were two pieces of a three-piece meal. Shannon Pushcart was the third wing, and the fries—the extra-salty add-on—was Carlos Greene. Carlos and Shannon were also in the bathroom, both leaning into the urinals but looking back at me, which, by the way, is a weird thing to do. Don't ever look at someone else while you're taking a piss. Doesn't matter how well you know a person, it gets weird.

"You partying tonight at Jill's, soldier-boy?" Carlos asked, clowning me about the ROTC thing.

"Of course I'm going. What about you? Or you got basketball practice?" I asked from inside the stall. Then I quickly followed with, "Oh, that's right. You ain't make the team. Again."

"Ohhhhhhhhhhh!" Shannon gassed the joke up like he always did whenever it wasn't about him. A urinal flushed and I knew it was him who flushed it, because Shannon was the only person who ever flushed the urinals. "I swear that's never gonna get old," Shannon said, laughter in his voice.

I unbuttoned my jacket—a polyester Christmas tree covered in ornaments—and threw it over the stall door.

"Whatever," Carlos said.

"Yeah, whatever," I shot back.

"Don't y'all ever get tired of cracking the same jokes on each other every day?" English's voice cut in.

"Don't you ever get tired of stroking your own face in the mirror, English?" Carlos clapped back.

Shannon spit-laughed. "Got 'im!"

"Shut up, Shan," English snapped. "And anyway, it's called 'stimulating the follicles.' But y'all wouldn't know nothin' about that."

"But E, seriously, it ain't workin'!" from Shannon.

"Yeah, maybe your follicles just ain't that into you!" Carlos came right behind him. By this point I was doubled over in the stall, laughing.

"But your girlfriend is," English said, with impeccable timing. A snuff shot, straight to the gut.

"Ohhhhhhhh!" Of course, from Shannon again.

"I don't even have no girlfriend," Carlos said. But that didn't matter. Cracking a joke about somebody's girlfriend—real or imaginary—is just a great comeback. At all times. It's just classic, like "your mother" jokes. Carlos sucked his teeth, then shook the joke off like a champ and continued, "That's why we gotta get to this party, so I can see what these ladies lookin' like."

"I'm with you on that one," English agreed. "Smartest thing you've said all day."

Off went the greenish-blue, short-sleeved, button-up shirt, which I also flung across the top of the door.

"Exactly. That's what I'm talkin' 'bout," Shannon said, way too eager. "'See what these ladies lookin' like,'" he mimicked Carlos, the slightest bit of sarcasm still in his voice. If I picked up on it, I knew Carlos did too.

"I can't tell you what they'll be lookin' like, but I can tell you who they won't be lookin' at . . . you!" Carlos razzed, still on get-back from Shannon being slick and for laughing at my basketball crack. It had been at least three minutes since I made that joke, and he was still holding on to it. So petty.

"Shut up, 'Los. Everybody in here know I got more game than you. In every way," Shannon replied, totally serious.

I kicked my foot up onto the toilet to untie my patent leather shoes. Just so you know, patent leather shoes should only be for men who are getting married. Nothing about patent leather says "war."

"Argue about all this at the party. Just make sure y'all there. It's supposed to be live," English said, the sound of his footsteps moving toward the door. He and Shannon didn't have mandatory basketball practice like usual, but were still going to the gym to shoot around because, well, that's what they did every day. For those guys, especially English, basketball was life. English knocked on my stall twice. "Look for me when you get there, dude."

"Bet."